Praise for *Sl...* *House*

'Excellent . . . an original plot, a character it's a
pleasure to spend time with, and the deployment
of the author's clever, ranging talent . . . a novel
drenched in that most elusive and valuable of
literary elements – atmosphere'
Spectator

'A genuinely creepy exercise in neo-gothic that flirts
with the supernatural and horror genres'
The Times

'Brilliant – a tour de force. Noon has taken the humble
police procedural, blended in a genuinely frightening
psychological element, added a layer of human
corruption and a piquant dash of insanity'
Fully Booked

'Unsettling'
Financial Times

'The obsessive world of pop culture becomes a dangerous,
dark, bewitching place . . . utterly brilliant'
William Shaw

www.penguin.co.uk

Jeff Noon trained in the visual arts and drama, and was active on the post-punk music scene before becoming a playwright, and then a novelist. His first crime novel featuring Detective Hobbes was *Slow Motion Ghosts*. His other novels include *Vurt*, *Pollen*, *Automated Alice*, *Nymphomation*, *Needle in the Groove*, *Falling Out of Cars*, *Channel SK1N*, *Mappalujo* (with Steve Beard), *A Man of Shadows*, *The Body Library* and *Creeping Jenny*. He has also published two collections of short fiction, *Pixel Juice* and *Cobralingus*. He lives in Brighton.

HOUSE WITH NO DOORS

Jeff Noon

BLACK SWAN

TRANSWORLD PUBLISHERS
Penguin Random House, One Embassy Gardens,
8 Viaduct Gardens, London SW11 7BW
www.penguin.co.uk

Transworld is part of the Penguin Random House group of companies
whose addresses can be found at global.penguinrandomhouse.com

First published in Great Britain in 2020 by Doubleday
an imprint of Transworld Publishers
Black Swan edition published 2021

A CIP catalogue record for this book
is available from the British Library.

ISBN
9781784163549

Typeset in Adobe Garamond Pro by Jouve (UK), Milton Keynes.
Printed and bound in Great Britain by Clays Ltd, Elcograf S.p.A.

The authorized representative in the EEA is Penguin Random House Ireland,
Morrison Chambers, 32 Nassau Street, Dublin D02 YH68.

Penguin Random House is committed to a sustainable
future for our business, our readers and our planet. This book is made
from Forest Stewardship Council® certified paper.

For Michelle

1962

A shroud had fallen over London, a thick layer of all-encompassing smog that covered both the suburbs and the central regions. This was the third day of its reign. The pitch-black fog reached into every street and alleyway, crawling through open windows and under doors, seeping into public houses and living rooms, causing people to cough and choke, even those who wore thick scarves or homemade masks of cotton gauze. The screens in the picture houses could barely be seen. Already a good number of people had died, ninety or so by the last count. More would follow.

The city was blinded. Visibility zero.

In the district of Soho people groped along with their arms outstretched in front of them, to keep from bumping into other pedestrians. Police officers shouted warnings, and car horns sounded continuously. A double-decker bus loomed out of the fog, then stopped with a squeal of brakes. Headlamps flared and died after a few feet. It was hopeless: there was no way forward. Two vehicles had collided. One of the drivers was trapped behind the steering wheel, and another man was trying to free him. The klaxon of an unseen ambulance made a harsh cry, but any kind of rescue seemed many miles away.

One young woman stood beneath a silver-blue neon sign, its diffuse glow lending her face the haze of a ghost. She could not move. Her eyes were wide in shock and she looked around in fear, as though expecting to be attacked at any moment. But she was alone. Alone within the crowd, as so many were on that day, in that great, overpopulated city. The smog held all in its grasp.

The woman murmured to herself. Her hands were cold and trembling.

The blood ran down her fingers.

PART ONE

1981

Blue with Yellow Flowers

Somebody slammed a drawer shut and let out a curse. Bollocks! One of the older guys was coughing his guts up. The Monday-morning blues. Cigarette smoke and cold coffee, and the blasted light that never stopped flickering over by the window. Hobbes was troubled. The phone call wouldn't go away: why had Glenda rung him at such an hour, still dark outside? What did she want? They hadn't spoken in so long. Maybe she— No, he cut off the thought. Once upon a time he'd known his wife's moods to a tee, but now she was a stranger to him. Yet it hadn't been that long since they'd split up. Half a year, that was all.

Damn it. Another mistake. He looked in despair at the letter – it was already marred with red crosses. He pulled it from the typewriter, rolled in a fresh sheet of paper and started again, hoping to concentrate this time. He'd written up enough reports and filled in enough arrest sheets over the years, but this was different: a friend was in need and he didn't have a clue what to say. He didn't even know how to address the recipient: first name, full name, or rank?

The telephone on his desk rang. 'Yes?'

'It's Latimer.'

'What's happening?'

'Something you should see.'

'Really?'

'It's a weird one.'

'Tell me.'

'You need to see it for yourself.'

That was enough to get him away from the desk. He drove over to the address DS Latimer had given him. It was a quiet day in Richmond upon Thames, the sky grey, almost sunless. A woman pushing a pram along the pavement. A street cleaner at his work. The last of summer. The rain had stopped, though. That was good. The trees of the parkland were lit with sparkles of water as he turned on to Palliser Road. Large houses set apart from one another, each with its own individual design. This was a well-off part of London. Old money. He parked behind Latimer's Viva outside number 17, where a curved path led up to an imposing structure, three storeys high and on top of that a dormer window in the attic. The house name, Bridlemere, was proudly displayed in iron scroll-work. A sprawling Edwardian family would have lived here in the good old days. The current residents seemed down on their luck, especially when you compared the house to the well-maintained ones occupying the rest of the street. Here, the brickwork was crumbling and the window frames were rotten in places, in need of a good lick of paint. One of the downstairs panes was broken, and patched up with a square of cardboard on the inside.

Latimer was waiting for him at the front door.

'I hope this is good, Meg.'

She nodded, invited him inside without a word and led him down a corridor that ran alongside a staircase. The banisters were peppered with woodworm holes, and the struts were scuffed and dusty, two of them cracked. They passed one room after another, all with their doors open, through which Hobbes saw a mixture of antique and 1950s furniture, all placed next to each other with no thought of matching styles. But there was nothing of the present day, as far as he could see. The people in this household had stopped buying things a few years back. His mind was already at work, even though he had no idea of what he was going to see. It was a rambling house, with lots of nooks and crannies, oil and watercolour paintings on every available wall space, along with framed black-and-white photographs from a former age, probably the first quarter of the century. Also on view were old-fashioned theatrical playbills, and a good number of Catholic icons: crucifixes and statues of the Virgin Mary. Only a grandfather clock in the long central hallway made any sound.

Latimer entered the large kitchen at the rear of the house. Hobbes followed her and was immediately struck by the stench of vomit. In this room one final battle had taken place, life against death. The usual winner.

The old man was slumped at the table, the side of his head resting on a linen napkin as though placed there in position. A pair of spectacles lay a few inches away, carefully folded. But his body had reacted badly to its final throes: a teacup had landed on the floor, smashed to pieces, and plates and cutlery on the tabletop were scattered about, probably pushed away by one of the man's arms as it spasmed outwards, seeking one last hold on the material world.

Jesus. What could you do?

Hobbes moved closer and leaned over. A fly was walking across the man's right hand. The detective shooed it away. He looked closely at his subject. The face was well creased, almost cadaverous, determination still etched into the features. He had the wiry, gnarled look of an ageing greyhound. His hair was pure white and sparse on top, the remaining strands overly long and untidy. It had been many weeks since he'd had a haircut. And yet he'd dressed himself in a blue blazer and matching necktie for this occasion: Hobbes had seen such behaviour before, people getting dolled up for their leave-taking. A military man, perhaps. At the very least a person keen to leave a good corpse. A stream of vomit had gathered and dried in the deep cleft of his chin, and on the table around his mouth, which was still open, caught in a snarl. Brown teeth, one visibly rotten, and a couple of gaps. A liver spot high on the brow.

A bottle of vodka had remained standing on the table, along with a glass tumbler. A number of white tablets had spilled from a small container.

'Sleeping pills?'

Latimer nodded.

For a moment Hobbes said nothing, but simply stared ahead at the kitchen wall. No, he never quite got used to it.

Latimer told him, 'His name's Leonard Graves. I'm guessing mid-eighties.'

'A good enough age to go.'

'I'd be happy with that. He lived alone. The lady next door found him earlier today. She's a bit of a saint, apparently. Comes in once a week to do a spot of cleaning, bring him food and make sure he's all right. She has a key.'

Hobbes nodded to himself. 'The poor sod. Probably thought he'd just fall asleep.'

'A common mistake. And the doctor agrees. Self-administered.'

'Time of death?'

'About two hours ago.'

'Yes, yes . . .'

Something on the table had caught the inspector's attention.

Latimer continued: 'According to Mrs Travis – that's the neighbour – he'd been poorly for a while, but always refused offers of medical help.'

Hobbes picked up the object. It was a lady's handkerchief, a lacy affair. White, with a monogram in lilac: M.E. It looked out of place next to an ashtray filled to the brim with Park Drive butts. But the cloth gave off an aroma – sweet, cloying, deeply engrained. His eyes scanned the table. Yes, there it was, near the milk jug, a dark-blue bottle labelled Midnight in Paris. He pictured the old man making this movement: his finger holding the spray button down to saturate a handkerchief with scent. And then perhaps the handkerchief raised to his face . . .

'I think his wife must've died,' Latimer explained. She seemed to be reading Hobbes's thoughts, something he'd noticed her doing more and more in the few months they'd worked together.

'So then, Meg. Why am I here?'

'First of all, this.' She turned the man's left arm from the table-top and pulled back his blazer and shirt sleeves, revealing a collection of scars on his forearm and wrist, each scabbed over or faded to a line of pale flesh. A large sticking plaster had been half peeled back, revealing a newer incision: a couple of inches long, it looked to be quite deep. Blood had recently dried around the cut.

'You seen anything like this before?' Latimer asked. 'Because I haven't.'

Hobbes considered. 'What do you think? A failed attempt at suicide? Or a few failed attempts over time, from the look of things. And then the pills.'

She let the plaster fall back over the wound. 'Well, that's not the right place to kill yourself.'

'No.'

'But here's the thing: he needed the blood. He squeezed it out.'

Hobbes frowned. 'Come on, Meg. What the hell's going on?'

'Follow me.'

They went back into the hallway and took a door on the right, which led into a spacious living room: one wall was lined with books, another with more of the old photographs, all of them framed, protected behind dusty glass. An upright piano in the corner, and a television that looked like it had been purchased in 1966 or thereabouts. A small chandelier hung down from the centre of the ceiling, the smell of years and years of cigarette smoke in the air, the once white walls now stained with a yellow tinge.

Latimer was standing to one side of the marbled fireplace. Hobbes followed her gaze down to the hearth rug. A woman's dress was laid out on it. It looked to be 1950s style, a blue background with a pattern of yellow flowers. Stretched out at the dress's hem was a pair of beige nylon stockings, with a pair of low-heeled blue shoes below them. A yellow scarf covered the neck of the dress. It was, to all intents, the figure of a woman modelled by her clothes. A vanished woman. Hobbes bent down and examined the most interesting part of the display: the right midriff area of the dress was torn and smeared with red. He touched the edge of the discoloured patch gently: it was slightly sticky.

'This is the old man's blood?'

'Looks that way. I can have it tested.'

'It's, what, a few hours old?'

'Probably.'

Hobbes nodded. He noticed a Gillette razor blade lying on the rug near the shoes. This, too, was stained with blood. 'Christ. So he cut himself?'

'That's all I can think. And then he took a plaster . . .' she pointed at the box that also lay on the floor '. . . and covered the cut.'

Hobbes stood upright. 'What was his name again?'

'Graves. Leonard Graves.'

'Let's see. Mr Graves collects together a woman's outfit, lays it out on the floor. Rips the dress.'

'It's cut. I'm guessing with the razor blade.'

'OK. And then he slices into his forearm, and lets the blood fall on the dress.'

'Drop by drop.'

'Some time later he takes an overdose of sleeping pills, smokes a cigarette, and drinks a glass or two of vodka. Kills himself.'

Latimer nodded. 'That's the picture.'

For a moment they both stood in silence, staring down at the set of clothes arranged so precisely and artfully on the floor of the living room. The scene lent itself to melancholic thoughts: the out-of-date furniture, the lonely-old-man smell in the place, the way the late-afternoon light shone through the half-open curtains. That damn fool piece of cardboard in the broken window frame: it wouldn't last out the autumn months. It was enough to make anyone succumb to despair.

Hobbes breathed out evenly. 'Well . . . this is strange.'

'It is. But there are some other things you need to see. Upstairs.'

'Lead the way.'

They climbed up to the first floor, and into the main bedroom at the front of the house. This showed evidence of a woman's touch, in the floral curtains, the matching bedspread and pillow cases, the doilies on the dressing-table. Hobbes stopped where he was, a few steps into the room. Another dress was laid out on the bed, again with a pair of nylon stockings and a pair of shoes at the foot, a scarf at the neckline.

'The scarf and shoes are different from downstairs,' Latimer said. 'But the dress . . .'

'It's the same?'

'The exact same design and size.'

'Hmm.' He stepped closer to the bed to inspect the torn area on the dress's right-hand side, and the blood around the tear. No, it wasn't blood.

'It looks like red paint?'

'This time, yeah.'

The paint was dry to the touch.

'What do you think?'

Hobbes couldn't answer. 'It's a mystery.'

'Maybe . . .'

'Meg, you have a theory?'

She pursed her lips. 'His wife died. And this is his way of com-memorating her. Hence the old perfume bottle in the kitchen, and the dresses.'

'We definitely know that his wife died, do we? Or is that an assumption?'

'The latter. But have a look in the next room.'

They walked along the landing into a smaller bedroom, this one entirely bare of any personal effects, no curtains at the win-dows, no carpet or rugs on the floor. No photographs or paintings. A single bed, a chest of drawers. That was it.

This time the dress was hanging on a wire coat-hanger from the picture rail, again accompanied by a pair of shoes, resting on the floor beneath. No stockings this time, but with a white silk scarf draped over the shoulders. The tear in the cloth was in the same place as it was in the other two dresses, and also surrounded by a dry smear of rust across a yellow flower.

'That looks like blood to me.' Latimer stood at the inspector's side. 'But I'm guessing a good few years old.'

Hobbes nodded slowly. He didn't say anything.

'Do you want to see the next?'

He looked at her sharply. 'How many are there altogether?'

'A dozen. Maybe more. I didn't keep count.'

'A dozen?'

'Always the same dress, same pattern, blue with yellow flowers. All laid out or hanging up, as this one is, and all of them torn or sliced in the same place.' She touched her own midriff. 'And all decorated with blood, or a blood substitute. Paint, lipstick, and even what looks like tomato sauce in one case.'

'Show me.'

Latimer directed him along the corridor and around a corner. The house seemed to be endless, one corridor after another, but all of them quite short: a labyrinth of angled floors and ceilings, dusty alcoves and hidden corners. The floorboards creaked with every step.

'So, Guv, have you seen anything like this before?'

'I can't say I have. It's very odd. And yet . . .'

'What is it?'

Hobbes shook his head. 'I don't know. But it does remind me of something. I can't think.'

They entered another bedroom.

Totems

Caroline Travis paused and looked down the hallway towards the closed door of the kitchen, as though she could actually see the cold, silent occupant through the panelling. But then she shook herself and moved on quickly into the living room, following DS Latimer.

Hobbes was waiting for them, standing in the corner of the room.

He didn't speak to the next-door neighbour, simply let her look around the room. He wanted her to notice the clothes on the floor for herself, wanted to see her reaction. It took her a surprising time, scanning the walls, the furniture, before her gaze dropped to the floor in front of the fireplace. For a moment she said nothing, her eyes creasing, her upper body trembling slightly.

'Oh dear,' she said. 'Oh dear.'

Hobbes could not decode the phrase. He asked, 'Did you see this earlier, when you found Mr Graves?'

She shook her head. 'I didn't come in here. I went straight to the kitchen.'

'But you have seen this before, or something like it?'

Mrs Travis looked at him. 'No. That is . . . yes, I have, but not like this.'

'And how have you seen it?'

'Well, I've seen the dress before, hung up in a wardrobe. There's quite a lot of them, actually. A lot of dresses, all of them the same.' Now she looked worried. 'It's not like I'm being nosy or anything, you understand? I do the cleaning for him . . . for Mr Graves . . . sometimes . . . once a week . . . just a bit of a tidy . . .'

She ran out of words.

Hobbes studied her. Caroline Travis was a fine, upstanding citizen, that was obvious. She was neatly dressed in cream trousers and a woollen cardigan with a home-knitted look. A heavy fragrance surrounded her. Her hair was frizzy and brushed upwards almost into a bouffant. Her eyes gathered light easily: they glinted as she looked at the figure of the absent woman on the floor. Was that a smile?

Latimer touched the woman's arm gently. 'That's fine, Caroline. We're just trying to work it out.'

'It's like a puzzle? Right. Yes, I see.'

Hobbes nodded. 'We're trying to work out why Mr Graves laid the dress out like this, with the tear in the cloth, and the blood spread on it.'

That final statement shocked her. Her eyes darted back to the dress on the floor and she shivered despite herself. 'You mean that's blood?'

'It is. Probably from Mr Graves's arm.'

Caroline raised a hand to her mouth. 'This must be . . .' She hesitated.

Hobbes took a step closer. 'Do you know why he killed himself?'

'Because . . . because of his wife. I don't know. I'm only guessing. Because . . .'

'His wife died?' Latimer asked. 'Is that it?'

Caroline Travis turned to her. 'No. No, she was taken away. A few years ago now. You know . . . He never got over it. Never.'

'Put in a home, you mean?'

Mrs Travis nodded vigorously, not wanting to say any more.

Hobbes and Latimer caught each other's eye. Latimer shrugged. Then she turned back to the neighbour. 'What can you tell us about Mr Graves, Caroline?'

'I didn't really know him, not as such.'

'Was he reclusive?'

'Oh, yes, very much so.'

'Since his wife went away?'

'Yes, but before that, even, the two of them together. Well, we hardly saw hide or hair of them from one day to the next. A woman used to come round, a care assistant, for a while. But then . . .'

Hobbes urged her on. 'What happened?'

'Mr Graves just sort of gave up, I guess. He didn't want anything to do with anyone, and he stopped letting the care assistant in. That's when . . . Well, that's when I took over. You have to do your bit, don't you, for those less fortunate?'

Latimer smiled and nodded as the neighbour rattled on.

'The poor man. He lived on the ground floor most of the time. He slept on a bed in the next room – you'll have seen that, right? But once I found him halfway up the stairs, struggling, panting for breath. So I know he went up there, still. Things were often moved around in the upper rooms.'

Hobbes frowned. He didn't like this. He didn't like the house, the atmosphere, the murky light and the countless rooms, like a series of chambers in a mausoleum, or even an overgrown doll's house. This wasn't a place where happiness dwelled. It was too cold, too self-enclosed.

And right there and then he understood what his wife Glenda wanted from him: she wanted a divorce. That had to be it.

Cold house, cold rooms. The heart shut up, tightening . . .

'Sir?'

It was Latimer, nudging at him.

'Right, yes.' He opened his eyes. 'Just a few more questions, Mrs Travis.'

'Of course. I'll do all I can to help.'

'Did Mr and Mrs Graves have any children that you know of?'

'I've seen a few people visit, now and then, over the years. Relatives, I suppose. But we were never introduced.'

'Had they lived here long?'

'I think they'd always been here, as far as I know. The family was born and bred in this house. We moved in – that's Andrew and me, and our daughter – we moved here, oh, nearly ten years ago now. I can't believe it's been that long! Anyway, no one else in the street seemed to care for the Graveses very much, from what I could tell, so I felt I had to help. What else could I do? He was so lonely, these last few years especially.'

'Was he ill?'

'He had a very nasty cough, and I was always telling him to get it seen to. But he was a hardy soul. The type of man who never surrenders. But here, you know . . .' she touched her chest above her heart '. . . in here, something had given in.'

Hobbes thought about this. 'Was he depressed?'

'How do you mean? He wasn't crazy –'

'I'm not saying that.'

'– or anything like it, not that I could tell.'

'I mean . . .' Hobbes hesitated.

Latimer came in to help him. 'Was he sad about his life, about being alone, and so on?'

'Well . . .' Mrs Travis considered, '. . . he missed his wife, but I said that, didn't I?'

'Anything else?'

Now she looked intently at DS Latimer. 'Leonard wasn't exactly a talkative man. In fact most of the time he just sat in the kitchen, mumbling to himself about the rotten state of the world. But on occasion he would speak to me, and he'd smile and laugh – he really was a nice man when that happened.'

Hobbes said, 'What did he talk about?'

'About the theatre. It was the one thing he loved. He was involved in it himself, when he was younger.'

'As an actor?'

'Maybe. Or more of a director. I could never get complete sense out of him. He spoke in opposite directions, if you know what I mean.'

She walked to the nearest wall and singled out one of the many framed photographs hanging there. 'This is him as a younger man.'

Hobbes went over to look at the image. It showed a man in his early thirties, darkly handsome with brushed-back hair, wearing a sharp suit and a tie over a white shirt. A glamorous woman stood at his side. She was wearing an evening gown; it was a black-and-white photograph but Hobbes could imagine the dazzle of the many sequins covering the outfit. The backdrop showed a bunch of other people, all well dressed, smoking cigars, supping champagne in a club of some kind, very like one of those upscale drinking dens he remembered from his youth, patrolling the streets of Soho.

'This is his wife, Mary.' Mrs Travis pointed to the woman in the photograph. 'Although he always referred to her as Mary Estelle, her professional name. She was an actress. Quite well-known, I think, in her day.'

'He spoke of her often?'

'Oh, yes. They were devoted to each other. She's very beautiful, don't you think?'

The inspector nodded. He turned to face the neighbour. 'Mrs Travis?'

'Yes?'

'When you were cleaning, and tidying things away, did you find anything unusual?'

'I didn't really look around that much.'

'Anything at all?'

Again, she hesitated. 'Does pornography count? Dirty magazines? Oh, I don't quite know what to call them! Anyway, it made me quite sick, finding them like that.'

Hobbes and Latimer exchanged another glance.

'But of course I never mentioned it to Leonard. After all, he was a man alone.'

She looked at the two police officers nervously, and added, by way of an excuse, or an explanation, 'They were very old. From the sixties, or the fifties, even.'

Hobbes nodded. 'I see. Anything else?'

'No, that's all.'

'You didn't take anything from the house?'

Caroline's eyes opened in shock. 'What? No, of course not! How – how dare you?'

Latimer moved in to calm her. 'That's all right. Don't—'

'Well, he shouldn't say things like that. He shouldn't!'

Hobbes stood there, looking at Caroline Travis, saying nothing. He couldn't decide if her indignation was real or a cover.

'You said before that there was more than one dress of this kind.' He pointed to the dress on the floor. 'Could you tell me where the others are?'

'They're in the back bedroom on the top floor, the one on the right. In the wardrobe.'

'Thank you. That will be all.'

Caroline Travis looked at him for a few moments, her eyes dark with hurt. Then she turned and left the room.

Latimer waited until she heard the front door close. 'So you think she was taking things?'

'Yes, but I don't know why I think it. She's certainly holding something back.'

'It's her perfume.'

'What?'

'Caroline Travis was wearing perfume.'

'I noticed.'

Latimer tilted her head and smiled. 'And?'

The light went on in Hobbes's eyes. 'Oh, it's the same kind.'

'Exactly.'

'Midnight in Paris.'

'There's your trigger.'

'Yes, yes. Maybe she took a bottle for herself. Damn it. How could I miss that?'

'Getting old.'

Hobbes smiled at her. 'Not quite yet.'

Meg Latimer was both his bane and his blessing: the one person on the team he could readily talk to, even if she was always undercutting his thoughts. Today she looked as untidy as ever, her dark hair uncombed and unruly, the 'hedge-backwards effect', she called it. She was rarely without a cigarette, as now, and her face creased a little, her eyes narrowed, as she saw him studying her. She gave him that fuck-you-too look in return. 'I need to clean my lungs of the smell of this place. Too much loneliness.' Hobbes nodded, not wanting the argument. He could never tell if she rated him, or whether she was playing a game. If so, she played it well. And, quite often, from their differing opinions a new idea would emerge.

'So then, Guv . . .'

'So. Indeed.'

'What the hell do we do?'

'There's nothing here, Meg – no crime, no dead body.'

'Apart from Mr Graves.'

'Yes.' His mind was absent.

'You've forgotten about him already, haven't you? Bloody hell!'

His head shook slightly. 'Anyway, so much for your theory of the dead wife.'

Latimer shrugged this off. 'I'll search for next of kin. Let them know.'

'Yes. Good. And could you arrange a photographer?'

'For the body? I don't think . . .'

'No. For the dresses. All of them, mind. Every last one, each in its place.'

'Sure. What's on your mind?'

'Nothing. Nothing at all, not yet.'

She let him ponder for a moment longer, then asked, 'Are you coming back to the station?'

'I'll stay here for a bit, I think. A tour of the house.'

Latimer looked nonplussed. 'Are you feeling all right?'

'As good as can be.'

'OK, so what the fuck is wrong, then?'

He looked away, his eye drawn back to the fireplace, the laid-out dress, the shoes, the scarf. The shape of a woman. The blood, the tear in the cloth. The pattern on the dress: blue background, yellow flowers.

That pattern and cut, that same design . . . years ago . . .

'Guv?'

'It's Glenda.'

'Glenda? Oh, right, your wife. Sorry, I forgot her name—'

'She rang me this morning, wants to meet up.'

'But that's good, isn't it?'

'Maybe.'

'Or maybe not?'

He wouldn't go any further on the subject. Instead he returned his attention to the house and its ghostly occupants. 'Something happened here, Meg. Something bad.'

She nodded. 'True.'

'It worries me. What if . . .'

'Go on.'

'The theatre scene. Actors, directors.' Hobbes gestured to the empty dress. 'What if all these dresses, each one created at a different time, the blood, the wound in the cloth, what if all this was a series of rehearsals?'

'For a crime, you mean? A murder? Or a series of murders?'

'Yes. Why not?'

'Perhaps we'll never know.' It was Latimer's final statement before leaving.

Hobbes frowned. He didn't like it one bit, the idea of never knowing. His entire being burned against such a notion. His hands rubbed against each other, palm on palm. Friction. He felt his heart tighten in his chest.

He stood alone in the middle of the room, willing the anger to subside.

It wouldn't. It wouldn't go away.

He suspected it never would, not until the final case of his life took him over, however many years away that was.

Damn it to Hell and back!

He walked the floors of the house for the second time that day, but on this occasion taking in every room. He opened cupboards and drawers, he peered inside wardrobes and behind panels and decorative screens. He examined the photographs that covered the walls, many of them showing Mary Estelle Graves on stage, always posed in a highly dramatic fashion. He glanced under beds and behind armchairs. But the truth was, he didn't know what he was looking for. But he was in his element now, working alone, fully engaged with the very particular atmosphere created when a death has occurred, the vacuum left behind. He lived for these moments. This was his chosen location in life: this emptiness, these shadows, the silence that followed him along the corridors.

The small ground-floor room that served as Graves's makeshift bedroom was as neatly set out as all the others, and quite clean. It had the look of a well-tended campsite. It was amazing: the old man really looked after his personal effects, and himself. Clearly, he was holding back the tide for as long as he could. Which begged the question: what event had tipped him over the edge, had had him reaching for the vodka and the pills?

Hobbes bent down and looked under the single bed. A chamber pot: he hadn't seen one of those since he was a small boy. Memories. The outside lavatory, far too dark for a night-time visit, but having to go there anyway. The fear of insects crawling on you as you sat down, lice, beetles, spiders. His mother shouting for him from the back door.

He walked upstairs, thinking of Graves struggling to get up here. The old man must have been in search of specific objects, items of sentimental value, perhaps. Maybe to set out the dresses, or to fetch a new one.

In a small cupboard Hobbes found a collection of perfume bottles, all the same brand, Midnight in Paris. This was where the neighbour had done her pilfering. And he was still thinking of her when he entered a back room and located a cardboard box, which held the collection of adult magazines – Mrs Travis really had made a thorough search of the place. Perhaps she was looking for something she'd heard about, something that Leonard Graves had mentioned to her. Hobbes had sudden visions of a hidden fortune. It was easy to imagine such a thing in a house like this: the old mistrust of banks, the stash of banknotes under a floorboard.

He skimmed through a couple of the magazines. They were indeed from the 1950s: see-through nighties, mild bondage, a spot of light caning. *Le vice anglais*, as the French called it. All very tame by today's standards, and Hobbes had to wonder why Mr Graves had kept them, so neatly tied together, like rare issues of comic books. In fact, every object in the house, every piece of furniture, every photograph was carefully arranged. Mr Graves was a stickler for neatness, and order.

The face and form of Mary Estelle adorned every wall. Often she was on her own in these images, at other times accompanied by her husband. And she was young in every shot: her older image had been banished. No children were portrayed. And yet the house was so big. Why would two people live here on their own? It didn't make sense.

A locked door here and there, at least one on each floor.

A nursery. Or the remains of one: the brocade wallpaper had peeled away in shreds revealing fairy castles and galleons underneath. It must have served for both boys and girls, in its time. Now only echoes filled the bare space. Next door was a boy's bedroom from yesteryear, complete with pictures of steam locomotives and cruise liners on the walls. He guessed twenties, early thirties.

Another corridor, each one leading off another. The higher the floor, the more maze-like the house was: a lot of additions to rooms and walls, some of the work professional, but more often quite homemade-looking.

A fly moved on the wall. Was it the same one he'd seen on the hand of the dead body, biding its time? Hobbes took a book from a nearby shelf and smashed it down on the insect. He muttered to himself, 'Humans one, decay nil.'

But, of course, decay was never out of action for long.

One room had a small raised platform, and it took him a moment to work out what it was: a stage. The family must have put on plays and sketches here. The costumes, the laughter and words of encouragement, children with wooden swords and papier-mâché crowns on cotton-wool wigs.

The next flight of stairs, the last. He noticed that a stair-lift had been installed to reach this final floor. He pictured Graves slowly rising upwards, his eyes gazing at the portraits of his wife on the staircase wall.

More bedrooms, more storage cupboards. An old Singer sewing-machine in one room. There was a pile of yellowing manuscripts stacked in the corner. Hobbes looked at the top two: playscripts, both written by Leonard Graves. And even more framed playbills on the walls. A lot of mirrors on this level, in all shapes and sizes, ornate, simple, cracked and dirty or polished, and one or two smashed completely, only jagged shards of glass remaining in the frames. Hobbes couldn't escape his own image as he walked along.

An attic door in the roof. A set of stepladders leaned against the wall, and the inspector was sorely tempted, especially when he saw that the door was padlocked. What was kept up there, hidden from whose hands and eyes? But he backed away. He had to keep in mind that no crime had been committed.

But, my God, this place spooked him.

So many dresses, each set out as though for a woman to step into, to wear for a romantic date, or a night on the town. He counted them as he found them, in one room after another, keeping tally. Thirteen, all told. Was the number chosen deliberately, he wondered, an omen of ill luck? Most were laid out on the floor, a few others held on hangers, or on hooks in the wall, the scarf and stockings draped over the shoulders, the shoes placed neatly on the floor beneath. Sometimes just the dress alone. And they all looked to be from different periods of time, years apart even, given the condition they were in, the amount of dust, the state of the blood or its substitute.

Thirteen ghosts. Thirteen wounds in the cloth, thirteen splashes of red.

In an otherwise empty room, he found the wardrobe that Caroline Travis had referred to: another ten or so dresses of the same design and size hanging on a rail. More scarves, more shoes, but these secondary items were of differing designs and colours. No, it was the dress that was important, that had to be the same each time, the exact same. The dress was the *totem*. It was a strange word to use, but he could think of no other. The dress was a metaphor. But for what? Which event, or which person?

Coming back downstairs, he paused on the first-floor landing and looked down on the back garden through a round leaded window. The sky had darkened with clouds, lending the house an even more morbid air. The garden was huge, the far end of the untended lawn lost in a tangle of overgrown bushes, hedges and brambles. A contorted elm rose from the wild flowers and vegetation, its trunk wound tightly with strings of ivy and its leaves in their October colours. Hobbes pressed his hands on the glass. There was something of interest down there, in the garden, hidden in the overgrowth. He descended to the ground floor and made his way to the kitchen. The ambulance team had arrived and were taking away the body, lowering it on to a stretcher.

'Could you check his pockets for me, please?'

One of the men did so, and found a folded sheet of paper. Hobbes opened it and read the single line of handwriting.

Dearest Adeline, I'm so sorry. For everything.

So, then: Leonard Graves's final thoughts were not with his wife, Mary, but another woman. A daughter or sister, perhaps.

A lover, a mistress. Perhaps the couple had not been so devoted, after all. One thing was clear: it wasn't for his wife's sake that he had ended his life.

Hobbes opened the kitchen door, walked out into the garden and made his way to the wilderness at the end. The rear of the house was protected by a high stone wall, impossible to see over, its top studded with diamonds of broken glass. Mr Graves really wanted to keep people out. Hobbes pushed on into the overgrowth, bending aside brambles and heavily scented weeds that clung to his clothes as he passed. Some of the leaves were already yellow and orange; a mulch of them squelched underfoot. It had rained heavily that morning, and now everything stank of rot and overabundance. Hobbes felt nauseous. He stepped in something soft, and his shoe vanished into it, almost to the ankle. An animal moved away through the tangled darkness ahead, causing the stems to tremble. Dark, slithery, unseen.

Hobbes was sweating by the time he reached the garden shed he'd spotted from the landing window. The wooden structure was almost hidden by clinging vines and tendrils. He stared through a filthy, fly-spattered window and saw only a dark space within, a grey mist. He walked around the side, again fighting his way through the plant life, and found the door. It was unlocked. He pushed it open against some obstruction, or just the weight of years bearing down on it. The air was foetid, damp. Cobwebs strung themselves around his head as he made his way inside. He brushed them aside and looked around. A workbench, rusting tools on the walls, many crumbling away at the edges. A vice, tins of nails and screws. Each item in its rightful place. But unused, unused for years. A metal bucket rested on the floor, filled to the brim with rainwater that had dripped down from a hole in the roof. The linoleum around the bucket was brown with rot. Hooked on the single overhead beam was a clothes hanger, with another dress of the same blue and yellow material hanging from it. Another scarf around the neck, another pair of shoes placed on the floor. The dress was moth-eaten, covered with dirt and cobwebs, barely an object in the world: a filigree, a web itself. One touch might crumble it. The bloodstain around the tear was ages old, its crimson paled almost to a shadow.

Number fourteen.

He walked back through the garden, keeping to the pathway he had made for himself. Graves had been taken away. A quick job, no fuss. The kitchen was empty. Inspector Hobbes stood by the table for a few moments, letting the atmosphere take him over.

A perfume bottle, some tablets, a bottle of vodka. A lady's handkerchief decorated with the initials *M.E.* Mary Estelle. The loving spouse. But a farewell letter to another woman.

Final rites.

We come into this world alone, and we leave this world alone.

He shook his head to clear it, then walked along the hallway towards the front door. He would drive round to his wife's house now, right now, and get it over with, and then he would know, one way or the other. Divorce, as seemed likely? Or maybe, was it possible, that Glenda might want to give it another shot?

His trouser legs were dark with rainwater and mud around the turn-ups, and his right foot squelched whenever he put it down. He stopped, thinking he might have to take it off, give it a clean in the car. And then he noticed the door built into the side of the staircase. There was a padlock on it, but it had been broken open, the bracket pulled loose from the wood of the door-frame. The door swung open easily, revealing another set of stairs, leading down into darkness. Hobbes groped around the inside wall, found a switch, and a light bulb clicked on below. With careful steps he walked down into the cellar.

It was a large space, taking up the entire foundations of the house. Crumbling stone walls, cold air, each footstep echoing. Another workbench down here, more tools. Lots of household items that the occupants could not bear to throw away: an armchair, a number of paintings, their faces to the wall, a tailor's dummy. A wine rack with a couple of dusty bottles left in it. But no sign of the telltale dress. He was almost disappointed. No more clues.

A great number of items were pushed up against the furthest wall: wicker baskets, bed sheets and blankets, rolls of wallpaper, an ironing board, cardboard boxes, books, an old canvas tent, and so on. In a darkened corner he found a small pile of bones. It was a skeleton, that of a domestic cat, by the look of it, its tail still curved around its body in death. The flesh was all gone, eaten away, although a few patches of mangled fur still clung to the bones. Next to the creature's body there was a metal bowl stained to the colour of rust inside, with a cut-throat razor laid across it. Hobbes grimaced at the sight. So old man Graves had used animal blood as well as his own, to adorn the dresses? Perhaps the cat's blood at first and then, in desperation, his own in the later years? Start with red paint, ketchup and lipstick, then move on to animal blood, and human blood. It made a kind of cruel sense, an increase of intent. Which made Graves seem like a lunatic – there was no other explanation. And yet the woman next door had painted a picture of him as essentially harmless, a little damaged in the head or heart, perhaps, by loneliness and despair. But the sight of the cat's bones told a different story.

But which story?

There was no easy answer.

Hobbes took one last look around the cellar. The household's subconscious. He laughed at this notion as he walked back upstairs. And then he stopped. He stood where he was, halfway up the stairs, and he waited as the cellar creaked around him, the bare bulb above his head already fizzing: this room wanted only to return to darkness, to silence.

Something nudged at him, a stray thought.

He really didn't like leaving things half done. *Check, and check again. Just in case.* Because he'd missed too many things when he was a rookie.

Hobbes went back down the stairs. He crossed the floor and, without hesitating, set to work on the pile of unwanted household goods, moving them aside one by one. It took him fifteen minutes. And now he stood and stared at the floor, at the patch of exposed cement, which had so obviously been disturbed some time before, perhaps years before, dug up and replaced in a roughshod fashion with cleaner cement, as best as could be done at the time.

Placed on the patch of lighter concrete was another of the dresses – number fifteen. It was torn and bloodied, as the others were, complete with accompanying shoes and scarf. No stockings this time. Hobbes bent down. A phrase in black lettering – previously hidden by the pile of rubbish – had been scrawled on the wall.

R.I.P.
ADELINE

Hobbes cursed. He should've been more careful, worked more slowly. Called Latimer back to take photographs. Now the scene was compromised. Yes, he was already thinking of it in such terms, a crime scene. His mind settled on one thought only. He stood up again, looked down at the dress and at the exposed patch of floor. And he knew: someone was buried under there.

He was certain of it.

Marks on the Skin

He stayed in the car for a few minutes just to steady his breath and to calm himself. He turned the rear-view to examine his face: the scar seemed darker today, more prominent, but he had to think that was just his nerves adding their own portion of blood. Well, there it was. His nose was crooked. Redness in the whites of his eyes. And the bloody recede didn't help! His wife hadn't seen him since he'd been attacked a few months ago: one brief phone call had sufficed, a quick asking of how he was, and if he needed anything. It wasn't really an offer, he could tell that from her voice. And now . . . and now Glenda wanted to see him again. He felt jittery, like he was going into the fray on a Saturday night after chucking-out time.

Leeside Road, Crouch End. Two up, two down, the last years of a mortgage ticking away. They'd always planned on moving up when a second kid came along, but that never happened. Just walking up to the path and pressing the bell set the memories going. He ran a hand through his hair, to pat it into place. And he suddenly realized he was holding his stomach in. Christ. *What am I doing here?*

He noticed the bruise on her eye straight off, a small mark on the rise of the cheekbone. Glenda had tried her best to cover it with powder, and for that reason alone Hobbes didn't mention it.

Still, it was a shock, and he felt his anger rising. Anger, and something he didn't like to think about, but he couldn't help himself: had a man done this?

In the living room she directed him to the settee, as she sat at the table, a respectable distance away. They didn't speak. He shifted about uncomfortably. It was strange to see her in this way, her face with its recent bruise, and his with the scar still healing. They had each received punishment: but who had done this to her? How could he ask?

Glenda coughed.

Hobbes managed a thin smile. 'You're looking . . .'

'Yes?'

He wanted to say, *You're looking good*, or *You're looking well*, or some such, but the bruise stopped him. It would be a stupid thing to say.

They fell back into silence.

No offer of a cup of tea, no biscuits, no niceties.

And then she turned away from him to stare at the decorative wall clock. She'd bought it when he'd been made detective sergeant. A celebration for the house. The room looked exactly the same: nothing new, nothing missing.

'How is your face?' she asked. 'It looks to be healing.'

'Yes, thank you.' What else could he say?

'Henry, I know what you're staring at.'

He nodded.

'Well, I must say, we both look a state.' She tried for a laugh and failed, and her voice caught. Her hand strayed to the bruise, then hurried away. 'It's not what you think,' she said.

'What am I thinking?'

Now Glenda turned to him and they stared at each other. Hobbes read so much into the shared look that he couldn't begin to untangle the feelings.

'It was an accident.'

He frowned. And then she genuinely shocked him.

'Martin did it.'

For a moment he thought he'd misheard. 'Martin . . .'

'Yes. But like I said, Henry, it was an accident, it really was.' Now she was speaking quickly, all awkwardness lost. 'He pushed me. We just sort of banged into each other, that's all, I swear to God.'

'He was here?'

She nodded. 'Yes, yes. He came round a few days ago. Friday night, it was.'

Hobbes stood up. He went over to the table and sat down near her. 'Glenda, tell me. What did he want?'

'He wanted . . .' Her eyes closed. 'He wanted help.'

'In what way?'

'I don't know. He wasn't speaking proper sense.'

'How often does he visit?'

She looked at him. 'Oh, he's only been here twice, only twice since you . . . since we . . . I mean, since you left. The first time he looked bad, far too thin, and really desperate. He can't be eating properly. He said he was in trouble, but he wouldn't say why. I gave him a few pounds, just what I had in my purse.'

'He didn't ask to see me?'

'No.'

'I could've—'

'He never mentioned you.'

'I could've helped him. Given him money. If that's what he needs.'

She started to speak, then stopped. In the silence Hobbes went over it in his mind: his son had taken the split badly, but then again, Martin took everything badly, having left home earlier this year, in the spring.

He'd only been sixteen, when he'd left.

Seventeen now.

Seventeen years old. What kind of trouble could he be in?

Despite his years on the force witnessing the simple way in which people slipped over into criminality, often by accident, DI Hobbes held an entirely innocent picture of Martin in his mind: it could never be dismissed, no matter who or what contrived to disprove it.

'And then he came back a second time?'

Glenda nodded.

'How was he?'

'At first I thought he was better. But then I saw him up close . . .'

She hesitated. Hobbes could see the worry playing at her eyes.

'What is it?'

'He looked ill.'

'Ill? In what way?'

Her head shook and she bit at her lip.

'Glenda, please.'

Now she looked at him again. 'Tired, grey skin. Unwashed. His clothes smelt bad.'

'That doesn't mean he's ill.'

'No, no. But his hands . . .'

Hobbes started to feel uneasy. But he said quietly, 'Go on.'

'He showed them to me, deliberately, like this . . .' She held both hands in front of her. 'And I could see that his fingers were . . . discoloured.'

'How do you mean?'

'They looked like they'd been . . .'

'What is it, Glenda?'

'They looked like they'd been dipped in ink. In blue ink.' She paused. 'All ten fingers. Dipped in ink nearly up to the first knuckle.'

'Do you mean his hands were damaged in some way? Or were they . . . They weren't tattooed, were they?'

'No, it wasn't that—'

'It must be one or the other.' His voice was insistent.

'Henry, don't shout, please.'

'I just need to . . . I need to understand.'

Glenda looked him steadily in the eye and said, 'He had blue fingertips. That's it. That's all I saw. And then he lowered his arms again.'

'He showed you this on purpose?'

'Oh, yes. He was proud. Or defiant. You know that look he gets?'

Yes, Hobbes knew it all too well.

For a moment neither spoke. He wanted to argue, to uncover every detail. Treat her like a witness. Christ. But their old house was used to such things, the raised voices. And the long silences that followed. Hobbes imagined all the words said in anger over the years, and the words of love. And he had to wonder which side had come out on top.

The same wallpaper, the same furniture: he never had got round to redecorating.

His mind focused. 'You think it's some kind of infection?'

'Maybe, yes. That's all I can think.'

'He's in pain.'

'No, I don't think so. Not physical pain, anyway.'

Hobbes felt the onset of darkness. A flicker at the edge.

Glenda nodded in response and, again, her hand went to her cheekbone, and this time it stayed there. He saw in her face the lines, the concern, the face he had loved and still loved. Together they had striven. Love grew from that, it deepened, but this last year had been too much: the balance had shifted. And his wife held the weight of worry.

'What happened, Glenda?'

'We argued. I asked him about his hands, but he wouldn't tell me. And the thought of not being able to reach him was too much. I shouted at him.' She took a breath. 'And then . . .'

'And then he hit you?'

'He didn't. I told you . . .'

'Glenda?'

'He was drunk, or on drugs, I don't know. Or maybe his illness, whatever it might be.'

'Tell me what happened. Everything.'

She did so, describing how their son had pushed past her in his frustration. 'And that's when we made contact.' The phrase made him bristle: making contact doesn't leave a bruise. More than that was needed, far more.

'I banged my face against the door jamb.'

As a police officer, he would automatically suspect this, and think it a lie, to cover up some deeper, more painful truth. But this was different: this was his own wife and child, arguing with each other. He would always want to understand, as best he could.

'Did he apologize?'

'No. No. He was too far gone for that. He just sort of collapsed into the seat, where you're sitting now, with his head bowed.'

'What did you do?'

'I stood here, and I watched him. I didn't know what to do. But then he looked at me and said the strangest thing . . . He asked about our wedding photos.'

'What?'

'I know, I know. It's odd, but that's what he wanted to see, our wedding album.'

Hobbes tried to process this. 'Why would he want—'

'He was very insistent. So I gave him what he wanted, of course. I was curious.'

'Yes, yes, I can imagine.'

Glenda went to the sideboard and opened a cupboard. She drew out a large book with a padded cover. She handed it to Hobbes. He placed it on the table and flipped through the pages: 1963, the year of their wedding. It was a small church affair and then a reception in a room above their local pub. Glenda's mum and dad smiling dutifully. And his old friends and colleagues on the force. Their faces . . . some he remembered, some he couldn't quite put names to. A couple were dead now: the line of fire, or self-inflicted.

But no one, not one person from his own family.

Glenda said, 'He sat where you are now, Henry, and he did exactly what you're doing.'

'He was looking for a particular image?'

'Yes. He took it away with him. The next page. You'll see.'

Hobbes was expecting to see an empty space in the album, but every single slot held a photograph. And then he noticed something strange: one of the pictures wasn't from their wedding.

'OK, I need help with this. Glenda?'

She spelled it out: 'Our son took away a wedding photo, and replaced it with that one. I didn't realize he'd done it, not until later, after he'd left.'

Hobbes examined the new photograph.

He asked, 'Which photo did he take? What did it show?'

'The two of us. Just me and you, Henry, outside the church. That's all.'

Hobbes found he was trembling slightly. What was going on? Why on earth should Martin want that photograph? The lad had never shown any interest in their wedding before. Was it a good thing that he was seeking out these old images from their relationship? Did he want to be reminded of something, of the family's better days? Was that it?

And why on earth replace it with a new image?

He looked at Glenda and asked, 'Did he leave then?'

She nodded. 'He was agitated. His mood kept changing, I couldn't keep up with him. He stood up, paced the room a few times, speaking to himself, and then he left. I called to him, but he just ignored me. The front door banged shut.' Her eyes suddenly opened wide, as though she could still hear the bang of the door against the frame. 'And then he was gone.'

She sat next to him on the settee and he took her hand in his.

Neither of them spoke a word. He could hear a radio playing through the wall. Radio 1. Pop hits. A bright, sunny tune. They always played it too loudly.

Her fingers curling around his.

That was good. He held on. This was the closest they'd been in half a year. His eyes closed. *That it took all this to make it happen* . . .

'Do you know where he's living?' he asked.

'In Peckham, I think. One of those illegal housing places.'

'A squat?'

'Yes. I think he mentioned someone called Oliver. A friend, maybe. I don't know.'

Hobbes made a mental note. 'Good. That's something.'

Her mood lit up, and he reacted to the signal, as he always would. 'I'll find him, Glen. I'll see what I can do. I'll help him.'

But in truth a strange mood had taken him over, dark-tinged. It was this room, the lost promises, a young man growing up too quickly. And not for the first time Hobbes thought of how the troubles of the past half-year had affected the boy: not just his parents separating, but also the problems at work, his father's face in the newspapers – *DI Hobbes called 'outright liar' in Soho attack case*. And even on the *Nine O'Clock News*, right here in the living room, with all three of them sitting in their usual places – father, mother and son – watching the television in silence. It had all started after the Brixton riot had devastated the city. Hobbes had stumbled on a group of fellow officers attacking a young black man. He'd blown the whistle on them, and been punished for it by his colleagues, high and low.

Police chiefs call for resignation of . . .

DI Hobbes blamed for . . .

Police Board to decide this week . . .

Oh, the poor lad, poor Martin: it didn't bear thinking about. His hand parted from Glenda's, and he said again, 'I'll find him.' It was enough. A promise.

The Stranger

Late night, no hope of sleeping. He had laid out a few photographs – the only ones he owned – on the coffee-table in his living room. One after another: Martin as a kid, knee-high to his dad, playing football. The usual fantasies – his son scoring a goal for England in the World Cup final. Happy families, holiday shots. The kid alone, growing shy as he got older, often turning away from the camera. He had his mother's good looks, thank God. Hobbes allowed himself a smile at that. And then his son with his friends, all male, not yet that interested in girls. In the final image Martin's face was pained in some way, caught unawares.

Hobbes levered the cap off a bottle of beer.

Other thoughts intruding.

The light seemed to dim in his tiny room and he adjusted the reading lamp slightly, angling the beam.

Photographs. One image swapped for another. Why?

And then a spark flared in his mind.

That dress.

That bloody dress. The blood on the dress, on the torn and bloody dress.

His mind could not keep still, not tonight.

Yellow flowers, tiny flowers, so many of them on the blue cloth.

Spots of red on the yellow, the blood . . .

His mind clicking on the various sightings, one room after another, the same dress, the same design, over and over. Fifteen dresses, nearly the same number of scarves, and then the shoes, the stockings. Add it all up. How many, in total? Maybe fifty items altogether. Leonard Graves laying them all out one by one, a patient old man at work. The pills and the vodka. And then Hobbes happened by chance upon a memory, as before, when Latimer had first shown him the dress laid out on the floor of the living room. His own past, a similar thing, but years ago, years, he couldn't quite place it . . .

He stopped his thoughts right there and stared at the photograph he was holding.

This was the new image, the one Martin had slotted into the album. It showed his son and a friend, a woman this time, but older than him by a good few years, somebody new. Late twenties, maybe more. Hard to tell. One arm draped over his son's shoulders, the other stretched out before her towards the camera. Smiling broadly. Martin also. A joke shared. A fragment of graffiti on a wall behind them: BAN THE. The photograph was taken recently, Martin looking older than Hobbes remembered, his hair longer. The thinness that Glenda had mentioned. A T-shirt with a Public Image Ltd logo on it.

This woman. Who was she?

He held the photo under the light and stared at the stranger's face intently. And then at her outstretched hand. The fingertips. The colour of them.

Could he really trust what he was seeing?

The Middle Child

The next morning he overslept, something he hardly ever did these days, and he groaned as he sat up in bed. And then he remembered the cause: on top of the can of beer, he had taken a couple of shots of whisky late last night. Another unusual occurrence.

There was a single thought in his head: *Martin. Find Martin.*

And then the day crowded in: the light, the traffic, the hustle and bustle of the police station. The constant attention to work, as one human being after another fell into temptation.

Cleaning up the mess.

As Hobbes caught up on his paperwork, he decided to spend a day or two at the most on the Case of the Fifteen Dresses, as he was now calling it in his head. If nothing was found out by then, well, so be it: the old man would lie in peace. So he was glad when DS Latimer came in and greeted him with the news.

'I've found a relative of Mr Graves, a son. Nicholas.'

'Oh, good. I'll go and see him. Address?'

'Actually, he's waiting to speak to you. Room Two.'

Hobbes smiled. 'You want to join in?'

'Too busy. And, anyway, this is your baby.' She turned towards her desk, adding, 'Just remember: the man's father has died.'

The inspector nodded. Latimer was always telling him to be

kinder to people. Or at least to be more aware of them. *Not every-one's a suspect.* That was the phrase she liked to use. But Hobbes had his own rejoinder: 'No, but everyone's to blame for some-thing.' And she'd told him he was a hopeless, irredeemable cause.

He got a coffee from the canteen, added two and a bit sugars, then walked along the corridor to the smaller of the two inter-view rooms.

Nicholas Graves was around sixty years old, and right now he was showing every mark and worry of every single day of his time on the planet. Hobbes sat down opposite to him, introduced himself, then said, 'I'm very sorry for the loss of your father.' He could never get the voice just right, despite so many years' experience.

Nicholas stared ahead. 'He killed himself. Is that correct?' Each word was slowly and clearly pronounced.

'It is, yes.'

'I don't understand, I must say.'

'He was very old.'

'He wasn't the kind to do such a thing.'

Hobbes said, 'He had reached the end of his life.' Blunt, but truthful.

'Yes. Yes, of course.'

'A certain kind of person prefers it this way. Still, that doesn't make it any easier, not for those left behind.'

Nicholas Graves stared at the detective for a good few moments. He started to breathe heavily; it sounded as though his entire body was starved of oxygen. He tried to speak, but then stopped. One hand was resting on the tabletop, the fingers clenched together, like an animal hiding in its shell.

Hobbes studied the other man under the bright light of the overhead tube.

Nicholas Graves was every inch his father's son: thin, almost frail, sunken at the key points – cheeks, eye sockets, the muscles of the neck. He had the haunted look that Hobbes had noted on the dead body. Father and son, both men who wasted nothing of what they ate, burning it all for fuel. But what drove them? What was the fire?

The only real outward difference was that the son had retained most of his hair, long and swept back with just a small recede at the temples: it gave him the air of an old-fashioned romantic artist, or a classical pianist. Had it been dyed?

Now Hobbes spoke in a quieter voice. 'I'm glad you came in to see us.'

'The other officer, the female officer . . .'

'Detective Sergeant Latimer.'

'Yes. She said there was a problem.'

'You've been to your father's house, I take it?'

'To Bridlemere? Yes. This morning.'

'And you saw the dresses. Can you tell me—'

'I'm sorry, the dresses?'

Irritation entered Hobbes's voice. 'The dresses laid out on the floor, and hung up from hangers. In the living room, various bedrooms, the cellar. You did see them?'

The other man nodded.

'This didn't strike you as strange?'

Graves frowned. 'There were some clothes scattered around the place, yes, but I don't quite see . . .'

'Scattered around? That's what it looked like to you?'

'My father could be—'

'Because to me they looked *arranged*. Very carefully arranged.'

Graves went quiet. Hobbes watched as he gnawed at his lips, almost hard enough to draw blood. His lined face was now very pale, and his sunken cheeks caught at shadows.

'I don't . . .'

'Yes?'

'I don't really see what the problem is. My father was eighty-five years old. Who knows what goes through a mind of that many years?'

'Granted.' Hobbes waited, saying no more.

'What I'm saying is . . . well, perhaps he went a bit strange, towards the end.'

'Yes, yes. That's possible. Certainly.'

Graves drew his strength together and stated, 'I really don't see what it has to do with the police. Has a crime been committed?'

'No.'

'Well, then . . .'

'Mr Graves, all of the dresses are torn in the same place. Like a wound. And there is blood on them. On just about every one. Blood. Or a symbol for blood.'

The room filled with silence, one man staring at the other.

And then Nicholas Graves stood up, his chair scraping along the floor. 'I feel like I should just leave, actually. Because – because I don't know why you're doing this to me. Why?' The paleness left the man's face as his anger rose and burst in a howl of pain. 'My father has just died!'

'Please, please, sit down, Mr Graves. I didn't mean to—'

'You have no right! No right at all.'

Now both men were standing. Hobbes felt only frustration, but he was willing to back down, to acquiesce. But then the door of the interview room opened and DS Latimer entered.

'Mind if I sit in?'

Her presence immediately calmed Nicholas Graves. He sat down without another word, and Hobbes followed suit. Latimer remained standing. She took charge.

'Nicholas, were you close to your father?'

'Not particularly, no.'

'So you didn't see him very often?'

'No, not really, not these days . . . now and then.'

Hobbes let his sergeant do the talking. She must've been watching at the glass the whole time: so much for not wanting to join in.

Latimer asked, 'When was the last time you saw him?'

'Oh, that would be, let me see . . . about four years ago. I don't have any children of my own, you see.'

'Right. No grandchildren, no reason to visit.'

A single nod in response.

'What about your mother?'

At this question there was a definite change in Nicholas's appearance: his whole face seemed to fold inwards, the sides of the cheeks almost touching each other. It was a startling thing to witness. Hobbes was staring at a man who wanted nothing more than to vanish into himself.

Latimer pressed the point. 'She's in a home, I believe?'

'Yes, that's right. She went in about . . . five years ago, it was.'

'For?'

'I'm sorry?'

'What kind of home?'

'Just an old people's home.' He paused, blinking. 'She isn't crazy or anything like that. Just, you know, a bit under the weather.'

'I see.'

And then Nicholas said something interesting: 'We took Mary Estelle away from him, from Father.' He ended the statement with a weak smile.

Hobbes nodded, giving nothing away. 'Do you have any siblings?' he asked.

'I have two sisters, Rosamund and Camilla. One older, one younger. I was born in the middle.'

'And did they go round to Bridlemere very much?'

'I don't know. I really don't know. We are a . . . *separated* family.' His voice took on a definite and very deliberate edge. 'We have, each of us, taken very differing pathways through life.' The skin around his eyes twitched at a sudden thought. 'Oh dear. I'll have to inform them today.'

Latimer took a seat at the table and smiled, hoping to draw him closer. Graves responded well to this: he leaned forwards just a little way.

'Nicholas, are you sure you don't know what the dresses might mean? You have no clue at all?'

He shook his head. 'I'm sorry, I really don't.'

'But you do understand our concern, if some of them have human blood smeared on them?'

'My father – our father, I should say – he was never a rational man, or a kind one. In fact, he was often the opposite. Leonard Graves was a creative person, a playwright. He was fêted in his day, before the fashion in drama changed in the 1950s. Like many of that generation, the first night of *Look Back in Anger* made him terribly out of date.'

Hobbes asked a question of his own: 'He was more interested in his job than in the family, is that what you mean?'

'No, not that. But he treated the family as a drama of his own making.'

Hobbes could sense that Nicholas was relaxing a little. He said, 'I saw a small theatre stage in one of the rooms of the house. Did your father build that?'

Nicholas nodded, but would offer no further information. The furrows appeared once more in his brow.

'Are you working at the moment?' Hobbes asked.

'I have had numerous careers, most of them artistic in some way. And most of them failures.' He laughed a little. 'At the moment I'm working in journalism, for the *Telegraph*.'

'I see.'

'In three years I reach retirement age.'

'So you're, what, sixty-two now?'

He nodded.

Hobbes drew a folded piece of paper out of his pocket and placed it on the table. 'Your father left a suicide note, a message to a loved one.'

Nicholas stared at the piece of paper without speaking. Then he picked it up and read it to himself, his lips moving with each word.

Hobbes asked, 'Do you know who Adeline is?'

'No.'

Latimer came in: 'Not one of your sisters' middle names? Or some other relative?'

'I've never heard the name said before, in the household, as far as I can recall.'

'Your father's mistress, perhaps?'

Graves looked up at the inspector. The pain had burned clean away from the man's face, leaving only coldness in his eyes. 'It might well be that. He was a randy sod.'

There wasn't an ounce of humour in the remark. An entire family history was contained within that one line: loneliness, despair, anger, a marriage breaking down, the young kids clinging together for comfort and security – sister, brother, sister.

Hobbes cut to the heart: 'What we'd like to do is dig up the floor of the cellar.'

Graves stared at him. His eyes never wavered.

Hobbes was about to repeat his words, but the other man cut in: 'I don't understand you, Inspector. Why on earth would you—'

'I believe,' Hobbes explained, 'that somebody is buried under there. A woman called Adeline.'

The staring match continued.

Latimer watched from the side, letting them play it out.

Without even glancing her way, Hobbes said, 'Detective Sergeant Latimer, would you explain the procedure to Mr Graves? Thank you.'

'I can do that.' She leaned over the table. 'It would entail the police employing a contractor, a trusted firm. They would drill into the floor, one section only, and take up the concrete. Afterwards, everything would be put back in place, probably even better than it now looks. There is no expense on your part.'

Nicholas Graves laughed. 'You think I'm concerned about the *cost?*'

'I'm simply explaining—'

'Do you have a search warrant?'

Hobbes answered this one: 'No. And I very much doubt that I would get one, not on the evidence as it stands.'

'The evidence? You mean some items of clothing left on the floor?'

Hobbes played his last card: 'And the words "R.I.P. Adeline" scrawled on the wall.'

This clearly threw the other man, and for one second Hobbes thought he'd managed it. But instead Nicholas firmed his jaw and spoke clearly: 'No. *No*, is the answer.'

It was his final word. Nicholas stood up from his seat and was about to make his way towards the door, when he paused and said, 'May I keep my father's note?'

'Of course. It's not police property.'

Nicholas held the inspector's gaze for one second longer, then left the room, the door banging to after him.

Latimer waited a moment, and then said, 'So that's that then. Back to normal.'

'Perhaps . . .'

'How do you mean?'

He shrugged and smiled a little, and she looked at him askance, and said, 'Bloody hell, you want to break in at night, don't you, when no one's around? With a pickaxe and a shovel, and do the job yourself. Is that it?'

'Nothing would give me greater pleasure.'

'Holy shit. I can just see you doing it, covered with dust, hands blistered.'

'Whatever it takes.'

Latimer tilted her head. 'You're a damn good copper, Hobbes, but a fool with it,' she said, with a fake movie-star accent to soften the blow. It worked a little. Still, he knew what he was, and he knew how people regarded him.

He smiled back. 'Let's sit here a while longer, shall we?'

'And do what?'

'Chat, discuss your current cases, your plans for the future.'

She looked at him as though he were cracked in the head. 'Well, I'd like Fairfax to be back at work, at least.'

'Yes, yes. I was trying to write him a letter, just this morning.'

'Fairfax? Saying what?'

'I'm not sure. I kept getting it wrong, having to start again.'

'You know he's moved back into his mum's house?'

'Where is that?'

'Deptford.'

'Get me the address, will you?'

'Sure. If you think it'll do any good.'

Hobbes looked aside. 'The thing is, Meg, nobody likes being under suspicion.'

'I'm sorry, what? Oh, you mean the son? Graves?'

'It eats away at them. Ah! Here we are . . .'

The door of the interview room opened and Nicholas Graves walked back inside. He was breathing heavily, almost a continual heaving sigh, and dots of sweat had broken out at his high temples. He spoke directly to Hobbes.

'Will you promise, if you dig up the cellar floor and find no sign of a dead body . . . is that it? Will you then leave me, and my family, and our house, alone? Will you?'

The inspector smiled. 'I give you my word.'

Nicholas looked relieved. But Hobbes thought he saw something else in the man's eyes: a kind of fear.

It lasted a moment only.

Too Much Noise

DS Talbot from the Peckham station gave Hobbes a tour of the local housing units that had been taken over by squatters. Sally Talbot was the new breed of policewoman, a no-nonsense professional playing strictly by the rules, while doing whatever needed doing when people's backs were turned. 'One foot on the greasy ladder, and no fat bastard up top is going to drag me back down.' It was the second time in half an hour that he'd heard her say as much. But he let it pass. She was ex-Charing Cross nick, as he was, and he was used to her outbursts.

'We had to do something to stop the slum landlords evicting people. So the law was passed, stopping them breaking into residential properties. And now we have the opposite problem – people taking over empty buildings, and making them their homes.'

'Is that such a bad thing?' Hobbes asked.

'Small fry, without a doubt. But they're not paying rent.'

'Nothing to do with the police, surely.'

'I'm paying top whack for my digs, Henry. Why the hell shouldn't everyone else?'

Hobbes laughed. 'You haven't changed, Sally.'

'Change? Why would I change? I'm perfect as I am.'

Now they were both laughing. She steered her Ford Granada into a side-street.

'Anyway, we keep as low a profile around the squats as we can, but some of these places, they're hotbeds for drugs, violence, political unrest, you name it. And now and then some young idiot gets him- or herself killed. Overdose, usually. Or else they fall off the roofs. They like to go up there and get high. They start dancing around, and splat!'

The talk of young people dying quietened Hobbes. They had visited three places so far, and the task seemed daunting, just from the outside: boarded-up windows, barbed wire, threatening graffiti, no one answering any of the doors. And if they did see someone, the usual response was abuse: *Fuckin' pigs! Cop filth!*

Hobbes had heard it all before, and worse, but it still got to him.

'Who is this guy you're looking for anyway?' Talbot asked.

'A long-time informant. He went off the map recently, but I know he has info for me on a case.' He had the story down pat.

Talbot pulled the car to a halt and turned to her passenger. 'Now why don't I believe you? You're pulling a stunt, aren't you? Come on, what's really going on?'

Hobbes shrugged. 'Hush-hush.'

'Personal, is it? Are you in trouble? Again, Hobbes?'

'Something like that.'

Talbot grinned. 'Christ, but you lead a shitty life.'

They got out of the car and walked to the edge of a rundown housing block. 'And here we are. Welcome to Cromwell House.'

Straight away, Hobbes knew this was the one. 'I thought I was looking for a person, a man.'

'How do you mean?'

'All I had was a name, a contact. Oliver.'

'Right, yes. Oliver's. Or plain Ollie's. That's the nickname the kids use for the block. They obviously think they're performing some kind of rebellion. Well, they are. But only against their nice middle-class upbringings.' Talbot smirked. 'Most of them come here from the suburbs, looking for excitement.'

Hobbes had stopped listening.

'Mind, I should tell you, this place is a bit different from the others. Well, you'll see.'

They walked into a large interior courtyard, surrounded on all sides by three-storey-high walkways. Every single window he could see was boarded up, as was every door. It was eerily silent, even in the middle of the afternoon.

'Are you sure people live here?' Hobbes asked.

'They do. But the Roundheads like to keep themselves to themselves. They're a private tribe, cut off from normal life, and even from the other squatting communities. They live by their own laws here, and there's not a lot we can do about it.'

Hobbes saw a line of graffiti spray-painted on a wall: *BAN THE BOMB*. It looked to be the same as the wording in the photograph Martin had left in the wedding album. The light was fading as a bank of clouds moved overhead, low down, laden with rain. A strong wind was blowing through the entranceway, and a swirl of litter was caught in an alcove leading to a stairwell. Hobbes felt as if he was walking on to the set of a movie when the filming was long over, or something more than that, far stranger, like an abandoned building in a dream world. And yet life was here: the further they ventured inside, the more he could sense it. It stirred behind the barriers and the boards, the faintest sign, the lowest sound, a whispering, the noise of hate or despair, he didn't know which.

And then the music started.

Quietly at first, a drumbeat, a few guitar chords. And then growing louder and louder, a song played from one of the flats. It grew in volume until the walls seemed to pound with the heavy bass. A different song started from the opposite side of the courtyard, playing at the same time as the other. Hobbes and Talbot stopped where they were. It was an aggressive act against them. A third tune came from the walkway directly in front of them. The sound was a maelstrom, an explosion of noise. And Hobbes was at the centre of it.

DS Talbot turned to him and raised her hands in surrender. 'I told you so. It's a hellhole.'

Her voice was almost lost in the continuing noise.

Another increase in volume drove the two officers out of the central courtyard and back to the car. Talbot drove in silence for a while. Words could not compete with what they had just heard or, rather, experienced.

'I guess they don't like us?' Hobbes said at last.

Talbot grunted. 'So what do you think? You still happy to go in there looking for your nark?'

Hobbes thought about it. He thought about his son hiding behind one of those boarded-up windows, peering out through a gap, watching his father as the noise rained down. Maybe he had even chosen a record, put it on the player, and turned up the volume. His own son's hands on the controls – it was certainly possible, aiming the music right at him. A punishment, or a warning to stay away.

'He's in there. I know it.'

They stopped at a red light, and Talbot snuck a sideways glance, but she didn't say anything. Hobbes's expression was too fixed in place, bound tight. Nothing would change it.

Five minutes later she asked, 'Is this about your kid? What's his name? Martin. Is it? I heard he'd left home.'

Hobbes didn't answer. Talbot drove on along Peckham High Street.

'You know what, Henry? Sometimes you just have to let them go.'

Hobbes nodded. The music was still ringing in his ears.

Down to the Roots

It was half past six in the evening by the time they got a team in place to start digging up the cellar floor at Bridlemere. Hobbes watched the first cracks appear in the concrete, but the dust got into his throat and he had to make his way back upstairs. He sat waiting with Latimer in the living room. The flowery dress had been taken up from the floor, along with the shoes and the scarf – most probably Nicholas Graves had cleared them away. He would have to have words with him, about not destroying the clothing, just in case they found anything.

Hobbes stood up and started walking back and forth.

Someone was hidden down there. He knew he was right.

The sound of the drill came up through the floorboards and the room trembled a little. Dust vibrated minutely on the table-top. Many of the framed pictures had shifted on the walls and were now tilted at different angles. A family askew. The whole house was settling into a new shape at this first sign of disturbance in years, and it suddenly felt like a very fragile structure.

How long had she rested there, this Adeline? How long buried beneath? What kind of state would her body be in? Bones, probably. Bones and dust and a few strands of hair. Or perhaps mummified. Yes, he could see it all quite clearly in his mind's eye.

'Christ!'

'What's wrong?' Latimer asked.

'I'm willing someone to be down there, buried. Which means . . .'

'Sure, you're hoping that some poor woman's been murdered.' He paced on.

'Sit down, for God's sake, Guv. You're making me nervous.'

Hobbes turned to stare at her. 'Nervous? Of what?'

'Of the house falling down around us. What do you think?'

But Hobbes couldn't keep still.

'Make sure photographs are taken.'

Latimer shook her head. 'You don't have to remind—'

'Of everything. Every single bloody thing! Go on, check on them.'

She left the room. He stayed there for a few moments longer, but didn't know how to keep still. He walked into the corridor. The sound of the workmen was even louder here, the air turning to fog at the top of the cellar stairs. He moved into the kitchen, where Nicholas Graves was waiting. He was sitting at the table drinking a cup of tea. After each sip he placed a saucer on top of the cup to keep it free of dust.

He looked strangely calm, now the digging had begun, all thoughts of his dead father apparently put aside. But his face belied him, when Hobbes asked if he'd removed all the dresses.

'Yes. All of them.' His eyes darted to the kitchen table, where his father had taken his last breaths.

'You haven't thrown them away, I hope?'

'I was going to.'

'Don't.' It was an order. 'Not yet.'

'They're in the wardrobe. Third floor. Blood and all.'

'Good.'

Nicholas gave Hobbes a cold look, but then relented. His expression had no hold on his tired skin. Memories kept returning, taking charge. And Hobbes noticed a set of photographs on the tabletop. He decided to help him along.

'Tell me about your childhood, your family life.'

'Life at Bridlemere was . . . abnormal, to say the least.' Nicholas spoke readily. 'We led a very isolated life. My parents had a morbid fear of visitors. There was an older woman who came in every day, to help my mother with things, with the children.'

'A servant?'

'Yes. But apart from that we were very alone, as a family. And in such circumstances, behind closed doors . . .'

'Go on.'

His brows crinkled slightly. 'By any modern standard, I guess you could say we were abused.'

'Physically?'

'Let's just say that Father and Mother were old-fashioned parents. They both had strict upbringings, and they forced the same rules on to their own children.'

'Beatings?'

Nicholas looked at Hobbes. 'Well, you know how it was. It was all perfectly accepted, a way of life.'

'Yes.'

'But it was more than that, more than any physical harm, I mean.'

'Explain that to me.'

'They liked to play mind games with us. The everyday cruelties.'

Nicholas took another sip of tea. This time he left the saucer on the table and watched as a layer of plaster dust settled on the surface of the liquid.

'It was a theatrical family. I think I told you that. Their fortune was built on play-acting, directing, storytelling, and so on. The children – all of us – well, sometimes it felt like we were characters in a play created by Mummy and Daddy. Of course, being kids, we took this further, and made up our own worlds, our own adventures, our own heroes and villains.' He turned the pile of photographs face up. 'I was just looking at these, when you came in.'.

'Let me see.'

Nicholas handed over the photographs one by one. They showed three children dressed up in costumes, holding props, standing on the stage in different tableaux. Two older kids, ten or eleven, and a younger girl perhaps half that age.

'This is you, and . . .'

'Rosamund. And the little one is Camilla.' A faraway look came into his eyes. 'We were happiest like this, playing together.'

'I can see that.'

'There was one particular summer, when it was all we did, one play after another. Some of them were things we'd read in books that we adapted. Others, we made up. Pirate tales, murder mysteries, romances, ghost stories. Our favourite was called *House With No Doors*.' He laughed at this. 'We were unstoppable. And so the days went by.'

Now his eyes came into focus, brightened by memory.

'I was the director, ordering my sisters about. Oh, God, I was such a bossy-boots!' It was an absurd thing to say, in the current circumstances, and it served to change the mood. Nicholas gathered up his mementoes. 'Anyway, it's all a long time ago now.' He wiped at his brow. 'I got out when the war started, and I enrolled in the army. That was my break. But my sisters . . .' He shook his head.

'It was harder back then for young women to leave the home?'

'It was. They usually left home to get married. That was the rule, in our stratum of society anyway. So they were stuck here. In fact . . .'

'Yes, what is it?'

'Rosamund was schooled at home. By Mother and Eileen.'

'Eileen?'

'The woman who came in to help. She was a kind of governess, I suppose.'

Nicholas smiled at his own thoughts. It was quite cold to begin with, this smile, and then it softened. He said, 'I used to love how we played out our little fantasies in secret. The three of us. How strange it was, thinking back.' His eyes drifted off target and his voice grew wistful. 'Well, all that is gone now. All gone.'

Hobbes made to ask another question, but just then a great clanging sound came from the cellar door, followed by a cry from one of the workers. Nicholas Graves grimaced, and his cup clattered against the saucer. It sounded like a bone cracking in two.

Hobbes said gently, 'I know this is difficult for you, Nicholas.'

There was barely a nod in response.

'Tell me, why did you change your mind?'

Nicholas turned in his seat. 'I'm sorry?'

'At first you didn't want us to dig up the cellar. And then you did.'

'Because . . . well, if you must know, I could see the kind of man you are.'

'Really?'

'You can mock me all you like, Inspector, but I know you won't stop hounding me until I prove my innocence.'

'Now there's an interesting turn of phrase.'

'I meant my father's innocence, of course.' But he looked flustered as Hobbes stared at him relentlessly. 'Actually, in all truth, I mean the innocence of the house. Bridlemere counts for everything. I was born and brought up here.'

'So, you really have a clue about what's down there?'

'A burst pipe, I should imagine. One that's been mended. Dad was always doing work about the house, not that he was any good at it . . . but rather his botched jobs than have someone come in, a proper worker. He could not abide strangers in the house.'

Hobbes filed this information away. He said, 'I think you're as curious as I am, about what's hidden down there.'

'I really have no interest in such things. Secrets bore me.'

'I don't think that's true, Mr Graves. Everybody likes to unearth—'

'No! Not at all.' Nicholas's voice rose in volume. 'I'm only interested in the here and now, in what I can see before me!'

Hobbes waited for a moment. Then he smiled and said, 'It's very good of you to help us.'

The other man grimaced. 'I just – I just want it over with! Once and for all.' It was said with such vehemence that Hobbes was surprised: sheer hatred had fed the words. But hatred of what? And once again, as the hatred died, he saw that look of fear.

Hobbes decided to hold back, for now. There would be time enough for questions, if needed, once the contents of the cellar floor had been revealed.

He excused himself, opened the back door and stood there for a moment to get a breath of air. The jungle of the garden, the hidden shed with the dress hanging from the beam, the mystery of it all, the sense of things still to be revealed. He was on the edge of discovery, and he loved the feeling of it, he always did, even if a dead body lay at the centre. From death he spiralled out and found meaning for himself, knowledge: this was his way.

He could hear Nicholas moving, his chair scraping across the floor. He half expected a blow on the back of his head and tensed. Instead Nicholas Graves stood close behind him and said, 'If there's nothing down there, nothing of interest to you . . .'

'A corpse, you mean?'

This was waved aside. 'If not, I'll keep everything you find. Do you hear? Hobbes? It's my property.'

The inspector didn't turn round. He said quietly, 'So you are interested, then?'

'I'll do it just to spite you.'

God, but that was a strange thing to say. It might have been a malicious nine-year-old boy speaking, not a man in his sixties.

Hobbes didn't bother replying. He stepped outside and walked down to the edge of the overgrowth. Life was abundant here, struggling amid the dank leaves and tendrils. A weird mushroom drew his eye. It was attached to the earth like a parasite, cream-coloured, the cap billowing out like a shroud, the surface decorated with a darker pattern. A Rorschach test. It looked poisonous. Probably called 'dead man's tongue', or some such. But of course he was no expert. He bent closer. The fungus stank to high heaven. Dozens of ants busied themselves under its shade. Nearby was a discarded toy, a plastic doll.

Hobbes went back inside. The kitchen was empty. He walked along the hallway and paused at the door at the top of the cellar stairs. The men were still working, still digging. But then the sound of the electric drill stopped. Hobbes placed his handkerchief over his mouth and walked downstairs, into the pit, the root of the house, the clogging air, the damp, that bittersweet incense of rot and mould.

There was no sign of Nicholas Graves.

DS Latimer was waiting at the edge of the work area, the lower part of her face covered with a work mask. She handed one to him. He slipped it on and stepped forward with her to where they could see down into the hole that had been dug. It was narrow, about five feet long, a trench or a grave – Hobbes couldn't help the thought once it had taken hold. One end of the hole had been opened wider than the other, and it was here that the foreman of the work team was bending down, inspecting something in the dust and rubble.

'Don't touch anything,' Hobbes said. 'Move back, come on. Let me see.'

The workmen stepped back so that Hobbes and Latimer could peer into the hole. He grabbed a torch from a man, and used that to help him see. The beam moved over some object lodged in the dark of the pit.

Latimer was leaning over. 'What is that?' she asked.

'Looks like a piece of cloth. Give me some gloves.' She handed him a plastic pair. He reached down into the hole and pulled at the cloth. It was heavy, dark in colour, but discoloured from the years underground. He pulled hard and a piece tore off in his hand, it was so weak and rotten. He lifted it out and he and Latimer stared at it. It wasn't anything like the flowery dress.

'It looks like curtain material,' she said. 'Ideal to wrap something in. A body, for instance.'

'Let's not jump ahead.' Hobbes turned to the foreman and asked him to dig down further, a few pieces at a time. 'And, for God's sake, be careful.'

But Latimer said, 'Let's stop now. We should get Forensics in.'

'Yes, yes. Just a moment.'

Hobbes was impatient. He wanted to know. He *needed* to know.

The foreman scraped at the side of the hole with a trowel, working carefully; he looked for all the world like an archaeologist at some important historical dig. He handed up larger pieces of rubble as they fell away. And then the hole was wide enough for Hobbes to ask Latimer to have a look. She did so, bending down and peeling back the torn layers of exposed curtain. He shone the torch over her shoulder.

She gasped, loud enough for Hobbes to hear.

'What is it? Meg? Talk to me.'

Her hand was on a fragment of material, not the curtain, separate from that, but also torn and frayed and very ragged at the edges. She lifted it carefully and handed it to Hobbes. And even with all the dirt and decay and the slow effect of the years passing, he could see the blue of the material and the remains of a yellow flower design.

Latimer was bending down into the pit again.

'There's something else,' she said.

'What is it?'

'It looks like – like a bone. A number of them.'

Hobbes was suddenly very still, unmoving. As always, at this moment, the moment of discovery, his mind took control of the case. He was a machine with one purpose only. There was someone down there. A body waiting to be uncovered.

A killing to be solved.

The Shiver

The two subjects vied for attention, and they ended up blurred, merging together in his mind. His missing son, and the results of the dig at the Graveses' home. His hands gripped the steering wheel and he was thankful when he had to pull up at a red light. One thing, then another: two lost people. At the Kew Road police station he picked up a set of the photographs that had been taken in the cellar. Latimer gave him a look, but said nothing. She carried on with her work. He was glad of it: some other officers were staring at him. One held back a laugh. So, he'd made a fool of himself, yet again. That bloody cellar! Hobbes was about to say something, to justify himself, but what was the use?

Every time he made progress with his colleagues, he slipped back a few steps.

But he couldn't stop now.

He said to Latimer, 'I'll be back in later today.'

'Where are you going? Or shouldn't I ask?'

Hobbes held up the photographs in their folder. 'Seeking help.'

He drove out towards Deptford. He kept south of the river all the way, rather than the quicker route of going north and then back down. And only when he was on the outskirts of Peckham did he understand why: hidden thoughts were steering him.

He parked outside Cromwell House and sat in the car, smoking a cigarette and letting his thoughts wander. He bought a sandwich and *The Times* from a newsagent, came back to the car and waited some more. He said to himself, One hour, that's all, but he was still there at eleven o'clock, tackling the cryptic crossword. Exactly two clues written in, and one was probably wrong. He threw the paper on to the passenger seat and did his best to resist yet another cigarette: the car smelt bad enough as it was.

The housing unit was all shut up, as it had been the first time he'd visited. From his vantage point he could see the main entrance and one outer wall of flats, all the windows boarded or barred. Not a single person came or went. It really was a strange place, eerie almost. And so different from the other squatting communities he'd visited on the job, which were usually lively places, driven by activism, revolution, creativity, the idea of forging new ways of being outside society's structures. This place was more like a castle under siege. But they had to eat, they had to buy things – booze, drugs, rolling tobacco, and so on.

And just past the half-hour he struck lucky. Two people came out of the entranceway, turning on to Cavalier Road.

Hobbes got out of the car and started to follow them along the busy street. It was easy enough, as they stuck out from the other pedestrians by way of their clothes and hair: the boy was a punk, still sporting the spiked hair, leather jacket and tight black trousers popular a couple of years back. The girl wore torn fishnet tights under a black skirt and a plastic jacket, bright green in colour. They both wore rust-coloured Dr Martens boots.

Hobbes followed a few yards behind. An interesting thing happened when they turned a corner on to Peckham High Street: now they looked at each other and came together in a kiss. Hobbes watched from a doorway until they parted again and walked on, this time with their hands clasped together. The milling crowd closed around them.

Hobbes kept pace, his eyes on the boy's spiked hair, the girl's green jacket. He saw it now: two young people in love, but a love that wasn't allowed in the squat for some reason. They had waited until they were out of sight of the building. Maybe one or both had another partner back at Cromwell House, and this time out was their only chance to connect.

They stopped outside a general store, looked at each other and laughed. Then they entered the shop. Hobbes stood in a bus shelter for fifteen minutes or so until they emerged again, carrying plastic bags, two each, loaded with produce. The squat's weekly shop, probably. They moved on to busy Rye Lane, where they bought things from market stalls and other shops. Hobbes kept his distance. And then they walked back along the street directly towards him. Now was his chance: he could step in front of them and get them talking. He could play it cool and ask misleading questions and gather whatever information he could from them, without them knowing; he could make certain that Martin was actually living at Cromwell House. Or he could take out his warrant card and play it tough, make up some misdemeanour to threaten them with. He might even give in to his feelings and plead with them to show him where his son was.

Instead he let them walk on towards the squat.

He remembered the advice he'd given to Glenda, to let Martin have a few days to make up his mind. Yes, that was the best thing to do, the best thing . . .

He set off towards his car, along the edge of a small park.

'Why are you following us?'

Hobbes turned and saw the girl staring at him from the line of grey trees. She was late teens, with straggly unwashed hair, ashen face, a little make-up. Her jacket was held closed with the strap of an army-surplus shoulder bag. A lapel badge showed her support for the Anti-Nazi League. She didn't move, or say anything further, just stood there looking at him, the two heavily laden shopping bags hanging from her hands. A car passed, then a woman pushing a pram.

When the squealing baby was out of earshot Hobbes said, 'I'm not from the landlord.'

The girl didn't respond.

'I'm a police officer. If there's anything you need help with . . .'

'All we want is to be left alone.'

'And boarding up every window and door helps with that?'

'We have to. If it's not the council, or the bailiffs, it's the cops. And if it's not them, it's the skins.'

'Skinheads?'

She nodded. 'They like to do night raids, beat up a few hippies and punks.'

Hobbes knew this was true: the youthful tribes of London at war with each other. He thought again of his son's welfare. 'Still, you've taken it further than most,' he said, 'locking yourself away in there.'

'What's it to you?'

The girl didn't wait for an answer. She set off, moving away from the trees, back on to the pavement.

He stopped her and asked, 'What's your name?'

'Get your hands off me!'

'You can make a name up, I don't care. I just need to talk to you.'

'I don't talk.'

One shopping bag fell to the ground, then the other.

'So why did you wait?'

'To tell you to fuck off.'

'I think something's troubling you.'

'You're wrong.'

'What about your boyfriend? Is he too scared?'

For a moment Hobbes saw something in her eyes, beyond the anger and indignation: fear. It was held deep, well hidden – but once he'd spotted it, persistent.

'What's your friend called?'

'Why should I tell you?'

'He's over there.' Hobbes nodded towards the park. 'Isn't that him?'

The girl turned and followed his direction. A young man was turning slowly in a circle beneath a plane tree. One of the girl's hands reached up as though to signal to him, but fell again. Hobbes saw the marks on the ends of her fingers, each one darkly covered. But he didn't say anything about it, not yet, not directly.

'What's wrong with him?' he asked. 'The usual, is it? Drugs?'

'You don't know. You can't know.'

'You'd be surprised.'

'Nothing we do is *usual*. Nothing!'

It was a simple statement, spoken in total anger, and Hobbes was intrigued by it. He tried a different tack, one worried person to another.

'I'm looking for someone, a young man.' He let the words sink in, waiting until she gave him her full attention. Then he continued: 'His family think he's run away to your place, to Cromwell House. They're old friends of mine, and they're worried sick, they really are. They've asked me to help.' He paused, to allow the half-lie to take hold. 'They just want to know if he's all right, that's all. Nothing more, I swear.'

The young woman stared right at him.

'Are you Hobbes? Detective Hobbes? Martin's dad?'

He was taken aback. 'I am, yes. How is he?'

She didn't answer, not right away. The fear was more present than ever, and her eyes moved from his. She couldn't face him.

71

'Is he in trouble?'

She bent down to pick up one bag, then the other, but the second slipped from her grip and spilled its contents over the pavement. She made a kind of heaving motion with her upper body, then bent down to retrieve the goods. Hobbes made to help her. She brushed his hands away at first, but then let him. He was surprised at the items he saw: not only the food and drink he was expecting, but a curious mixture of objects – a beaded necklace, a pair of spectacles with no glass in them, a Chinese-style fan, a hairnet, two copies of a history of London's hidden rivers. He couldn't quite work out the rationale behind the purchases. He picked up sachets of powdered milk and a box of eggs.

'One of these is broken.'

She sobbed freely at this, way beyond what such a breakage should entail.

'What's wrong?'

Still she wouldn't look at him. Her hands grabbed at chocolate bars and tinned beans. 'I can't talk to you, I can't! I'm not allowed to.'

'Because I'm a cop, is that it?'

Her sobs mixed with laughter: she was a mess.

He held one of her wrists and put a little pressure on it, enough to stop her moving and to make her look at him.

They were still kneeling. His face was close to hers. He saw a glimpse of the girl she'd once been, before this present adventure. Blonde hair, blue eyes, clear skin. He remembered Sally Talbot's talk of a lot of the kids being middle-class rebels, running away from their nice homes. And, of course, that was true of Martin as well. It was an act of escape as old as mankind, dressed up in different clothes for each generation.

The girl was shaking quite badly now and her eyes were glazed, and he wondered if she'd taken anything. But it wasn't really a physical effect, more a psychological state.

'Tell me your name, at least.'

She drew in a heavy breath and said, 'Esme. That's what people call me.'

'Esme. OK.'

It was a start. He stood up and she followed him. There was a bench near by and he led her to it. They sat down. He said, 'You'll have to get a new badge soon.'

'What?'

'Word has it that the Anti-Nazi League are on the verge of breaking up. The Socialist Workers Party have fallen out with them.'

'Divide and conquer?'

Hobbes smiled. 'Oh, the left are very good at doing that for themselves. From Marx and Engels onwards, they've loved fragmentation. All those tiny differences of belief. And people wonder why nothing really changes.'

'But something new will arise. Won't it?'

'Of course. A new name, the same old struggle. It never ends.'

Esme breathed a little easier. She said, 'We all know about you. About you being a cop, I mean. Martin told us all, one night. He was ashamed to admit it.'

The words cut into Hobbes, but he remained silent.

'We have these sessions, where we're meant to tell of our troubles, any worries or complaints we might have. Nadia insists on it, once a week.'

Nadia. Hobbes filed the name away.

'That's when it came out, about you, during one of these meetings. Your job, and all that.'

Now he turned to her. 'Did it get a bad reaction?'

'What do you think?' She started to roll a cigarette, but shreds of tobacco kept blowing away. Her fingers were trembling.

'Esme, I swear to you. I only want to know if Martin's all right.'

Her answer wasn't what he expected. 'You spoke out, didn't you? Against the other pigs.'

'That's one way of putting it.'

'You know, Martin tried to keep his identity secret, to begin with.'

'But someone found out?'

She nodded. 'So then I was curious.'

Hobbes was worried. 'He told you the story, did he?'

'No. He wouldn't. I looked it up in the library, in the old newspapers.'

'Right.'

'So I don't understand. Why is he so upset? After all, you did a good thing. You told the truth.'

Hobbes considered his answer carefully: he knew he was getting closer to her, and nearer to finding out about his son. 'It took a long time for the *truth*, as you call it, to come out, a very long time. And even then, there were suspicions on both sides. In between . . . well, my family suffered. And that's when he ran away.'

Esme frowned. Her roll-up collapsed. Hobbes offered her one of his Embassy Reds, which she took with a nod and a smile, telling him again, 'I *really* shouldn't be talking to you.'

'You said that.' He lit her cigarette. 'Nadia's very strict, is she?'

It was a guess, a good guess, and it hit home. Esme's face creased into a frown.

'What is she? The queen bee of the hive?'

The girl tutted. 'You think you're a clever bastard, don't you? You've got it all worked out.'

'Can I show you something?' Hobbes took a photograph from his jacket pocket, the one Martin had inserted in the wedding album. 'Do you know who this woman is?'

She didn't answer, but he saw her eyes widen slightly.

'I'm guessing she lives in the squat with you. Is this Nadia? Is it?'

'I can't help you.' Her tone was flat.

Hobbes shook his head sadly. 'Esme, I've been interviewing people for too long now, for too many years. I know a lie when I hear it.'

'Good. Because I'll never tell you the truth.'

'She's standing next to my son.'

'So?'

'Look at Nadia's hands, the marks on her fingers. You've got the same condition. And I think Martin's the same.'

'So what?'

Esme was closing up. Hobbes blew out a breath in frustration. 'All that matters to me is my son. Nothing else. And you still haven't told me if he's all right or not.'

'He's fine. Martin doesn't need—'

'Here, let me give you my number, my home number. Just in case.'

He wrote it on a page torn from his notebook, but Esme pushed it away, repeating almost to herself, 'He's fine. We all are.' As some kind of evidence of this, she held out both her hands, first palm up and then down, and she let Hobbes see the marks, each finger looking – as Glenda had described it – as though it had been dipped in blue ink. But he could see the marks were ragged, not a pure colour but mottled, each one slightly different in shade and shape on the skin and fingernail.

'Don't you think it's lovely?' she said, in a whisper.

'What is that? What causes it? Does someone paint your skin for you?'

'It's a mark of love.'

'Love of whom? Your leader? Of Nadia?'

She frowned at this.

'What then? The group? The tribe? Your little band of rebels?'

He couldn't find a way in. Esme just looked at him with disgust on her face. 'You'll never understand.'

'Try me.'

'You're too far away.'

Hobbes felt a knife twisting at his heart. 'And what about Martin? He's suffering from the same thing.'

'It isn't suffering!' Her voice broke. 'It's joy and beauty and a great release.'

Hobbes tried to control himself.

Esme smiled. It was quite cold. 'Thank you for the cigarette.' She grabbed her bags and stood up. She called to her friend, who was still circling the trees. 'Joe! Come on, we're going.'

The young man took his order willingly, and walked across the grass to meet her. He carried his own shopping bags like a servant at a task.

Hobbes felt a sudden panic. 'Esme, wait!' But she would say no more. He watched them walk away, more worried than ever about his son. But he made no attempt to follow, knowing full well Esme's fear of being seen too close to home with the enemy, a cop.

Boy and girl, neither glanced back.

Hobbes looked at the page with his telephone number scrawled in it. He screwed it up and threw it into the gutter. Useless. Bloody useless! He went back to where his car was parked and sat in the driver's seat for five minutes, thinking over the conversation. He stared at the photograph, willing it to give up its secrets.

The woman's left arm was stretched out to show off the markings on her hand, the blue at the end of each finger. And that smile in place, that was the worst thing, as though the sickness meant nothing at all to her. She revelled in it. And her right arm around Martin's shoulders, the clutch of possession.

Hobbes felt his anger rising.

In the Dark

Deptford marked the south-eastern boundary of old working-class London, before the greener plains and townhouses of Greenwich and Blackheath took over. Here the old terraced houses and workshops still existed, and the air was gritty and grey. Rain speckled the windscreen, first a few drops and then a downpour. He had to lean forward in his seat to peer out through the always disappearing arcs of clear glass left by the wipers.

It was good: the rain, the need to concentrate, to locate the address that DS Latimer had given him. It stopped him brooding too much.

There it was – 37 Parchment Street. He pulled up at the kerb and waited for a moment, hoping the downpour would let off a little. It didn't. He lodged the cardboard folder under his jacket and got out of the car. Even walking at speed, he was drenched in seconds. It took a while for the bell to be answered, and he was on the verge of walking away when the front door opened.

'Mrs Fairfax?'

'That's right. I was just getting ready to—'

'I'm Detective Inspector Hobbes. I'm here to see your son, Thomas.'

'You're going to arrest him, are you? About time!'

'No. Not at all. I just want to—'

'I'm joking!' The door opened fully. 'Well, come in then! Hurry up – you're getting my hall carpet wet.'

Hobbes tried to remember her name. Had DC Fairfax ever mentioned it?

He followed her into the hallway. Mrs Fairfax was dressed to the nines in a fancy red dress and a fake-fur stole. A string of pearls circled her neck and her face was done up in rouge and lipstick. It was two in the afternoon. 'It's my day off,' she said, in answer to his look.

'Where are you working?'

'Maureen's Salon, on the high street. Hair stylist. But right now I'm going down the West End.' A ready smile took over her face. 'Window-shopping to begin with. A spot of dinner. A few drinks. And then a club. Husband-hunting. Lovely.'

He pulled a name from his memory. 'Delia?'

'Yes?'

'I didn't know you were . . .'

'What?'

'Divorced. Tommy never said.'

'A year last Thursday.' She patted her hair while looking in the hallway mirror. 'I'm so glad you've come round, Inspector Hobbes.'

'You don't need to call me—'

'Only I'm awful worried about Tommy. See, he's not been himself lately.'

Hobbes nodded. 'He's in, then?'

'He's watching tele.'

She led the inspector to the living room and whispered at the doorway, 'Now don't let him talk improper to you. He's been terrible for that, lately.'

'I won't. Thank you.'

The doorbell rang. It was a signal for Delia Fairfax to pull on a coat. 'That'll be Gladys. She's on the prowl as well.'

'Good luck.'

She smiled one last time and left the house.

Hobbes looked through into the living room. He could see Fairfax sitting down in front of the television, his back to the door. If he'd heard any of the conversation in the hallway, he'd made no reaction to it. The screen flickered with an afternoon chat show. The remains of egg and chips sat on a little table at his side, with an open can of lager.

Fairfax suddenly made a noise. 'Oh, please! Everyone knows what the capital of Brazil is! Idiot.'

Hobbes entered the room. One of the chat show's guests was being asked a series of general knowledge questions. 'Tommy? It's me.'

'It's Rio! Rio de Janeiro! Come on! It's for charity, for fuck's sake.'

'Tommy?'

'Yeah.' It was more a grunt than a word. 'Get me another one, will you?' He held out the now empty can of lager. 'Fridge. Kitchen.'

'I don't think so.'

'Fuck.' For the first time Fairfax looked up at his superior officer. 'What the fuck?'

'You've had enough.'

'Really? Is that all you've got to say?'

'Pretty much. Except that it's Brasilia.'

'What is?'

'The capital of Brazil. Brasilia.'

'You're making that up. You're having me on.'

Hobbes shrugged.

Fairfax glared at him. 'What're you trying to do? Humiliate me?'

'Of course not.'

'Then what the hell are you doing here?'

'Seeing how you are, Tommy.'

'Well, now you've seen. So piss off.' The younger man's gaze returned to the screen. 'Ah, I've missed it now – I've missed the bloody answer.'

Hobbes studied his colleague for a moment.

Fairfax had changed in these last few weeks. 'Compassionate leave', they called it, a catch-all phrase covering so many different kinds of hurt. It can tip the balance, being taken off duty like that; it can make an officer doubt what they're doing. Too much time to think, that was the problem. Some people come back stronger from it, while others sink into despair. Detective Constable Tom Fairfax had taken the latter course. His once immaculate appearance had given way to coarseness and untidiness. His usually neat and ever-present stubble had grown out into a rough beard, and instead of the smart jackets, shirts and ties he used to wear, he was now sitting around in tracksuit bottoms and an old cardigan, with beer stains down his vest. His hair was unwashed and it needed a trim.

'Meg was asking after you.'

Fairfax pursed his lips.

'She's worried. She'd love to see you.'

'Latimer's an old cow, she really is. What else has she got to do but worry?'

'Ah, Jesus.'

'What? What now?'

'You're still on the force, DC Fairfax.'

'Barely.'

'I won't have you being disrespectful of a senior officer.'

A sneer took over the man's face. But then he relented, and muttered, 'Yeah, I shouldn't have said that. Meg's all right, actually.' He stood up and pushed past Hobbes, making for the doorway. Hobbes followed him into the kitchen, where Fairfax was searching inside the fridge, and cursing. 'Oh, shit. There's none left. No fuckin' beer.'

'Sit down, Tommy. Come on. That's an order.'

'I told her to keep it stocked—'

'Sit down!'

There was sufficient force in the inspector's voice to compel Fairfax to take a seat at the kitchen table. He sat there with his arms propped up and his head lowered into his hands. He groaned and started to speak, but then stopped. And groaned some more, quieter now. Some internal sadness had taken him over.

Hobbes sat down at an angle to him. He placed the folder on the tabletop, saying, 'This is a case I'm working on.'

'And?' More a grunt than a word.

'I thought you might take a look.'

'A look? Is that it?'

'I need your help. A fresh eye.'

'Come on, Guv. I can't.'

'All I want—'

'I'm done. Do yer hear me? I am done. Done with it all. No more.'

'A setback, that's all—'

'No!'

He pushed his chair away from the table and made to get up, but Hobbes reached out, grabbed his wrist and held him there. The two men stared at each other, neither giving in. Hobbes felt his fingers tightening around flesh and bone. So close, he could smell the unwashed stench of Fairfax, the cigs, the drinking, a splash of Aramis to try to cover it, a pointless exercise.

'You did a good thing, Tommy. You tracked down a cop.' Fairfax grimaced, hearing this. Hobbes kept on: 'A bad cop. A killer. You got a confession out of him.'

'I beat him up to get it, damn near killed him.'

'But you didn't.'

'I had a tyre-iron in my hand!'

Hobbes blew out a breath. The lecture was having little effect, but he had nothing else to offer, except persistence. 'I'm not going anywhere, Tommy. I'm not leaving.'

'I can't—' But Fairfax stopped speaking. His mouth trembled.

'You can't what?'

'I can't fuckin' *stand* myself.'

The words were said in quiet anger. It was the truth, Hobbes saw that, and he let the statement remain unanswered. Fairfax sat down and stared at the table, his body limp in the chair. Hobbes looked at him. He couldn't help feeling angry, seeing the younger man like that. It sickened him. But he mustn't let anger get the upper hand.

He made a decision. 'Tommy, I'm going to tell you the truth.'

Fairfax made a dismissive noise.

'I don't think you're a good cop. In fact, in many ways, I think you're a fuck-up.'

'Jesus. And the same to you.'

'But I believe you have the potential to do better one day. But here's the thing . . .'

Now Fairfax looked at him.

'What are you, Tommy? Twenty-seven?'

'Twenty-eight.'

'You'll need to buckle down. And work hard. But one day you'll shame us all.'

'Oh, yeah? How do you work that out?'

'I used to know a copper just like you, name of Collingworth. By all accounts, he started out as a first-grade twat, like yourself.'

'If you think you can—'

'But then a change came over him. He got down to work,

serious work. Made chief inspector. That's when I knew him. He was the man who taught me the ropes. Near strangled me with them, mind, if I did wrong.'

A flicker of light came into Fairfax's eyes. 'I've heard you mention his name before.'

'Sure. I still follow his advice.'

'What happened to him? You still see him?'

Hobbes paused. He'd started off honest, so thought it best to carry on in the same manner. 'They threw him off the force, corruption charges.'

Fairfax laughed. 'That must have hurt.'

'Sure. He messed up. Which pissed me off, no end.'

'So, what are you saying?'

'I'm not certain. But in those years, when I knew him, there was none better.'

Both men were quiet for a moment. And then Fairfax said, 'It's a fuckin' knife-edge, that's what it is. Good, or bad, black or white.'

'And which way to go.'

'Ah, fuck it. Fuck it all.' Fairfax reached for a cigarette, lit it, then nodded at the folder on the table. 'What's all this palaver, then?'

Hobbes opened the folder and placed the first photograph on the table. He went over the story of Leonard Graves, as he laid out further images, talking about the old man's final position, the pills, the suicide, and then the fifteen dresses they had found around the house, and even in the garden shed.

Fairfax stared at the photographs without speaking.

Hobbes tapped at one image. 'This is the cellar of the house. I cleared some rubbish away from the wall and found these words scrawled there: *R.I.P. Adeline*. And a patch of the floor, which had been re-concreted at some point.'

There was still no reaction.

Hobbes carried on: 'So I ordered the floor to be dug up. I really did think a body would be buried there. But I was wrong.' He placed the next photograph on the table, showing the final results of what the team had found underneath the cellar. 'Another dress. The same dress as the others. Number sixteen. Buried here inside an old curtain, less than two feet down, along with a pair of shoes and a scarf. The same thing. The same bloody thing, Tommy! The same effigy, whatever it was. Buried. A dress. Torn, just here on the midriff. The exact same place. Probably stained with blood, or a blood substitute. We can't tell, it's too old – the cloth's too ragged and worn.' He considered a thought. 'It's been there for a long time, that's for certain, but for how many years, I can't say.'

He studied Fairfax's face.

There was no expression.

'And there's nothing further I can do. There's no crime, no corpse. I've spent funds on this, for God's sake! Man-hours galore. The super's going crazy. And all for no good purpose. I'm at a loss, I really am. I mean, why would anyone do this? Why would they go to all that trouble of digging down into solid concrete just to bury a dress?' He swore. 'I just don't get it.'

Fairfax licked his lips. He looked like he might speak, but he shook his head.

Hobbes added, 'But there's a couple of variations this time. First of all, these . . .'

His finger pointed to a photograph of a pile of small off-white objects. 'Bones. Probably from some bird.' He breathed in. 'A set of bones wrapped up inside the dress.'

Fairfax leaned forward slightly. His eyes searched the image.

'So, what do you think?'

Silence. Then a murmur. Hobbes asked him to speak up.

Fairfax looked at Hobbes. 'Which kind of bird was it?'

'What? I don't know.'

'If it's a chicken, that's one thing. You can buy that at the butcher's. If it's a canary or a budgerigar, that's easy as well. Just reach into the cage. It's pretty gruesome, though.'

'There was a cat's skeleton in the cellar as well.'

'Right, right.'

'But we think that was killed for the blood, to mark the dresses.'

Fairfax nodded. For the first time his eyes had taken on light. He continued with his thoughts: 'If it's a pigeon, that's more difficult. If it's a blackbird or a sparrow or a crow, that's fuckin' serious. You need some real time and effort to catch it. And a lot of luck.'

Hobbes nodded. He was pleased with the response.

Fairfax picked up the photograph and stared at it once more. 'The bird represents the body, the missing flesh and blood.'

'So you think someone was murdered? That's your opinion?'

Fairfax stared at the inspector. 'A woman,' he said. 'It has to be. And she's out there somewhere. Hidden in the dark. Buried deep.'

Hobbes had to agree. But how would he ever locate her? He added, 'We found something else in the grave.' He made no excuse for the word. 'It was laid next to the dress, where the tear in the cloth was.' He placed another photograph on the table. The object depicted was a small container of some kind. Fairfax studied the image. For the moment, at least, he had lost all interest in booze and chat shows.

'It's a decorative box. A jewellery box, I think.'

Fairfax looked up at his boss. 'And there's something inside? What is it?'

Hobbes smiled. 'Well, now, that is a puzzle.'

He handed another five photographs to Fairfax.

Object of Desire

Hobbes woke up in the kitchen, standing at the sink, his hand on the cold tap, the water running. The sound of it, bouncing off the dirty dishes, had stirred him awake. The moonlight cast the room in a cold shiver of light. Oh, God. He couldn't remember how he'd got here, the steps taken. His head ached. It had been a while since his last bout of sleepwalking. Really, he'd thought it a thing of the past. He cursed out loud. And once the anger had passed, he felt drained of all feeling. Emptiness. And then a memory . . . yes, that was it: he'd been dreaming of the hole in the cellar floor, and what they had found there, the senseless nature of it. Literally: it was *without sense*. He abhorred the very idea of an object devoid of meaning. Nothing should be left uncovered, nothing at all.

His shadow trembled on the floor.

The kitchen clock: a quarter past midnight.

Thank God, nobody here to . . .

A resident animal moved behind the skirting board, scratching away, always unseen.

He drank a glass of water, then turned off the tap.

The silence.

Within it, a voice. Quiet, barely heard. And then getting louder, calling to him from the shadows of the room.

He listened.

It was an old man's voice saying over and over the same few phrases: *Dearest Adeline, I'm so sorry. For everything. Dearest Adeline, I'm so sorry. For everything.* A final message. But sorry for what? A broken promise, something lost, or stolen . . . or for pain given, a life taken? Hobbes knew the words would keep on repeating, whenever he was still and quiet enough to listen, until this case was done, and the ghost in the blue and yellow flowered dress had been brought into the light, or laid to rest. Whichever might be appropriate.

And then his breath caught in his throat.

Hobbes tensed.

Somebody was outside, moving around. Feet on concrete, the fall of something heavy against the wall. Hobbes was by the door in seconds, his entire body leaning forward. The presence was there, he knew it, just on the other side of the door. Somebody waiting in the dark outside, listening, as he was. For a sign.

Hobbes clicked on the kitchen light, hoping to startle the person outside into action. But there was no further noise. He waited a moment longer, then opened the door.

'Who is it? Who's there?'

A figure scurried back, his hands already reaching to pull up the bicycle that had fallen over. Hobbes stepped out – feet on the pavement, gritty, cold – dragged the person upright and twisted him around to see his face.

It was Martin, his son.

Neither spoke. They stared at each other.

Hobbes kept it cool, as best he could. 'Do you want to come inside?'

Martin looked down the alley, to the street. A way of escape. But then he turned back, and nodded.

'It's all right,' Hobbes said. 'Leave the bike there. It's safe.'

The lad followed him inside. Hobbes steered him to the living room. 'You've never been here before, have you?' Hobbes was suddenly ashamed of where he'd ended up. 'This is only temporary.'

Martin looked round in a vague manner. He hadn't yet spoken.

'I didn't think you knew where I lived. Did your mother tell you?'

Still no response.

The teenager's face showed evidence of the grey pallor Glenda had mentioned. It was true, the lad didn't look too good. Hobbes glanced at his hands, but they were covered with cycling gloves.

'Give me a second, will you? Just one second.' Hobbes went into his bedroom, put on his slippers, and found his dressing-gown. He paused at the door, collecting his thoughts.

Don't blow this.

He went back into the living room, all smiles. 'Would you like a drink? A cup of tea?'

A shake of the head.

'OK. It's just – it's just really good to see you, son.'

They both stood there. Hobbes knew he had to play this a certain way. One false word and the lad would take off in a hurry. And perhaps never come back.

'You're shaking.'

'Yeah. I'm cold. Freezing.'

A reaction, good. At last. Hobbes said, 'I'll put the fire on, shall I?'

But Martin lowered his voice and said, 'No. I can't stay . . . I can't stay long.'

'That's fine. As long as you like.' Hobbes thought about sitting down, but was scared of tipping the balance. He said, 'Is there something you want to talk about?'

Martin looked down at the table and saw the photographs set

out there, including the one he'd placed inside the wedding album.

Hobbes spoke carefully. 'You went to see your mother, I hear.' Martin nodded. 'You left that picture behind for her.'

'It's for the both of you, really.'

'Oh. And why's that?'

It took a while for the thoughts to come. 'You went to Cromwell House.'

'I did, yes. I talked to a friend of yours, Esme.'

'Please don't. Stay away.'

'You think that's possible?'

The lad gritted his teeth. Hobbes had never seen him so determined, a different kind of strength.

'I have new people now, a new family. They will look after me.'

'Martin . . .'

'You need to listen to me, Dad, and closely. I have new friends, a new place to live.' He picked up the photograph. 'Look, you see here . . . I'm smiling. Laughing. What I'd like is whenever you doubt me, or think I've failed, just look at this picture.'

He was suddenly mature: he'd grown up without Hobbes knowing it.

Martin added, 'That's all you need to know.'

He was perfectly capable of expressing himself, but Glenda's fears – that their son was taking drugs – was a fair assessment: the lad's mind followed its own crooked pathways. This whole thing with the photograph made sense, but only to himself.

'And who's the woman? Is that Nadia?'

Martin stared at his father directly. It was their first real contact, and Hobbes drank freely of it. But instead of answering the question, Martin said, 'I need something from you. One last thing.'

'Anything at all. You know that.'

'Your wristwatch.'

Again, Hobbes was taken aback. His hand went to his bare wrist. 'My watch? It's, erm, it's in the bedroom.'

'No, not that one. The one you wore when I was young. You know, silver, with a blue face.'

'That old thing?'

'I used to play with it.'

'I remember. I'd curse you sometimes for over-winding it.'

'Do you still have it?'

'Yeah, somewhere. But why?'

'I just need it, that's all. I can't tell you why.'

'OK. Let me find it for you.'

Hobbes walked into the little room where he stored most of his household goods. It was filled with cardboard boxes and piles of clothes and books: he still hadn't sorted things out, perhaps never would. And he was worried that his son would leave.

He called, 'Martin!'

'Yes?' The lad appeared at the open doorway.

'I'm not sure where it is.'

'Please, you have to find it. It's important. Fabian needs . . .'
And he stopped speaking.

'Who's Fabian? Someone from the squat?'

'A friend, that's all.'

'OK, OK. It's here.'

Hobbes took the wristwatch from its resting place in a wooden box filled with signet rings, tie-pins, cufflinks and the like. He handed it over. 'I don't think it works any more. If you're thinking of . . .'

'I'm not going to sell it, don't worry.' Martin looked at the object avidly, his face filled with happiness. 'This is good. It's just right! Thank you.'

The wristwatch rested on the palm of Martin's gloved hand.

Hobbes spoke gently. 'Son, show me your hands.' There was no response. 'If there's anything wrong, you know you can—'

Martin groaned. 'Perhaps I shouldn't have come here. You won't stop.'

Hobbes felt a sudden desperation. 'If you need help, anything at all . . .'

'I won't bother you any more, don't worry.'

And his eyes were held so wide open that the light itself was swallowed within them: dark, dark. This was a young man with a different plan for life.

He moved away, along the hallway.

Hobbes tried to stop him, to hold on to him. He called, 'Wait!'

But his son had already made it to the front door. He was running up the side alley, wheeling his cycle alongside. Hobbes went after him, but Martin was too quick, and he managed to swing a leg over the frame of the bike and to carry on in the same movement, pedalling furiously, turning on to the road and making his escape, riding erratically as though drunk or high on life.

Hobbes watched until the figure had vanished around a corner.

A night sharp and clear under the streetlamps and a cloudless moon.

Everyday Strangeness

There were only four people around the open grave, and that included the priest. A pitiful turnout. Hobbes watched from a way off, half hidden by a copse of trees at the cemetery's edge. He wasn't sure what he was hoping for: certainly, more people. And then a twitch of nerves maybe, something that told him a malign presence was near. But he felt nothing, no sensations other than cold and the usual ache in his heart whenever he attended a funeral.

It had rained earlier in the day and now the air was grey and misty, a perfect setting for the end of a lonely life. The priest made the usual gestures, the same pattern, no matter who had died, and his words were hardly audible at this distance. A spell to ease the pathway ahead, through the darkness.

Nicholas Graves stood with his head held high, a proud man suddenly. Perhaps it was a show for the woman at his side, no doubt one of the two sisters he had mentioned in his interview. She was a little older than him. Standing slightly apart was a younger man, perhaps one of Leonard's grandchildren. There was a slight family resemblance.

There was no sign of the other sister. Or of the mother, Mary Estelle. Perhaps she had had trouble getting away from the old people's home.

The priest finished the service and the coffin was lowered into the ground.

The woman moved away first. There seemed to be little connection between the three mourners: they had not spoken at all, or made any bodily contact. The grandson left next, following her. Nicholas remained for a while longer, looking down into the grave, and then he, too, walked away, taking a different path from the other two.

Hobbes went over to the grave.

The wooden cross was temporary, a simple affair.

Leonard Graves
1896–1981

Eighty-five. A good innings. But he couldn't help thinking of the last such marker he'd seen, a week and a half ago, scrawled in black ink on a cellar wall. No dates on that one, only the woman's name, *Adeline*, and the usual comfort of *R.I.P.* Was it heartfelt? he wondered. Did they really want her to rest in peace? He couldn't get the idea out of his mind, of a victim lying hidden somewhere, in secret, decaying or decayed.

Hobbes turned away and walked back towards the car. As he did so, an absurd little ditty came into his mind.

Graves in his grave. Grave Mr Graves, in his grave.
On this grave day, grave Mr Graves in a grave lay gravely . . .

And then he stopped.

A woman stood a little way off, looking right at him. She was young, still in her teens, with long black hair parted neatly in the middle. She had taken off her raincoat and was holding it over her arm. It was an odd thing to do, on such a cold day.

Hobbes knew there was something familiar about her straight away.

She was wearing a blue and yellow dress: a blue background with yellow flowers.

It was the exact same style as the ones laid out in the Graves household.

He walked quickly towards her, but she saw him coming and stepped back. One of her hands rose to her face. Yet still he followed her, conscious that he was acting strangely, even threateningly, but he couldn't stop, not now. He called to her: 'Hello there.'

She paid him no attention, moving into a grove of trees. Her shape flitted between the trunks and branches, a flash of blue here and there. He couldn't help thinking of Alice in Wonderland, hurrying from one adventure to another, the strangeness of the everyday.

Hobbes reached the trees and entered the shadows.

She was nowhere to be seen.

He stood where he was, listening, listening . . .

All was still.

The last of the raindrops fell from the branches.

A single bird sang a few bittersweet notes, and fell silent.

He heard a twig snap.

To his right.

He followed the sound, deeper into the trees. They were planted thickly here, and soon he reached the high wall that surrounded Richmond Cemetery and had to turn back. For a moment, he thought that two people moved ahead of him, quite separately. But both vanished at the same time: an illusion of some kind. He moved on at a pace, hoping to catch a true sight of the young woman. But soon he came out of the grove and stood at its edge. He had reached another area of the grounds, one with many old tombs set closely together, a tumble of stones draped in moss and ferns.

He was alone.

Hobbes was sweating from the exertion. He took a winding pathway that he hoped would lead him back to his car. And then he saw the teenager again, walking ahead towards a gate. He hurried after her and almost caught up, just as she left the cemetery. By the time he'd reached the gate, he was alone once more, standing on Lower Grove Road, with the traffic roaring by. Where was she? Which way had she gone?

He chose to turn right, following the wall for a while. Across Queens Road he saw a bus shelter. The woman was waiting there. The dress made her easy to spot: it was a pattern imprinted on his brain. But she was putting on her coat. A bus was approaching. Hobbes tried to cross the road, but a rush of traffic was coming towards him – he couldn't make it. He moved along, hoping to cut across when there was a gap.

He saw that four or five people were waiting at the stop. It wouldn't take them long to board, and the bus was already pulling up. He took his chance and darted into the road, dodging an oncoming car.

The bus pulled away from the kerb.

The shelter was empty.

She'd gone. He'd lost her.

Hobbes watched the bus moving off down the road, leaving him there, hunched over, trying to catch his breath. His mind swirled with images. Confusion. He saw a light flickering at the edge of his vision. He had to take more care of himself, that was obvious. Maybe do more walking, for a start . . .

He came back up to his full height.

And there she was.

Just a few feet away. The woman. The dress. The blue and the yellow. The flowers. Her face looking at him, her youthful face, her eyes so clear and full of life, and she stared at him and nodded in some kind of recognition. A smile crossed her lips. And he knew then, in that instant: a memory was triggered. He had seen that dress before, somewhere, long ago, so very long ago. The thought startled him. It wasn't so much the pattern or the colour, but the rip in the side, and the blood. Another victim, perhaps, from an earlier case. But he couldn't think from where or when: the idea would take on neither weight nor form.

And then the young woman turned and walked through an open doorway in a side wall. She moved quite slowly now, gracefully even.

He went over and looked through into a small enclosed garden.

He walked a narrow twisting pathway between tall hedges and bushes until he reached an ornamental fountain at the garden's centre.

Water trickled from the mouth of a stone cupid.

It was the only sound, the only movement.

The woman had vanished.

All That Remains

At half past nine on Sunday evening, Hobbes was in his living room listening to a discussion programme on Radio 4, all about the meeting points of art and science. But his mind was elsewhere when the phone rang, and he couldn't help but wonder if it was Martin, calling to say he was all right. He hadn't heard or seen anything of him in the past week, ever since the late-night visit.

But the call was from DS Latimer.

Within a minute Hobbes was at the wheel of his car.

He'd been instructed to head for the east gate to Richmond Park, the only one the park officials had left open for the police to use. A number of uniformed offers were already standing around just inside the entranceway. Hobbes wound down his window, spoke to one and was directed along an access road. On both sides the fields and trees faded away into the dark. He knew that deer roamed these woods and banks, but all he could see was the road in his headlamps.

London's largest enclosed parkland, a vast green space.

Once he was past the Pen Ponds, it was easy to see where the activity was. A spotlight had been set up and other lights – torch beams – moved around a police van and a number of other vehicles, both marked and plain. Hobbes drew up his car and got out. He looked around, trying to find his detective sergeant, then made his way to a command post. A constable came up to him and handed him a pair of plastic gloves. 'Evening, sir.'

It was PC James Barlow, one of the few officers Hobbes had managed to get close to during his short time at the station. The young man's hair was plastered to his brow. It was raining heavily.

'What's the situation? Where's DS Latimer?'

'This way, sir.' Barlow set off along a pathway. 'Oh, that's the couple who found it,' he said, pointing to a man and a woman standing in the light of the police van's open back door. The woman was holding a dog on a lead.

'It?'

'I mean the body, sir.'

'The dog. More probably.'

'What? Oh, right . . . yes. Of course, sniffing about.'

This was Barlow's first major crime scene. The young PC seemed nervous – he couldn't stop blinking when he spoke. Hobbes wondered just how much he'd seen.

They walked off the pathway into woodland. Hobbes's shoes sank into a layer of mud. Barlow held up a length of cordon tape that stretched from one tree to another so the inspector could duck underneath.

'We need to find out about access,' Hobbes said. 'To the park, I mean.'

Barlow already had the information: 'It's open twenty-four hours a day to pedestrians. But vehicles can't get in after dusk.'

'Right. Thank you. And there's no sign of a car parked anywhere, I take it?'

'No. Nothing at all.'

They moved on, out of the spotlight's reach. Darkness enclosed them. This was one of the less cultivated areas of the parkland, a patch of wilderness. A ring of smaller lights had been set up and a tent erected a few yards ahead, to stop the rain getting in.

Hobbes stopped moving.

Barlow realized and stopped as well. He watched the inspector.

Hobbes's face was blank, unforgiving. He started to move in a circle around the tent, keeping a good few yards away from that central point. His gaze took in all of the trees one by one, then the muddy ground at his feet. He seemed to be surveying every square foot of soil and plant growth.

He came to a halt once more, shook his head and mumbled something.

'Do you need anything, sir?'

Hobbes didn't answer the constable straight away. And then he looked up and wiped the rain from his face and eyes. He frowned. 'The whole area should've been covered. It's a fuckin' mess!'

Barlow was perplexed by the inspector's tone of voice.

'Do you have any idea what happened here, Constable?'

'I'm sorry, sir, we had to get to the body. We had to walk over the ground. There was no way of knowing—'

'Not that! Not that, for God's sake. I mean, do you know what *happened* here? Read the signs.'

Barlow tried. He looked at the ground, but the earth was churned up with boot prints, one over the other in a chaotic pattern. 'I think—'

'Come on, I need a second pair of eyes.'

Barlow stood up straight. 'The body wasn't dragged here.'

'Right. Good. There are no drag marks. None of the plants anywhere around are broken or bent over. And there's no trail along the ground.'

'So the killing took place where the body lies?'

Hobbes nodded. 'They met here. And the struggle, or whatever it was, took place right here.' He looked at the tent. It was bright yellow, a stark intrusion into this world of muted colours.

'Right then. I'll take it from here.'

Barlow nodded and moved back through the trees. Hobbes collected his thoughts, then slipped inside the tent.

The atmosphere changed. The air was stale and hot. Sweat broke out on the inspector's brow and neck immediately. The canvas billowed and snapped in the wind, like a yacht's sail. He could smell rubber, damp, mildew. And plant life roused by the night's rain. But no decomp. That was something. Recent, then.

Hobbes waited on the threshold.

The body lay on the ground, with its own negative energy, drawing every last shred of hope and goodness from the small enclosed space.

DS Latimer was there, alongside a couple of crime-scene officers.

He asked simply, 'Time?'

'The doctor said around eight o'clock.' Latimer frowned. 'So he'd been here for about an hour, that's all, before discovery. Rigor hasn't yet set in.'

Hobbes's face showed no reaction.

'Anything been touched?'

'We've kept it clean. As clean as we can, given the circumstances.'

'Right.' Hobbes stepped to the side. 'Meg, you know what I need.'

She nodded and spoke to the forensics team. There was no argument, no nasty looks or gestures: they were used to, or had heard of, Hobbes's mannerisms by now. The three people filed out through the tent's opening.

The inspector was alone.

Alone with the body.

This was how he worked best. He knew it was unconventional – everything was teamwork, teamwork, teamwork these days. But he had to do it this way. By some intuitive process, he could *feel* the murderer's intent in the air, just waiting to be grasped. By Christ, but he wished he'd got here earlier, the first on scene. He hated all the clutter: the doctor and the whole crew and the tramping feet and the noise and the endless speculations. His ideal, he often thought, would be to arrive five to ten minutes after the perpetrator had fled the scene. That would be so perfect. Everything untouched, pristine. He needed time to get close, to find the thing that mattered, the *one* thing.

The message, the traces left behind. He pictured words floating in the cold air around a corpse, readable for a time, but then fading.

The life once lived, now ruined and reduced to this, a lump of flesh.

Dead. Unmoving.

He had not yet taken a step. He stood there, perfectly still. Only his eyes moved, as they looked here and there, pulling in all the details, first from a distance.

Overview.

The body was lying face upwards in a tangle of weeds and brambles. The man's arms were spread out on either side. The overcoat was ripped at one lapel. There was no jacket under the coat, only a cream shirt, a few buttons of which had popped open or been ripped apart. He was dressed for the weather: wet but humid.

A night stroll in the park?

Or a rendezvous under the trees?

OK, so the time of death was eight o'clock, approximate. Fairly dark by then. And not many lights around. A strange place to meet someone. Mind, that couple had been walking the dog, so people did come here this late.

His mind clicked back to the body and its immediate surroundings.

Move in, focus. Surmise. Put it together.

Plants trampled, bent over. Snapped at the stems.

Leaves crushed into the mud.

Broken twigs.

A struggle or a fight or an argument had taken place, right here, and one person had attacked another, and that person, a man, had fallen on this spot. Here, the final moments of his life had played out.

The rain hit again with a vengeance, playing a drumbeat on the canvas of the tent.

Hobbes shivered.

There were more footprints all around, churned up in the mud, and the mud drying now under the canvas, in the gathered heat: so many criss-crossing patterns.

Hobbes bent down close and looked at the man's face.

Nicholas Graves. Sixty-two years old.

Son of Leonard Graves, recently deceased of this parish. Following unto death . . . and so on and so forth.

The damage to the face and head was total, and brutal, an attack of extreme passion. Broken skin, bones showing through, the bones themselves broken, especially around the left jaw. The eyes were glued shut with blood. The skull was crumpled in a number of places and the hair was black, filthy, matted with God knew what. The nose had been shattered and was bent out of shape. The mouth had also taken a blow and Hobbes could see the cracked teeth behind the peeled-back lips. Every wound was gritted with bits of stone and dirt.

Christ, but someone had really gone for him. One of those

hard-driven attacks. Sudden. No planning. Slow to start maybe, but then very quickly leading into overkill as the anger burned and raged. Vengeance, maybe.

The murder weapon was lying on the ground to one side. A rock. One of many dotted around this area – he'd seen them on his way through the trees. Light grey, ornamental. Brought here specially, Hobbes thought, to set off the flowerbeds, or to emphasize the artificial wildness. It was covered with blood, clumps of hair and shredded skin. A weapon at hand: carefully chosen while waiting in the shadows, or grabbed in the moment?

Rethink: maybe this was self-defence. The killer was attacked first by Graves, and knocked to the ground, the rain falling – no, no, it wasn't raining at eight – knocked to the ground and the fingers grabbing blindly at whatever they could find . . . a rock . . . fighting back, the two people rolling over until the killer had the upper hand . . .

'Guv, we're getting soaked through out here.'

Hobbes ignored Latimer's voice. *Let them wait.* He shifted his focus from the victim's head, down to his right hand, to the object gripped in the fingers, clenched tight.

All that remains, nothing more.

It was a fragment of cloth, coloured blue with yellow flowers.

That pattern, that same pattern.

Hobbes stood up. He took one last look around, and muttered a few words to himself. It was a habit he had, a prayer, a promise made. He spoke the last sentences directly to the corpse: 'Nicholas Graves, I will find out who killed you. I will bring them to justice.'

And then he noticed Latimer peeping in at the tent flap. For a moment he looked embarrassed, but threw it off quickly and said, 'Can you hear that, Meg?' His voice was a whisper.

She was wet through and tired and it showed in her face.

But Hobbes carried on: 'The words, the story in the air. The murderer knows more than we do. It's a story. A long, twisted tale.'

Now she was worried. 'You OK?'

'What do you think?'

'I think . . . you've been through a lot lately.'

There was no response.

'I need to know that you're going to be all right, Guv, that you'll do the job well, no mistakes, no messing about.'

He stared at her.

Shrines

More than an hour later, Hobbes was ringing the bell of 17 Palliser Road, the house called Bridlemere. Police Constable Barlow was with him. They waited for a moment, then used Nicholas Graves's key to let themselves in. It was dark inside, every light switched off, and the long hallway was quiet but for the ticking of the grandfather clock.

'Nobody home,' Barlow said. 'Looks like.'

Hobbes shrugged. 'Yes. I thought one of the sisters might be staying here. I saw her at the funeral.'

'You went to the funeral? Of the man's father?'

'Of course I did.'

'Why, sir? That was before anything bad had happened.'

'Oh, there's been bad things happening in this family for a long time now, years of it. Can't you feel it in the house?'

They were both standing in the hallway, near the closed door to the living room.

Barlow looked hesitant. 'I'm not sure . . .'

'I'm not talking about ghosts or anything. So don't give me that look.'

But they were both whispering.

'Come on, let's begin. Every room, mind, every drawer and cubbyhole.' He handed Barlow a photograph. 'I'm looking for this item in particular. It's a jewellery box, a distinctive design. Made of copper. Do you see?'

Barlow nodded.

'If we're lucky, Nicholas Graves kept everything we found in the cellar floor, including this box.'

'Why didn't you take it away?'

'There wasn't a crime, back then. That's why. Now, look, it might've been hidden somewhere. Or he might have thrown it away.'

'We could try the bins, you never know.'

'Good idea. You see to that.'

'Yes, sir.'

'And the dresses, of course. All examples. Whatever you can find.'

'I'll get on to it.'

The constable walked along the hallway corridor. Hobbes thought of going upstairs, but instead chose the living room. He turned on the light and started to search, opening drawers in the Welsh dresser and looking in the various ornamental boxes set on the bookshelves. His thoughts settled on one subject. He couldn't help thinking that he'd overlooked something with Nicholas Graves. The man had been in the station, in the goddamn police station, sitting across a table from Hobbes. In his mind, the inspector played over and over the man's words during that interview, trying to work out the flaw, the tiny thing he'd missed. He felt certain that if only he'd acted even slightly differently Nicholas would still be alive.

There was nothing to be found here. He moved on, passing the open door that led to the ground-floor room that old Leonard Graves had used as a makeshift bedroom, during the final months of his life. Barlow was in there, looking through the drawers of a cabinet.

'Anything?'

'A lot of dust. Old pennies, toy soldiers. Oh, and a ration book.'

'That's going back some.'

Barlow nodded and carried on with his work.

Hobbes climbed the stairs to the first landing, making his way to the boy's bedroom, with its posters of steam trains and cruise ships, the preserved atmosphere. His hunch proved correct: Nicholas Graves had set up house here, sleeping on his old childhood bed, surrounded by the things of yesterday. It was a comfort, after his father's suicide. Or sheer force of habit. Fear, maybe? The only place in the house the ghosts couldn't visit. There was a suitcase on the floor, the lid open, showing a few items inside. A couple of shirts and a jacket hanging in the wardrobe. The eiderdown on the bed was ruffled, the sheets pulled back.

Father and son, both taken from the world in the space of a week.

What was the connection?

Why was Nicholas Graves murdered? Was it inevitable, once his father had died, a plan set in motion?

The questions were beginning, one by one. Soon the house would be overrun by police officers, and the forensics team, searching for clues to intruders: fingerprints, footprints in the dust, smears on the walls, anything that might point to someone having been here with Nicholas. But, for now, the building was quiet, the shadows still settling.

Hobbes started with the suitcase, but there was little of interest: dirty socks, yesterday's *Telegraph*, a clothes brush and a packet of liver tablets. He tried the drawers of the cabinets, the wardrobe, the pockets of the jacket. He looked under the bed. Another chamber pot, this one decorated with a picture of a bulldog, God knew why. The Bulldog Breed, perhaps. Ah, well, I suppose we should . . . just in case . . . He pulled the pot from under the bed and looked inside. A couple of dead flies and a still-living spider, that was all. He tipped the spider on to the floor and let it live on. The bedside cabinet held a traveller's fold-up alarm clock, nothing else. He stood in the centre of the room, reluctant to leave: he really needed to find that jewellery box, and the objects it contained. At least he'd had the wherewithal to photograph them at the time of the excavation.

And then it came to him where they might be – it was quite simple, really.

Hobbes left the room and made his way to the staircase. He went down to the ground floor, where Barlow was just coming in through the back door. He had a torch in his hand.

'Nothing here, sir. Nothing of interest.'

'The bins?'

'Emptied out. Recently, from the look of it.'

'OK. Carry on upstairs. I've done the first floor, so start on the floors above. There's, erm, there's an attic as well. I'd like to get in there at some point.'

'You think there are secrets hidden away?'

'We'll see.'

Hobbes's mind was elsewhere. He opened the door that led to the cellar. Walking down the stairs again was like revisiting a dream, an action that wasn't usually possible, even in sleep, not in such a knowing way. The air was filled with dust, and he could hear tiny sounds, creaking noises, a skittering as something moved away from the light. Probably a mouse. The bare bulb hung low from its fitting and he had to duck his head as he passed through, into the main space of the cellar. The hole in the floor had been filled in, the concrete cleaner and lighter compared to the floor around it. The pile of rubbish lay in a jumble to one side. The words were still written on the wall above the damaged area, urging Adeline to her eternal peaceful rest. And directly below this message lay a small metal box, a copper box. Hobbes knelt down. He could feel that the objects were still inside, hopefully all five of them.

Sheer curiosity had made him open it, as soon as they had realized that the cellar held nothing more than another dress, so he knew the contents. But, then, Nicholas Graves had taken claim of all the things they'd found down here. Hobbes had kept his promise on that. But, crucially, somebody had brought the box back down here and placed it on the site, as near as damn it to the original resting place. Sacred objects returned to the place of worship, was all Hobbes could imagine.

He sealed the box in an evidence bag.

Barlow was moving around on the floor above, and then his footsteps were loud on the cellar stairs, his voice calling, 'Sir, sir? Where are you?'

'I'm down here.' He stood up and moved to the steps. 'What's wrong?'

Barlow appeared at the cellar door. 'I've found something. I think you need to take a look.'

Hobbes climbed up to meet him, and together they ascended the stairs to the top floor of the house. They left behind the realm of photographs and entered the realm of mirrors, so many of them. Barlow led the way into a back bedroom. It was the one with the wardrobe, where the extra dresses were stored. No other furniture. A single framed playbill on the wall. But now a dress had been laid out on the bare floorboards. The same dress, of the same colours. But no shoes this time, and no scarf: the dress alone. The tear in the side was visible. But no blood. This was a new specimen. Clean and without creases, no doubt taken from the wardrobe. Hobbes stood in the doorway, reluctant to enter.

The room was a shrine. Or a chamber of madness.

There were no curtains at the window and the clear moonlight shone through on to the floor. The dress lay in its glow. The sleeves had been stretched out on each side, and both of them were fixed to the floor: drawing pins had been pushed through the cuffs, into the floorboards. Two further pins had been driven through the hem of the dress, on the right and left sides, causing the lower half of the dress to flare out.

It was easy to imagine a woman lying there.

Every Contact

Through half-closed eyes, he saw the woman lying on the floor, her body wrapped in the blue and yellow dress, torn, the cloth extended over her head to cover her face.

Through half-closed eyes, he saw the house of Bridlemere empty of all life, except that which can never be seen clearly, can never be tested for, or found by any forensic analysis.

Through half-closed eyes, he saw Adeline rising from the floor of the cellar, her skin clothed in ash and dust, her lips sealed with clay. Her flesh was torn where the dress was torn, and the blood had once flowed, but was now dry, dry as the bone that lay exposed within.

With half-closed eyes, he walked the corridors and hallways of the house, from room to room, seeing one after another, each dress, each pair of shoes, each scarf, and he saw the dresses moving of their own accord, empty, empty of all warmth and flesh, the cloth itself animated, the blue and the yellow flowers and the blood on the petals.

Through half-closed eyes, he saw the bodies of all the victims he had ever witnessed in his career, the hopeless ones, the lost, those still clinging to life, helplessly; the ones he had helped and the ones he had failed, the closed cases and the ones still open, all the way back to his mother, whom he had found dead on the floor of their kitchen when he was sixteen years old.

Through half-closed eyes, he saw the metal jewellery box being opened and the various objects tumbling out, five in number, each one different, each one a mystery.

Through half-closed eyes, he saw the woman in the dress, as he had seen her at the funeral, breathing, young, strong and vital, her face always hidden in shadow, no matter where she turned, and no matter how close he came to her.

Through half-closed eyes, Hobbes saw his own son's face disfigured, the skin as blue as his fingertips.

Through half-closed eyes, he saw his own bedroom as he woke in the gloom, stilled and silent, the walls, the ceiling, the dawn light struggling through the curtains, the facts of the case heavy on him, a weight, holding him down in the sheets.

Through half-closed eyes . . .

Hobbes got up. There would be no sleep now, his mind was working.

A shower in the tiny cubicle, as cold as he could bear it.

A quick shave.

Through half-closed eyes, his own face in the mirror, staring back at him.

He tried to imagine the victim's childhood, from hints given, evidence gathered.

It didn't look good. What was it he'd said? *Abnormal, by any modern standard.* Was that it? *You could say we were abused. Old-fashioned parents. All perfectly accepted, a way of life.* Christ, but he wished he'd recorded that interview now. If he'd known . . .

What else? Think!

They liked to play mind games with us.

Yes. And something more. Something important . . .

The everyday cruelties.

That was it.

Everyday cruelties. A double meaning. Accepted cruelties. Or cruelties every day.

And somehow or other those cruelties were still being administered.

Hobbes drove to the police station through the quiet streets. It wasn't an uncommon experience, waking up early and coming into work before the morning shift had properly arrived. The nick was more his home than anywhere else these days.

His desk was piled with forms to be signed, reports to be finished, bits of paper with memos written on them in someone else's handwriting. He couldn't read the notes.

His head was a cage. Thoughts were animals, birds, trapped there.

He was still in the dream in some way, still peering out through his half-closed eyes at the wall in front of him, one or two night-shift officers sitting at other desks, working quietly, ignoring him. Good. He needed time. He wanted to be alone. The wall board was blank. He used a black marker to write two words: *THE DRESS*. He stared at this for a moment. Far off, a clock was chiming: he checked his watch. Six. An hour or so before the team arrived. His eyes closed, his head bowed forward, and the fingers of one hand stretched out, to rub at both temples.

The dress. The blue dress, yellow flowers. No, not the flowers, not that, not the dress itself but something else, on the edge of memory, long ago, years. Damn it. The image flickered into view, and then away.

Mist. Fog. He couldn't see forward . . .

When was that? 1961? '62? Later, maybe. Why was he thinking of that? The last of the London pea-soupers. Smog. Yes, he remembered being on duty that day, barely seeing his hand in front of his face . . .

Hobbes sat down and pulled an evidence bag from a drawer. Within a few hours this would belong to Forensics, but for now it was his to examine. He pulled on a pair of thin plastic gloves, although he hardly knew why: the box and its contents had been buried deep inside concrete for so long. Still, someone had touched it since then – someone had placed it on the floor of the cellar. Probably Nicholas Graves. But wasn't there an off-chance that the murderer had done it? And that one chance meant that Hobbes had to handle the material carefully; he mustn't add his own traces.

Every contact leaves a trace. That was how they put it. Otherwise known in the trade as 'Locard's Principle of Exchange'. Jack Collingworth had taught him this, the DI who had taken Hobbes under his wing back in the sixties. *Exchange, lad! Monsieur Locard got that spot on. Tit for tat. You just need to work it out.* The perpetrator always leaves something behind at a crime scene, and they always take something away; there are no exceptions. *The Old Conundrum*, in Collingworth's words. To wit, lad: a strand of the victim's hair snagged on the killer's clothing, in exchange for a scraping of the killer's flesh under the victim's fingernails. No, not 'killer': Jack always used the word *bastard* for any male perpetrator. *The bastard's flesh.* And there it was, the pure equation: a flow of give and take across the borderline where life and death merged as one. *You just have to work it out properly, that's all, lad. And the bastard's done for!*

Hobbes pressed at the clasp that kept the box closed. The lid clicked open. He switched on a desk lamp and angled it just so, directly over the contents. With utmost care, with his fingertips, he lifted each item from the box, placing it on his desk. Now they lay in a line for his scrutiny.

OK. Good. Now then, let's see, let's work this.

Five items altogether.

Five objects, given a power and an intensity beyond their everyday scope simply by context. By mystery. For some reason these items had been gathered together in a box, and then placed, along with a dress and a pair of shoes and a scarf, oh, yes, and a dead bird. The whole collection wrapped in a curtain and buried beneath the floor of the cellar, out of harm's way, out of sight. But why? Why?

Hobbes thought of the old Anglo-Saxon burial ritual. *Grave goods*. That was the phrase. Items placed with the body, to accompany the dead person on their journey.

He leaned forward slightly, the better to examine the objects.

Item number one was a Player's cigarette card, depicting the film star Greta Garbo.

Item two was a lipstick tube. Gold-coloured, mottled with black. Hobbes unscrewed it, revealing the dried-up remains inside. Crimson Sunset, something like that. Scarlet Temptation.

Item number three was an old coin from before decimals were introduced: a threepenny bit. Silver, smaller and lighter than the later brass edition. It was dated 1919.

Item four was a military medal, a coat of arms on one side and the phrase *Distinguished Conduct in the Field* on the other. It was attached to a very tatty blue-and-red-striped ribbon.

The final item was a lady's brooch, silver inlaid with three rubies. There was a hollow where a fourth gemstone had once nested.

On whose lapel had this once been pinned?

Who had stared at Garbo's face in wonderment?

Who had painted her lips, or had them painted for her?

Who had earned, but never spent a small coin?

Who had been honoured with that medal, for what bravery, in which campaign?

Why had these particular items been placed in the box and buried alongside the dress?

Hobbes frowned. Too many questions were clouding his mind.

Together these five items made up a life. But whose life?

1962

The smog had closed in on Saturday, and two days later it was still clinging on, as thick and as deadly as ever. Hobbes had been called out to a car crash on Wardour Street, one of the numerous slow-motion collisions that had taken place in the darkened streets. The chaos seemed overwhelming. What could he do? People were standing around at the kerb or moving away already, stumbling into each other. The young detective constable directed a team of three uniformed officers to help where they could. His own job was to comfort the driver of a blue sedan, a middle-aged man barely conscious, his eyelids fluttering. His body was twisted, crushed around the middle. It seemed hopeless. Maybe just to be there, that might be enough, standing close by until at last the welcome sound of a klaxon pierced the darkness of day.

Hobbes stepped away from the vehicle as the ambulance crew took over. This was his first week as a DC and it wasn't what he'd expected, to be out on the street still, helping people like this. And then a voice had called to him from the murk of an alleyway. He turned and took a few cautious steps forward, until the woman's face emerged as though from behind a curtain. Her cheeks and brow were spattered with droplets of red, and when she held up her hands, he could see they also were stained with blood. How stark and terrible it looked, amid the sulphurous air.

She was in shock, her eyes wide open, her arms and upper body trembling.

The smog closed around them both.

Hobbes held her by the arm and tried to get her to make sense, but her words were garbled, almost mute. His own eyes were smarting and his throat was clogged. They were alone on an island, himself and this woman. Everyone else had faded away, even the ambulance and the two crashed cars. And then he felt a slight tug on his sleeve and he knew she was offering direction. Without thinking, he let himself be led further into the narrow alleyway, stumbling forward, his one free hand reaching out to scrape along the brick wall. Keep contact. Don't get lost. But Soho was riddled with these dark, twisting back-streets, and he was new in the district, unsure of his way. It was bad enough in clear daylight, but in these conditions it was impossible. They turned a corner, the woman stopped, and he almost bumped into her. Now he saw the fear in her eyes. She was the same age as him more or less, mid-twenties, but the day's events – whatever she had seen or found – gave her a sinister aspect, like something terrible drawn from a dream. For a moment she looked empty of all expression or feeling.

The alleyway was suddenly quiet. All of London had vanished down to this moment, her hand still in his, held tight against the coming danger, whatever it might be. Only her ragged breaths were audible.

'What is it?' he asked. 'What's happened to you?'

She made no answer.

'Show me. Are we near?'

'I'm scared,' she replied, her first words.

Hobbes looked round helplessly. He was scared himself, but couldn't dare admit it. *Last week I was in uniform. That was protection. But now* . . . His outstretched hand disappeared into the haze of yellowish-grey fog. He could see only the woman's face, as it moved from side to side, her hair long and draggled over her eyes, the strands discoloured from a weekend's exposure. He tried to smile, to look in charge. 'It's all right,' he said. 'Let's retrace our steps – we can find the road again.'

'No. No, you have to help me!'

She was suddenly focused. And, without a word, she set off once more, further down the alleyway, her form soon merging with the smog. Hobbes followed, taking one corner after another. This might as well have been the Victorian era: the same phantoms, the same demons prowled the streets.

'Here,' she said. 'This way.'

There was a door ahead, a metal fire door at the end of the alley. It was wedged open with a wooden block, and the woman pulled at it, opening it further. She was about to step inside, when he stopped her and asked, 'What's your name?'

Her face hovered in the dark of the doorway.

'Glenda,' she answered. 'Glenda Jones.'

'I'm Detective Constable Hobbes. Has somebody hurt you?'

She didn't reply.

'Glenda, you have blood on your hands. Is somebody injured? I need to know.'

In answer she moved into the gloom of the building. Even there he could see traces of the smog. It got everywhere, into the lungs, the hair, the eyes, the rooms where people were living and working. At first Hobbes felt that he'd been abandoned. A sudden thought came to him: was this a trap? Oh, Jesus, would he ever get better at this?

He called, 'Glenda!'

Her voice answered: 'This way. Quickly! Down here.'

A set of stairs took him down into the basement of the building. He stepped forward, feeling his way with his hands on the walls, and walked through an open door into another room. There was a flickering light, images dancing. A bank of seats. It was a small cinema of some kind. The seats were almost all empty, but the film continued on the screen: a masked woman, a whip, and was that a saddle? Christ. And then he looked down and saw a figure lying on the floor, a little way down the central aisle. It was a woman. Hobbes stared ahead, unable to move. The blood, the wounds to her stomach, the torn clothing.

Glenda was kneeling close by. She said, 'Marge, I've brought someone, a policeman. Listen, darling, stay awake, will yer? Please, Margery. We're here to help you.'

At last, Hobbes snapped out of his trance. He bent down, and examined the wounds. A lot of blood had been shed. It had splashed on to Glenda's dress.

'What happened? Glenda! I need to know.'

'It was a punter. He went crazy. We get that sometimes, but never like this.'

'And Margery, she works here?'

'Oh, yeah. She's an usher, like me.'

'What about the weapon?'

Glenda had a drained expression. She was staring at her friend, unseeing.

'What did they use? A knife?'

'Yes, yes. I think so. A flick knife. He was a Teddy boy.'

Hobbes didn't have a wireless on him. He attended to Margery as best he could, and told Glenda what to do, to keep pressure on her wound.

'Don't worry, she'll be all right. We'll look after her.'

He walked to the back of the cinema and found a telephone in an empty office. The projector was still whirring around. As he waited to be connected, he looked through a small window into the auditorium. Maybe fifty seats in all. A tiny place. And despite everything, there were still one or two customers gazing at the screen. And now he knew why. Almost for the first time, or for the first conscious time, he took in the nature of the film being shown – the bare flesh, the groans of the soundtrack, the sleazy music, the grimaces on the faces of the performers.

He spoke into the mouthpiece of the phone, giving instructions. And all the time his eyes were staring at the screen.

PART TWO

1981

Bedsitter Land

After the morning meeting, once he'd given out his orders for the first full day of the murder investigation, Hobbes set off alone for an address in New Cross. As he searched for the house number he realized he wasn't that far away from DC Fairfax's current abode, at his mother's house. A pang of guilt: he had neglected to follow up on his last visit. If Tom Fairfax didn't come back to work soon, they would have to seek a replacement. And so his mind was beset, as he walked from his car to the front door of the terraced house on Shipyard Lane. He took a set of keys from his pocket and tried each one until the door lock clicked open. The hallway was filled with piles of junk mail, empty beer bottles, pizza containers and other such debris. A rusty, chainless bicycle propped against the wall. The smell of damp. Peeling wallpaper. Hobbes took the stairs to the first landing and again searched for a key, this time to fit the lock on flat number three. He could hear music from the next flat along.

Down the way a door opened and a young man peeked out. 'Can I help you?'

Hobbes stated the case: 'Police.'

This brought worry to the man's eyes. 'Police? What . . . why?'

'Detective Inspector Hobbes. I'm looking for Mr Graves. Do you know him?'

'Mr Graves?'

All he could do was repeat Hobbes's words without purpose.

'You mean Nick?'

'That's right. Have you seen him recently?'

A game was being played, but maybe the young man didn't know it yet. Somewhere between the known and the unknown was the truth. It was a question of teasing it out.

Hobbes had still not found the correct key. He gave up and approached the other man. The scent of marijuana wafted from the doorway.

'What's your name?'

'Colin. Colin Beck.'

He was in the second half of his twenties, with badly cut hair and a creased shirt-front. His chin and cheeks were troubled by a combination of spots and stubble. Bloodshot eyes. His hand tightened on the door of his flat and he pulled it further to, possibly ashamed of what might be found within. Now his face was the only part of him visible.

'I'm looking into a crime.'

'Do you have . . . do you have identification?'

Hobbes showed him the warrant card. 'That good enough for you?'

A nervous little nod.

'Answer the question, please.'

'The question . . .'

Hobbes was getting irritated. He hardened his voice. 'When was the last time you saw the occupant of flat number three?'

'Not for a week now. Something like that. He came round to pick up something. I could hear him through the walls. They're paper-thin.'

Yes, Hobbes thought. Nicholas Graves was probably collecting the suitcase and a few belongings to take with him to Bridlemere.

'And he hasn't come home since? You didn't see anything?'

'No. But I heard something . . .'

'Go on.'

By now Colin Beck was keen to pass on the information, seeing a way to be useful, to gain points.

'It wasn't him. I mean . . . someone was banging on his door.'

'Who was it?'

'I didn't know. But they called out for him.'

'A woman?'

'No. A man. But . . .'

'How many?'

'Sorry?'

'How many people?'

'Just the one. One voice.'

'What day was this?'

'It was the day before signing-on day.'

'Which is?'

'I was brassic, skint, like, so—'

'The day!'

'Thursday.'

So, three days before Nicholas was killed. It might not mean anything . . .

'Thank you. And what did he say?'

Beck looked confused. 'Who?'

'This man, the visitor, when he called out, what did he say, precisely? Come on!'

'Wait. Let me remember . . .'

He came fully out of his flat, but he kept his door pulled to behind him.

'Did you see him, this visitor?' Hobbes asked.

'No, I didn't come out, not that time. And he left after a minute or so, getting no answer.'

'Have you remembered yet?'

'What?'

Hobbes sighed. 'What was said?'

'Oh, yeah, yeah. He called out for Nicholas. That was it.'

'Not Mr Graves?'

'No, I'm certain of it. *Nicholas*.'

That didn't make it any easier, Hobbes thought. Maybe a relative, or a friend. But Nicholas, not Nick . . .

Hobbes softened his voice: 'Colin, what is Mr Graves like? Do you get on with him?' Still keeping to the present tense.

'He keeps to himself. Old people can get like that, I think.'

'You think he was old?'

'Course he was. Getting on, getting on. And you know how it is, when they end up alone in life? Right? But he's friendly enough, when we meet in the kitchen, or on the way to the bathroom. We share the facilities . . .'

'I see. So all the flats are bedsits?'

Beck nodded. 'Sure, that's right. But I was never invited inside. Not once. Like I said, Nick was the private type.'

'How many other people live here?'

'There's Josie, upstairs, that's the top flat. And Mavis and Tom downstairs. They're a couple, boyfriend, girlfriend. And, erm . . . the other downstairs flat is empty. Apart from Mavis, we're all on the dole . . . This government, eh?'

'You're saying that Graves didn't have a job?'

'That's right. He stayed in, mostly. Except for signing-on day.'

Hobbes mused on this. So Nicholas's talk of being a journalist for the *Telegraph* had been a lie? One thing was certain: he'd come down in the world since the glory days of Bridlemere. 'Any other visitors? Regular ones?'

Beck shook his head.

'Come on, there must've been someone. Didn't he have any friends, relatives? Lady friends, overnight guests?'

'What? Nick? No, no, nothing like that. Not that I saw, anyway. That's why, see . . . that's why it was unusual, when that man came calling, banging on the door. And you, today. That's why I came out, to see . . .'

Hobbes went back to trying keys in the lock. He found the right one.

'Inspector?'

'What is it?'

'Will he be coming back soon? Only . . .'

'Yes?'

'Only Nick's got food in the fridge, see. Maybe I should eat it, what do you think?'

'He's dead.'

'It'll go off, otherwise— What did you say?'

'Nicholas Graves was found dead on Sunday evening.'

Hobbes studied the tenant's reaction. It was pure surprise, shock even. No guile. For form's sake, he asked, 'Where were you, on that night?'

'Sunday? Me? In here. Indoors. Why?'

'No matter.'

'Mavis and Tom saw me at teatime, we chatted in the kitchen. Fish fingers.'

'What's that?'

'That's what I ate. Fish fingers and beans.' It was offered as proof of alibi.

Hobbes smiled. 'Thank you for your time.'

He waited until Beck had re-entered his bedsit, and then he opened the door of flat three. The dead man's place of residence.

The detective stood on the threshold, concentrating, seeking out every detail, even before taking a step. He knew that the room held something of import – all rooms did – but such clues were often hidden or, if in plain sight, not of obvious significance. It was a case of sorting through the chaos. But Hobbes saw straight away that his job would be very different this time.

The room was almost bare. He stepped inside.

There was a single bed in the corner and a wooden chair next to a desk, a wardrobe, a rickety bookcase. That was it. No pictures on the walls. Very few personal belongings on view. The wardrobe held one jacket and a pair of trousers, a couple of shirts, a few items of underwear, socks, a brown tie on a rack. Nothing in the pockets of the jacket.

Talk about the greasy slope. A life almost down to zero. And there was Graves Senior, lumbering around in that giant house all alone. Maybe Nicholas had been resentful.

Hobbes looked under the bed and found a single issue of a body-building magazine. He checked the drawer in the table. A few sheets of blank paper, a biro. His UB40 card. Some spare change. No sign of a typewriter or any other evidence of journalistic activity. Nothing much to show for the struggle, the years put in, the dreaming. Did he welcome those few nights he had slept at Bridlemere, after his father died, in the comfort of his childhood room? Or perhaps he liked the dismal life. Hobbes knew that some people just give in one day, and lead far better lives for doing so: no lead weights around the neck.

Inventory of a dead man.

Four cigarette butts in an ashtray.

That body-building magazine. Presumably of erotic intent?

A dark stain on the ceiling.

Grey, almost transparent curtains. No shade on the overhead light.

Only the bookshelf showed evidence of an individual at play: all three shelves were crammed with books, most of them hardbacks. It took Hobbes a moment to realize that he was looking at the same title, repeated on every single book, very often the same edition of the same novel. One copy lay flat on the top shelf of the stand; perhaps Nicholas Graves had been reading it recently. Hobbes picked it up.

A Spell of Darkness.

The author's name was Mary Estelle Graves.

He turned to the inside back cover, where a photograph showed the novelist's face beautifully cast in half-shadow. A caption read, 'Mary Estelle Graves achieved fame as "Miss Kreeley" in the theatre play *The Moon Awakes*. Many other roles followed, both classical and modern. She is esteemed by audiences and critics alike. *A Spell of Darkness* is her first novel. She lives in London with her family.' Hobbes flipped to the opening pages of the book and saw that it was a first edition, published in 1958. The title page was signed and dedicated.

To my loving son, Nicholas, on his birthday.
Your mother, Mary Estelle

Hobbes sat on the bed and read the first paragraph of chapter one:

Leigh Park Manor had a reputation for being haunted even before the Parnell family moved in, and their stay there did little to rid the local townspeople of their fears, for the family was seen, from that very first day in the midsummer of 1897, to be the carriers of a curse. Over time suspicion turned to fear and the large three-storey building at the end of Lumb Lane was shunned by all. It was a house of mysteries, within whose shadowy rooms and corridors a family of peculiar nature went about their secretive business. Indeed, we might never have known of the exact nature of that peculiarity if a certain young lady had not walked up to the ornate front door and pulled on the bell rope some two years after the Parnells had taken up residence.

The cover of the book showed a proud-looking woman in profile, a large dark house behind her, an overgrown rose trellis partly obscuring her white gown. In her hand she held a lighted lantern, which shone a yellow light on the book's title.

Hobbes's mind was active with new thoughts, all vying for attention, but none would come into focus. And then he bent forward slightly. From his position on the bed he could see under the table: a wastepaper basket was pushed against the wall. He pulled it out and rummaged through the sheets of crumpled paper it contained. When these were opened and spread out on the desktop it became obvious that Nicholas Graves had been composing a letter, or at least trying to. After several false starts, he had managed at best a half-paragraph. But Hobbes read this with great interest.

For the third time in this case he saw the name written down: *Adeline.*

The Dreamers

Mrs Rosamund Kepple lived in Plumstead, in a small house at the end of a row. DS Latimer accompanied Hobbes. The front door was opened at the first ring of the bell, as though the householder had been waiting for them in the hallway. She led them into the living room, which was compact, neat and tidy, and spotlessly clean. Everything that could be polished had been polished. The air was scented. Not a speck of dust disturbed the whiteness of the carpet. Hobbes had never seen so many knick-knacks before – porcelain figurines and brasses dominated, with a few souvenirs of holidays in Spain slotted in, all arranged in rigid lines on shelves, tabletops and inside glass cabinets. It was a collector's den. A portrait of the Virgin Mary took pride of place above the mantelpiece.

Latimer perched on the edge of her seat, looking uncomfortable. This wasn't a house to feel at home in. Hobbes found himself staring into the eyes of the abyss, and it was garishly coloured, in the shape of a shepherd boy with a flute. And then Rosamund Kepple came in carrying a tray. She sat at the coffee-table next to Hobbes and served tea and biscuits. There wasn't a sign of mourning, not on her face or in her body language. This could be just another day: tea with acquaintances. But her first words cut through this atmosphere of politeness.

'Detectives, I'd like to answer the most obvious question for you straight away, so as not to prolong your stay here.' She didn't wait for Hobbes to respond, but carried straight on. 'I didn't kill my brother. I had no reason to kill him, none at all.'

Hobbes waited a second and then he asked, 'Do you have feelings for Nicholas, for his passing away?'

She thought for a moment. 'I can't say I do. I'm trying to, I really am. I'm trying to feel sad, but it's a difficult emotion for me to summon.'

Latimer came in: 'So you didn't like your brother?'

'I wouldn't say that, exactly. But . . .'

'Go on.'

'We're not that kind of family.'

'Which kind?'

'The kind that cares very much for each other.' Her nose crinkled in distaste. But then she softened, or at least made an effort to do so. 'Please, don't get me wrong. Sometimes I'm truly jealous of friends who burst into tears at the mere mention of a relative being ill, or made poor. But mostly I'm glad that my mother and father raised me as they did, raised all of us as they did, to be strong-willed, and not to live beholden to our hearts.'

Rosamund Kepple sat bolt upright in her seat, a delicate teacup perched on her lap, one hand resting lightly on the chair arm. She was slight in the body, dressed in a pair of mauve trousers and a white blouse under a purple cardigan. A thin decorative silk scarf was wrapped around her neck. Her hair was tied back in a bun. Her face was distinctive in that Gravesian manner: finely etched, drawn in at the cheeks. Her eyes never blinked. Hobbes knew she was sixty-three years old. She seemed younger. Willpower played a large part in this: she had the look of a person who was holding back time by the sheer force of mind. Her brows would crease with the effort, then suddenly uncrease when she realized she was frowning. Rosamund was keeping account of herself, moment to moment. Because of this, Hobbes could easily believe everything she was saying, for she spoke simply and plainly, stating the facts. He had to be on his guard.

He said, 'Let's go back to basics.'

'Please do.'

'Where were you yesterday evening around eight o'clock?'

A tiny smile played on her lips. 'You mean, when Nicholas was killed?'

'Just answer the question, please.'

'I was here, at home. On my own. As always.'

'Your husband is . . . ?'

She shook her head. 'Andrew died in the war, I'm afraid.'

Latimer was taking notes. She said now, 'So nobody can confirm where you were last night? Is that right?'

'It seems that way. But I've already told you I didn't kill Nicholas. I barely knew him at all, these days.'

Hobbes asked, 'What about the man I saw at the funeral?'

'You were . . .'

'Who was he?'

'You were at my father's funeral? But why?'

'The man at your side?'

'That was David. My son.'

'You brought him up on your own?'

'I did. With a little help from the family.'

Latimer asked, 'Could you let us have his address?'

'Of course, but I can't see what this—'

'We're making sure that all areas are covered.'

'Right. I see. Yes.' Mrs Kepple gave out her son's address.

There was a pause. The room was very quiet. No clocks ticking, no sounds from any of the other rooms. Lace curtains covered the bottom half of the windows.

The outside world was shut away.

Only the occasional crackle of a piece of coal in the fireplace broke the calm.

Hobbes asked, 'When did you last see your brother?'

'At my father's funeral. I came home straight after.'

'There was no wake?'

'No. For what purpose? We all went our separate ways.'

'But you met up prior to the funeral, surely?'

'Yes, Nick called me and told me of Father's death. I came to Bridlemere the next day, and we consoled each other, as we could.'

'Did you stay there?'

'No. I drove back that evening. Nick was staying there. But we talked.'

Latimer asked, 'Did Nicholas mention any worries?'

'Of course. His father had just killed himself.'

'Yes, but apart from that?'

'No, not really. Not that I can recall. We went through the house together.'

'Looking for?'

'Nothing in particular. We spoke of childhood memories, of the games we used to play.'

'Did you find a last will and testament?'

'We did. Hidden among his papers. But it's handwritten, and without witness. Our father distrusted all lawyers, solicitors, judges, any figure of authority. Even policemen.' A smile aimed at Hobbes. 'So I'm not sure what validity the document will hold.'

'Do you have it with you?'

She sighed, then stood and walked to a chest of drawers in the corner of the room. 'It really isn't of much use.'

Hobbes took the piece of paper from her. It was a personal document, a few handwritten lines in blue ink.

I, Leonard Graves, of sound or sound enough mind, leave all my worldly goods to my daughter Camilla, to do with as she sees fit, for the good of the family.

It was dated 2 June 1967. Then a gap, and in the same handwriting but a different colour of blue, it said:

Nothing to Nicholas or Rosamund. They have taken Mary Estelle from me.

This later entry was undated. The word *nothing* had been underlined.

Rosamund's face betrayed no emotion as she said, 'There you have it. Father in all his glory.'

Hobbes waited a moment. 'And how did that make you feel?'

Latimer added, 'Angry, I imagine.'

Rosamund shrugged. 'His fortune is paltry by now. And the house . . . well, it will fetch a price no doubt, but you've seen the state it's in. And so . . .'

'Yes?'

Rosamund's face twisted up. 'Let Camilla have the house, and let her rot in it.'

Hobbes wondered if that emotion ran deeper, beyond bitterness. 'And how was Nicholas during this search?'

'I would say . . . Yes, I would say he was sadder than I was, by a good few degrees.'

Hobbes shivered, he couldn't help himself.

Latimer said, 'We're trying to get in touch with your sister.'

'With Camilla?'

'Have you any—'

'I have nothing to tell you, I'm afraid. I haven't seen her in years. Decades.'

'And you have no address for her, or a telephone number?'

'Nothing. To be honest . . .'

'Yes?'

'. . . I'm surprised she's not still living in her father's house.'

'How about a photograph of her?'

'I have no photographs of my family.'

'None at all?'

'Such things have never interested me.'

Latimer frowned. 'How old would Camilla be now?'

Rosamund worked it out. 'Oh, I don't know. She was born in 1926, I remember that. What does that make her?'

Latimer gave the answer. 'Fifty-five.'

'Is she married?' Hobbes asked.

'I really couldn't say.' Now Rosamund sounded irritated. 'Don't you like these questions?'

She dismissed his remark with a wave of her hand. 'I doubt Camilla would invite me to any ceremony, marriage or otherwise.'

The two officers looked at each other.

Hobbes dug in. 'Rosamund, do you know of anyone who might want Nicholas dead, or wish him harm in any way?'

The question appeared to disturb her a little.

Hobbes and Latimer watched her closely. Was something of significance coming?

But no. She regained her sense of self, and said plainly, 'I really know very little of my brother's life. He left home in his twenties to fight in the war. Since then I've seen him only a few times, at family get-togethers and the like, but even those stopped after a while. That house was never inviting.'

'Bad memories?' Hobbes asked.

'Oh, the usual things. Family life . . . and all that . . .'

'The everyday cruelties?'

'I beg your pardon?' Her brows knitted once more and, this time, she forgot to rectify the problem.

'It was something your brother said to me, about your upbringing. *Everyday cruelties.*'

'I see. Well, that is a strange thing to say.'

'You think so?'

'I do, yes. We were no different, I'm sure, from any other family of the time.'

Hobbes stared at her. He said, 'Mrs Kepple, I think you're lying.'

At last he had her attention. She held his look for a second or two. Distress flickered around her eyes, which then closed. It was the first proper emotion she'd shown, small as it was, and held tightly within her own body.

She said nothing.

Latimer asked her, 'Rosamund, are you all right? Would you like a glass of water?'

There was still no response.

Hobbes made to ask another question. But Rosamund was already speaking quietly to herself. He had to lean in to hear the words.

'Oh dear, another funeral.' Her head was bowed, hiding her face. Her shoulders were hunched. 'Another funeral to arrange.' Her downturned head shook a little.

Hobbes watched her closely. Latimer took over. 'I know this is difficult. But your brother was murdered. We need all the help you can give us, even the tiniest remark or action might be useful. Anything at all that he might have said or done in the last few days?'

Rosamund looked up. But not at Latimer. Her eyes had gathered anger, which she directed at Hobbes. 'You called me a liar.'

'What the inspector meant was—'

Hobbes raised a hand to halt his sergeant. He spoke simply.

'I believe that Bridlemere is a house of secrets. And that some very bad things might have happened there, in the past.'

'I really don't know what you're basing this assumption on.' Control had returned to her body and voice.

Hobbes played his most important card. He took a photograph from a folder.

'You're not going to show me . . . are you?'

'What?'

'Nicholas's injuries.'

'No. Of course not. Although there is an injury involved. Of sorts.'

He placed the photograph on the coffee-table. Rosamund leaned over to look at it. Then she picked it up and stared at it without speaking.

'Does that dress have significance for you?'

She didn't reply.

'We found fifteen examples of it on the day your father died. Another buried in the cellar. And since then my officers have found another eleven copies, stored in the attic. And all of them have the same cut or rip in the material at the same place on the body. And the blood in the same place. Do you see? Just here.' He tapped at the photograph.

Now Rosamund nodded.

'That's twenty-seven dresses, altogether.' Hobbes's voice was quiet and insistent. 'We may yet find more. Do you think we will?'

She glanced at him. 'I'm sorry. I don't quite understand . . .'

'Do you think we'll find more copies of this dress around the house, hidden away, mutilated in the same way, and stained with blood?' His voice never wavered.

Her answer took a moment to form on her lips: 'Yes. Maybe.'

The photograph was trembling in her hand.

Latimer asked, 'How many should we be looking for?'

'I really can't say. It was an obsession.'

'On whose part?'

'My father's.' Having said this, she breathed out. As though relieved of a burden.

'Please explain.'

She looked at Hobbes and then at Latimer. 'It's difficult to speak about.'

Hobbes's eyes held no joy, none. 'Still. Let us speak.'

Rosamund smiled weakly. 'The dress belonged to my mother, Mary Estelle. I think she wore one very like it when she was young, when my father first met her. And I suppose over the years it had taken on symbolic value for him.'

'Did he have the dresses specially made?'

'Oh, yes. He gave her the same dress every year. My sister Camilla made them. She's the seamstress in the family.'

'Isn't that a strange thing to do?' asked Latimer. 'A strange gift?'

'I suppose so, yes.' Rosamund summoned courage. 'But as children we took it as simply a part of life, perfectly normal. In fact, it was a necessary thing to do.'

'So your mother enjoyed the same gift every year?'

'She loved it. In fact . . .' Rosamund dabbed at her lips with a fingertip '. . . our mother demanded the gift, the same gift. She would scream blue murder if he tried to buy her anything else.' Here she looked at Hobbes with some vehemence. 'If there was madness in our house, well, Mother was its focus, and its true cause.'

Nobody spoke for a moment. Latimer was going over her notes, turning back the pages, while Hobbes closed his eyes and tried to concentrate. Mrs Kepple smiled absently, and then stared into her empty teacup.

Hobbes brought his attention back. 'What about the cuts in the dresses, and the blood?'

'That I can't explain, I'm afraid. Not truly.' She placed her cup on the table.

'You don't remember this from your childhood, or from later years?'

'Oh, of course I do. Of course. It was all part of the ceremony.'

Hobbes shook his head. 'That's the second time you've used that word.'

'I don't understand.'

'You said you doubted your sister Camilla would ever invite you to any *ceremony*.'

Rosamund's face was frozen, bereft of all emotion. 'What, precisely, are you implying, Inspector?'

'I'm surmising . . .'

'I can see that.'

'Let's say, then, that your father attacked your mother with a knife.'

'And why would he do that?'

Hobbes carried straight on: 'One year he attacks her, injures her, and then each year after, the same ritual is undertaken. The same *ceremony*, as you called it.'

She smiled broadly, then turned to DS Latimer and said, 'Do you have to put up with this every day?'

It was an expert remark, and neither officer knew how to respond at first. Until Latimer returned Rosamund's smile and said, 'He's been known to be right. On occasion.'

'Well, this time, he's wrong.'

'Do you mean there's another explanation, the correct one? And you're not willing to tell us? Is that what you're saying? You're hiding it from us?'

Now the two women stared at each other, neither willing to back down. Hobbes let the silence play out.

And then Rosamund laughed gently. 'There may have been a

sexual element at play, the dress as a fetish object, who knows? Something that we, as children, could have no understanding of. Didn't Freud say something along these lines, that none of us can face the sexuality of our parents? We can only be appalled.'

Here she paused, looking from one officer to the other. 'I know this: our mother was a woman of great passion. She used that passion on stage, to create her wonderful characters, and to connect with her audience. She specialized in the kind of fiercely dominant female popular at the time. All black cats and lace veils. Very Bette Davis. But Mary Estelle had her own voice, and her own fashion. It brought her fame. But later on, after her career dwindled, and time took hold of her beauty, and lightened her auburn hair, this passion turned inward.'

Rosamund's entire face was taken up by a passion of her own now, every careful rule of behaviour cast aside. Her features were creased and coloured as the anger seethed through her. Her hand moved before her, clutching an imagined weapon.

'The knife of hatred was pointed at the world. But now it turned towards her . . .'

Hobbes was fascinated. 'You mean . . . you're saying your mother injured herself?'

'Perhaps. Yes, why not? I imagine she was capable of such an act.' But then Rosamund shook her head, to erase the feelings from her body. Control took over again, even colder than before. 'Well, it is one explanation. The one I prefer, when I think back on my younger days.'

Latimer took up the idea. 'So every year this self-*mutilation* was replicated, on the dress, as a way of, what, preventing it from happening again, for real?'

'Yes. Why not?' Rosamund Kepple's voice was icy. It might have been an automaton speaking. 'I'm sure Nicholas told you a little of the theatrical nature of life at Bridlemere.'

Hobbes said, 'He did.'

'Every day was filled with miniature dramas concocted by our parents. And later on, by a natural process, we children took on our own creative roles.'

'It must've been hell.'

'Actually, it was quite fun.'

Hobbes changed tack. 'Your brother claimed to have no knowledge of the dresses.'

'Well, that's Nick for you. Always wanting to hide the truth of Mother's madness. He was the apple of her diseased eye, and she loved him dearly. Her little boy-child.'

Latimer said, 'We'd like to speak with your mother. Would that be possible?'

'You can try. I'll give you the address of the old people's home.'

'Thank you.'

'It's called Riverdale House, in Greenwich. The best David could find.'

'Your son?'

'That's right. He found his grandmother a place there, and he pays all the bills. Really, he's turned out a good boy.'

'We'll go to see her, I think.'

'Of course. But I must warn you, my mother isn't very responsive these days. She makes little or no sense.'

'You don't get on?'

A simple shake of the head was her only answer.

Hobbes considered for a moment. 'We know very little about Nicholas. What was he like, as a person?'

'Artistic, sensitive. He was always working on some scheme or other, but none of them came to much. He wanted to follow in his father's footsteps.'

'Into the theatre?'

'Yes, or the arts in general. He had an interest in films. But the old man cast a heavy shadow. Nick could never quite escape his father's influence, although God knows he tried.' She took a breath. 'I always thought he needed a woman in his life. But he wasn't the marrying kind, if you take my meaning.'

'I think so, yes.'

'Of course, he might have married, just to spite himself. Or to hide his true nature. But no. I genuinely think he preferred loneliness. Or, of course . . .'

'Affairs?'

'One-night stands, I suppose. He mentioned a few. And afterwards . . . the shame.' Rosamund folded her hands in her lap. 'Now, if we're finished here . . .'

Hobbes shook his head. 'Not quite.'

'Really? Do you think you're progressing?'

'One more thing.'

'Very well. If you must.'

'About the dress we found buried in the cellar. I take it your brother mentioned that to you?'

'He did.'

'Well, then, I'm curious about that.'

Rosamund looked at him for a long time. Finally she spoke. 'Yes. So am I.'

'You're saying you know nothing about it?'

'That's right.' Stony-faced. 'Father was always working down there. As children, we were never allowed down the stairs, not even supervised.'

Hobbes groaned. He wiped sweat from his face with a hand.

He took a hardback book from his bag and placed it on the coffee-table. Rosamund looked at it. Then she picked it up eagerly. 'My Lord! I haven't seen a copy of this for so long a time.'

'Your mother wrote it.'

'Yes, she had an idea she would become a novelist, that it would be a second career, when her acting days were over. But it was her only book, sadly. The critics didn't take to it. And it never sold very well.'

'I found it in Nicholas's flat.'

'I see.'

'I also found this.' Hobbes opened a sheet of paper. 'It was in the wastepaper basket. He was attempting to write a letter. He tried several times.'

Rosamund's expression was wide-eyed, a mixture of surprise and fear.

'I'll read it to you.'

She nodded. Hobbes read the words slowly: ' "Dear Adeline. I hope I can call you that. I've been thinking about you a lot, these last few months, I don't know why. Getting old, I suppose. I wish I could see you again. I really do! Who knows, a second time around, we might even . . ." '

He paused. 'Here the letter breaks off. What do you make of it, Mrs Kepple?'

'Nothing.'

'And yet this is the third time we've seen this woman's name mentioned. First in your father's suicide note. Which said, *Dearest Adeline, I'm so sorry. For everything.* And then the same name was written on the wall of the cellar, where Adeline was asked to rest in peace. And now this.' He brandished the piece of paper at her.

But Rosamund would not respond, only to widen her eyes still further.

Hobbes continued, 'You see, when I saw that epigraph on the wall, I naturally assumed that Adeline, whoever she might be, was dead. But this letter, I don't know, it seems to throw some doubt on that.' He stared at her. 'So. What do you think?'

With a great effort Rosamund said, 'That isn't a letter. It's a journal entry, a *musing*, if you like. An attempt by Nicholas to make sense of his feelings for someone long lost.'

'So Adeline is dead? Is that what you're saying? Rosamund, talk to me.'

It took an effort: 'She can't be dead . . . because she was never alive.'

Hobbes looked at Latimer, who was as puzzled as he was.

'You're saying that— Let me get this straight. You're saying that Adeline doesn't exist?'

'That's right. Our family created her. She's a character in a play. A play set not on the stage, but in reality. In the reality of Bridlemere, our family home.'

Hobbes couldn't quite grasp it.

Latimer said, 'OK, I'm having trouble with this, I'll freely admit it.'

'Yes, it must be puzzling . . . to outsiders.' Rosamund's voice was icier than ever.

'So could you explain it a little more clearly?'

'I can try. Yes. Adeline was . . .'

But then Rosamund stopped talking. Hobbes watched her carefully.

Her eyes closed, the lids firmly pressed together.

Her hands twisted in her lap.

She might have been alone in the room, for all the attention she gave the others. And when her eyes opened again, Hobbes saw that the light had gone from them. The force of nature had left her body. She had given up.

It was the only way to describe it, as an act of surrender.

She looked at Hobbes and said matter-of-factly, 'Our family has created itself. From a dream.'

He asked for explanation.

She answered: 'We have created ourselves, and we can so easily do the opposite.'

It struck him as a warning, but one whose nature was still hidden. And again he asked for information. 'What do you mean?'

When he received no answer, Latimer spoke sternly: 'Mrs Kepple. If you're withholding evidence that later leads to a conviction, you will be held responsible. I hope you understand me.'

Rosamund smiled. And then she stood up and walked over to the doorway.

'Where are you going?'

'There's something I need to show you. I won't be a minute.'

She left the room. Hobbes could hear her ascending the stairs. He turned to Latimer and asked, 'What do you make of her?'

'She's nuts.'

'Apart from that?'

'Oh, God, I don't know. Maybe the whole family is mad. Can that be possible?'

'There have been cases, yes. Have you read R. D. Laing?'

'No, I haven't bloody well read R. D. Laing! When do I have time—'

'He has some interesting theories . . .'

The sergeant grimaced. 'That look on her face is a bit scary, isn't it?'

'But do you think she's capable of killing her own brother?'

'The mark of Cain?' Latimer thought for a moment. 'Maybe. She looks strong enough.'

Hobbes nodded. 'Yes. And Nicholas was very frail.'

'Actually, she reminds me of someone.'

'You're not going to say me, are you?'

'A little bit.'

'I'm not – there's no way—'

'Just here and there, that's all. Now and then ... a certain phrase.'

'Jesus.'

'Don't worry, Guv.' Latimer was smiling.

'OK. Very funny.'

'She's taking her time, isn't she?'

Hobbes stood up and walked out into the hallway, where he looked up the stairs. He called, 'Mrs Kepple?'

He took the stairs at a pace, suddenly worried, and he couldn't think why. At the landing he called her name again, more softly this time. He pushed open the nearest door and saw a bathroom. He walked along the landing to a bedroom door.

Rosamund was lying on her back on the double bed, perfectly still, her limbs composed as a corpse's might be, her legs straight, pressed together, her hands crossed on her chest.

Hobbes came into the room and looked down at the bed.

For a moment he wondered ...

But, no, she was breathing evenly. Her closed eyelids were flickering. And then she opened them slightly. A smile played on her lips.

There was a pair of scissors lying on the eiderdown.

Hobbes bent closer.

Rosamund Kepple had used the scissors to cut open her blouse, on the lower right-hand side. That special place. The blades, or one of the blades, had continued through the material and entered the flesh. She had cut herself. It wasn't a deep cut, not to look at, but the white cloth was stained red.

Suddenly, Rosamund reached up and grabbed Hobbes as she spoke in a low voice, drawn from deep down: 'We are born from the night flesh.' She stared at him, her eyes ablaze. 'We crawl from the skull, from the shadows of the skull. From the sick dreams in the dark of the skull, we shall arise.'

Her smile broadened. Milk-white teeth, a fleck of lipstick on one.

Hobbes pulled himself loose from her grip. Latimer came into the room, to take charge of the situation, pressing a hand over the wound on the woman's stomach.

The sight of blood meant nothing to Hobbes, or next to nothing, but the words she had spoken made him feel sick.

Decay Factor

Later that day, Hobbes drove to Richmond Park. It was around the time of the murder, according to the estimate. Eight o'clock in the evening. He liked to see things as they were, when they were, in the hope of connecting to the perpetrator's intent and mood.

There was still a small police presence, PC Barlow among them. Hobbes asked the young officer to join him and they ducked under the tape to make their way off the beaten path into the wooded area. Neither spoke as they walked along. Hobbes listened to the last of the raindrops as they trickled through the branches. The smell of the autumn air always carried a sense of things ending, nature reminding us that all things must pass.

They stopped at the cleared ground. The tent had been removed.

Crime scenes after the fact: he knew them well. Another lesson from DI Collingworth.

Always go back, lad, once the hurly-burly's done. Once they've carted the body away and the backroom boys have scraped the place clean.

You never know what you might find.

Hobbes stared at the black earth, the tufts of uprooted grass, patterns in the mud. The holes in the soil where the tent poles had been inserted. And over there, claw marks: another bloody dog sniffing about probably. Or something wilder. He looked to the surrounding trees; he looked up at the sky, darkening in a circle where the branches didn't quite meet.

Barlow asked, in a quiet voice, 'What are we looking for, sir?'

'I'm trying to work out why *here*, why the deed took place here, in the park, in this particular place, these trees.'

'Right.'

'Look, I'm Nicholas Graves, OK? You're his killer. Maybe I asked you here, or maybe you asked me. But this is a meeting place, I'm sure of it.'

'You mean . . .'

'Think it out.'

'Right. They didn't meet by chance.'

'No, of course not. They knew each other, or they knew of each other.'

'His wallet wasn't taken.'

'Exactly. This wasn't a mugging or anything like that. They *met* here. By arrangement.' He turned a full circle. His hand reached out and touched the bark of the nearest tree. 'Why this place?'

They stood in silence. There was no easy answer.

Barlow took up the thought. 'Well, didn't Mr and Mrs Graves live in Richmond all their lives?'

'She did, definitely. In the same house. I'm not sure where Leonard came from.'

'But the kids grew up here, so they would know the area well. They knew the park.'

'We're close enough, a couple of streets away.'

Barlow nodded. 'So they probably came here quite a lot when they were young, the three of them.'

'What are you thinking?'

'I'm not sure, sir. Just getting things straight in my head. They must have played here, running about.'

Hobbes smiled to himself. 'I have a wish, a fantasy. I'd like to get a giant bloody digger in here, churn up this soil, uproot the trees and dig down deep, this whole area.'

'Looking for?'

'The woman in the blue and yellow dress. Adeline. Her bones.'

'You think . . . you think she's buried here, really?'

'No, of course not. Well, I doubt it. You can't just carry a body into Richmond Park and dig a grave. No. But something . . . something about this place . . .' He stopped, and shook his head in frustration. 'And, anyway, from what I heard today, she might not even be real.'

'Sir?'

'What is it?'

'We're being watched.'

Hobbes peered into the trees, following the constable's direction. At first he could see nothing out of the ordinary, but then the branches trembled and a dark shape moved across, from one trunk to the next.

'Who's there?'

There was no answer.

Hobbes stepped forward. The figure was now standing perfectly still, half visible amid the tangled web of twigs and branches. It was a man. He was smoking the last of a cigarette. Then he threw down the butt, ground it into the mud and came forward, swaying on his feet a little.

Hobbes cursed. He couldn't believe what he was seeing. 'Fairfax?'

'All right, Guv.' DC Fairfax grinned. He looked ill-kempt, as before, his hair plastered to his skull, his jacket mud-stained, his beard bare in patches, as though eaten away by some creature.

'What are you doing here, Fairfax?'

'Same as you, Guv, surveying the scene.' He was concentrating on each word. 'This is connected to the dresses you found, yeah?'

Hobbes turned to Barlow. 'Did you let him through, Constable?'

'No, sir, I swear. It's the first time—'

'There's more than one way through the woods.' Fairfax laughed. 'How's that for a bit of philos—'

He couldn't complete the word. Hobbes realized that Fairfax was drunk, badly so. His voice was softened and slurred by it.

'Phil-os-o-phy.' He slowed the word down, so he could pronounce it properly. He was proud of his effort. 'There it is. Philos— Ah, fuck it.'

Hobbes came close. 'Fairfax, you need to—'

'I need to pee, actually.'

He was unzipping his fly as Hobbes grabbed his arm. 'Get away from my crime scene, Tommy. Well away!'

'But I thought – I thought you wanted my help. You need my help. You said so, didn't you?' Now he looked peeved.

Hobbes kept a tight hold of him and dragged him through the trees. 'Give us a hand, Barlow! Come on!' The constable hesitated, then joined Hobbes in the task. DC Fairfax had started to sing in a raucous manner. *Show me the way to go home!* His weight settled low in his body. He slumped down, so that the other two men had to hold him up forcibly.

It started to rain, hard, the drops easily piercing the canopy. Hobbes and Barlow were both soaked in a moment, and their burden was even heavier. Hobbes slipped, almost fell. Barlow had to help him up.

By now Fairfax was leaning against a tree trunk, muttering to himself.

Hobbes brushed some of the mud off his trousers and raincoat. 'OK, Barlow, let's get him out of here.'

'Wait, sir.'

'I need to get indoors. There's nothing we can do here.'

'But, sir, listen to him. Listen to Fairfax.'

Hobbes did so, holding his face close to the drunken man, but any words he could hear were slurred, free of meaning. 'Tommy, what are you saying?'

'There's another . . .'

'Come on, let's have it.'

'There's another body.'

Now Hobbes fell quiet.

Fairfax gathered his words together, one by one. 'Over there, on the pathway.' A vague gesture. 'I nearly trod in it. Flesh. Decayed.' His head lolled to the side.

Hobbes wiped the rain from his face. His sight was blurred in the downpour.

Barlow said, 'He's pretty far gone, sir. Off his head. Do we believe him?'

'Best make sure.'

The constable nodded, but he still looked doubtful.

'Jump to it, Tommy. Show us the way. Let's get this over with.'

Fairfax followed these instructions well enough, weaving a route between each tree trunk, below the low-hanging branches. He led them the way he had come, back into the dense overgrowth, further away from the police tape, from the lighted walkways. But soon enough they hit another path, one made by people over the years for their own use, the grass and plants trampled down into the soil. They walked along it a little way. Already Hobbes could smell the rot. But it didn't smell like normal decomposition, or not the kind he was used to at any rate. He stopped breathing, to keep from throwing up. It really was a stench, and it rang a vague bell in his mind.

Fairfax was holding up well now, trundling along at his own speed. Barlow and Hobbes followed a few steps behind. The downpour stopped after a few minutes, turning the trees into a kind of spectral orchestra made of the sound of dripping water, the creak and crackle of the twigs finding their rightful patterns. The evening birds had started up again with a flurry. The earth was dark and rich.

Then they came upon the sight.

The thing was half buried in the dirt, partially covered with roots and tendrils. Some strange-looking fungi had taken root in the flesh. It was this that gave off the terrible smell, for the body had been there for a time, some weeks, that was obvious.

'It's just a dog,' Barlow said.

Hobbes nodded.

Fairfax mumbled, 'I told you, I told you so.'

'It's a fuckin' dog.' Barlow hardly ever swore but he looked well pissed off. He turned his face from the thrust of the wind.

Hobbes murmured, 'I don't believe it.'

'I told you, right? Another body.'

'Yeah, you did. Brilliant, Tommy.'

'It's probably significant, right? It probably ties in with . . . you know . . . the murder case, the . . . erm, what is he called? The victim? Oh, shit, my feet are soaked.'

Hobbes turned to Barlow. 'Take him away, will you? Get him out of my sight.'

But Fairfax had other ideas. He pushed the constable's hands away, suddenly angry. 'Watch it, kid. I'm not under orders, right, you see that?'

And he took off, moving further along the pathway, deeper into the woods. Hobbes watched him go – a half-broken figure stumbling to avoid the branches that reached down to entangle him. The sound of twigs cracking. And Fairfax swearing continuously, his voice growing quieter with every step. Until, at last, the woods were silent.

Barlow banged his arms against his sides to keep warm, but Hobbes didn't move, not yet. He bent down and examined the dead animal. Something large, an Alsatian or a golden retriever, maybe. Patches of fur still visible here and there. He stared at the fungi, the cream caps with a swirl of black shapes. And that smell . . .

How long had the dog been there?

How had it died? An accident, old age? Or was it killed?

Why hadn't it decomposed completely?

He carried the image of the creature with him, all the way back to his car, back home to the flat, and all the way through the late-night television shows, through the taste of the cigarettes that he smoked one after another, hoping to get the stench of death out of his mind. Even in bed, even asleep or half asleep, the image plagued him. The sight of it merged with the phrase Rosamund Kepple had used.

I am the night flesh.

And right on the edge of waking up in the morning, on the edge of his final dream, he remembered where he'd seen the dress, the flowered material, the tear in the cloth and the blood, so long ago, in the fog, the fog on the streets . . .

But the knowledge slipped away.

An Actress Prepares

The double doors at the end of the corridor opened on to a large airy room, filled with mid-morning light from the extensive windows. Armchairs and settees were dotted around, and a central table laid out with biscuits, cakes and tea in paper cups. It was warm, uncomfortably so. Hobbes cursed to himself.

'What's wrong?' Latimer said.

'I can hardly breathe.'

According to the day manager, there were more than thirty patients currently, all women, all over sixty. And most of them, it seemed, were sitting in a circle of chairs at the far end of the room. Hobbes and Latimer approached; they could already hear the voice of the woman who stood at the centre of the circle. She spoke loudly and clearly, in a skilled voice that still had some power to it, enough to draw the two detectives closer. They stopped a short way from the chairs.

Mary Estelle Graves was eighty-three years old, and looked frail, with a walking stick held in one thin-boned hand. But she was still lively, moving her arms around and bending her back when necessary. She used the stick both as occasional support and also to jab home a point in her dramatic monologue. Or maybe monologue was the wrong word, for her voice changed from one character to another with ease, deepening to play a man, lightening to become a child's delighted cry. And then Mrs Graves rose to her fullest height, seeming to add inches to her slight frame, and her voice rang out, trained as it was to reach the back rows of theatres and music halls.

'I gathered my children to me, all of them, so sweet they looked, and I took them into the parlour in order to play a game of hide and seek. The house rang out with their laughter, and then with whispers of their hiding places. Of course, I found them all, except for crafty little Abigail. She was always finding a new place to hide. "James," I said, "James, we must lock the doors tonight, for the wind is fearful and the rains may come again and the flowers shall wilt in the garden. Too late the sun came, too late the days of light. Oh, what shall I do, James? For our autumn years are coming to an end, only winter awaits us. The old house will have to live on without us, and the childhood ghosts find their own long-lost friends."'

Here she stopped, held the moment with a gesture of her hands, and her stick, then gracefully bowed. Her audience of attentive women, fellow residents of the home, all burst into applause. Many a handkerchief dabbed at wrinkled cheeks. And then a nurse clapped her hands vigorously and said to them all, 'Ladies, that is all for now. I'm sure Mary Estelle is very tired. But, my, what a lovely performance!'

More nurses appeared to take charge of wheelchairs and to help the weaker patients to their feet, leading them over to other activities, or out of the lounge. Gradually, the room quietened. Mary Estelle Graves was left sitting alone. She looked exhausted, now her performance was over. All the energy had drained from her body, and the powerful actress that Hobbes had just witnessed had been replaced by a little old lady, struggling to catch her breath. She was dressed in a long gown, plainly coloured but set off by a string of gaudy beads around the neckline. Her hair was cropped in the urchin style, entirely grey, and circled by a cloth band decorated with yet more beads. She had retained, or gone back to, the 1930s style of her youthful days. Her spectacles were the arched type, designed to give a catlike appearance to the face.

The manager of the home was talking to a nurse, and pointing to the two detectives. Then they were called forward. The nurse spoke to Mrs Graves in a soothing voice: 'These two people are police officers. They want to talk with you, Mary Estelle. Would you like that?' In response the old lady stared first at Latimer, then at Hobbes. She kept her gaze on him for a long time. He felt he was being analysed by those steely grey eyes that never blinked. But she didn't answer the nurse's question. Hobbes didn't know if he should move forward or not. And then Mary Estelle made the slightest of nods, a signal. Hobbes and Latimer sat down, facing her across a small card table.

'Am I in trouble?

Her voice was cultivated, old-fashioned. Received pronunciation, they used to call it. Queen's English. Her demeanour went well with the voice, born of the desire to present herself to the world in the best possible light. But her features were her own, given in the blood: aquiline nose, thin, almost straight lips, her eyes still sharp with life and hope.

'No, Mrs Graves, you're not in trouble.'

'I sincerely hope not.' She added a little chuckle to the end of the line, a perfect expression. She must have had many such tricks in her repertoire, learned over the years of stage work.

'Not at all, Mrs Graves. We only—'

'Please, you must call me Mary Estelle. Everybody does.'

'Mary—'

'Mary Estelle. If you would. The full name.'

'Very well.'

'I suppose you want to know about my husband, Leonard, and why he killed himself.'

Hobbes hesitated. Her statement surprised him. He didn't know how much she knew of the events of the last few weeks. Looking at her, he was struck by her compassion, and her obvious intelligence. He couldn't help wondering about Rosamund Kepple's description of her mother as a crazed individual incapable of making proper sense. The truth was very different, or at least it appeared so on the surface.

Latimer took over. 'Do you know why he killed himself?'

'*Shame*, I imagine. It finally gathered up inside him. Poor Leonard, he was always a one for carrying burdens.'

'Why would he feel shame?'

'I'm sorry?'

'Why would your husband feel ashamed? Do you think he did something wrong?'

The question was met with a look of distaste. 'I never said that.' Her voice hardened. 'I would never say such a thing.'

'I only meant to—'

'Do not take such a tone with me, miss. I dislike it.'

Latimer felt it best to look down at her notepad, and say nothing.

Hobbes spoke carefully. 'Mary Estelle, do you know about your son, Nicholas?'

'My son?'

'Yes. On Sunday night, I'm afraid he was—'

'I don't have a son.'

Her face had taken on a very different aspect now, one of complete certainty in the stated fact. And she said again, 'I don't have a son. I have two daughters. Or is it three?'

And the certainty left her eyes. She was perplexed.

A moment passed.

Hobbes watched her closely, as her face struggled to express itself once more. A famed actress, searching for a mask.

And then she turned to the nurse and asked, 'Deborah, dear? How many children do I have?'

'Three, Mary Estelle.'

'Yes, I thought so, I was correct.'

'Three children, all grown-up now. Their names are . . .'

'Yes?'

'Can you remember?'

'Rosamund?'

'That's right. And?'

The nurse was treating her like a child, but the approach seemed to be working.

'Rosamund, Camilla and . . . Nicholas!'

The names were exclaimed with delight – delight at having reached into her memory so well, and so deeply. Her eyes refocused and she looked at Hobbes, then at Latimer. 'Are you my daughter? Which one are you?'

'Mrs Graves, I'm a—'

'Which one are you? Rosamund or Camilla? Which one?'

Hobbes looked at his fellow officer. He could see that Latimer was feeling at a loss. He felt the same. The interview was proving difficult. He looked at the nurse for help, receiving only a raised hand in response.

Go easy. Go slow.

He really didn't feel like doing that.

Mary Estelle laughed. She said in her politest tone, 'I am so sorry. I mustn't raise my voice, I know it disturbs people.' She smiled. 'Did you enjoy my performance?'

Hobbes nodded. Latimer said, 'I did. Was it a role you used to play?'

'Several of them, actually, all jumbled together. I can never remember the lines, not in the correct order anyway. Everything gets terribly mixed up.'

Hobbes said, 'Mary Estelle. I have to bring you bad news.'

She looked at him.

'Two nights ago, on Sunday evening, your son, Nicholas, was found dead.'

'Oh.'

It was a quiet cry. Hardly that. More an exclamation of surprise.

'Nicholas? Little Nicholas?'

'Yes, I'm afraid so.'

'How he used to play on his hobby horse, wooden sword in hand, like brave St George. He loved to fight the dragon!'

And now she was lost. Mary Estelle had drifted away into the distant past. She was rocking back and forth gently in her chair, holding an invisible form in her hands, perhaps a child, perhaps a precious object, someone or something she had once loved.

The nurse bent to her. 'Are you tired? Would you like to lie down for a while?'

'No. No, thank you.' She spoke in a whisper. 'I have things to do.'

And she continued the rocking motion, the stroking of a child's hair.

Hobbes felt certain she was doing just that.

Nicholas.

In her hands, still.

Even now.

Latimer leaned forward in her seat and said gently, 'Mary Estelle, we'd like to show you something, if that's all right?'

'Of course. I only want to help.'

Latimer drew an object from her bag. It was an item of clothing, carefully folded. Mary Estelle received it tenderly. She held it at two places, her fingers lightly clasping the left and right shoulders, and she flipped it outwards so that the dress unfolded like a wing and then settled, hovering for a moment, until the hem dipped and fell slowly to the floor.

And there it lay half suspended, yellow flowers on a blue background.

There was no tear in the cloth: Latimer had chosen this one from the wardrobe, from the rack of identical items, a supply for later times, perhaps.

The dress shivered in the old lady's grip. Her hands were shaking.

Mary Estelle Graves was crying.

She said, or barely said, or tried to say: 'Adeline.'

Hobbes didn't catch it at first, and he asked her to repeat the name.

She did so, a little louder: 'Adeline.'

The name trembled in her mouth, as the dress trembled in her hands.

Latimer made to speak, but Hobbes stopped her with a raised hand, not wanting to break the mood.

So he waited.

Suddenly the rain came down hard, turning the windows into a series of grey sheets. The air inside the lounge darkened. Mary Estelle turned to the sight. Her lips were tightly closed. Her hands let go of the dress, and it fell to the floor.

Then she stood. 'Inspector, would you accompany me?'

'Where to?'

'Just to walk a little way.'

'Of course.'

He stood up, and Latimer did as well. But Mary Estelle shook her head. 'Please, the gentleman alone. If you wouldn't mind?'

Latimer shrugged. She bent down to retrieve the dress and said, in a low voice, 'You go off and enjoy yourself, Guv. I'll have a poke around, ask a few questions.'

'OK. I think you've got the better job.'

'Inspector? If you would . . .'

A harsh note had crept into Mary Estelle's usual politeness. Hobbes went to her. She slipped her hand through the crook of his elbow, and they set off at a sedate pace. Hobbes had to take far shorter steps than he was accustomed to. In this fashion, they made their way to a corridor.

'It would be nice if we could walk around the garden. But this weather . . . I think God is punishing us.'

'Perhaps you're right.'

'I wonder what our crime is? Pride, I shouldn't wonder.' She frowned. 'I often think of what the coming months will bring.'

'How do you mean?'

'At my age, Inspector, every winter might be the last.'

He was tempted to say something of denial, but he stopped himself: he had the impression that this woman had time only for the truth, whatever that might mean, given her current circumstances and the extent of her mind.

They walked on in silence for a while, turning a corner into another corridor. It was a large building, and members of staff passed them, often with other residents in hand. Many of them smiled and nodded at her.

At last they came to a doorway, where she stopped and said, 'This is my room. Will you come in? It isn't much, I'm afraid.' She pushed open the door and entered. Hobbes followed. The smell was evident, as soon as he stepped inside: sweet and tangible, a scent he had experienced before. It took him only a moment to work it out. Midnight In Paris. The same perfume they had found on the table in Leonard Graves's house. A few bottles of it lined a small shelf next to the bed. Mary Estelle sat down in a wicker chair, and gestured for Hobbes to close the door. He did so, then perched on a stool next to the dressing-table. He noticed that her spectacles were decorated with tiny diamonds along the arched brows.

She looked at him for a good half-minute. Then she said, 'I have a confession to make. It's a secret. I wanted to tell you, and you alone. Not the lady officer.'

Here she paused and took a heavy breath, and he could hear lungs working to gather sufficient air.

'I am, to all intents and purposes, *compos mentis*. Do you understand what I'm saying?'

He nodded.

'You may speak, Detective Hobbes.'

'You're putting on an act?'

'Exactly. There is nothing wrong with me, beyond the usual ailments that come with being a woman in your eighties. And, alas, I have a somewhat fleeting memory. But let me assure you, my thoughts are lucid. A bright light shines through me.'

'And yet . . .'

'I have to put on this *act*, as you call it, to make sure that I can stay here, in the comfort of this home.'

'I see.'

'I am, as I'm sure you know, an experienced actress.'

'Yes.'

'Of course, one must try to avoid succumbing to the role. I have known great actors and actresses who have let their characters take them over completely to the ruination of their everyday lives.'

'But you know the difference, I presume.'

'To a point, yes. The necessary point.' A little smile. 'You have seen already that the old biddies here adore me. They make a fine audience. Once, I performed Gertrude's description of Ophelia's death for them, from *Hamlet*, and somehow or other it all got mixed up with Lady Macbeth.'

'Two very different expressions, I should think. One all languid and forlorn . . .'

'The other sheer rage, and greed for power. Indeed, yes!'

Hobbes nodded. 'I would have liked to see that.'

'A policeman who knows his Shakespeare? I knew you were a person of learning, Inspector. I saw it in you.'

'Self-taught. I read a lot of books when I was younger.'

'I do admire a man who betters himself.' Her eyes sparkled gently.

'Actually, I know you wrote a novel, Mary Estelle. *A Spell of Darkness.*'

'Oh, that old thing! Really, I'm embarrassed that you even mention it.' And yet she allowed herself a little smile.

'I found a copy at Nicholas's bedsit.'

'You did?' She was genuinely interested.

'Several copies, in fact. He must have been an admirer of your work.'

'Well . . . I am surprised, I must say. It's been long out of print.' And she smiled broadly now, brightly enough to thrill the people in the back stalls.

Now that he'd relaxed a little, Hobbes asked, 'So, you don't want to go home?'

'I am home!' It was the most vehement she had been. 'I would hate to live elsewhere. Especially that old dump Bridlemere.' Her upper body shook with disgust.

The sudden emotion took something out of her, for she lolled against the back of the chair and placed a hand on her chest.

Her eyes closed tightly, crinkling around the edges.

Her other hand joined the first, and her linked fingers rose and fell as she struggled to breathe.

Hobbes gave her a moment to recover. He looked around the room. It was sparsely furnished, with only a few choice personal belongings scattered about: a hairbrush, a stand with beaded necklaces draped over it, the blue bottles of perfumes. There was the faint air of a penitent's cell, a feeling enhanced by the statuette of the Mother of Our Lord hanging on the wall, the sole decoration.

'Tell me, Mary Estelle, did you love your husband?'

Her eyes opened. 'I thought you were a detective?'

'I am.'

'Not an agony aunt.'

Hobbes couldn't help smiling. 'Are you avoiding the question?'

'Probably. Well . . . let me see. Did we love each other?' She reflected, and then quoted: '*Love is not love which alters when it alteration finds, or bends with the remover to remove. O no! it is an ever-fixed mark.*'

'Shakespeare again. Let me think. Sonnet . . . 112?'

'116.'

Hobbes nodded. 'Of course. The marriage of true minds.'

'I would say that we loved each other more than adequately. In our own way.' Here she seemed to change the subject. 'My family name is Layne. Perhaps you've heard of us.'

'I can't say I have.'

'Really? We were mentioned in the Domesday Book, you know. *The goodlie Laynes of Shropshire.* Yes, we became quite prominent in *society.*' She said this last word with an air of disgust. 'We made the bulk of our fortune importing tea from China. Poor dear penniless Leonard married into my family's money, and was happy to do so. In turn, I gained a manager, and a stage director, and most of all the creator of my finest roles. He really did understand me, in terms of my art. We made each other famous.' Passion entered her voice. 'We *created* each other.'

'You're saying, what, that the marriage was a business arrangement?'

'Partly, yes. But we did love each other, and it grew over time, this love.'

'But you didn't go to his funeral?'

'Dr Cleveland said I was too poorly. Can you imagine that? That it might be too much for me.' She tutted.

Hobbes watched her as she spoke. She was a great actress: how much of her demeanour was true, how much a well-practised role? 'It's been a difficult week for you. With the loss of your husband. And now Nicholas . . .'

'Do you find it musty in here?'

'I . . . Yes, a little. I can open a window?'

'No, please. I chill easily.'

She reached over for one of her perfume bottles and gave the room a generous spray. Hobbes almost gagged before he asked his next question. 'So you knew that Nicholas was dead?'

'Yes. David came to see me yesterday. He told me.'

'This is David Kepple? Your grandson.'

'He's the only one who ever visits. Mind you, I'm thankful for that. I cannot abide Rosamund, and as for Camilla . . . Well, she lives by her own rules, and I can't blame her for that . . .' Her voice trailed off, the thoughts lost.

Hobbes asked, 'How did you feel when you heard about Nicholas?'

'How did I feel? I am his mother. I was saddened.'

'Do you know who might have killed him?'

'I have lived here for the last five years. I am cut off from the world.'

The inspector concentrated. 'Mary Estelle, who is Adeline?'

It took only a moment for her to answer: 'She is my daughter.'

Hobbes waited for more information. None came. 'You mean . . .'

'Yes, my youngest child.'

'You mean Camilla? Is Adeline her middle name?'

'No, no. Adeline is my fourth child. Didn't I tell you that?' Her eyes flashed with anger. 'Weren't you listening?'

Ignoring this, he asked, in a clear voice, 'How many children do you have, altogether?

She took a breath, as though to speak, to pronounce the truth . . . and then she hesitated. Her whole body was stilled, held in place. She had not yet exhaled.

'Mary Estelle? Would you like a glass of water?' Hobbes looked around the room, failing to spot a washbasin, or a water jug. 'Shall I call for a nurse?'

But she breathed once more. 'No, no. A momentary lapse, that is all.' She looked at Hobbes as she might at a complete stranger. 'Who are you? What are you doing in my room?'

'Hobbes. Detective Hobbes.'

'Of course, yes, I know that. Oh, this memory of mine. It will not work properly!'

'You were saying?'

'Was I?'

'You were telling me about Adeline.'

'There is no such girl, no such, no such, no such, no such, no such . . .'

Now she was trapped in the circle of herself. Hobbes wanted to reach out and touch her, to jolt her out of this repeating pattern of behaviour, but he thought such a move might not be appropriate. Instead he raised his voice and asked as direct a question as he could manage: 'Is Adeline dead?'

It worked as a reverse charm to break the spell. Mary Estelle stopped chanting. She was sitting bolt upright in the chair, her eyes looking directly at the wall in front of her.

Hobbes kept on: 'Is she dead, your daughter?'

'I believe . . .' She turned to face him. 'I believe she must be, for she has not been to visit me, not in so long a time.'

He asked his next question without pause. 'And how old was she when she died? A girl? A young woman?'

'She was . . . she was . . .'

'Go on.'

'She was a late child. Oh, the shame, the shame of it! Such a terrible affliction.'

'You mean the child was ill, or disabled?'

'The dreams wither.'

Her mind kept skipping. But Hobbes couldn't let her rest. 'And the dress we showed you, with the flowers on it? Did she wear that dress?'

'Camilla made that for her, yes. It was Adeline's favourite.'

Her eyes would not shift away, or blink. Hobbes stared back into her gaze, and saw the darkness he would have to explore, to uncover the truth in this case. Nothing was as it seemed in this family. Each person he spoke to told a different tale. And then, as he looked at her, a teardrop appeared at the corner of her right eye. It lingered, then rolled down her cheek. She made no attempt to wipe it away . . . or the next. The first reached the corner of her mouth; it made her speak.

'*I love thee with the breath, smiles, tears, of all my life; and, if God choose, I shall but love thee better after death.*'

Hobbes searched his memory. 'I don't know that one.'

Mary Estelle nodded. 'Elizabeth Barrett Browning. Sonnet forty-three. But I know it better from *A Streetcar Named Desire*. Mitch has that line engraved on his silver cigarette case, which he shows to Blanche DuBois. She is very taken by it.' Her lips tightened. 'I so desired to play the part of Blanche. It would have been my parting gift to the West End. But the producers deemed me too old. Can you imagine? That I was losing my looks.'

'Isn't that the point? With Blanche, I mean. About her looks.'

'Yes, yes, of course!' She wrung her hands together, another theatrical gesture. 'Oh, those imbeciles. Olivier included! He was to direct it, you see.' She scoffed. 'Sir Larry! Men like that, they turn their own incompetence into a religion. And they glory in it!'

It took her a moment to calm herself. She drew a handkerchief from the sleeve of her gown and wiped her lips and cheeks with it, a delicate action. Then she smiled. She revealed the handkerchief to Hobbes: he recognized the letters embroidered on the corner – M.E. And she said, 'Leonard always used to laugh at this. "Mary Estelle," he'd say, "only you would have the word *Me* as a monogram!"' And she laughed again.

Hobbes studied her. He did something strange: he asked a question for the second time.

'Mary Estelle. How many children do you have, altogether?'

The answer came instantly: 'Three, of course.'

'And their names?'

'Rosamund, Nicholas, and young Camilla.'

Perfectly said, without hesitation. The truth. Until the sands next shifted.

'Do you know Camilla's whereabouts?'

'She came to see me. Once only.'

'She did?'

'Oh, it was a long time ago now, I can't remember when.'

'But you don't know where she lives?'

There was no reply. Mary Estelle blinked repeatedly.

Hobbes tried to keep her focused. 'Is she married? Is Camilla married?'

She raised a hand. 'I find these questions distasteful, of a sudden.'

It might have been a line from a play, performed exquisitely. And yet it was all artifice: there was little true feeling behind it, Hobbes was sure.

Now she picked up the bottle of perfume once more and gave her neck a spray, first on one side, then the other. And then her wrists, one and two. The cloying smell gathered around her, like a shroud. Hobbes felt sick. He got up from the stool. The room seemed far too small, more like a trap. With the door closed he felt he was a resident of the home, a long-term patient. And although in his career he had faced down some powerful gangsters, and brutes, and callous murderers, there was something about Mary Estelle Graves that worried him deeply. He couldn't state it plainly, even to himself, and it had nothing to do with her mind's afflictions, but with the weight she carried, the weight of the past, and what it might mean for present-day events. That certain events, long lost, buried deep, might have led to the murder of her son, Nicholas.

The air was thick with the perfume: it was a ghastly smell.

He thanked her for her time and headed for the door.

'Do you have to go, Inspector?'

'I do.' He spoke curtly.

'I see.' Her mood changed, settling into melancholy. And loneliness. But she had one last piece of stagecraft. 'I might have a photograph . . .'

It made Hobbes turn back. 'Of whom?'

'Why, Adeline, of course. Yes, I'm sure I do, somewhere . . .'

He came to her. 'I would like to see that.'

'In the cupboard, the right-hand side, I think.'

He went over to a small cupboard next to the bed. Inside were books and cardboard files, and among them a photograph album. He drew this out and handed it to her. Quickly she flipped through the pages.

'Now, let me see . . . Where would it be . . . ?'

Hobbes registered the flicker of images as the pages went by, sepia, black-and-white. The history of the family in her hands. He couldn't help but think of Glenda and their own wedding album, and how he'd—

'Oh . . . oh dear!' Mary Estelle made a gesture of surprise.

'What is it?' Hobbes moved closer, braving the perfume.

'It's been removed, do you see?'

He looked at the double-page spread and saw that one photograph had gone. She moved on a few pages, and Hobbes saw several other empty spaces where photographs had been removed from their brackets.

'They're all missing, the pictures of Adeline.' She looked up at him. 'Do you think somebody stole them? How wicked that would be.'

He couldn't answer freely. The photographs might never have existed: Adeline remained a ghost, neither alive nor dead, real and unreal at the same time.

Hobbes stood up straight. He rubbed at his eyes with finger and thumb.

Mary Estelle sighed. 'I'm so very sorry, Inspector. I really thought I might be of help to you.'

'Never mind. But I would like a photograph of Camilla, and one of your family all together. Would that be possible?'

'Let me see . . . Yes, I think we all look presentable in this one. And here is Camilla alone. Hmm. An intriguing face, don't you think? Not exactly pretty.'

'Thank you for these.'

'Of course, Rosamund possessed a greater beauty. That was her downfall.'

'Mary Estelle?'

'Yes?'

'Tell me, does the phrase *night flesh* mean anything to you?'

'Heavens.' Her voice was weary now, and she looked tired: her eyes were closing. 'It's an age since I've heard those words. My mother used to say such things to me . . . and her mother before her, I imagine.'

'Your children picked it up from you?'

'Yes, I suppose so. I wrote it down for them.'

'As a lesson?'

'In my novel. Did I tell you that I wrote a novel?'

Hobbes answered carefully: 'Yes, I think so.'

'I put my whole being into that work.'

'And what does it mean, the night flesh?'

She made a last effort at wakefulness: 'It's madness. Possession. To be taken over by something beyond one's self.' She shuddered at the memory.

Hobbes recalled Rosamund's exact words: 'And so, to be *born* from the night flesh, what would that mean?'

One hand fluttered, birdlike, at her brow. 'That madness has made you what you are, from birth onwards. Passed on like a sickness in the blood.'

'A kind of fate, or destiny?'

'The most terrible kind.'

Hobbes nodded, and turned, and walked out into the corridor, glad of the fresh air. He met DS Latimer in the car park. As they drove out on to Maze Hill she brought him up to date: 'I talked to members of staff, and to a doctor they have on call. Mrs Graves seems well enough liked, or they were all being diplomatic. No visitors apart from her grandson, David Kepple. And she was here on Sunday evening. So you can stop fantasizing that an eighty-odd woman went out one night and bashed her son's head in with a rock.'

'That never entered my mind.'

'I know your mind. It stinks. You always think the worst.'

'She might have employed someone.'

'There you go.'

'What did the doctor say?'

'He wasn't forthcoming, which is fair enough. But he hinted that she hasn't got long on this earth.'

This time, Hobbes didn't respond.

'Something puzzling you?'

'What? No, no, just thinking. Look, Meg, take us back via Peckham, will you?'

'Any particular reason?'

'Something I want to show you.'

They stopped at a zebra crossing. An old man took a while to get across, dragging a shopping trolley behind him.

Latimer asked, 'What did you learn from talking to Mary? Sorry, Mary *Estelle*. She was very strict about that.'

'Yeah. It was her stage name, I guess. The name she was known by, at the height of her fame.' At last the car moved on. 'She told me a whole bunch of stories, but I don't know which are true. And, worse than that, I don't think she does either. She claimed Adeline was the name of her fourth child.'

'What? That's amazing.'

'Maybe. But one minute later she had gone back to three kids only. Then she wanted to show me a picture of Adeline. But all the photos of the girl, or the woman, were missing from the album.' He could not get the smell of the perfume out of his nostrils. 'I think she removed them herself, to be honest.'

'Not the full shilling, then?'

'Perhaps, but she's only a halfpenny short. There's a clear mind at work in there, I'm certain of it.'

'Maybe . . .'

'You've got an idea?'

Latimer had an eager look about her. 'Yeah, I'm thinking back on what Rosamund told us, that Adeline wasn't real, that she was a fantasy child. Maybe the kid died at birth, stillborn, something like that, yet in Mary Estelle's mind she's still totally real. So the family play along with this, to keep their mother happy.'

'Keep going.'

'They have a stage in one room. A friggin' stage! I mean, can't you just picture them all, playing out this little drama, conjuring up a missing child. Adeline. And – and I can see Mary Estelle right there, in the audience, sitting on a chair . . .'

'An audience of one?'

'Yes, maybe! Think about it! It makes sense, right?'

'Sure. A kind of sense.'

'I'm not hearing much from you, theory wise.'

He laughed. 'True.'

They took Shooters Hill Road, along the edge of Greenwich Park. The trees were losing their greenery, getting ready for the colder months ahead.

The talk stayed on Rosamund Kepple. Latimer said, 'The wound in her stomach wasn't deep, and she's had a few stitches. Casualty took care of it. I stayed with her in the waiting room, but she wouldn't talk to me, not a word.'

'Nothing more about the night flesh?'

'Nothing.'

'Mary Estelle claims it's a kind of madness, passed down in the blood.'

'God, that's one fucked-up family.'

Hobbes nodded. 'I know Rosamund's got more to tell us. If we could just—'

'Let's bring her in, treat her mean for an hour or two.'

'I'm not sure that would work. Too much armour.'

'There's always a weak spot.'

'Hmm.'

He fell silent. Latimer met his mood and drove on for a while without speaking. Along Deptford High Street, he said, 'Oh, by the way, I saw Fairfax last night.'

'Tommy? Did you?'

'Yeah, it was weird. He turned up at the crime scene.'

'You mean . . .'

'Richmond Park, where Nicholas Graves was found.'

'What was he doing there?'

'He wouldn't say.'

'But this means he must be—'

'Let's not jump to—'

'He must want to come back. What do you think?'

'Maybe. But listen, Meg, he wasn't looking too good.'

'No?' She pulled up at a red light and turned to Hobbes. 'In what way?'

'He was drunk. I mean, really pissed up. Stumbling about, ranting and the like.' He decided not to say anything about the dead dog in the woods.

'Poor Tommy.'

'I think he's done for.'

'Don't say that.'

'Meg, we need to replace him.'

'No, no, just no!'

'Meg . . .'

'What now?'

'Green light.'

'Oh, right, sure.'

The car behind was honking its horn. Latimer shouted, 'Christ, I'm moving, I'm moving! Fuckin' twat!'

Hobbes tried to laugh it off.

'No one can hear you, only me.'

'Oh, bloody hell, Hobbes. I can't believe you've given up on Tommy.'

'I haven't given up. But he's digging himself into the ground.'

Latimer made a noise. It wasn't a nice sound. Hobbes thought of arguing further, but knew it wasn't worth it. His detective sergeant must have agreed, for she concentrated all her efforts on the traffic.

When they got to Peckham, he directed her to Cavalier Road and they parked across from the Edwardian block of flats.

'What now?'

'We wait. If you don't mind.'

'What is this place?'

'This is where my son is living.' After a moment: 'It's a squat.'

'Right. Some of them aren't too bad, I've heard. But others, well, they're shitholes.'

'This one is weird. It's locked up, virtually impenetrable. Cut off. The residents are up to something, but I don't know what it is, and I don't know how to find out.'

'Martin . . . how old is he?'

'Seventeen.'

'That's young.'

'Yeah, I know. And he told me he's happy there.'

'Well then?'

Hobbes looked away.

Latimer persisted: 'Look, Henry, if your boy wants to come home, he will. But if you go in there gung-ho, don't you think you'll drive him further away?'

He didn't answer her. His eyes swept over the crumbling walls, barred windows, and political slogans painted on the plasterwork.

'Is this why your wife asked you round last week?'

Hobbes was desperate. 'Partially.' The hopelessness was taking him over. 'I need to do something.'

'It's another world.'

'What's that supposed to mean?'

'In there.' She pointed to Cromwell House. 'You don't know the rules.'

'I have two names. Nadia. And Fabian. I think Fabian's a friend of Martin's, but the woman, Nadia, I believe she's in charge of the place.'

'Boss, you're going crazy. What's the use?'

'The use? He's my son.'

'If he comes back, he comes back. That's it. Otherwise . . .'

Hobbes brooded on his anger. 'Come on. Let's get moving. For fuck's sake.'

'I'm just telling it—'

'You think I don't know that?'

'Give the lad a chance. That's all.'

'Like Fairfax? You're all heart these days, Meg.'

She jerked round in her seat to face him. 'What the fuck is wrong with you?'

And he saw in her eyes the man he was becoming. She had used the same look on DC Fairfax when he'd played silly buggers.

'OK.'

'What?'

'I'm sorry.'

'You should be.'

'Just . . . Martin, you know . . . and the case . . . the cellar.'

'Give it a break, Guv. Go out and get drunk or find someone to shag. Whatever it is you do, when you need to unwind.'

Hobbes didn't respond: there was nothing. That was the truth. No exit point.

Instead, he said to her, 'I have an appointment to see Rosamund's son, David Kepple, this afternoon. Do you want in?'

'No, I think not.'

'You're going it alone, are you?'

'If you must know, there's something I want to check out.'

'A lead?'

'Remember that story you told me, of the young woman in Richmond Cemetery?'

'The one wearing the dress?'

'Yeah. I have an idea about that.'

But she would say no more, and the journey continued in silence.

Latimer dropped him back at the police station on Kew Road, and he spent an hour or so going through the case notes. It was a mess, chaotic, no through line, like one of those avant-garde plays he used to watch in Soho when he'd first arrived in London as a young man. And yet, as always, he kept in mind the simple human desires. He drew a diagram, a family tree, on the board.

Leonard Graves ———— *Mary Estelle Layne*

Rosamund —— *Nicholas* —— *Camilla* —— *Adeline?*

David Kepple

The diagram was surrounded by photographs of the crime scene, and close-ups of the wounds on Nicholas Graves's head. Other photos showed the five items found in the jewellery box, and the mysterious dress. Two pieces of the dress material were pinned to the board, one showing the pattern clearly, the other containing the tear in the cloth and a splash of red substance, found in this case to be paint. But in Hobbes's mind, everything rested on one single item: the question mark after the name *Adeline*. It got to him so much, he added another two: *Adeline???* Was she real, or unreal? If he could answer that, he felt sure the case would start to make sense.

For a moment he considered the items found in the jewellery box. Forensics had told him that the box had last been handled by Nicholas Graves, and that partial prints had also been found on the drawing pins used to fasten the dress to the floor in the top bedroom. So Nicholas had conducted one last set of rituals before he met his death. Hobbes hadn't really put any effort into the five items, as yet: they seemed too detailed, too personal. And if people didn't recognize the dress, why should they know about the box and its contents? There was too much going on, that was the problem: too many bloody angles.

The hardback novel he had taken from Nicholas Graves's bed-sit was half hidden by a fan of papers. *A Spell of Darkness*. He picked it up now and considered, then flicked through the pages. The book fell open easily where a card was hidden between pages. It advertised the services of one *Nick Greaves, Artist, Film Maker, Screenwriter*. Greaves? A single letter added. This must have been Nicholas's pseudonym when he was making films. Rosamund had mentioned such a thing: her brother's career, or his attempt at one, in movie-making. But the card was old and tatty, a remnant of former times. Another dream lost. Hobbes turned his attention to the page that had fallen open. One passage was underlined in red pen:

Yvonne would often take the children aside and speak to them in sinister tones, out of hearing of her husband. She felt that she was in charge of their discipline. If they ever misbehaved, she would say to them, 'The night flesh will get you. It will burrow into you and make you its own.' It was said as a threat. Sometimes she would stand over their bed and whisper these same words into their ears, even as they slept. Perhaps they heard it in their dreams. This was Yvonne's abiding hope, that she might influence her children, that she might plant such terrible thoughts in their heads, and then live to see the outcome as they grew older.

Jesus. It made you wonder where reality began and ended for the Graves family. Was this an example of *everyday cruelties*?

Hobbes could hear that voice clearly in his imagination, Mary Estelle's softly lilting tone, as she spoke in that darkened room . . . and the children, Rosamund, Nicholas and Camilla, in their beds asleep. And their dreams, and the things learned in dreams. The things that can only be learned in dreams.

There was a fourth bed in Hobbes's mind, and a fourth child sleeping.

But her face was still invisible.

The Nine Stages

The gallery was a small but fancy establishment off Regent Street with the name Kepple & White painted in an almost unreadable script. The window held a sculpture of an oversized poodle made from plaster of Paris, coloured here and there with orange and pink splashes of paint. The current exhibition was called *Lana Devine, Sculptures and Images, 1974–81*. Detective Inspector Hobbes peered through the glass – the place appeared empty. But when he stepped inside, he felt immediately ill at ease. A woman sitting at a desk stared at him as though he were a piece of litter, something blown in off the street. She was beautiful, and remote, an abstract work of art in human form. Hobbes asked to see Mr Kepple. She nodded. She didn't speak. She didn't move a muscle. But some kind of signal must have been sent, for the gallery's owner soon appeared from a side door. He introduced himself: 'David Kepple. Inspector Hobbes, I believe. It's very good of you to see me here.'

Hobbes looked around. 'You're not exactly busy?'

'We've had two customers in already today, proper ones, and both bought something.' He turned to the young woman. 'Thank you, Samantha, you can take a break now. I'll look after things here.' Soon, the two men were alone. 'Are you an art lover, Inspector?'

'Not the visual arts, no. More poetry, and the novel.'

'I showed no interest in painting when I was young, none at all. I know you've seen my mother's home. All those ornaments, the chintz, the bric-a-brac?'

'Yes.'

'That was my milieu. It was quite stifling. But at the age of eighteen I had, to use an old-fashioned word, an epiphany.'

Kepple was in his forties, a well-dressed man in a designer suit and tie. He had taken his looks from the grandfather's side of the family: handsome in a Gregory Peck sort of way. His haircut had probably cost more than Hobbes earned in a week, and his body was trim, his skin polished and ever so slightly tanned. Strangely, a touch of Cockney was in his voice: probably an affectation that went with the job.

The two men walked among the sculptures.

'Lana Devine is one of the new breed of artists. Have you heard of postmodernism?'

Hobbes shook his head.

'You will. Eventually.'

'Is that a put-down? Because—'

'Of course not.'

'Because you should be aware that I really don't care.'

'I already know that. From the way you treated my mother.'

'You think I caused her to take a pair of scissors to her own flesh?'

'Well, something prompted it.'

'How about guilt?'

Kepple peered at him over the top of a five-foot-tall multi-coloured guinea pig. A slight frown took over his face, but it lasted for a second only, to be replaced with the man's best professional smile.

Hobbes said, 'I'm sorry for your loss, Mr Kepple. Or *losses*, I should say.'

'Thank you. Yes, it's been a difficult couple of weeks.'

'What can you tell me about Nicholas?'

'Uncle Nick? He was a disappointed man.'

'He expected to do more in life?'

'Let's say he had aspirations. To write his own plays, poems, even make films. A lot of them funded, of course, by his father, who poured money into his son's ambitions, more fool him. Oh, yes, Nicholas had an artistic bent, but would you like to hear our family's dirty little secret, Inspector?'

'I'm sure there's more than one.'

'Nicholas made quite a few films of . . . shall we say a "continental" nature?'

'Dirty movies?'

In answer, a sardonic grin played on Kepple's lips.

Hobbes asked, 'Did he use the name Nick Greaves as a pseudonym?'

'Yes. Yes, he did. My, you are doing well!'

'One extra vowel. Was that enough to escape his father's influence?'

'I suppose there's nothing worse than being the child of a great artist, for stifling the creative genius. But, sadly, the new name brought him little success, outside the top-shelf market. And even there . . .'

A thought came to Hobbes. 'Mr Kepple, did you visit your uncle last week, at his flat?'

'I did, as it happens.'

'What day was this?'

'It was . . . last Thursday, I think.'

'Yes, good. You were heard knocking on the door, by the neighbour.'

'Well, yes . . . but Nick wasn't in.'

'Why did you want to see him?'

'To find out how he was doing, if he needed any help. I was concerned about him.'

Hobbes nodded. 'Did Nicholas have any enemies?'

'In the old days, maybe. The skin game could be a little cut-throat, back in the sixties. But nowadays, I very much doubt it.'

'And within his own family?'

'That's different. All of them, at various times, could have killed each other without regret. But at others they would close up tight and, under the guise of love, protect each other.'

'You saw this at first hand?'

'Now and then. My mother and I visited the family home perhaps five or six times in my childhood.'

'Your father died when you were young, is that right?'

Kepple moved on to study an image of a bird of paradise. The materials were listed as *felt-tip pens, sequins, glue*. He looked to be studying every little mark, every imperfection.

'My mother left home when she was twenty-five to marry Andrew Kepple. I was born a year after. Despite our family's history, I like to think I've turned out fine.' Again, the smile. He kept it in place, even as he said, 'My father was killed in action at the Battle of Hamburg, one of the last offensives of the war.' A slight pause. 'I was a year old.'

'It must have been tough.'

'For my mother, yes.'

'Why did she wait so long to leave home?'

'I think it was difficult to escape. Bridlemere has thick walls, and sturdy doors. And many locks. Even Nicholas, the male child, had to wait for the war to start before he could get away, by joining up to fight. As for Camilla . . .'

'What about her?'

'She was nearly forty when she left.'

'And do you know where she's living, right now?'

'I wish I could help you, I really do. But she's become a mystery. Dearest Camilla. I rather liked her on the few occasions we met. She had a bit more . . . gumption than Nicholas or, indeed, my mother.'

A young couple opened the door of the gallery, took a glance around, and exited again. They looked embarrassed.

Kepple smiled. 'We get that a lot.'

Hobbes said, 'What do you remember of the times you visited the house?'

'As a child? Just dimly lit rooms, endless corridors, sealed doors. And the smell, of course. That fascinated me. Camphor, lavender, mildew. Always the aroma of tobacco, which seemed to follow me around like some half-visible wraith. My grandfather smoked a pipe in his middle years. He used to scare me with his tales of the ghosts of Bridlemere. He talked of a hidden room, with no doors, no windows, and how a voice could be heard speaking from behind the walls. That gave me nightmares, as a child. Of course, I loved the thrill of it, really.'

'Anything else?'

'We never stayed long. One time I remember a grand dinner. Six courses. Over dessert, a terrible argument broke out. I haven't a clue what they were talking about. I was six or seven at the time, sitting on my own at a little side table.'

'What about Adeline?'

Kepple's expression gave nothing away. 'Who's that? I'm sorry?'

'You never heard anyone in your family talking about her, about Adeline?'

'I've never heard the name until now. Who is she?'

'It doesn't matter.'

Kepple led the way to another exhibit, a pile of paperclips, each one a yard long, each painted a different colour of the rainbow. The piece was called *Charles Darwin Argues With President*

Kennedy. The gallery owner continued, 'Later on my mother stopped visiting, and she banned me from going on my own. Something must've happened between them all, something nasty. But when I reached the age of eighteen, I decided to pay a visit. I was curious, as only a person of that age can be.'

'What year would that be? Early sixties?'

'Sixty-two.'

'And what did you find?'

'Camilla was still living there, pushing thirty. Granddad and Grandma had quite separate lives, I think. Their own bedrooms. Not a lot of talking. But I got on best with Mary Estelle. She was a hoot. She made me laugh with her tales of theatreland, you know, the dreadful things that actors and actresses got up to in private, and in public.'

'You didn't see . . .' Hobbes didn't quite know how to put the question. 'You didn't see any children in the house, or teenagers. Girls?'

'No. Of course not.'

'She might have been wearing a blue dress with yellow flowers on it. Like this.' He pulled out a photograph.

Now Kepple looked confused. 'I really don't . . .'

'Think carefully.'

'This is ridiculous. Why are you asking me these things?'

'It might be important. Did you ever see this dress laid out on the floor?'

'No, nothing like . . . Oh, would that be . . .' Understanding flickered in Kepple's eyes. 'Is this to do with Adeline, whoever she might be? Is there something I need to know about, some secret?'

'We're exploring various avenues.'

'Did Adeline kill Nicholas?'

Hobbes didn't reply.

The two men stared at each other.

Kepple said, 'You've set yourself a pointless task, you do know that?'

'You think so?'

'Postmodernism works against the sureties of narrative, of linear progression – ultimate goals, beginnings, middles and ends. I truly believe that a coming age will despise such notions. There is no *one* truth, only a mist of possibilities. We are lost among the various meanings, and we should celebrate that.'

The detective spoke clearly: 'I will discover the person who killed your uncle. That will be truth enough for me.'

'Beware of false endings, then. Come, let me show you another piece.'

Kepple led the way into a second room, smaller in size and containing only one exhibit: a large glass-walled container, perhaps six feet long by four in height and width. The tank was entirely open at the top. It was filled to about the halfway mark with branches cut from trees, and twigs, and dead or dying leaves, a whole mass of them.

The two men stood looking at it in silence.

And then Kepple said, 'So, are you impressed?'

'It's a glass box filled with bits of wood. How should I interpret it?'

'Look more closely. Peer within. Go on. It's rather fun.'

Hobbes did so. He found that his sight quickly became lost in the criss-crossing of the branches. And then one moved, shifting out of position, then another, and one more, until the whole assemblage moved into a new configuration. And right in the centre of it all, there was an eye peering out at him: a human eye, blinking.

The inspector moved back a little, in his surprise.

'What is that?'

Kepple was delighted at the reaction. 'It's all part of the

exhibition. Miss Devine works with a number of volunteers, both male and female, on a daily rota. She applies the pieces of wood to the volunteer's body, and—'

'You're saying that people *volunteer* for this?'

'Why not? They are amply paid, and it's only for three hours at a time.' Kepple smiled broadly. 'Rest assured, I do let them out for the call of nature. If needed.'

Hobbes leaned over to peer down into the tank. It was like looking for an insect with a camouflaged carapace. But he saw now that the person inside was a woman. He could make out very little of her, for almost her entire body was clothed in the twigs, leaves and other materials.

Kepple explained, 'This is Nell. She was very excited to be here today.'

'Why?'

'Because I told her a real-life police detective was coming to visit, to view the exhibit.'

Hobbes had to smile, a little. And in response the figure in the box moved again, the twigs crackling and almost snapping in places. Dust and seeds floated here and there. Her face was briefly seen – time enough for a smile – then hidden once more.

'It's very impressive,' Hobbes said. 'I admire her resilience.'

'But, you see, you cannot make her out properly. No matter how hard you look, the pattern will always change. That is the whole point: in this new age of which I dream, the patterns will never settle, they will never be decoded.'

Hobbes frowned. 'But what if I should buy this piece?'

'I doubt you could afford it.'

'Of course not. But if I did . . . would the person inside be included?'

'Ha. No, sadly not. You have to provide your own occupant. It would make a fabulous talking point at a dinner party.'

'Or the purchaser might take their own place in the box.'

Kepple clapped his hands together. 'Yes, why not? If they so desired.'

They moved away from the glass box, back into the main gallery area. Hobbes said, 'You mentioned before about having an epiphany, when you were young. What was that?'

'It's quite simple. My grandmother saw something in me, some potential. You'll have seen the various paintings in Bridlemere? It's quite a collection.'

'Yes. She gave you one?'

'Actually, she asked me to choose ten for myself. Any ten. Can you imagine?'

'And you did?'

'Of course. And one of them turned out to be a Max Ernst, an original. I don't know if either Leonard or Mary Estelle knew what they truly possessed. Anyway, I sold the painting at auction, and that set me on my future career. I owe it all to Mary Estelle.'

'Did you visit much after that?'

'Only now and then. The house remained as it ever was, a fortress. When Camilla left home, my grandparents more or less bolted the doors against all intruders.'

'But you helped your grandmother later, by finding the old people's home, paying her bills?'

'It was the least I could do. Although, in truth, I thought it was Leonard who should have been put in a home. Mary Estelle *deserved* that house.'

Hobbes considered. 'I would like to talk freely, Mr Kepple.'

'Of course.' He looked nervous.

'First, can you prove where you were on Sunday evening?'

Kepple didn't flinch. 'My wife will confirm I was at home.'

'I'll need a little more than that.'

'I don't have—'

The detective held up a hand. He said something extraordinary. 'It seems the night flesh hasn't yet touched you.'

Kepple's eyes opened wide. 'I beg your pardon?'

'You don't seem crazy.'

'Right. Erm . . .'

'Your grandmother told me that the night flesh is a kind of madness that affects members of the Graves family. She hinted that it might be genetic.'

'It's the first I've heard of it.'

'Your mother, Rosamund, used the phrase as well, a couple of days ago. When she cut herself. She's never mentioned it to you?'

'No. No, I . . .'

'What is it?'

'No one told me, but I'm sure I . . . Yes, I must've read it somewhere.'

'Where?'

'I don't know. I can't help you. I wish I could.'

'Perhaps you read it in Mary Estelle's novel, *A Spell of Darkness*.'

'Yes, maybe. Is it mentioned in there? I really couldn't say.'

Hobbes gave him no chance to relax. He stepped a little closer and said, 'Nicholas, Rosamund and your grandmother . . . There's no easy way to say this but they're maddened by the world, each in a different way.'

Kepple spoke softly, brokenly. 'Yes . . . yes, I agree.'

'But you seem to have escaped that fate.'

'Perhaps . . . on the surface.'

'And underneath?'

Kepple moved back slightly, to give himself breathing room. For a moment he looked uneasy, or doubtful. Hobbes couldn't quite read his expression.

A moment of silence. Neither made a move. Hobbes kept his gaze on Kepple, allowing no escape. He thought the other man might be on the verge of speaking, of confessing to something. 'You look worried, Mr Kepple.'

'Me? Well, you know, the police . . .' He took a breath, and found a little strength within it. 'I must say, I find your approach rather aggressive.'

'Sometimes it's necessary.'

'Quite. With hardened criminals.'

'Some of the cruellest people I've met are well-dressed, and well-mannered.'

'Perhaps you're right.'

'Is there something you want to tell me?'

Kepple looked around the empty gallery. He said, 'I'm going to lock the door, and put up the *Closed* sign. Is that all right?'

'Of course. If it makes you feel safer.'

'It's not that. But I have some artworks that might throw a light on my family. I'd like you to see them.'

He locked the gallery's front entrance, then headed for a door behind the reception desk. Hobbes followed. They went upstairs into an office space. Another door led into a small private art gallery. 'I only allow the true aficionado entry to this space.' Hobbes was expecting to see erotic or even pornographic images of some kind, and indeed there were a few of those dotted around the walls: women, and men, in sultry poses, some more explicit than others. But the main wall was taken up with a number of inked drawings, nine altogether. They made a series.

Hobbes had never seen anything like them before.

David Kepple explained, 'These paintings are part of a Japanese practice known as *kusozu*. The contemplation of bodily decay.' He turned to Hobbes. 'A dead body was taken out into the woods and left to rot. People would travel out there every so often to view the body as it decomposed. In this way, we are reminded that life is precious, made up of a few fleeting moments. *Kusozu* insists that we make the most of those moments before we die.'

Hobbes went up to the first of the images, to study it more closely.

Kepple continued, happy to play the part of a guide, 'The series is known as *The Body of a Courtesan and Her Physical Decay in Nine Stages*. It was painted in 1850 or thereabouts. This first image shows the courtesan at the moment of death. Her body is falling back against the cushions on her couch.'

The two men moved on to the second image.

'Here, we see her recently deceased, the body still fresh. As you can see, the top part of her kimono has been stripped away, revealing her breasts and shoulders.'

Each image was contemplated and described in turn.

'The third image is difficult to take, I find. It shows extreme discoloration of the body, bloating, and the onset of decomposition.'

Hobbes murmured to himself.

'What's that?'

The detective nodded to the third drawing. 'The title of this one might be *The Night Flesh*. What do you think? The skin is very dark.'

'Yes, yes. If you say so.' Kepple gathered his wits. He moved down the line. 'Next we see blood leaking from the body. And here, in the fifth image, the lady's skin is coming loose. We also see marbling of the flesh, and liquids being purged. Her clothing is now quite disintegrated. And, look carefully, the artist has painted in the flies and other insects, attracted by the smell of rot. Some will feed here, others lay their eggs in the flesh.' Kepple beamed. 'Exquisitely detailed, don't you think?'

Hobbes had seen several dead bodies in his time as a police officer, but to have the process of decomposition turned into art was a step too far for him. At the same time he couldn't help being fascinated.

'Are you quailing, Inspector?'

'Not at all. Carry on.'

'The sixth drawing shows the abdomen caving in, and the exposure of various internal organs. We can imagine the many worms working at her flesh. Image number seven depicts animals scavenging at the corpse – a dog, a fox, a crow. They are treating the human body as a meal, nothing more. Decomposition is now well and truly advanced.'

They had almost reached the end of the series.

'At last the flesh has rotted clean away, leaving only a bare skeleton. And here, in the final image, we see only a few small bones remaining, and a cracked skull. The rest is dust, scattered on the wind.'

Hobbes stepped back to take in the series as a whole. 'So let me guess, these are the nine other paintings you took from Bridlemere.'

Kepple nodded. 'As I mentioned, the Max Ernst I sold on for a tidy sum. But this exquisite *poem* of decomposition, I could not bring myself to part with it.'

'And these were actually on view in the house?'

'They were, all nine of them. Not hidden in the attic or the cellar. But proudly displayed in Leonard's study. Any of the children would have seen them, every day of their lives, I imagine. My mother included.'

Hobbes turned to him. 'That shows a . . .'

'Yes, Inspector?'

'I'd call it cruel. But that isn't the right word.'

'No, it isn't. In a certain way it might almost appear enlightened. In our current practice, we tend to hide the darker aspects of life from our children. But at least now you will have a clearer picture of what life must have been like at Bridlemere, when Rosamund, Nicholas and Camilla were young.'

'Yes. Thank you for this.'

Hobbes was in a contemplative mood. The images had acted upon him as they were designed to, as a *memento mori*. He shivered slightly. Kepple picked up on his mood, saying, 'In other examples of *kusozu*, the final image depicts a memorial for the dead person, to mark the grave.' He allowed himself a grim little smile. 'I like to come up here, once a month, say, entirely alone, and think on the nature of life, and of my place in the world. For soon, soon it will all be gone.' He paused, then said, in a low voice: 'Rest in peace, Uncle Nick. And Granddaddy. May you both have a safe journey.'

Hobbes felt he was intruding on a private ritual.

They were standing close together, and to move away now would seem rude.

For the first time he noticed that a rather strong odour rose from David Kepple's body. It was unidentifiable.

Kepple was apparently aware of this. He stepped to the centre of the room.

Hobbes walked back to the start of the series, and made a study of the first image, where the woman was seen in the very act of dying. He didn't speak.

'Most people concentrate on the later images,' Kepple said.

'Not me.'

'What are you looking for?'

'I'm wondering about the cause of death.'

'What?'

'There are no visible wounds. You can see that clearly in the second and third image, where the flesh is exposed. There are no puncture marks.'

Kepple laughed politely. 'I always thought she'd died of a

sickness. Well, to be honest, I've never actually thought about it before.'

'She's only a subject matter to you. To me, she's a potential victim.'

'Maybe she killed herself – some kind of drug?'

'Yes, it's possible. But, as with your grandfather, the police would have been called in. Just to make sure.' Now Hobbes examined the second and third images more closely. 'Hmm. Interesting.' His face was almost touching the surface.

'What is it?'

'Her lips are coloured in this second picture. Perhaps evidence of vomiting.'

'Let me see.'

Kepple came forward again and stood beside the detective. 'I've never noticed before. It's very subtle.'

Hobbes nodded. 'I'm thinking some kind of opiate. Something that put her to sleep, or that caused a slow paralysis. Something derived from a plant, I imagine, given the historical period. Hemlock, for instance. The poison that took the life of Socrates.'

'I'm not sure if it grows in Japan.'

'Do you see here?' Hobbes pointed to the first image. 'Her limbs look stiff, crooked to the body.'

'Evidence of a struggle, you think?'

'Only with herself, those final moments as the soul surrenders.' Then he frowned. 'I wish I could send off a sample of her blood for testing. A tox report would settle it.'

'Are you toying with me?'

Hobbes looked serious. 'Whenever I see a dead body, my first questions are always the same. How did they die? Are there suspicious circumstances? And . . .' he turned to David Kepple '. . . if she was murdered, who was the perpetrator?'

'Surely, you can't work that out just from a painting?'

'My first instincts would say . . . the artist. Who else?'

Kepple was dumbfounded.

'You said she was a courtesan?' Hobbes asked.

'That's right. According to the title.'

'So, a high-class prostitute? Is that correct, for the period?'

'Yes. Very popular in the age of the Japanese Empire. They were trained in etiquette, arts and crafts, dancing, singing.'

'So, then, I think the artist paid for her favours. And killed her, just so he could portray her body, as it decomposed, over weeks, months, or longer.'

'The artist as murderer? That's an interesting concept, Inspector.'

'Of course, this is all supposition.' Hobbes gave a slight smile.

The two men had stepped back so they could look at the images in a row. Kepple said, 'I suppose you think me very morbid, collecting such things?'

Hobbes didn't answer straight away. He considered the nine pictures one last time, each in turn. 'These were painted in, what was it? Eighteen . . . ?'

'The 1850s. We're not certain of the actual year.'

'That gives it distance. Another time, another culture. It no longer shocks us in the way it might have, back then.'

Kepple nodded at this. 'Your point?'

'If these were painted today, by one of your artists, they would have much more of an impact. And imagine if these were photographs, not drawings or paintings. Glossy photos, blown up, framed, as these are, and presented in a gallery. Better yet, let's imagine them taken out of the gallery context, and placed in a home, a domestic setting . . . perhaps your home, Mr Kepple.'

The gallery owner wiped his face with a hand. His skin was damp. 'What would that mean to you?'

'We wouldn't be having this conversation here. We'd be in a police station, in a room with no windows.'

Kepple tried to regain his calm. 'You think me a prime suspect? A man with murderous tendencies?'

Hobbes gave a slight nod. It was an ambiguous gesture. Then he turned and walked back downstairs. Kepple followed him into the main gallery space.

'If anything else comes to mind, let me know. About Nicholas, and anyone who might want him dead.'

'Of course.'

They were standing near the door. Kepple clearly wanted the inspector to leave. Hobbes held his stance for a while longer. He didn't speak.

Kepple held the door open for him.

Hobbes looked into the man's eyes. 'Why do you think Rosamund stabbed herself with a pair of scissors?'

'I really have no idea. It shocks me.'

'I don't know her that well,' Hobbes said, 'but I see her as a woman in pain. I think something happened to her when she was younger, in that house, in Bridlemere. And I've seen it happen before, many times: past events coming back to haunt us. And forcing us to act. In ways she might regret.'

It took a moment. 'You're not saying she killed Nicholas, are you? Her own brother?'

Hobbes shrugged.

'She's innocent, I know she is! My mother would . . . she would never do such a thing. Don't you believe me?'

'Belief irritates me, Mr Kepple. I seek proof. Nothing more.'

Five minutes later the inspector was walking along Regent Street, pushed and pulled by the crowds of tourists and shoppers, the office and store workers hurrying towards the tube stations at Piccadilly Circus in one direction, and Oxford Circus in the other.

Hobbes hardly saw a single person.

He was alone.

The Living-room Theatre

Dark skies over London. No rain. Just the feel of it on the air, waiting. A twilight moment. The room darkened without the two officers fully realizing. Neither bothered to turn on the light. The clock ticked loudly from the hallway. Otherwise silence. Latimer was sitting in an armchair, while Hobbes paced nervously about, his eyes skipping from one item to another on the walls. Portraits, landscapes, playbills. *Presenting a new stage play by Mr Leonard Graves,* The Silent Guardian. *With the much-admired Mary Estelle Graves in her finest performance yet.* The face of the actress in profile, stark black-and-white, shadows, smoke drifting in from a hidden cigarette.

Another glance at his wristwatch.

'She's not coming.'

'Have faith.'

'We can go round, knock on the door.'

Latimer contemplated the empty fireplace. 'She wants to meet us alone, away from her mother. That's the deal.'

'There's a deal?'

'Just sit down, Hobbes. You're making me tired. And yes.'

'What?'

'There's always a deal, you know that. Of some kind, or other.'

He could no longer see Latimer's face clearly. He switched on the overhead light. Now the room was too stark, too bright. He was reminded of his first time here, seeing the dress laid out on the carpet, the sheer surprise of it.

Another playbill: When Dreams Unfold, *a searing exploration of forbidden love. Only at the Aldwych Theatre. Opening: 2 September 1939.* That would be right after the war started. The theatres stayed open, though, where and when they could. He knew that. Even during the Blitz.

'Calling Planet Hobbes.'

'What?'

Latimer had got up from her chair. 'She's here.'

Hobbes shook his head to clear it. He could hear the front door opening. 'She has a key?'

'That proves something, right?'

He turned towards the hallway, but Latimer held him back. 'Let me handle this.' He raised his hands in mock-surrender and moved aside.

A young woman came into the room. A teenager. Latimer greeted her, then looked over towards the inspector. He nodded.

Yes, it was her. The girl he'd seen in the cemetery, the girl in the flowery dress.

Latimer took charge. 'Joan. It's good of you to see us.'

'I can't stay long – I mustn't, or else my mum will have a go at me. She doesn't like me coming round here. She never did.'

Her voice denied everything genteel her mother had taught her: this was an accent learned from the playground, the bus stop and television. All the airs and graces cast aside: these days, everyone wanted to be working class, or at least to appear that they were.

'Do you want to sit down?'

'Don't mind if I do.' She was chewing on gum, and she kept moving it around her mouth as she spoke. 'Thanks very much.'

She dropped into the most uncomfortable chair available, a rickety wooden one at the table. It creaked as she shifted about, one of her arms dangling over its back, the other playing with a long strand of hair, which had a frayed look about it: a favoured site of worry.

Latimer took a seat at the table. Hobbes remained on his feet.

It was strange. In the cemetery he had seen this young woman as a mysterious creature, something out of a dream almost, but now, seeing her in scuffed jeans, a blue sweatshirt and a purple bomber jacket, Joan Travis looked exactly as she was: the girl next door. Greasy black hair, a few spots on her chin, soft features. Her face was not yet fully formed.

She looked at Hobbes directly. 'You're the man who was chasing me.'

'I wasn't.'

'You were – at the funeral of Mr Graves. I saw you.'

'I wasn't chasing you.'

'You gave me a fright, you did! I thought you were, you know, a perv, like.'

'Oh, Christ.'

Latimer smiled. 'Yeah. Believe me, he really isn't.'

'I can see that now, looking at him.' She was examining Hobbes from head to foot. 'He's just, like, *normal.*'

She made it sound worse than being a perv, somehow or other.

'Mind you, that scar's quite interesting.'

He touched his face, the movement unbidden. 'OK, can we just get on with this, please?'

'You don't have a ciggie, do you?' She took the gum out of her mouth and squashed it on the underside of the table. 'Only, Leonard used to let me smoke in here. Mum's not so keen.'

'Joan?'

'Yeah?' She turned to Latimer.

'We have some questions to ask you.'

'Right. Fire away.'

'How old are you?'

'Eighteen.'

'And you used to come round here quite often, is that right?'

'Sure, yeah, now and then. I liked Mr Graves. He was interesting, you know? Like, he'd written plays, and directed them, and all that. I'd like to be an actress one day. Can you imagine it, walking on stage and every single person watching you? Oh, my God, how cool would that be? Or a writer. That would be neat, like making up stories and things.'

'Joan!' Latimer put an edge in her voice.

The girl took a breath. 'Sorry, I chatter. Never know what else to do.'

'When did you start visiting Mr Graves?'

'A year ago, maybe more. My mum used to come here once a week, to give it a bit of a clean, and to make sure the old codger was all right. Well, I came along with her one time, and I got talking to him while she was upstairs, and it turns out he wasn't *just* some old codger. He told me the story of how he got his first play put on, how he waited outside the stage door of the Savoy Theatre for two and a half hours in the wind and rain, oh, my God, waiting for Terence Rattigan to come out – that's another playwright, by the way, I learned that. Anyway, Leonard thrust his playscript into Terence's hands—'

'Excuse me.'

'Yeah?'

'Sorry, love, but we need to keep on track.'

'Right, of course. So, yeah, that's how I got started on coming round. In secret, mind. My mum wouldn't like it, if she knew . . . You're not going to tell her, are you?'

'No, it's nothing to do with her.'

'You're right there. Nosy old bat.'

Hobbes watched all this from across the room, holding his tongue.

Latimer leaned back in her chair. She waited a moment before asking her next question. 'Joan, where did you get the dress from?'

'Where do you think?'

'You stole it?'

'What? No. Who do you think I am? My own mum, always rooting around for what she can find? Yuck, no. Mr Graves gave it to me. Honest, it's true, swear to God. It was a gift.'

She looked from Latimer to Hobbes, seeking confirmation.

'That's all right, love, we believe you.'

'Well, I hope so. I'm not making things up, you know.'

'So, you talked to him quite a bit, I imagine.'

'Oh, yeah, like once a week.'

'What did you talk about?'

'Theatre and stuff, like I said. Poetry, art. It was the first time I had someone proper to talk to, you know what I mean?'

Latimer nodded. 'What about his family, his children?'

'Sure, yeah, now and then he'd talk about stuff like that.'

'Did he mention his son, Nicholas?'

'This is the bloke . . . the guy who was killed in the park, right? Yeah, he was mentioned, in passing.'

'Did you ever see Nicholas around here?'

'No.'

'You never saw any visitors?'

'Now and then, maybe. But not often.'

'Who?'

'I don't know. What do you want, that I should be asking for names and addresses, or taking photos of them?' Joan was getting fidgety. She slid further down in her seat, her legs splayed. The chair creaked loudly.

'Why did he give you the dress? Was there any special reason?'

The girl didn't answer. She was gazing into space.

'Joan? Is there a story attached to the dress, anything that Leonard mentioned?'

'Oh, yeah, sure. He went on about that a fair bit.'

'And what did he say?'

Now she stared at Latimer intently, then at Hobbes. Her eyes narrowed. 'Is this important, like? The dress? It's nothing to do with his son being killed, is it?'

At this point Hobbes stepped in. 'It has everything to do with him being killed.'

Joan went quiet. She held his stare, then faltered, blinking. 'But that can't be right . . . Why would it be right?'

Hobbes knew he was lying, a little bit, or, more, *allowing* his convictions to become truth, a kind of truth in the moment of being said. 'I believe it to be true,' he added.

'Look, I'm happy to come here, really, I'm happy to chat, but I don't know what you want from me.'

Hobbes stood close to her. He bent down slightly.

Latimer said, 'Hobbes, leave it. Let her be.'

The girl sneered. 'Yeah . . . *Hobbes*. Leave it, like the lady says.'

The inspector raised his hands.

Latimer said to him, 'Let's allow her to talk.'

Hobbes gave a nod.

Latimer turned back to Joan Travis. This time she spoke in a monotone, knowing she had to shock the girl. 'Nicholas Graves was killed without mercy, his head beaten repeatedly with a rock, until his skull caved in. I saw the body, as close as I am to you this moment.'

Joan stared at the detective sergeant.

'Somebody is to blame for this terrible crime. We will catch them. Believe me when I say that. And you, Joan, you will help us. Because . . .'

Joan carried on with Latimer's thought: 'Because he was Leonard's son?'

'That's right, love. So, what do you know? What are you holding back?' Without either of them realizing it, Latimer had leaned over and taken hold of Joan's hand. Her next words came out softly: 'Don't worry, Joan. I'm here for you.'

And that was the key. Joan Travis told a secret. 'He liked to watch me dance.'

A pause. The two detectives stayed silent.

Latimer's grip tightened ever so slightly on the girl's hand.

'He liked me to wear the dress and to dance around in it. Right here in the living room. First . . . first of all, he asked me to close the curtains.'

Hobbes groaned. He couldn't help it.

'Carry on,' Latimer said. 'Don't let anything worry you.'

Joan nodded, more to herself than anything. 'He watched me dance. He put a record on the gramophone, that one over there, usually a waltz, or something old, like a nice romantic tune. It sounded very crackly. Very slow . . . like a dream . . . and I danced. I *danced*. Around and around the carpet, just following the music, making it up as I went along.'

Latimer still had hold of Joan's hand. 'What did Leonard do?'

'He sat in the armchair over there and he watched me, and he smiled. And sometimes . . . sometimes he would direct me, tell me what to do, which movements to make, like I was on the stage.'

'And then?'

'And then the music stopped. The needle would make this repeated hissing noise, but Leonard seemed to be frozen. And he didn't want me to move either, so we both just sort of stayed like

that for a while. It was like a magic spell. A spell in the daytime.'
She paused. 'I think he was lost in the past. Far away, far away . . .'

For a moment no one spoke.

Joan's expression had softened. Her head was tilted to one side.
'Did you dance again for him?'

'Yes, a few times. Not many. I got the feeling that each time he
was happy, but that each happiness lasted only for a while. And
then . . .'

'That makes sense.' Latimer thought for a moment. 'You said
you knew the story of the dress.'

'Only a little. Leonard said it had been made by his daughter,
Camilla. That Camilla made all of the dresses.'

Hobbes asked, 'Did Leonard ever mention where Camilla was
living?'

'Ooh, it speaks.'

'Joan . . . ignore him. It's me you're talking to. Just me.'

'OK, fair enough, I'd prefer that.'

'Me too.'

'Can't we ask him to leave?'

'Sadly, no.'

Joan frowned. Then she said, 'I think Leonard mentioned
Southend one time. The seaside.'

'In regards of Camilla?'

'What?'

'That's where Camilla was living?'

'Who knows? Maybe. Is it that important? Oh, right, she's the
killer.' The girl's eyes widened. 'Oh, God! She killed her own
brother! That's incredible. I wish I had a brother, I bet we'd hate
each other.'

Hobbes and Latimer looked at each other. They didn't need to
speak.

'This is good, Joan. You're being very helpful.' Latimer smiled to put the girl at ease. Then she asked, 'Did you see any other dresses around the house, similar to the one Mr Graves gave you?'

'Of course I did. He had a whole load of them, didn't he, in a wardrobe upstairs.'

'Did any of them have a rip, or a cut? Just here.'

The girl shrugged.

'What about a dress with a stain on it, a red stain?'

'You mean like blood? Or meant to look like blood?'

'Yes, perhaps.'

'Sure, I helped him to make that one.'

Hobbes stiffened. Latimer looked surprised. Joan could tell she'd said something of note. She was eager to spin her tale. 'Leonard told me it was for a role in a play. A stage play he'd written years and years ago, *The Moon Awakes*. The main character was called Anna Kreeley. And Leonard wanted to see the part acted out.'

'That must've been exciting for you.'

'It was! Oh, God, yes. I ran upstairs for him, and brought down a new dress. And I worked at the table here, doing what he told me, making the cut with a pair of scissors and applying the red paint. Just so. He said I was a natural, and that I should work in the theatre, one day.'

'What happened then? Did he make you wear the dress?'

'He didn't make me. I did it because I wanted to.'

'Where did you change?'

'In the room next door. And then I had to make an entrance, and I had to say the lines he'd written down for me. I can remember them by heart.'

'Why don't you perform for us now?'

'I suppose I could . . .'

'You don't need to put the dress on or anything. Just say the lines.'

'Right, then. Here goes. Oh, I'm a bit nervous.'

'You don't need to be.'

Joan Travis prepared herself. She got up from the chair and stood in front of the fireplace. Her body took on an angular shape with jutting limbs, and her face set in a very different expression. The two detectives looked on. And then Joan started to speak, or rather to intone, to murmur, to chant, to bare her teeth and at one point to shout, 'I would rather see myself alone for ever than to be a part of this marriage any longer. You sicken me! The very thought of having to look at your face for one more day fills me with dread. And to think, James, that I once professed to loving you. Such feelings belong to a different woman, one I cast aside many months ago. I am a ghost. Our love is haunted by the past, by your past. All those hideous friends of yours . . . if only you could see how boring they are. Maybe then . . . maybe, yes, we might have had a chance. But sadly, the day wanes . . .'

Here she stopped and looked embarrassed. 'Oh, Miss Kreeley goes on a bit more after that, but I can't remember it, sorry, and there's me saying I had it all in my head.' She looked to Latimer for approval, and then to Hobbes. 'I think it's because Leonard is dead, that he killed himself, I think that's why I've forgotten it. He's taken the words away with him.'

'I liked it,' Hobbes said.

Latimer agreed. 'Yes, it was very good.'

For the first time Joan Travis looked entirely innocent, and desperate to be loved. 'Really? I've done it much better, at other times.'

Hobbes asked, 'How did Mr Graves take your rendition?'

'He gave me lots of notes, tips and the like, ways to improve. I suppose that's all over with now.'

'You can still pursue it as a career,' Latimer told her. 'Go to drama school.'

'Yeah, I suppose. Leonard said the same. There was one weird thing he did, though. It made me think he was losing his mind a bit, becoming forgetful.'

'Something he said?'

'Yeah. Once, after I'd performed the piece for him, he called me Adeline.'

Silence in the room.

Latimer made a note. Hobbes was going to speak, but then he stopped.

Joan looked at them both, one after the other.

Finally, Hobbes asked her, 'And did he say who this Adeline was?'

'No, he just called me the name. And then he apologized, and said he'd got me mixed up with someone else, someone—'

'Who was it?'

The steel had come back to Hobbes's voice.

'I don't know.'

'Was it his daughter?'

'His daughter? No, of course not. He hasn't got a daughter called—'

'Joan, you have to tell me.'

'I am telling you, for fuck's sake! I'm telling you that I don't know. What's wrong with you? Jesus.'

Latimer interrupted them. 'OK, Guv, I think I need to talk to Joan on her own for a bit.'

'Aye, that's right. *Hobbes. Guv.* She does.'

Hobbes raised his hands in surrender. He left the room and stood in the corridor. He felt guilty for his behaviour. He thought of going back in and apologizing but, no, best leave Latimer to it. He headed for the kitchen to make a drink, but then changed his mind. He took the stairs down into the cellar.

There was the shape of the pit on the floor, covered over with clean concrete. And below this, the empty grave. This was the prime site, he knew that now: of all the dresses laid out as ritualized objects, as magic charms, the one buried in the cellar was the most important, perhaps the very first.

He had read the preliminary report: a best estimate put the burial in the 1950s, maybe earlier. Thirty years or so in the ground.

And still no body, no flesh and blood.

A suicide note: *Dearest Adeline, I'm so sorry. For everything.*

A screwed-up letter in Nicholas's bedsit: *Adeline . . . I've been thinking about you a lot, these last few months . . . I wish I could see you again.*

Father and son, both obsessing over the same woman.

Adeline, Adeline, Adeline . . .

He remembered David Kepple's words about the missing final image in the *kusozu* series: a memorial for the dead. Human emotions working against decay. Perhaps the dresses served such a function: an act of remembrance.

Hobbes climbed the stairs. Enough of this place. He poured himself a glass of water at the kitchen sink. And he looked through the grimy window at the back garden. Without thinking he went out through the kitchen doorway. Dusk had settled heavily on London. He walked across the remains of the lawn to the overgrown section. Here he bent down, to part the damp stems and branches. The fungus was still there, now joined by a smaller partner. Yes, it was the same as the one he'd seen in Richmond Park, growing on or around the body of the dog. The same Rorschach-style markings: black on cream. This one was growing from the rich dark wet soil, attended by its colony of ants. Hobbes reached down, grabbed a section of the plant and pulled at it. There was a resistance at first, a determination to remain in place. He could almost think that a human hand beneath the soil was mirroring his action, and this made him shudder. But he pulled harder, dragging the fungus free of the soil, or nearly so. It was attached to something buried in the earth. Hobbes dug deeper, moving the soil away with his bare hands. The fungus crumbled under his touch. It sounded like blisters of soft skin popping open. There was a cloud of yellow dust in the air: the particles got into his nostrils and he almost sneezed. His eyes were watering. And now he saw what the fungus was attached to . . .

It was a bird. Just a common blackbird, as far as he could tell. Long dead. But only a small part of its body had been reduced to bone. The bulk was still composed of flesh, or mutated flesh: the fungus was growing all over this section. As with the dog in the park, the rate of decay had been slowed. Somehow the fungus had made its home in the flesh of the bird, and was changing the creature, transforming it into something new and strange.

Hobbes stood up. He had a section of the fungus in his hand.

It stank. It was just horrible. Top notes: sweetness. Base note: rot.

Some kind of sap on his fingertips, dark, putrid.

Dirt under his nails, and soft pulp.

It was sticky.

But he didn't care. Not just then.

The garden was held perfectly silent in that moment.

There was a haze in the air.

A thin yellow mist.

Perhaps the spores of the fungus, glistening . . .

He felt them on his face, on his skin.

The blackbird lay on the ground, already half hidden as the plants slowly curled back over it, forming a canopy.

The garden shed was visible through the tangle of branches.

Hobbes turned to face the house.

He felt light-headed.

The dress danced before him across the lawn, a flutter of blue in a human shape, empty, empty of life. And then gone, drifting away.

He saw the rear of the house through a kind of thin yellow-grey mist. His eyes moved from one window to another, as he thought of David Kepple's story, how his grandfather had scared him with rumours of a hidden room. Could such a thing be true? Would he have to bring a sledgehammer next time, and attack the walls, seeking a hidey-hole?

A single noise in the silence: a bird calling from a tree, in prayer to its dead partner.

The first drops of rain.

Warm on his skin, his neck, the back of his hand.

He looked up.

Someone was standing at a window on the third floor of the house, a woman, looking down into the garden, staring at Hobbes. She made a gesture, a wave of the hand. But he couldn't make out her face. Was it Latimer or the girl from next door?

He went back inside. The two women were talking in the living room. Neither turned to look at him.

He took the stairs, one flight and then the next.

Vacated rooms, one after another.

No one. No one there. His footsteps echoed. And yet around every corner he could hear noises: scrapings, whisperings, fingernails against glass.

His mind filled the emptiness with imagined life, with ghosts.

A shadow moved.

And stopped.

And moved again.

But there was no one there to cast it.

The corridors were empty.

Now and then he knocked on a wall, hoping to hear a hollow sound, evidence of the hidden room Kepple had mentioned. But all the walls were solid brick, and sturdily built. Perhaps he could find the original building plans of Bridlemere, the layout of the walls and floors, and thereby locate a secret door . . .

Now he found himself on the third floor, in one of the rear bedrooms. He stood at the window, looking down into the back garden.

A woman was standing on the lawn, looking up at him.

She wore the dress, the blue and yellow dress, the only dress possible.

The two people stared at each other across God knew what kind of threshold.

The rain fell between them as a curtain of grey.

The figure in the garden shivered, and almost broke apart. A phantom.

And Detective Inspector Hobbes knew then: the house had taken possession of him. The spirits of the family, the occupants. If he made his way back downstairs and peered out through the back door, the garden would be empty; and if he walked across the lawn and looked up at the third-floor window, the same woman would be there, looking down at him, waving, and so it would go on, this dance between them, always, always . . .

Her face obscured.

Contamination of Evidence

As they walked out of the house, Hobbes asked Latimer to drive. He handed her the keys.

'Why? What's up? You not feeling too good?'

'I'm fine. Just a bit . . .'

'What? Knackered?'

'Yeah.'

'Overdoing it, Guv. Bound to happen.'

'OK. That'll do, Sergeant.'

'Actually,' she glanced at him over the roof of the car, 'you look terrible, if I'm being honest.'

'For your honesty, thank you.'

'You're shaking.'

'I'm not.'

'You really are. What is it? Delirium tremens?'

'Christ. Will you please shut up?' It was said with a laugh but, still, he meant it.

'Not until I find out what the trouble is.'

They got into the car, and Latimer started the engine. 'Come on, then. Tell Aunty Meg.'

'OK, if you must know, I think I saw a ghost.'

She laughed out loud.

'And that's why I didn't want to tell you.'

'Henry, I never had you down as a—'

'She was in my mind, not in the house.'

'She?'

He sighed. 'I'm saying no more.'

'Ah. The woman in the dress. The blue and yellow dress. Adeline.'

'She was standing at the top-floor window, looking down at me.'

'Really? Oh, shit . . . What's that stink?'

'Eh?'

'What's in the bag?'

He had placed a plastic shopping bag on the back seat, its handles tied together in a knot. But the smell still escaped.

'Oh, it's evidence, I think.'

'Well, it's horrible.'

'Sorry. Should have put it in the boot.'

'What is it?'

'Something I found in the back garden. A plant. A fungus. Is a fungus a plant?'

'Haven't a clue.'

'Anyway, I think that's why I saw the ghost.'

'Because of a plant? You mean, like magic mushrooms?'

'Maybe. Fairfax found the same thing growing near to Nicholas Graves's body. I don't know . . . I want to get it analysed.'

'It smells like – like someone poured aftershave on a dog turd.'

'Jesus.'

'What? It's true. Thank the fuck it's not my car.'

'Your car stinks of Silk Cut and Cornish pasties. And hairspray.'

'The holy trinity. Which reminds me, light us one, will yer? In my bag.'

Hobbes found her cigarettes, lit one and handed it to her.

'Cheers. This'll hide the smell of your drugs. I hope we don't get pulled over, or we're done for.'

Hobbes was glad that Latimer was back in her usual good mood. Maybe the problem of DC Fairfax would sort itself out: let the guy run his course. And if he leaves the force, well, Meg will come round, eventually.

He asked, 'So how was your chat with Miss Travis? Anything untoward?'

'Untoward?'

'I'm guessing that's why you wanted me out of there.'

'Oh, right, yeah. It's clean. The old geezer never touched her, nothing inappropriate. I think he was just a lonely old man happy to have the company of a young woman for an hour or two. Must have perked him up no end.'

They were moving along Queens Road, past the cemetery where Leonard Graves had been buried. Hobbes was reminded once more of how Joan Travis had appeared on that day, as a magical figure among the trees. 'It was strange, though, their relationship.'

'Sure. Maybe. But she got something from it as well, in terms of knowledge, and I'm guessing self-confidence. You've met her mum, hardly a free spirit.'

'Hmm. And what do you think of her story? About Leonard calling her Adeline.'

'My granny used to do the same thing, get her two daughters all mixed up. It's common enough, once you reach a certain age.'

'So you're saying?'

'I think Adeline is Leonard's daughter. Mary Estelle Graves had a fourth child. But she died, at some point, probably quite young. And the family has kept her alive, ever since, in their minds. In their stories.'

Hobbes pondered this. 'But why are her siblings so adamant that she never existed?'

218

'Solve that, and we can close this case.'

'I'm not sure.'

'You don't think Adeline is the daughter?'

'Maybe. OK, probably. But there's definitely something else going on here.' Hobbes watched the road ahead, the shops and houses passing by, people going about their lives. 'Meg, can you have another go at Rosamund? Keep on at her.'

'Will do. What about you?'

They turned into the police station car park. Latimer drove into Hobbes's usual space. The car settled. But the inspector made no effort to get out.

'Henry, what's on your mind?'

He didn't answer. He was staring through the windscreen at a brick wall.

'You still suffering from your drug intake? Seen another ghost?'

'Hmm?' His mind was elsewhere.

'Come on. I need to get out of here. Whatever you have in that bag, it's making me feel sick.'

'I've seen it before,' he said. His voice was curiously flat.

'Seen what?'

'The dress. I've seen it before somewhere, in the past. The same cut, the blood. Or not so much that, but more . . . It was significant. A significant detail. Damn it, I can't think.'

'What was it, a former case?'

'Every so often the fog clears. And I see it. And then it's gone again.'

'How do you mean, fog?'

'I don't know . . . It's foggy in my mind, that's all I can say. Like in sixty-two.'

'1962? What about it?'

'That's when the smog came down. The last of the London pea-soupers.'

Latimer nodded. 'I remember now. I was still in uniform back then.'

'It was my first year as detective.'

'Stretch out your arm so far, and your hand vanished.'

'Yeah. Look, Meg . . .'

'What is it? You've got that tone of voice. Is there something wrong?'

They were walking towards the station entrance.

Hobbes spoke quickly. 'Next week, I'll start looking for a new detective constable.'

'What? No. It's too soon. Tommy's still—'

'He's finished.'

Latimer stopped and turned to him, her eyes glaring.

'Meg. I can't hold his place any longer.'

'Fuck it. You've always had it in for Tommy, right from the start.'

'He was—'

'Right from the fuckin' start!'

He was going to answer back, but there seemed little point. They looked at each other in silence. Latimer's face showed every single expression she could muster, one after another. It was quite a thing to see. In truth, Hobbes felt as bad as she did. But he kept it secret.

Latimer hurried inside.

Hobbes followed at a steadier rate. He bumped into PC Barlow. 'Ah, good, there you are. I have a job for you.'

'To do with the Graves case?' The young constable's eyes lit up.

'Maybe. It's a bit of a strange one.'

'Let me have it.'

Hobbes handed over the plastic bag. Barlow's nose crinkled.

'I know, I know. Don't go on. I've had Latimer telling me off already.'

Barlow untied the knot in the bag and peered inside. 'What is it? A toadstool?'

'A fungus of some kind. Like the one we found on the dead dog in the park.'

'OK. What do you need?'

'I want to know what it is. Species, habitat, effects on the psyche. The lot.'

The two men went their separate ways. Hobbes climbed the stairs to the second floor. His desk was covered with papers. He was searching through the top few sheets, hoping there was something of interest, when Latimer appeared at his side.

'Meg, no more arguments. Please.'

Her face was set, cold. 'Actually, this just came in.' She handed over a folder. 'Report from St Catherine's House. I asked them to look for birth certificates for anyone called *Adeline Graves*, within a reasonable set of dates. And this is what they found.'

It was a copy of a birth certificate. Hobbes read off the entries.

'Date and place of birth: *Third November 1936. Richmond.* Name: *Adeline.*'

Latimer allowed herself a little smile. 'There she is. Finally.'

He nodded. 'A girl. Father is . . . *Leonard Albert Graves*. Mum is *Mary Estelle Graves, formerly Layne*. Father's occupation: *Author*. Nothing listed for Mary Estelle.'

'They didn't bother with the mother's occupation back then.'

'Right. And *Informant*?'

'That's the person who provided the information for the certificate.'

'Listed as *Leonard Graves*.' He waved the sheet of paper around. 'So there was a fourth child. Excellent.'

'We're getting somewhere.'

'Is there a death certificate, by any chance?'

'I have an officer working on that. But nothing up to now.'

221

Hobbes looked again at the details of the birth: '1936, November. So if she's alive, Adeline would be what now ... mid-forties?'

'Forty-four. With a birthday coming up.'

'Good. This is excellent. A few more details, and we can start to—'

'*If* she's alive.'

Hobbes was adamant. 'Until I find a body, she's alive. That's the rule.'

Latimer nodded. 'I'm calling it a day. I'll try Rosamund Kepple in the morning.'

'Yes. Thank you, Meg.'

His mind had already moved on. He read again each element of the birth certificate, as though any one of them might hold the secret, the key. His eyes were irritated, and a dull pain took over the exact centre of his skull. That's how it felt – a very particular pain, in a very particular place: targeted.

The telephone on his desk rang. It sounded like a klaxon.

'Yes?'

'Oh.' A woman's voice, anguished. 'Is that . . . ?'

'Who is this?'

'Inspector Hobbes, is that you?'

'What do you want?' He rubbed at his brow, pressing hard with his fingertips.

'It's Delia. You know . . .'

'Tommy's mother?' He felt a tightness in his chest, awaiting bad news. It was always the same with Fairfax. 'What's wrong? Is Tommy all right?'

'Can you come round, Inspector? Do you have time?'

'Of course. What is it?'

'Please. Just come round.'

He drove east, to Deptford. The rain kept off for a while, and the streets were packed. He had to concentrate all his focus on the road ahead, trying to avoid the haze that sometimes descended. The pain in his head had lightened, a little. But his eyes ran with tears.

It took him a while to get there. Delia Fairfax was waiting for him on the doorstep of her home. She looked anxious. 'I came back from work, and he wasn't here.' She was talking even as she led him into the hallway.

'Isn't that good?' Hobbes said. 'That he's getting out of the house?'

'That's not the problem. He's out every day, for hours on end.'

'So then?'

'You don't understand. Come on, I'll show you.'

Delia led the way upstairs and into a small bedroom at the rear of the house. It was a mess, with clothes scattered everywhere, half-eaten plates of food, and screwed-up papers all over the floor. One wall was pinned with newspaper clippings, all relating to the Richmond Park killing. Photographs were pinned up here and there, all taken by Fairfax. They showed the area around the crime scene where Nicholas Graves had been found, including the dead dog with its fungal coating.

Hobbes wiped his face with his handkerchief. His skin was damp.

'He doesn't like me coming in here,' Delia said. 'Not at all. Forbids me even to give it a quick clean. Can you Adam and Eve it?'

A desk was covered with sheets of notes, all concerned with one thing only, or rather, five things: the objects found in the jewellery box in the cellar of Bridlemere. Fairfax had become obsessed with these, more than with any other part of the case. He must have spent a good few hours in the library. He'd identified the silver medal and ribbon as being a Distinguished Conduct Medal, bestowed for *exceptional acts of gallantry* during the First World War. The name *Leonard Graves?* was written alongside this information. The Greta Garbo cigarette card had first been issued in 1934, part of a collection of famous movie stars. Fairfax's notes wove a complex story, a fantasy, from the items and what they might mean for the mystery girl in the flowered dress, and for the Graves family in general. It wasn't at all based on reality, but on a kind of fevered dream in the detective's head. In many ways, Fairfax had conducted the perfect investigation, but one that was utterly useless, based as it was on spurious ideas and imagined connections.

'I don't understand.'

'Neither do I, Inspector. I've given up trying to—'

'No, I mean I don't understand what Tommy is doing here. He's trying to solve a current case, but he won't come into work. It doesn't make sense.'

'I've told you, he's a proud man.'

'His position will be taken over, maybe next week.'

'You mean he'll be out of work?' Delia was stricken by the news.

'Yes.'

'He'll have to . . . he'll have to sign on?'

'Or get a job.'

'But what would he do? Tommy's only good at one thing. Being a copper! That's it.'

Hobbes picked up a set of five photographs, depicting the objects found in the jewellery box. He felt a pang of guilt. Fairfax had worked from these images: his starting point for his own personal investigation. And Hobbes had given the photographs to him. He'd made a mistake. He should never have used the Graves case as a temptation.

Delia Fairfax was fretting at his side. 'I need your help.'

'Of course. But what's the real trouble?'

She stared at him, her eyes filled with worry. Then she bent down to the bed and peeled back the bedclothes: there were bloodstains on the sheets.

Hobbes tested them. They were dry, but still retaining some of their colour. Probably a few hours old.

'Did Tommy come in last night?'

'No, I don't think so. He must've come in this morning, after I'd left for work. The towels in the bathroom are also . . .' Her voice trailed off.

Hobbes wondered how much to tell her. 'I saw him around seven, yesterday evening.'

'You did? How was he? Did he look—'

'He was drunk, Delia. Very drunk. He made a bit of a fool of himself in front of a constable.'

'Oh, he wouldn't like that.' Her face showed her concern. 'I know my boy.'

Hobbes looked again at the bloodstain. 'There's not much of it,' he said. 'Maybe he got into a fight.'

'Aye, I can picture that easily enough. The silly fool.'

'A couple of blows, that's all. I think he's all right.' Hobbes stood up straight. 'I'll see what I can do. Does he have a favourite pub, a local?'

'No. Not really. He doesn't have many friends. Not drinking buddies. But . . .'

'Yes, what is it?'

Delia's shoe was nudging at a copy of *Mayfair* that was poking out from under the bed. 'I really don't know why he needs these things when he has a girlfriend.'

'He does?'

'Oh, yes, well, on and off, you know? Meg, she's called. An older woman . . .'

225

Hobbes was taken aback. 'Meg? Are you sure?'

'She's one of your lot, I think. She's been round a number of times. But I don't know where she lives.'

'I'll find her. Yes, maybe she knows something.'

'Thank you, Inspector Hobbes.'

'Henry . . . please.'

'Tommy always said you were a good man.'

'He did?'

'Nothing but praise. Nothing but! When he wasn't calling you an idiot, that is.'

'Right. Fair enough.'

Hobbes said his goodbyes to Delia, promising once more to do what he could for her son. But, in truth, he wasn't sure what action to take. And as he drove along, he was overcome with a fearsome jealousy, which he could hardly explain.

No, that can't be it. There has to be some other explanation.

Christ, but she's too old for him . . .

Was he jealous that Fairfax and Latimer had got together, however that might be, and did this mean he had feelings for Latimer? Or was this a more universal emotion? How come other people can find love, or at least comfort, with each other while he—

A car hooted its horn at him.

He had veered a little towards the opposite lane.

And why the hell hasn't Meg told me about this? That rankled.

The Graves case flickered away from his mind. And he thought of Glenda, and Martin. His family. It was almost enough to make him stop the car and take his pain out on the nearest troublemaker, some poor sod. But, no, he drove on. It was all he could do, following roads and turnings he barely saw. The rain had started again with a vengeance, pelting the windscreen. It sounded like he was under attack from some unseen enemy. And with the rain came a sudden darkness.

He pulled up outside the little two-storey house on the back-street. He'd been here only once before, when he'd given DS Latimer a lift one morning. Now he sat in his car, looking at the house with its downstairs window lit up brightly. He knew that Meg had a lodger, DC Harris, who worked on fraud and embezzlement. Kathy, that was her name. He remembered it just as she opened the door to him.

'Is Meg in?'

'Who is it? Step forward a little.'

Typical cop behaviour. He followed her order and brought his face, drenched from the rain, into the glow of the porch light.

'Oh, it's you. Inspector Hobbes. Sir.'

He waved the title away. 'I just need to see Meg – DS Latimer – about a case.'

'She's not in.'

'Do you know where she is?'

'Probably still at work. You didn't try the station?'

'Yes. I'll do that.'

'Or maybe she's out with her man.'

'Right. A man?'

Kathy Harris laughed. 'Some girls have all the luck.'

'There's no one else here, is there? Inside the house?'

Now Harris looked suspicious. 'What's that supposed to mean?'

'Nothing. Nothing at all. Don't worry about it.'

'I'm not worried. I'm curious.'

He left it there. No more questions. Back in the car. A strange mood. One thought after another. Nothing connecting. He stopped for a doner kebab on the way, bolted half of it standing outside the café. Rain dripping from the edge of the awning, a couple of other customers alongside, doing the same. Their voices cut off from him: private jokes. He threw the rest of his meal into the bin. A funny taste in his mouth.

The next shop along was an off-licence. He did something he hadn't done in a while. He bought a half-bottle of whisky and drank a mouthful, neat, sitting in his car, the rain drumming on the roof. A second mouthful. Burning. Soothing. He started the car and pulled away from the kerb. Drive carefully, drive carefully, don't get pulled over. Make no mistakes. Keep going, one road at a time, one minute, one hour, one clue at a time, but all was lost, one kiss at a time, until love appears before you. No. All lost. No way forward.

He could smell the sickly aroma of the fungus.

At the back of his throat.

Head swimming with random pictures.

One above all. Of course. He could never escape it.

A flutter of blue and yellow cloth.

Were the spores still affecting him?

He had no sense of where he was going, but in the end there was only one destination, and he was guided there by feelings he had never encountered before.

Number 17 Palliser Road, Richmond.

Bridlemere.

He had a copy of the house key in his pocket.

Nobody home.

He turned on the hall light and climbed the stairs. He saw the playbills of Mary Estelle Graves's triumphs on the stage, including *The Moon Awakes*. And he noticed for the first time that the actress was wearing a dress in the photo, *the* dress. Even though the shot was monochrome, he could recognize the style and the pattern, brighter flowers on a dark background. The dress had had a long, long history, before it had arrived in this murder case, as an item of obsession.

One shadow after another. He walked up to the landing above, then the next flight, until he found the room he needed. The old bedroom. Here in this room he had seen her, from the garden below. A vision. Here, in the semi-dark . . .

Ghosts in the silence.

A girl's voice.

Adeline, calling to him.

Help me . . . rescue me . . .

Some ridiculous fantasy he carried.

But he was no one's saviour, never had been.

The room was lit by a wash of pale moonlight halfway across the floor.

The shadows moved of their own accord.

Tiny scraping sounds. An imagined breath being drawn.

He walked over to the wardrobe.

There they hung on the wooden bar, one dress after another, packed in.

Each one pristine, unstained, uncut. Made for some private ritual that had now come to an end. And yet Hobbes was part of that ritual. He had a role in it, a part to play. What was that role? He pulled down one of the dresses, held it and stared at it. He walked into the glow of the moonlight, so the yellow flowers were seen clearly on the blue cloth.

And for a moment, a stray thought came to him, that the dress had nothing at all to do with the killing of Nicholas Graves. That he had made a mistake, that he had forged a connection where there was none.

But the idea drifted away, and then certainty came over him.

The room. The shadows.

A man with an old-fashioned dress in his hands, just standing there. A police officer.

The window, with its wide-open curtains.

A woman's voice in his head, talking to him, whispering.

He spoke in a soft voice. A prayer, of a kind. An old habit. He had said it once already, on Sunday, as he stood over the body of Nicholas Graves. And he said it again now, with a different name, a different purpose.

Adeline Graves. I will find you. Alive or dead.

If you're alive, I'll find out why you have to hide yourself away. And if you're dead . . . I will find out who killed you. I will bring them to justice.

This I promise.

He looked at the dress. If anyone had walked in then, or watched him from a hidden corner, they would have supposed him a man caught in a spell, or a fetishist even, a madman fixated on one object alone. But Hobbes had no such rationale for what he was doing. He was at the mercy of other forces, beyond his reason. Beyond all reason.

And then he lowered his head. At the same time he raised his hands. Until his face and the dress met, and he drew in a deep breath. He took in the aroma of the cloth, and he let the material fold against his face, softly, softly, until his head spun with light.

Now, now he understood.

A film, a few moments in a film. The title came to him.

The Spell Makers.

Yes, that was it. Memories, until this moment forgotten.

The hook to his own life. This case.

And the fog, as it had closed in all those years ago.

1962

There was a whole gang of officers in a small windowless room, watching a film as it played out on a screen pinned to the wall. The twin spools of a 16-millimetre projector spinning, making a soft clicking sound. The men making lewd comments and nudging each other with their elbows. The air thick with cigarette smoke. Detective Constable Hobbes stood in the doorway. He felt slightly apart from his colleagues and their activity, and although he dearly wanted to enter into the spirit of things, something held him back. He didn't know what it was: he hoped it wasn't snobbery, and he hoped it wasn't hypocrisy. But the simple truth was this: the images on the screen sickened and excited him at the same time, and the clash between the two sensations caused him pain.

This was one of the films picked up from the unlicensed cinema that DC Hobbes had found that afternoon. More than seventy movies hidden in a cupboard, almost all of them illegal. It made him think about the injured woman he had helped: Margery Pollard. She was still in the hospital, but the latest news seemed good. She would live.

'Rookie! Close the door, mate. You're letting the smoke out.'

One or two of the men turned to him from the screen, expecting him to join in, to come back with a suitable riposte. He couldn't think of one. And then a great ribald cheer went up. Hobbes looked at the screen to see why.

For ten seconds, fifteen, his eyes took in what he was seeing. Then he walked away.

DC Hobbes wrote up his report. His mind wandered in a pleasant way to the usher, the one who had led him to Margery. Glenda, that was her name. Something in her eyes, her face, the way she held herself, despite the blood on her hands, and the nature of her friend's wounds. Hobbes couldn't stop thinking about her. He'd interviewed her, after the victim had been attended to, just a few questions, and hadn't gathered much in the way of information. *When did you first notice . . . can you describe the miscreant . . . what direction did he . . .* Christ, had he actually used the word *miscreant*? What an idiot! No wonder the lads called him a prig. But, still, it had been good to talk with her. He'd even made her laugh at one point. Or at least smile. What was the line, what had he said, to get that reaction? He couldn't remember now. Ah, well, there it is.

He finished the report. His colleagues invited him out for a drink, which he agreed to, and they spent the night in the Lamb and Flag, and people kept buying him drinks. Star of the Hour! He downed a couple too many and slipped away without anyone noticing – they were all in their cups by then.

Her face, those eyes in the glow of the beam . . .

He made his way to Regent Street and crossed over, enjoying the night air. The fog had lifted since this morning, but remnants still remained, clinging on, giving the streets a spectral feel, and surrounding the neon signs with halos of mist. His head cleared a little, as he walked back to the police station on Savile Row. He always felt the change of mood as he crossed the road, leaving the glare of Soho behind, the shouts and cries of the hawkers, the whispered entreaties of the girls plying their trade from doorways. In contrast, a young couple strolled by, arm in arm, dressed in the new mod fashion, a riot of colour in the drab back lanes and alleys.

Glenda. Glenda Jones.

And he wondered what kind of woman ended up working in a cinema that showed dirty movies. Perhaps he should just forget her.

He took the stairs up to the second floor of the nick and entered the bullpen. The night shift had settled in, and he listened to a couple of officers chatting about a robbery with battery on Brewer Street. Every fourth word was an expletive. He retrieved the file from his desk, and quickly looked up Glenda's address. The beer gave him courage, and he thought of himself as a bold young man just finishing his first week as a detective, goddamn it, yes, why not? He had as much right as anybody!

She must've seen everything there is to see . . . those films . . .

As he walked back along the corridor, he passed the room where the viewing party had taken place earlier. A light was flickering under the doorway. The beam of the projector and all the promises that it held.

Because he'd never, not really, not fully . . .

A few fumbles at a cold bus stop.

And since moving to London, well . . .

Quietly, he opened the door and peered inside.

A film was playing on the screen.

Only one man was watching.

Hobbes froze to the spot, his hand on the door jamb.

He could see the man's face.

It was Detective Inspector Collingworth.

Hobbes hadn't spoken to him yet, not one word. But he knew the man had a fearsome reputation. The warnings had been freely given not to get on his wrong side.

A stocky well-built man, shaped like a barrel. Long, thick swept-back hair, slick with Brylcreem. A face prematurely lined. A misshapen nose, ruined by drink and one too many punch-ups. They said he'd taken down villains single-handedly, no back-up. And done the same to recalcitrant cops. A working-class bruiser wrapped in a detective's ill-fitting suit. That was his reputation. But just now that brutal face took on a different aspect.

Hobbes was shocked.

Jack Collingworth's eyes glistened in the light, staring ahead. Tears ran down the grooves of flesh.

He was crying.

PART THREE

1981

A View of Dreamland

Arlington House rose above the town, like a concrete sentinel, its sides undulating in and out, copying the shape of the waves that splashed on to the nearby beach. The high-rise was a loyal protector of the seaside resort, yet it must have inspired hatred over the years, for its beauty was well hidden behind its brutalist façade. There had been a shopping centre at its base, back in the sixties, and its remains were still there with most of the shops boarded up and covered with graffiti. A ladies' hairdresser and an off-licence were the only ones still operating as businesses.

Eighteen floors. One hundred and forty-two flats. There was a concierge's desk, but no concierge. Hobbes pressed on the intercom panel for flat 15B and waited. He pressed again, and this time a woman's voice responded.

'Hello.'

'It's Henry Hobbes. I'm here to—'

'Oh, you're early!'

The door popped open. He walked into the lobby and waited for a lift to arrive. The tiled floors stretched away in a strict geometric pattern. As the lift ascended he reflected on the last time he had seen his former boss: the man who had more or less single-handedly taught him how to be a copper, a *real* copper. Hobbes was nervous suddenly. He wiped his brow and adjusted his tie. Ridiculous. The man must be sixty or thereabouts by now. Surely the old ferocity had diminished.

Would they even like each other any more?

After all, they hadn't exactly parted on the best terms.

The lift door opened. The fifteenth floor.

His feet echoed on the tiles.

A woman was waiting for him outside flat 15B. She was dressed in pink from head to foot and her hair was the colour of freshly made Bird's custard. A large misshapen pendant hung at her neck; it looked like a magic amulet.

'Henry! It's so good to see you. Please come inside.'

Hobbes had never seen her before in his life, but already he was being treated as an old friend.

'Could you take your shoes off? Would you mind, my dear?'

'No, of course not. Erm . . .'

'Jack hates the floor to get scuffed.'

She pointed to a stand near the door and Hobbes placed his brown brogues on it.

'I'm Rita. I'm sure Jack mentioned me?'

'Oh, yes, of course. Rita.'

They shook hands a little awkwardly and then she came in for a hug. He caught a waft of perfume, a mixture of lemon blossoms and bubble gum. Her hair frizzed with a static charge. Hobbes liked her immediately. She gave him a big smile and looked him up and down. Her eyes lingered for a second on the scar on his face, but she moved on quickly. 'Yes, you'll do!' She led the way into the living room.

Jack Collingworth was sitting in a swivel armchair, his body perfectly still, his arms and legs arranged in straight lines. He looked to be immobile, but at the sight of the visitor he jumped up with as much energy as he could muster and grabbed Hobbes's hand in a tight, two-fisted grip. 'My God, it is you! Henry bloody Hobbes. I never thought . . .'

'Jack.'

'Let's have a look at you. Yes, indeed, every inch the chief inspector.'

'I'm not chief.'

'I know that. Yer daft ape. I'm shoving my oar in early on, like.'

'What can I say, Jack?'

Collingworth had to turn his head sideways to favour his right ear.

'It's a disgrace, that's what it is! Not making chief! What the fuck happened? Sorry. Just let me . . .' He fished in his pocket and pulled out 50p, which he tossed into a jar on the coffee-table. 'Rita doesn't like me swearing.' The jar was more than half full.

'Ah, you know me, Jack.'

'Pigheaded?'

'I never could play the game.'

'Aye, the one thing I could never teach you. Well, come on, sit, sit, sit!'

Hobbes was guided to the settee. Collingworth returned to his armchair. It gave Hobbes a chance to appraise him. He was thin. The weight he used to carry around, the belly he used as a weapon of intimidation, was more or less all gone. He now looked empty of air, wrinkled around the jowls and cheeks. The fat had simply dissolved, leaving pockets of loose skin. Only his hair remained as it was in memory, still as thick, not one speck of a recede.

'Don't look at me like that, Henry. I know I look ill.'

Before Hobbes could respond, Rita came in carrying a tray with cups and a plate of cakes and biscuits.

'Here she is, the love of my life. Did you know I got remarried?'

'No, not at all. I'm happy for you. For you both.'

'Best thing that ever happened to me.'

He pulled Rita to him and she perched on the arm of his chair. She was ten years younger than her husband, a good-looking woman with that ready smile, a dash of make-up and immaculately groomed hands. They looked perfectly matched. And Hobbes was suddenly aware that they'd dolled themselves up for his visit. The flat was spotless. Collingworth's face gleamed fresh and pink from a recent shave. His hair glistened.

Hobbes sat there in his creased shirt and his threadbare socks. There was a hole in one of them.

Rita poured the tea and served refreshments. Hobbes's slice of fruit cake was half the size he was used to. If he wasn't careful, he'd swallow it in one.

'Thank you. This is very nice.'

Collingworth slurped at his tea. 'Did you have a good journey? How was the A299?'

'I didn't—'

'You know we call it the Thanet Way? I'm guessing it was quiet, this time of year?'

'I got the train, Jack.'

'The train? No, no. I thought you'd have a driver, some keen detective constable out to prove himself.'

'I had to read on the way.'

'Do you remember I used to have you driving me everywhere? Especially when I'd had a few too many, eh.'

Collingworth laughed heartily. It took over his entire upper body and soon transformed itself into a racking cough. His tea spilled on to the carpet. Rita rubbed her husband's back gently. 'Now Jack, you know what the doctor said.'

'Oh, don't go on, not in front of the young 'un! It's nothing. Nothing at all. Right as rain.'

Rita got to her feet. 'I shall leave you boys to it. Duty calls.'

'I run a haulage firm these days, Henry. Just half a dozen wagons, but it keeps the wolf from the door. Mind you, Rita does most of the work.'

'Only until you're fit and ready.'

Collingworth nodded and smiled. Rita made a little wave. 'It was very nice to meet you, Henry.'

'The same.'

Once his wife had left and they heard the front door close, Jack Collingworth's mood changed. First of all he asked about the scar. 'A recent addition?'

'It is.'

'The line of duty, I suppose?'

Hobbes nodded. He didn't want to talk about it.

Collingworth had already helped himself to another slice of cake, and he spoke with crumbs on his lips. 'I can't believe they haven't promoted you yet, those bastards. Is this to do with that business earlier this year, after the Brixton riot?'

'Probably, yeah.'

'Aye, I read about it in the *Mirror*. Dreadful. But did you do the right thing, blowing the whistle?'

'I guess.'

Collingworth grinned. 'You're like that man in the fairy tale.'

'Which one?'

'The pauper who sees a big lump of excrement on the road, and instead of walking on like anyone else would, he bends down and picks it up and carries it into the palace and presents it to the Queen, saying, "Your Majesty, I do believe someone has taken a dump on the royal road."'

Hobbes couldn't help smiling.

'And I can't believe I managed to tell that story without swearing. I must be getting soft.'

'Rita's had a good influence on you, I can see that.'

Collingworth nodded, but his expression darkened. 'Exposing police corruption. Never a good career move.'

'And being corrupt is, I suppose?'

'Aye, well, we can't all be squeaky clean.'

Hobbes felt his anger burning. 'You taught me! You taught me how to be good.'

'I did. It's true.'

'And all along you were taking your own share.'

'Not all along. And you know that. Only later—'

'You let people off, for services rendered.'

'No one serious.'

'Christ. The old excuses.'

Collingworth raised his voice. 'Things changed. In my life. I had some . . . difficulties. I needed money to sort them out.'

Hobbes made to reply. He couldn't believe they had got off on such a bad footing. 'Jack, I'm not here to—'

'To what? To rake over old coals?' Collingworth grunted. 'Because, Henry my lad, I really don't give two shits and a squirt of piss what you think. Oh, sorry. I'd better put something in the jar for that. Rita empties it at the end of the month and spends it on the slot machines.'

Clink.

Clink, clink.

He stood up and walked to the window. Hobbes joined him there, and for a moment or two they looked out at the scenery.

'You don't have a fag on yer, do you?'

'Are you allowed?'

'Not strictly. But you know how it is. Old habits.'

'Sure.'

Hobbes handed over a cigarette and lit it for him. Collingworth opened the window and blew the smoke outside. 'I'll give my teeth a brush before Rita gets back.' He tapped a fingernail against the glass. 'A clever design, this window. Every resident can see the countryside and the sea.' There was pride in his voice.

It was absurd. And painful.

Hobbes didn't know what to say. He could find no easy way of broaching the subject, the reason he'd come to Margate.

He looked down at the beach. The tide was coming in and only a thin strip of sand was visible. A few moving dots indicated locals out shopping, or walking the dog. There was a small run-down amusement park that called itself Dreamland. It was closed at the moment, the rides empty. Glenda and he had holidayed here, when was that? 1965, '66? Early on in their marriage. He remembered laughter, and bright colours, cries of delight. But now, on a drizzly day in late October, a deep melancholy hovered over the town.

Jack Collingworth had a different view. 'Margate in the rain. Is there any place better?' He threw the cigarette into the outside air and closed the window. 'Brrr. It's chilly.'

'I was thinking about when we first met, Jack.'

'Oh, aye? Long ago and far away.'

'It was the same day that I met Glenda.'

'Was it? Oh, God, yes! I remember now. Vaguely. She had some kind of unsavoury job, didn't she?'

Hobbes nodded. 'She worked in a cinema.'

'A dirty-film show, that was it.'

'Anyway, Jack, it got me thinking.'

'Uh-huh.'

'It connects to a case I'm working on.'

'What does?'

'The day we met.'

Collingworth turned to look at him. They were standing only a foot apart. 'Now you've got me curious.' Worry settled on his face, as though he already knew what was coming.

Hobbes steeled himself. 'Jack . . .'

'Yes, what is it?'

'I'm here to talk about Georgie.'

Collingworth's hand pressed on the glass. The fingers splayed. He groaned. His whole body seemed to strain against some exterior force, and he wouldn't let go, wouldn't give in. Only the glass kept him from tumbling clean away. *Fifteen floors*. Hobbes wondered if his old friend had ever been tempted.

'I'm sorry. I'm sorry to bring this up now. I know—'

'What? What do you know?'

Bitterness had taken over Collingworth's voice. His hand was still pressed against the window. It looked to be stuck there. 'I found him, you know.'

'Who, Jack?'

'The bastard who took my son from me.'

Hobbes was shocked. He didn't know how to respond.

'1975, this was. December. Late one night on the Millwall Docks.'

'Jack, you didn't . . .'

The hand left the glass, bunched into a fist. 'Oh, don't worry, Henry. I won't *burden* you with the details. Whatever happened, I'll take it to my grave.' He made a soft noise, and a gesture: something falling into water.

Splash.

And then his voice took on a melodious tone. '*Sweet Thames run softly, till I end my song.*' He smiled, showing crooked teeth. 'Poetry, Henry. Your kind of thing, I seem to recall.'

Hobbes took a step back. He tried to reconcile what he'd just heard with what he knew of the facts. George Collingworth was Jack's son. He died in September 1962, a victim of a street brawl outside the Blind Beggar pub in Whitechapel. Beaten to death, his wallet taken. Someone spat in his face as the blood flowed. He was eighteen years old.

Collingworth was still standing there, his face turned away. Hobbes had no clue what he was thinking.

'Jack, come on. Let's have a sit-down, eh? Take the weight off.'

Collingworth responded, but in the strangest and most unexpected way. He turned and stepped towards Hobbes and, without any warning or sign, he attacked him. It was a pitiful assault, all told, but it came as such a surprise that Hobbes was caught off guard. There was a brief struggle, if it could be called that. It was all over in a few seconds, Collingworth's fists flailing about, hardly hitting any target. And then he half collapsed, the wind gone out of him.

Hobbes was now holding his former boss up, his hands under the shoulders.

Without him, Collingworth would have slid to the floor.

'Fuck it. Fuck it all to Hell and back.'

Spat out, whispered.

Not a single coin entered the swear jar.

Hobbes steered him back to the armchair. He looked around and saw a small cocktail bar in the corner of the room. He chose a brandy and poured it into a glass. Collingworth sipped, then took a bigger gulp. 'Christ, you're seeing me at my worst.'

'Yeah, I know that. But you're a strong bugger. That hasn't changed, has it? Eh?'

Collingworth nodded. He finished the brandy in a mouthful. 'What is it you want?'

Hobbes remained standing. He said. 'There was a film you used to watch. Your son was in it. He was an actor.'

'I know the one.'

'Jack, this is going to sound weird, but do you still have that film?'

There was no response.

Hobbes went on, 'We found it during the raid on the cinema

that day, when we first met. It was stashed with a pile of porn movies.'

Collingworth winced.

'But it wasn't a dirty film, was it? It was something else. A proper movie. A story, a drama. But made by the same director as the skin flicks.' ·

A single nod in reply.

Hobbes stepped closer. 'I know you used to watch it quite a bit. And later on, when we knew each other, you told me the story of it, and of your son.'

Collingworth stirred in his seat. 'You think this connects to a current case?'

'I'm sure of it, Jack. It's a homicide. A man in his sixties, beaten to death in a park. Truth is, I'm getting nowhere. There might be another victim, an earlier death.' He shook his head. 'I'm just not sure.'

'Sometimes you have to dig deep. At other times, all you have to do is brush away a single layer of dust. That's all.'

'Still with the lessons, Jack?'

'You look like you need it.' Collingworth managed a smile.

A moment passed.

Then he said, 'The second bedroom. There's a whole bunch of stuff in there. And an old projector. It still works.'

'Thank you.'

'But you can't take the film away.'

'No, no. Of course not. I'll watch it there. Is that OK?'

'Go on. But I won't join yer. Too painful.'

Hobbes felt awkward about leaving the room, about wandering around the flat unattended, but needs must. The second bedroom was tiny, filled with unwanted furniture and piles of books and magazines. A collection of films rested on a shelf, mainly Super 8 and 16-millimetre. Their boxes were marked with titles: *Georgie,*

7 yrs old; *Brighton holiday 1955*; *Georgie, first day at grammar school*; *George playing football, 1961.* Hobbes chose the final film in the row. He turned to the projector, which sat on a raised stand, and slotted the spool on to the empty spindle. He tried to thread the film through the machine, but couldn't quite work it out. A voice called, 'Christ, but you're hopeless. Here, let me, before you break something.' Collingworth was standing in the doorway. He took over the projector, while Hobbes closed the curtains at the window. The screen was already in place, against the far wall. Hobbes waited. He had viewed a few scenes of the film, those that involved George Collingworth, at Jack's behest, but that was a long time ago. Nineteen years! He didn't have a clue what he was going to see, or even if his assumptions were valid.

And then the film started, its monochrome images darkening the beam of light, spilling on to the screen like ink on water.

The Spell Makers
A film by Nick Greaves

Yes. This was it! That name. Directed by, written by, produced by. Hobbes gasped. The truth might now unfurl, unspool right before his eyes in fluttering pictures, in shades of grey, in the forms and faces of the young men and women who moved and danced and kissed and argued and even came to blows on the screen. But the imagery was cut-up, back to front, non-linear. It was like something by Godard, for Christ's sake! Was it a deliberate ploy on the director's part, to fragment reality in this way, to make a point about life . . . or was it a series of fumbling accidents? But all the viewer had to do was concentrate. Try to make it come together, to make sense in the mind. Because Hobbes knew that somewhere in this chaos lay a hidden truth.

There were four main characters, all young, teenagers or early twenties: one boy, three girls. Siblings. Their parents seen only now and then. They all lived in a rambling old house called Leigh Park Manor. Hobbes remembered that name from somewhere, and the name of the on-screen family: Parnell.

Of course! Mary Estelle Graves's novel. The film was a loose adaptation of *A Spell of Darkness*, removed from its original turn-of-the-century setting, relocated to 1962, and filled with the energy of that period. Yes, it was filmed in a different house, with actors playing the Graves children, but, still, this was Bridlemere in spirit. A realm of clues, of half-glimpsed shapes in the dark. What was it they said at the end of movies?

Any resemblance to actual persons, living or dead, is purely coincidental.

But sometimes it was deliberate, a metaphor.

The teenage boy in the film was called Kenneth. The three sisters: Ivy, Samantha and Belle. Three sisters, not two. Belle was the youngest by a good few years. Did she represent Adeline Graves? Hobbes found that his whole being was focused on her every appearance, every word she spoke.

But then Collingworth spoke at his side, breaking the spell. 'There's my boy now.'

George Collingworth played a minor character: one scene, only a few lines of dialogue. A visitor to the house who was teased by Samantha Parnell, and made fun of by Kenneth. But Hobbes could sense that Jack had relaxed a little, as this scene played out. His next line came in a whisper: 'This was the last proper thing he did in life, appear in this film.'

Hobbes didn't say anything.

'I did some digging around, after Georgie's death, but I could never find any trace of Nick Greaves.'

'No, it was a pseudonym. His real name is Nicholas Graves.'

'He's involved in your case, is he?'

'He's the victim.'

Collingworth nodded. Now that his son's appearance was over, he'd lost interest in the film. A few minutes later he left the room and closed the door behind him. Hobbes carried on alone. His eyes drank in the beauty of what he was seeing, the madness, the surreal nature of the poetic images, the startling changes of mood and perspective.

He witnessed the image he had viewed all those years ago, when he'd walked in on DI Collingworth and seen him crying. It was shortly after the character played by George had left the house.

A series of rapid jump cuts.

A dress lying on a table.

All the Parnells standing around.

Ivy Parnell using a pair of scissors to slice into the dress, at the midriff.

Samantha painting the cut with either blood or red paint.

Kenneth picking up the dress and hanging it from a hook on the wall.

Belle Parnell staring at the dress, her eyes wide.

The clock ticking, the sound of it overly loud.

A sudden splash of blood on Ivy's face.

A few more shots of the corridors of the house, a shadowy figure walking them, candle in hand. It was Belle. She sat on the floor of a bare room and placed the candle beside her. A flickering circle of light. Five small objects were placed one by one on the floorboards.

A cigarette card depicting a famous actress.

A silver medal.

A tube of lipstick.

A threepenny bit.

A brooch.

This was the final image.

The Spell Makers was a short film, perhaps half an hour long, probably unfinished. No end titles, no final credits, actors and crew members unnamed.

Hobbes changed the spools, rethreaded the film, and watched it again, or at least the first ten minutes. There was one image he wanted to examine in detail, now that he knew the story, or the lack of it, overall.

It was a kiss.

A kiss that took place in a darkened room, in a niche in the wall, hidden away: a kiss between brother and sister that went far beyond sibling kindness.

The Devil Himself

It was a kind of rage, a feeling that couldn't be explained. It came to him on the train journey back towards London. Hobbes was reading his copy of *A Spell of Darkness*. He'd started it last night in bed, and read a good chunk of it on the outward journey. Now he read the book in a different light, comparing it to the film he'd just seen. The two were related, but not in any obvious way. Taken on their own, neither would have caused much concern, but together, the fact that they had connecting points made Hobbes think that some hidden event or series of events had led to them both, novel and film. Mary Estelle and her son Nicholas had reacted to this event each in their own particular way.

One question: what was this central event?

A second question: why did its true nature have to be kept hidden?

He started to skip through the pages, seeking keywords that would give him a deeper insight. The Parnell family were as damaged as the Graveses, perhaps more so, exaggerated into a Gothic expression of tangled vines and dripping wounds and illicit meetings in moonlit gardens, and dreams of monstrous beings and *femmes fatales* and stunted passions. Everything in the novel – the house, the belongings, the food, the flesh – was ruined, broken, rotten to the core. And as Hobbes read the words on page

164 – *the room was too warm, the air too languid, nothing could be done, no movement made, and the night birds sang without melody on the branches of the birch trees* – it all became too much. He thought of Jack Collingworth and how he'd ended up, through mistakes of his own, of course, but still. There had to be a better way to end a life on the force.

And he sat there, his eyes half closed to the landscape flashing by the train window, in speckles of sunlight. He was fighting the anger, as he could. Jack, Glenda, Martin, the Graveses and their madness. But another feeling waited its turn, in the shadows. Layers of desire. He peeled them back, without meaning to. The memories of last night came to him, of standing in that room at Bridlemere, holding the dress to his face . . . and he was ashamed, ashamed of his own behaviour.

A woman across the way was staring at him.

Had he been mumbling out loud?

He smiled at her, turned away. Hoped she would do the same.

He tried to read, concentrating on Mary Estelle's story, but the meaning shifted in his mind and he could not grasp it.

The train moved on, in sight of the coast: sunlight thickening, but the clouds fierce and dark over the water.

Without realizing it, Hobbes had torn a page from the novel.

It was raining hard by the time they pulled into London's Victoria. He rang DS Latimer from a phone box outside the entrance. He asked about Rosamund Kepple.

'Nothing new, I'm afraid.'

'Still silent?'

'She hasn't left her home since getting out of hospital. Her son's been looking after her.'

'David?'

'Uh-huh. For whatever reason, she's living in fear.'

'Of what?'

'Retribution, probably. For killing her own brother.'

'You really think—'

'I felt like battering her one time, I really did. But you know me . . .'

'OK, don't worry about it. I have some thoughts.'

'I'll see you in a bit, then.'

Hobbes checked his watch: half past three. He had a bite to eat at a station café and read a few more pages of the novel. He drank two cups of terrible coffee, hoping to burn away the feelings that had taken him over on the train. It did little good, putting a veil on it, nothing more. But now . . .

An idea was forming in his mind.

A different way of seeing the mystery of the Graves family and their history.

Page 192 of the novel gave the vision substance.

He made his way to the railway station's car park. By the time he'd got back to Richmond, his head had cleared a little and his hands were firm on the wheel.

London was a welcome sickness after the seaside air of Margate: dark, overcrowded, noisy, vibrant, dangerous, a poem of good and ill.

Latimer greeted him at his desk. She was quick to speak. 'Where have you been?'

He shook his head at her, not wanting to explain. His meeting with Collingworth was too personal.

'You keeping secrets, Guv?'

'Same as you.'

'What does that mean?'

He didn't really want to push it, but the feelings were too strong, too deep. They couldn't be explained, not unless they were cut open.

'I went round to Fairfax's place last night.'

'Oh, yes? Any luck?'

'Tommy wasn't there. But his mum's worried.'

'She's always worried about something or other.'

Hobbes shifted some papers around on his desk. 'Tommy's working the Graves case on his own.'

'Well . . . didn't you want to involve him?'

'Yes, but—'

'But nothing, Guv. You started this.'

'He's going off the rails.'

Latimer gave him a cruel smile. 'I don't know what to make of you. There's always something new going on, and poor Tommy—'

'Yes. *Poor* Tommy.' There was bitterness in his voice.

They looked at each other.

It took a while, and then he said quietly, 'I know, Meg.'

'Do you? About what?'

She was playing it cool, but Hobbes could see the tiny quiver of a muscle above her cheekbone. 'I think . . .'

'Christ, what now?'

'I think you're going out with him.'

She laughed. That was all she could do. It came from nowhere, just mocking laughter.

'Going out with him! Really. What are you talking about?'

'His mum said—'

'That old bat, what does she—'

'Old? Really? She's not that much older than you.'

'What's that supposed to mean?'

'I think you know.'

They were both speaking quietly, hissing at each other. The other officers worked on at their desks, busy with their tasks.

The rain hit the windows at a sharp angle.

'Oh, God, is this why you came round last night? Is it? You were bothering Kathy.'

'I wasn't *bothering* her.'

'She said you looked crazy.'

'Well, is it true? You and Tommy? Is it?'

'How can you think that? I've got fourteen years on him!'

'Meg?'

Latimer looked away. Her mouth was set in a tight line, the lips almost invisible. And when she turned back, her eyes were fiery. She grabbed him by the arm and pulled him into a side office, little more than a storeroom. 'You've got a nerve,' she said.

'Yeah.'

He noticed that she hadn't closed the door: a way out?

'Let's hear it, Meg.'

'You wouldn't understand.'

And then she looked at him, her eyes deep and black, never blinking. She spoke from a true place.

'We get together, now and then—'

'I really don't—'

'Will you let me finish, please.'

'OK, I'm sorry. Go on.'

She took one more look at the bullpen through the open door. She waited until an officer had walked by, then said, 'You know . . . it's not that kind of relationship.'

'What kind?'

'The kind you're thinking of.'

'I'm not thinking anything.'

'You're thinking the worst thoughts. I know you.'

'So?'

'We never . . . not like that . . . Oh, God, it was just strange . . . weird.'

'Why am I feeling nervous?'

'He wanted me to re-enact the events.'

'What?'

'To play out the events, you know, of the night when he . . . when he attacked that cop, with the tyre-iron, and everything. We had to play it out, going over the lines again and again, with Tommy changing it slightly each time.'

Hobbes couldn't believe what he was hearing.

'You went along with this?'

She nodded. 'I wasn't sure, at first.'

'No, I can imagine.'

'But later, as we—'

'This happened more than once?'

'A few times, yes.'

Hobbes groaned. He rubbed his eyes. Images swirled in his head. 'And which part did you play? Oh, God, please tell me he didn't handcuff you to the radiator. Like . . . like . . .'

'It was play-acting, that's all. And, anyway, often we swapped roles.'

'Well, that's something.' He sounded bitter. 'You took turns?'

'That's good, isn't it? It makes it less . . . *weird*. Well, I thought so, anyway.'

'Of course.'

'And one time . . .' Her voice lowered further. 'One time he rented the room, you know, in the hostel, where it all happened. Two nights running, actually.'

'Jesus.'

'The true effect. The moment itself. It was amazing!'

'That's how you're describing it?'

'I mean, it helped Tommy, it really did.'

Hobbes wanted to laugh. 'The other night he was drunk, off his head, stomping around a crime scene like an idiot.'

'Because . . . because he's better now, he's working. He's searching.'

'This is fucked up, Meg.'

'Oh, totally. You couldn't get more fucked up. But here's the truth.' She had Hobbes's complete attention. 'The truth is, I do love him. I love Tommy. It's not the sort of love his mum's thinking about, nothing like that, nothing at all. But there it is.'

Having said this, Latimer sighed. She lowered her head. He could see her hands, one worrying at the other, spinning a silver ring around an index finger over and over. 'I'm forty-two. Divorced. No kids. This shitty job.'

'What's that got to do with anything?'

'Like it or lump it, I can do what the hell I like. And further-more,' she drew a hard breath, 'I don't give a monkey's arsehole what you or any of the other guys say about me.'

Hobbes nodded at this. He knew it was true. 'You and Tommy seem to hate each other. Most of the time.'

'We do, when we're not having a laugh about it. But lately . . .'

'He needs help?'

'We're cops. And we stick together. And that means for good or bad.'

Hobbes remembered that Fairfax had said a similar thing: *It's a knife-edge. Good, or bad.* And for a copper, that was the most difficult of all balancing acts. Christ, but it got to you! It was so easy to tip, one way or the other . . .

'You'll have words with him, Meg?'

'About what?'

'Tell him to stop. To stop looking into the Graves case.'

'You started that, showing him the photographs.'

'Didn't you encourage him as well? I've seen his room. There's stuff in there – names, addresses, details – only you could have given to him.'

Latimer was irritated. 'I don't get you, Guv. Do you want him back in here? Or not?'

Hobbes walked out of the office. His voice was cold. 'My only concern is to make sure Fairfax doesn't cock up our investigation.'

'He won't.' She followed him out. 'I'm sure of it. I won't let that happen.'

'After what you've told me today, I just don't know . . .'

'One last chance. That's all.'

'I'm sure you've said that before, about him.'

The telephone was ringing on Latimer's desk. She snatched it up. 'This had better be good!' And then she went quiet, and listened. Worry crossed her face.

Hobbes came close.

She said into the phone. 'He's here? Really?'

And she listened some more. 'No, keep him there. I'll be right down.'

She put the phone in its cradle.

'What is it?' Hobbes asked.

'The devil himself.'

'You mean—'

'It's Tommy. Down in Reception.'

'What does he want?'

'I don't know, but he wants to talk to me.'

'I'll come along.'

'Aye, I think you should, Henry. Oh, God, I hope he's not drunk again. Or worse.'

'Well, let's see.'

They took the lift down to the ground floor. Hobbes really didn't know what to expect, but the sight of Fairfax shocked him. Dishevelled wasn't the word for it. He was filthy, head to foot, his jeans covered with mud, his jacket wet through. The collar torn. His hair was long and tangled, water dripping from it into his eyes. He raised a hand to wipe it away. His fingers were caked with dirt. There was a bruise on his face. A day or so old. Christ. What now?

Latimer went to him first; Hobbes held himself back.

But Fairfax wanted them both; he tried to speak, and failed. But his mouth was lit up in a huge grin. It was absurd, gleeful beyond measure.

What the hell was he laughing at?

Latimer was talking to him, keeping it low. His hands were on her shoulders, then her waist. Hobbes had had enough. He came forward. 'What the hell are you doing here?'

Fairfax turned to him. 'Boss.' His eyes widened. 'I found her! I *found* her!' He was almost dancing.

'Found who?'

But he didn't answer. Latimer tried to keep him still. 'Tommy? Who did you find?'

'The sister.'

Hobbes wasn't sure what he'd just heard.

'You mean . . .'

'The one, the only. I found her!'

Fairfax turned around, his arms waving madly. He drew them both over to a row of seats. And sitting there, beneath a poster advising against letting strangers into your house, was a woman with a certain look about her, a familial likeness.

'Camilla Graves.' Fairfax introduced her with a bow. 'I found her, Meg, do you see?'

'Yes, yes, I do, Tommy. I see that. You did it.'

The woman on the seat stared at Hobbes, unblinking, her face set in one expression.

It was a look of pure hatred.

A Gift from Grandmother

Tommy Fairfax sat in the chair at Latimer's desk. Someone had brought him a cup of tea from the machine and now he sipped it. His shirt was still wet and he stank of the downpour, of dirt and rain. A whole bunch of officers had gathered around, watching the scene, muttering among themselves. Hobbes told them to get back to work.

'Well, then . . . Fairfax. What have you done this time?'

The answer came in a breath, and Hobbes had to lean in to hear it properly. 'What did you say?'

'My duty. Sir.'

It was crazy. A stupid answer.

'Did you harm her in any way? Did you lay a hand on her?'

'No. No. Meg, tell him I'm not like that.'

'I know what you're like,' Hobbes said, 'and that's the trouble. How come you're so filthy?'

'I fell over. It was muddy. That's all.'

'You smell of booze.'

'That's yesterday's. It's hard to clean off.'

'You didn't force her to come here?'

'I did nothing!' His voice rose, causing the other officers to look over again.

'Let's take this somewhere quieter,' Latimer said. 'Maybe it's best—'

'No. No, we keep it clear. Above board. He's a liability.'

'What? Me?' Fairfax looked from one to the other. 'I found her for you. Me! I did it. I need to be . . .' His voice trailed off. Then he found his vigour again. 'I need my reward.'

'Oh. For fuck's sake.'

Hobbes moved away. He stood with his back to the desk, his hands clenched. He felt like punching a hole in the wall. But instead he drew in his breath, turned back and said, in a calm tone, 'I need to know everything you did, Fairfax, from the beginning.'

'Of course. Whatever's best.'

'Go on.'

'It's simple. I did what needed to be done, my civic duty. Like I said.'

'And what was that?'

'I waited for her. I waited, and I waited. I sat there on the bench with my sandwiches and my Thermos, and I waited.'

'Where was this?'

'The cemetery.'

'You mean Richmond Cemetery?'

Fairfax nodded. He took a gulp of tea, which calmed him a little. 'Right there, where Leonard Graves is buried.'

'When was this? Today?'

'Every day. Every single day since the funeral, because I thought, you know, why wouldn't the children turn up? They had to, eventually, in private, like, or at least that's what I thought, right? Meg, you tell him, make him believe me.'

'I think he does.' Latimer laid a hand on his shoulder. 'Just tell your story.'

'Yeah, so there I was, every day. I chose to sit there at lunch-times, and then later on in the day, just in case she was working, Camilla I mean, or maybe she was retired, I didn't know, I didn't know anything. So then I started coming earlier, and leaving later, and then, today this was, I decided to get there at eleven and stay as long as I could. I brought my flask with me. Tea, mind. Nothing stronger.' He seemed overly proud of this fact. 'So there I was, on stake-out, like.'

Both Hobbes and Latimer were quiet now, letting Fairfax speak. 'I waited!'

It was said in the same manner another man might announce, *I stood my ground and let the enemy approach, my rifle at the ready, bayonet drawn.*

But his worry soon returned. 'I didn't touch her. I said that, didn't I?'

'You did.' Latimer comforted him.

'She took off, once I made myself known, tried to get away. Made for the trees. I went after her, but I slipped. Oh . . .' He seemed to notice the state of his clothes for the first time. 'Oh, God, look at me. This is really bad.'

He brushed at his jeans ineffectually.

Hobbes asked him, 'So why did she come with you, Tommy?'

'She gave up, I think. That's how I see it. She stopped moving suddenly. Like she was waiting for me to catch up.'

'Did she say anything? Then, or in the car?'

'I didn't have a car. I took a taxi. Oh, yeah, can I get expenses for that, or what?'

'Tommy . . .'

'Only I'm a bit skint, you know what I mean?'

'What did she say to you?'

'One thing.'

'What was it?'

'That it was time now. Time to tell the truth.'

Hobbes stepped back a little. Latimer came to his side. She spoke quietly: 'So what do you think?'

'I don't know what to think.'

'But he did good, didn't he? Admit that.'

'No. No, he didn't—'

'Hobbes, come on. He found her, which is more than we managed.'

'He stumbled into her, that's all. He waited around until she—'

'What difference does it make?'

He stared at Latimer and shook his head. And then they looked at Fairfax, who was getting to his feet, his voice clearly heard: 'When do we start? Let's do it.'

Latimer took hold of him. 'What is it? What do you want?'

'I want to interview her. I want to sit in.'

'No. No.' Hobbes shook his head. 'No, Fairfax. You're going home now.'

'Home?'

'That's right.'

'But I did my bit.'

'You did, and I'm pleased that you did.'

'I did well.'

'You did very well.'

'So I can come back, right? Is that what it means?'

'Maybe. I don't know.'

Fairfax nodded at this, as though he couldn't quite work out what it meant. He started to speak, stopped, took a thought, and said, 'OK, OK, boss. I'll get myself a sarnie in the canteen, and I'll . . . I'll wait around for news of when you've finished. That's it.' He looked at Hobbes with such intensity. 'Would that be suitable, uh, suitable behaviour?'

Hobbes sighed. 'Yeah, sure. Get yourself something to eat.'

'I will. I'll do just that.'

Fairfax smiled broadly. He looked around the room, the snake pit as he called it, the bullpen, his old stomping ground. And he called to an officer: 'Chadwick! It's me. I'm here. I'm back.'

The officer in question looked over and raised a hand in greeting.

Hobbes spoke kindly this time. 'Come on, then, let's get you sorted. Meg?'

'I'll look after him.'

Latimer led Fairfax away. Hobbes watched them go, until the door had swung closed. He gave it a moment, to gather his thoughts. His hands were shaking; he hadn't noticed until now. Then he went into the corridor and took the stairs to Interview Room B. He looked through the one-way glass at the subject in question.

Camilla Graves.

There she was. Face cold. No expression. Nothing. Only that sense of hatred. A statue. Eyes directed straight ahead.

A female constable stood to attention near the door.

Camilla was staring at her.

Hobbes watched as the constable shivered a little.

Camilla Graves was fearsome. This would not be easy.

Black hair, long, loose, no real style to it.

Eyes deep set, cheeks drawn in, the Gravesian look. An animal preparing to pounce. Perfectly still.

No cigarette, no tea. Not even a sip of water. None of the things that people usually reached for at times like this, with the police bearing down.

Dress functional: trousers, shirt, a jacket, all dark, muted.

No jewellery, not even a ring.

What was she? Mid to late fifties? This was a face that had held time at bay, quite naturally. Very few lines, brow clear, a wrinkle at the neck when she bent forward.

A fingernail scratching at the tabletop.

It's time. Time to tell the truth. Wasn't that what she'd said to Fairfax?

Well, then, let's see. Let's test her.

Latimer came into the room and stood at Hobbes's side.

'Are we ready?'

'I hope so.'

Together they entered the interview room. Hobbes dismissed the constable, thanking her. He clicked on the tape recorder and sat down, Latimer next to him.

Hobbes placed a hardback book on the table, its front cover uppermost, but turned away from Camilla Graves. She didn't even look at it.

For a moment no one spoke.

Then: 'Your name?'

'Camilla Graves. Although . . .'

'Yes?'

'I'm not known by that, these days.'

'You're married?'

'I used to be. But I'm still using his name.'

'Which is?'

'Is this important?'

'Everything's important.'

She swore under her breath, then gave her answer: 'Camilla Greene.'

Hobbes stared at her. 'You're very secretive.'

'I like to hide myself away, that's true.'

'Why?'

'I don't want my brother and sister bothering me. So I never gave them my address.'

Latimer asked, 'You don't like them?'

'They don't like me.'

'This is why you didn't turn up at your father's funeral? To avoid them?'

Camilla nodded.

'Why don't they like you?'

'Because of what I know, the things I saw, the things they did. That we all did.'

'Which is what? What did you do?'

But there was no direct answer this time, only: 'I imagine they hate me.'

And then silence.

Latimer asked, 'Did you know your father left everything to you, in his will?'

She seemed genuinely surprised. 'Really? I didn't know that.'

'He says that you should, quote, *do with it as you see fit.*'

'I'll follow his instructions.' Then she laughed to herself. 'I would love to have seen Rosamund's face, when she found out.'

Hobbes took over. 'How old are you?'

'Fifty-five.'

'And you're working as . . .'

'I run a guesthouse, in Southend.'

'Children?'

'No. I'm alone in life.' Her eyes closed momentarily, the lids flickering.

'Mrs Greene?'

'There's no one.' It was said quietly, as though to herself.

Hobbes nodded. He was keeping this straight, professional, as cold as Camilla was, in return. But he knew there would be gaps, where the truth might be hiding, the real truth, beyond what she might offer.

He said, 'If I asked where you were on the night your brother Nicholas was killed, how would you answer?'

'I was at home.'

'Is there proof of this?'

'Well, I have no guests at this time of year, with this weather we've been having.'

'Can anyone vouch for you?'

Her eyes locked on his. 'I can vouch for myself.'

'That's not good enough.'

'I didn't kill Nicholas.'

It was said with utter conviction.

Hobbes matched her mood. 'Still, we need more than that.'

'There is no more.'

He let it go. For a moment no one spoke. And then: 'You're the daughter of Leonard and Mary Estelle Graves, Is that correct?'

'It is.'

Hobbes leaned over slightly, asking, 'The youngest daughter?'

Camilla stared at him. The hatred was back in her face. It seemed to be habitual, a physical fixture that was only occasionally masked.

And then she smiled.

'No, not the youngest. The second youngest.'

And so it began.

'Who is the youngest child? Her name, please.'

'Adeline. Adeline Graves.'

'Is Adeline alive, or dead?'

'She's dead. Sadly.'

'Did she die of a stab wound?'

'That's right.'

'Is she buried in a dress of blue and yellow flowers?'

'She is.'

'Where is her body?'

That smile again, the teeth on view. They were quite yellow, the only real evidence of age on her body, of time passing, of decay.

'Camilla. Where is the body of your sister? Do you know?'

She wouldn't answer.

Latimer asked, 'Do you know who killed her? Will you tell us that?'

Still no response.

'And what about Nicholas? Do you know who killed him?'

'I can only imagine he overstepped the mark in some way. You must know by now that he had somewhat unusual . . . tastes.'

'You think a stranger killed him? Someone he tried to pick up?'

She brushed this aside with a cold gesture. 'I'm not here to talk about Nicholas. I have no feelings for him. Only for Adeline.'

'You said to the officer who found you today that you wanted to tell the truth.'

'I do.'

'So?'

'I'm trying to.'

Latimer's voice grew harsh. 'Try harder.'

Camilla scoffed. She held Latimer's stare and wouldn't let it go. Hobbes could see that Camilla needed to be in charge of this, of the interview, the whole situation. She was used to such things, to being in control.

He said, in a gentler voice, 'Why don't you tell us the story?'

She took a moment before answering, and her words were surprising. She said, 'Tell me, Inspector, have you ever heard of Jules Cotard?'

'Is this important?'

'He was a French neurologist. In 1880, he described a new condition, a delusion. He called it the Delirium of Negation.'

'Why are you telling us this?'

'Because it explains why Adeline had to die.'

Latimer asked, 'Was she suffering from this delusion?'

'Yes, I believe so. But I only knew this later, when I did my research in the library . . .' She caught a breath. Stopped speaking. And a great sadness came over her features, and a weariness.

Latimer pushed on, or tried to: 'What form does this delusion take?'

But Camilla would not answer.

Hobbes had to prompt her again. 'Do you or do you not want to talk to us?'

'Of course. Of course I do. I desperately do.'

'Well, then?'

'It's too . . . too painful. Too much is at stake.'

Hobbes nodded. 'Yes, I can see that.'

'If I tell you, there will be consequences. And that scares me.'

'That someone might be punished?'

'More than that. Much more.'

The heat had been turned up in the room. It was sweltering.

Hobbes tried a different tack. 'Can you talk about your childhood?'

He felt sure that Camilla Greene was going to divert the question yet again, but instead she brought her hands into sight on the tabletop and locked them together. She spoke in a strained manner, recalling past events, as from another life.

'Our parents were strange in so many ways. Mother was a devout Catholic, my father a serious artistic type, very much a Bohemian, at least in his own mind. They made a bizarre coupling. But I do believe they were in love, enough anyway to produce four children.'

'There was a gap before Adeline came along?'

'Yes, a long gap. I was ten years old by then.' Camilla nodded.

'Yes. A lovely child. I took to her, I must say. She was closer to me than she was to Rosamund.'

'Rosamund didn't like her?'

'Not really. No. But she was a teenager at the time, so she had other things on her mind. As did Nicholas.'

'What about your parents? How were they with the child?'

'They welcomed her, at first.'

'And then?'

'Father was at his peak as a writer, and a director, and he often worked late, or travelled the country with new productions. So he wasn't home for stretches at a time. But he was always very kind to Adeline, whenever he was around, bringing her little presents.'

'And Mary Estelle?' Hobbes asked.

Camilla hesitated. 'You have to understand. Mother was nearing her forties. Her career had stalled. I think she resented Adeline's presence. She could hear the tolling of the bell, if you know what I mean?'

Latimer nodded. 'She was getting older?'

'In terms of being a theatrical presence, yes. For women on the stage, it is a difficult transition. And she wasn't getting the older female's roles, sadly. But Leonard's plays were still doing well, and he was now working with younger actresses, in the roles that Mother first played and made famous. They were always very good-looking, these new young actresses, and, well, you can imagine how Mary Estelle must have felt, seeing them on the stage, and watching her husband directing them.'

'She was jealous.'

'Yes, of course, although she would never admit it. She became quite reclusive, rarely leaving the house. Keeping to herself, locking herself in her room. So we had the run of the place, myself and little Adeline. We would play Hide and Seek for hours on end. Bridlemere was filled with little cubbyholes and alcoves.'

'So you became a kind of mother figure to your younger sister?'

A look of regret came over Camilla's face. Regret, tinged with anger. 'Well, someone had to do it. But I was glad. Yes. I enjoyed playing with her, teaching her things, making up stories and little plays, acting them out together.'

She looked from one officer to the other, her eyes slightly unfocused. 'That house . . . It was so large, and so dark, filled with shadows, and ghosts, and old stories. You could feel the dead residents in the air like so much dust you might choke on at night. Such feelings . . . they would make me shiver.'

Hobbes asked, 'Did you have a nanny, or a governess?'

'We did. Mrs Braithwaite. She lived with us, and had done for years. She even helped Mother with the births, bringing each of us into the world. There were women like that, back then. Servants, retainers, helpers. In their way, mistresses of the house.'

'What happened to her, this Mrs . . . ?'

'Braithwaite. She retired. And died soon afterwards. Which meant that Adeline and I had the freedom to do as we liked.' Camilla fell silent. And then she said, 'I would like some water, please.'

Latimer filled a plastic tumbler and pushed it across the table.

'Thank you.' She drank it all in one go. 'It's very difficult,' she said, 'talking about Adeline. It's a story of such pain and strife. It's a wonder she lasted as long as she did.'

Latimer asked, 'There was something wrong with her?'

Camilla looked up. Her eyes were full of darkness. 'Not at first. We all thought she was a wonderful child, but then we heard that she was having problems at school.'

'With discipline? Or learning difficulties?'

'Both. But she wasn't . . . I mean, she wasn't stupid. She was intelligent, I think, in her own way. But something was holding her back. And sometimes, at home, she scared me, even when she was seven or eight . . . She would play the strangest games, mutilating her dolls, setting fire to books.'

Camilla shook her head, in shame of remembering, and of bringing such private things into the light.

'It all came to a head when Adeline reached puberty. By that time, she had left school, and was living at home. She was quite the young beauty, having some of Mary Estelle's looks. She was the only one of us girls to inherit our mother's auburn hair. I was always jealous of that.' A tiny smile at this thought. 'I tried to teach her things, to keep her up to date. But she was very self-contained. She was moving away from me.'

Her hands shook. She reached for the tumbler, saw it was empty, and didn't seem to know what to do, or even what to ask for. Latimer poured her more water.

Camilla sipped it without speaking.

Hobbes gave her a moment. He glanced at his watch. They'd been speaking for less than thirty minutes, and he felt that Camilla Greene was beginning to crack open. There was a great amount of pain in her body, and her mind.

Now he rapped his fist on the tabletop quite harshly and spoke without compassion: 'Shall we continue.' It wasn't a question.

Camilla looked at him. For a moment she seemed not to recognize the inspector at all, or Latimer. And she said, 'I am alone now. Nicholas has gone. Father has gone. My mother is lost in her own world. Rosamund and I will never speak to each other.'

'What about Adeline?'

'Adeline . . .'

There was a puzzled look on her face.

'I'm sorry, I don't . . . I can't . . .'

Hobbes studied Camilla, her every twitch, every little flicker of her eyes. She stared back at him, clearly uncomfortable under his gaze. She was fearful. He saw that now.

A scared woman, lost in her own loneliness.

He took a few easy breaths and held her gaze. Without emotion, he said, 'Camilla . . . I don't believe you. Not one word.'

He could sense Latimer tensing at his side, but he didn't look her way, no, he kept his eyes forwards. He forced his suspect – yes, he saw her that way now – he forced his suspect to lose control.

'I don't . . . I don't know what you mean.'

He didn't let her finish. 'I don't believe you. You're lying – about the house, and your childhood, and about Adeline, and about Adeline's parents.'

And at this last statement, those few words, an extreme reaction took over, a craziness held barely at bay: her shoulders hunched and her hand squeezed the paper cup until it crumpled in her grasp. A sob escaped her lips.

'Camilla, talk to me. What really happened?'

She shook her head. 'I can't.' She looked like a broken doll trying to come alive, and failing miserably. 'I cannot tell you.'

Hobbes pushed the novel across the table. He quoted the title to her.

'*A Spell of Darkness.*'

'Yes.' Camilla worried at her lower lip with her teeth.

'Is this what you're under now, a spell? A long-lasting spell cast by your family, your parents, many years ago. Are you still caught up in it?'

'Yes.'

The single word was a dark breath only. And then repeated. 'Yes, yes.'

'Well, you have to talk. I need to know the truth. Because – and I'm going to state this plainly – I am puzzled. I have no clue as to what happened in that house, with the dresses, and the rips in the cloth, the bloodstains and the cellar.' His words bit down hard. 'There was a dress, buried in the cellar! A woman's dress.'

Camilla flinched at his tone. She trembled. 'I cannot. We will not. You have no right—'

'I have every right!' he shouted at her. His words echoed in the tiny space, and then died, and in the silence Camilla Greene collapsed into herself – head bowed, face hidden, both hands gripping the table's edge. And she would not speak. Her fingers tightened. Her nails might break.

She was eaten by pain, halfway to darkness.

Latimer spoke softly: 'Camilla, look at me.'

She did so, and she said immediately, 'I am here of my own volition. Isn't that true?'

'Of course.'

'So I can leave. I can just walk away, and that's that?'

'No. Not quite.' The more Latimer spoke, the more her voice hardened. 'If you've done something wrong, or if you know of any wrongdoing, we need to hear about it.'

The two women stared at each other.

Until at last Camilla's hands relaxed, her grip loosened. Hobbes took this as a sign. He tapped at the book's cover, saying, 'This morning I watched a film. It was called *The Spell Makers*. You know of it, I presume?'

Camilla nodded.

'You've seen it?'

Another nod, smaller than the first.

'So you know what the film was about?'

'I do. And it disgusts me.'

Hobbes put a hand on the novel. 'Now, this book by your mother, and the film by your brother, they both deal with similar ideas and themes. They might almost be circling around the same subject. But here's the thing. That subject matter is hidden. In both cases. Hidden below the surface. But on occasion it seems to rise, to be put almost on view.' He looked at her. 'Camilla, can you help us with that?'

Her face was set, but it was a struggle to keep it so.

Hobbes kept on, giving no leeway: 'Have you read *A Spell of Darkness*?'

'No.'

'I find that difficult to believe. You own mother's—'

'I've read a few pages. I don't need . . .'

'What?'

'Our mother used our lives for her own ends. Her own children's lives! She tried to make money from us, to forge a new career for herself, from our travails. And then Nicholas tried the same trick.'

Hobbes nodded. 'But I imagine many artists do that.'

'There's no excuse. And, thankfully, in both cases the attempt failed. The book did not sell well. And the film was never finished.'

Hobbes opened the novel at a marked page. 'I'd like to read you a passage.'

A shrug. But she tensed as Hobbes started to read: ' "The night closed around them. The two of them, man and woman, brother and sister. The night enclosed them and kept them warm in their loneliness." ' His voice was soft, intoning. ' "Not a word passed between them. Their embrace went further than either of them thought it should go. They were breaking a law, a law of the house, and a law of the land." '

Camilla Greene stood up from the table.

Hobbes stopped reading.

He watched her as she turned her back on him.

Just standing there.

Nothing.

No sign of any life or emotion. Other than the turning away.

He carried on reading, finishing the passage: ' "The wild shadows of that long night, the flesh of the night, when they had both faced the wrath of their father, were now settled. Only the darkness remained; the darkness, and the dreams they shared, and the love that might yet be roused." '

A single word: 'Enough.'

Hobbes followed the request. He closed the book.

Camilla turned to face the two officers.

She'd been crying.

She sat down at the table and looked at them both, without blinking, her eyes still wet.

Latimer said, 'Camilla, I think you have something to tell us. A secret of some kind. But something is holding you back. Is that true?'

A quick nod in answer.

'What do we have to do to make you speak?'

'I want him to leave.' She looked at Hobbes. 'I will speak to the other officer, the one who found me.'

'Detective Fairfax?'

'Yes.'

Hobbes made to speak, but Latimer placed her hand on his sleeve.

Camilla Greene was smiling at him. There was an edge of cruelty to it.

He stood up and walked out of the room. Latimer followed him, and she arranged for the female constable to return to her watch. Hobbes was staring through the glass.

'Christ, Meg.'

'I know, I know.'

'We're so close. She just won't speak.'

'So then?'

'But he's a mess. Fairfax! He'll fuck it up, I know he will.'

'He sat in the rain, in the land of the dead. Would you have done that?'

'That isn't how police work is done.'

'Ah, to hell with that. What choice do we have?'

He couldn't answer that one. Latimer gave him a moment, then said, 'Look, he's still an officer, isn't he?' Hobbes nodded. 'So DC Fairfax is still on the books. His leave of absence has been worked through. We're not doing anything wrong.'

He could think of arguments against her reasoning, but none of them mattered, not really, not when he looked back into the interview room and saw Camilla Greene sitting there. It was enough. He said, 'OK. Let's try it.'

'You want me to fetch him?'

'No, no. I'll do it.'

He took the lift down to the basement level, where the canteen was situated. His mind was filled with doubt still, and he had this stupid petty fear as well that when he entered the canteen DC Fairfax would be surrounded by his colleagues, the men laughing at his ribald jokes, the women gazing at him, smiling . . .

But Fairfax was alone.

A cup of tea. No 'sarnie'. A half-eaten custard tart.

Hobbes sat down opposite to him.

Neither of them spoke.

Fairfax went for a cigarette, decided against it. 'Well, here we are.'

'Indeed.'

Fairfax sipped at his tea. 'What was it Kennedy used to call this stuff? Sump feed, bilge water, cat piss. He had a hundred names.'

'Kennedy?'

'Yeah, DS. First name, Dan. Danny Boy. Dan the Man.'

'Before my time.'

'Right. Right. Of course.'

And the conversation petered out.

Hobbes rubbed at his eyes. 'Your mum's worried about you.'

'You think I don't know that?'

'There's blood in your bed, on the towels.'

'Ah, Jesus.'

'What happened? You get in a fight?'

'Yeah, some bastard was badmouthing us, disparaging Her Majesty's finest, you know what I'm saying?'

'I do. You were drunk?'

'Aye, generally pissed off at life. I don't know where, some old pub or other.'

'Fairfax?'

'Yeah?'

'What did you say to Camilla Greene?'

'Oh . . . not much.'

'You persuaded her to come in. How did you do that?'

'The usual rigmarole.'

'I just need to know what you said to her.'

Fairfax finished his tea, and finally went for that cigarette. He lit it with the match that Hobbes offered. And only then did he speak.

'She was crying. Crying at the graveside, wiping her eyes with a handkerchief. That gave me my first clue. So I sauntered over. First of all I asked for her name. Or rather, I offered her name to her. Like . . . *Camilla Graves?* And she turned to me and looked surprised. And then I said, "I'm with the police." You notice, I hope, sir, I didn't say I *was* police. I said I was working *with* the police. Without my card on me. You see, I know the rules.'

Hobbes nodded. He didn't say anything.

'It had started to rain by then. And it all got a bit nasty. Nasty word-wise, I mean. She called me something I don't like to hear a woman say, or a man. Unless it's Latimer, of course—'

'Fairfax.'

'There was a bit of a struggle.'

'Christ, I asked you—'

'No, more like I just slipped. It was muddy! All churned up. I was in a right old state.'

'And?'

'Sure, right. The story. The details, as requested. So then I tried to calm her down. I said, "Actually, I'm not with the police, not as such. I lied, just a little. They kicked me out, leave of absence, and I'm still wondering whether I should go back or not, or whether my boss would even have me back."'

'You said all this?'

'That I did. Words to that effect. Anyways, I think that calmed her down a bit, like she wasn't expecting me to arrest her or anything stupid like that. So then I went for my killer line.'

'Which was?'

Fairfax's eyes sparkled. 'I said, "Are you the lipstick or the brooch?"'

'What?'

'The five objects, in the jewellery box, right? You gave me the photographs.'

'Yes, but—'

'Haven't you worked it out yet? They each represent a different member of the family. The medal is the father's, Leonard, obviously. The cigarette card of Greta Garbo, that's Mary Estelle, the great actress. The threepenny bit . . . that threw me a little, until I noticed the date on the coin: 1919. The year Nicholas Graves was born.'

'Did Latimer tell you that?'

'Nah, it was in the *Sun*. Nicholas Graves, aged sixty-two.'

Hobbes had to smile. He said, 'So that left the brooch and the lipstick?'

'Correct.'

By now Fairfax was in his element. He was leaning forward, puffing at his cigarette between phrases, the other hand moving constantly to express his excitement.

'Each member of the family placed an object in the cellar grave, with the dress. An object that meant something to them, that represented them. It's so fuckin' pure. Oh—'

And he stopped.

'What's wrong now?'

'I hope Meg won't get in trouble? She gave me some information, when I asked.'

'Don't worry about that.'

'Good. Good. Because I wouldn't—'

'You were saying, Tommy: lipstick or brooch?'

Fairfax nodded. 'Camilla didn't answer me at first. We'd walked on a bit by then, and she was looking down at another grave. So I made a guess. I said, "I'm reckoning the lipstick belongs to Rosamund, the elder daughter. But the brooch, I don't know, it's old-looking, an antique." And she spoke then. She said, "Yes, it belonged to my grandmother, Philippa. She gave it to me a few days before she died."' Fairfax smiled, and he said to Hobbes, 'That was the name on the grave, you see, where she had led me. Philippa Layne. The grandma. Died in 1934, according to the stone.'

'I see.'

'But that wasn't enough. No. I needed to . . . Well, the last detail, you know? I remember you saying that once, Guv. It's the very last detail that counts.'

Hobbes shrugged.

'So I remembered, right, that one of the gems was missing. So

I said to her, "Camilla, did you lose a ruby from the brooch?" And she nodded, and told me yes, that she'd been playing with it one day and had managed to prise the stone free and it rolled under the sofa. She never could find it, and she was upset by that, wondering if Grandma might be watching her from above. "It must still be there," she said, "somewhere in that house, that terrible house." And then she . . . well, Camilla just kind of gave in. She wanted to talk, to tell everything, to be taken to the police station.' Fairfax kept his gaze on Hobbes. 'And that's it. That's the story.'

Hobbes didn't say anything.

A moment passed.

He took something from his inside jacket pocket.

It was a black leather folder with a police warrant card inside it.

He slid it across the table.

Fairfax looked at it. His hand reached out. 'What do you want me to do? Talk to her?'

'No. *Listen*. Listen to her. The occasional word of encouragement.'

'OK. I can do that.'

'No messing about now, Tommy, no games, no tactics.'

'Absolutely.' Fairfax smiled.

'Because if you cock up again, I swear, you'll be gone. And gone for good.'

'Right. Sir. Noted.'

'What changed your mind? About coming back.'

'This case. Nothing more. The puzzle of it all.'

Hobbes kept his face cold. Even now, he couldn't help feeling he'd made a mistake, but the move was there to be made. He led Fairfax back up to the second floor. Neither man spoke on the way.

Latimer was waiting for them. 'Are we good?' she said.

'I hope so.'

Ten minutes later DC Fairfax was sitting at the table, opposite to Camilla Greene. DS Latimer was standing in a corner, keeping herself to herself.

This tiny space. Interview Room B.

It was all about one thing only: a woman talking.

The Hidden Room

She started quietly with the sentence, 'I wandered the corridors alone.' And she kept the same hushed tone for the first few minutes, until she had found a flow and then she spoke more easily. Soon after this Camilla's conviction faltered again and she made a visible effort to keep the story going. Her face would screw tight at these times, and her hands would clench. Twice she lit a cigarette and smoked each one only halfway down, stubbing it out with a look of disgust on her face. Fairfax kept quiet for most of this, nodding at certain points, sipping at a glass of water, asking an occasional question. Latimer stood against the wall, perfectly still, perfectly upright, listening intently.

'I wandered the corridors alone at night, staying up as late as I liked. Nobody cared for me, really. I was a free spirit lost in that ugly house, in the shadows.'

Hobbes stood in the dark of the viewing room, his face almost touching the glass. He never took his eyes off Camilla; he never stopped listening. Every word, every detail.

'And sometimes when I awake, even now, all these years later, I find I have dreamed myself back there, to the house called Bridlemere. Those same corridors, the same shadows and the clock ticking on the first-floor landing.'

Now Camilla stopped, her story momentarily lost.

Fairfax urged her on gently. Hobbes paid no attention to his words, only to the woman, her face, her expression, those hidden thoughts.

She made a decision and said, 'I was nine years old. It was early in the year of 1936. Leonard, our father, was on tour with a play. He'd been away for a week or more. Mummy had been her usual self, getting drunk, staying in her room, shouting at us from afar in that glorious voice of hers, screaming sometimes, God knows for what purpose, or why. But Rosamund always took the brunt of it. She was always being called to the room, and told off for some imagined crime. Mary Estelle's dreams had turned on her, and were eating her alive. It's pitiful, thinking back. But I was a kid, a child, what did I know of adult feelings? Nothing at all. Instead I revelled in my freedom, which I stole nightly, slipping from my bed after lights out. The house was mine. Ghosts crept the halls with me and I was happy in their company. I far preferred them to any of my living relatives.'

Here she paused, and reflected to herself, before continuing.

'Rosamund was eighteen years old, Nicholas a year younger. They had not yet escaped the house, and its rulings.'

It was a strange thing to say, almost as though she had jumped in time a little. But it soon became clear where the story was heading.

'I saw them. Well, actually, I *heard* them first.'

Camilla's voice had dropped low, in memory.

'I knew every nook and cranny of that building, every narrow passageway, every door that didn't quite close, the crooked walls. I stood at the doorway of a back bedroom, one that we hardly used, and I saw them standing there, close, embracing. Their faces in the moonlight, softly glowing, and their lips . . .'

Camilla seemed to have stopped breathing.

'They were kissing.'

Again, she paused.

Fairfax asked simply, 'Your brother and sister?'

She nodded.

'Together?'

Yes.

The single word, the admission, was nothing more than a breath. And then louder, angrier: 'Yes, together. I felt sick, and shivery, and yet . . . oh, I could not turn aside, could not look away.' Her eyes closed and her hands settled on the table, close to each other.

Hobbes was holding his breath, hoping for the truth to be spoken. He needed to be sure. Could he dare to believe her, even now?

The nature of the tale weighed the storyteller down. Camilla's hands now seemed to be almost digging into the tabletop. She would scratch her way out of there, if she could.

But there was no way out.

None.

She looked up, this time staring at the one-way mirror.

Hobbes felt she was looking at him.

Her own brother and sister . . .

The image of that kiss was burned in her eyes.

'I was . . . I was disgusted by it. But I didn't know why. Because I didn't know what they were doing, not truly. I was too young, too innocent.'

It could not be stated but she had to state it.

She *had* to.

And then she cried out: 'God help me!'

Fairfax leaned forward. But no prompt was necessary: Camilla's pain burned quickly away as she breathed deeply, recharging herself. And when she spoke again, this time the words came more freely. She was almost serene.

'A few months later, I felt that something had changed in the house, the way my parents were talking, and my sister and brother. Lots of whisperings, sudden cries of pain and anger. I felt that some great secret was being kept from me. As it was, of course.'

She nodded at Fairfax, and he poured her another tumbler of water. She took a sip to refresh her voice.

'I saw it in Rosamund's . . . *shape*.' She made a grimace, saying this last word. 'Her body was changing over time, as the months passed. And the way she was acting. In the meantime, Mary Estelle was busy hanging more and more crosses on the walls, and images of Our Mother of Sorrows. In preparation for some terrible or joyous event, who could tell which?' Camilla looked over to Latimer. 'Mary Estelle could not have any more children, you see. I have learned since that my birth damaged her. She would often remind me of this, in later life, as though everything that had happened was in some way my fault.'

Latimer didn't respond.

'In fact, two years after I arrived in the world, she suffered a miscarriage. Often, she would claim to hear this child, crying in the house at night. A ghost in the corridors. I believe that explains her welcoming this new daughter into the house. And her religious beliefs, of course, which told her that every life was sacred.'

Camilla took a moment to reflect.

'Rosamund was confined to the house as soon as the pregnancy showed. And then to her bedroom. Bridlemere seemed darker than ever, and more enclosing. I felt I could hardly breathe. Not until the baby was born. And then . . . oh, and then everything changed, and for the better.'

She smiled broadly, her first such emotion.

'Sweet Adeline! I have such fond memories of those early years, when I looked after her, watching her grow, playing games with her, telling her stories. We were very close, the two of us. Yes, very close. And so the years passed . . .'

'What about Rosamund?'

'Rosamund? Oh, she played the loving mother at first, and took to the role well enough. But that didn't last long. She was too young, and by now too anxious to escape the house.'

She took a breath. 'I would like to stand up, please.'

Fairfax nodded. Camilla got to her feet and stretched her arms. She moved away from the table a few steps.

'I have mentioned our nanny, Eileen Braithwaite. She helped with the birth, acting as midwife, and she played along with the secret.'

'Go on.'

'To avoid a scandal, Adeline was known as the daughter of Leonard and Mary Estelle, and grew up believing that was the case. I confess, in my youth, I tended to forget her true parentage. I never thought of her as my niece, only as my younger sister. To this day I think the same. And I was happy with that relationship.'

Hobbes stood at the glass, taking this in, willing Fairfax to ask the right questions. He wanted to be in the room, to engage with the emotions, but knew that Camilla might easily close up into her shell. And so he listened.

'There is an element here,' she said, 'that is very important.'

Fairfax asked her what that was.

'We were brought up as a theatrical family. We were encouraged from an early age to view life as a play, and ourselves as players, or actors, that by following this path we would always be in control of our lives, always be the masters of our fate, and never the victims of circumstance. Everything flows from that notion, which raged strongly in Leonard and in Mary Estelle. It was the guiding force of the house.'

'I understand.'

She nodded. 'So this idea, of a grandparent playing the role of a parent, came easily to them both. They might even have revelled in such an undertaking. And it wasn't that strange an occurrence back then, a common way of covering up embarrassments.'

'I've heard about such cases. It still happens today.'

The longer the interview went on, the more Fairfax settled into it, the more he spoke, and the more questions he asked. Hobbes watched his progress, hoping he kept on the necessary track.

Camilla continued, 'Nicholas left home to fight in the war. After VE Day, he found a place of his own, in Bayswater. And Rosamund got married in 1943. Can you imagine, a mother leaving her child like that, without a thought in her mind?'

'So then it was just you and Adeline?'

'Yes. Auntie and niece. Sister and sister.'

Fairfax lit a cigarette. 'Let me guess, if I can . . . Adeline found out the truth? About her real parents?'

Camilla frowned at this. And she started to pace about the room.

'Who told her? You?'

'No. No, our nanny did. Mrs Braithwaite. It was one of the last things she did, before she retired. I don't know why she did it, perhaps out of some kind of guilt. But there it is.'

'How old was Adeline when this happened?'

'She was fifteen.' Camilla frowned suddenly. 'I was twenty-five. Can you imagine? Still living at home, looking after my sister who wasn't really my sister. It doesn't bear thinking about, looking back.'

She was biting at a fingernail.

Fairfax tried to calm her. 'Why don't you sit down? Come on. Join me.'

She did so, keeping her gaze away from the mirror.

'It must have been a shock for Adeline, finding out?'

'Yes, dreadfully so. Dreadfully. At first she was angry and wouldn't stop screaming. She kept threatening to run away all the time, to tell people the truth, people outside the family. But she didn't have the courage for such things. Adeline was a fragile girl, very thin by this time, and weak. She was depressed, saddened beyond hope. You left school at fifteen back then, and she just remained indoors, keeping to her room. She was never a popular child, with few friends, if any.'

'Except yourself?'

Camilla looked at Fairfax. 'We grew apart, I'm afraid. I was a member of the family, the people who had created this drama, this terrible tragedy. She took to her room and would stay there for hours, sometimes for days on end. Weeks. She would lock the door, and refuse to open it. I'd leave a tray of food for her, a drink, and she would take that, but only after I'd gone away. I would try to talk to her through the door, but she never answered, not at first.'

'Later on she did?'

'Yes. Sometimes she'd come out to use the bathroom on that floor, the top floor of the house. But she always did that when she was alone. I imagined her peeping out, checking the corridor. So the conversations we had would always take place through the closed door. I'd pull up a chair and sit there, listening to her voice, and telling her tales about what people had been up to, or items from the newspaper. Little things. Tittle-tattle. Anything to keep her connected to – to life, I guess. Yes. To *life*.'

Fairfax spoke quietly. 'Did Adeline let you in, at all? Did she open the door?'

A nod in reply. 'It took a while. I had to be very gentle with her, and not push her. But yes, eventually, the door was opened. She was sixteen now, maybe seventeen. She hadn't left the house for a long time, not even for the doctor or the dentist.'

'What did you find?'

'The room was clean, tidy. I was glad of that, to see that she'd made an effort. But she wouldn't look at me, not directly. She sat at her dressing-table, staring at her reflection in the mirror. As though she couldn't see herself or was staring at a stranger. You know, like a cat will treat a mirror?'

'I know.'

'It was like that. Like she had no sense of herself. And we talked for a while, in that manner, with her never looking away from the mirror.'

'That must have upset you?

'It did. To see someone you love, someone who has been hurt, to see them lose all sense of what's real and what's unreal, yes, it's painful. But Adeline had a way of fighting back. Around that time she started to dress up. She liked to take the costumes that Mary Estelle had worn on the stage – there were a number of them around the house – and wear them, taking on one role after another, becoming someone new each time, as she whispered the lines from the playscripts to herself.' Camilla smiled, remembering this. 'There was one particular costume she liked above all others, the dress worn by the character Anna Kreeley in *The Moon Awakes*.'

'The blue dress with the yellow flowers?'

Her smile broadened. 'That was her favourite, yes. She seemed to be calmer at such times, when she was dressed up, or acting as someone else. Her psyche was very fragile, and playing a role helped her to survive from day to day, at least a little.'

'The effect didn't last long?'

'She was . . . Adeline had to be constantly *reminded* of her own life, of her value in the world. Looking in the mirror, and seeing herself as Miss Kreeley, or some other character, Ophelia, say, or Lady Macbeth, at such a moment she was fully alive.' Camilla took a deep breath. 'Anyway, that was when I started to make the blue and yellow dress for her. She needed more and more copies of it, as they got worn out or damaged.'

Fairfax thought for a moment. 'What about her mum and dad, Nicholas and Rosamund? Didn't they come to visit, to see their daughter?'

'They did come round, yes, on occasion. Family get-togethers. It was all very strained, ill-tempered, and Adeline never put in an appearance. She stayed in her room, the door locked. She was the great unspoken subject, haunting the party.'

The story faltered. Camilla's eyes had taken on a faraway gaze. Fairfax asked if she'd like to take a break.

But she refused this. 'No. I want it to be said. It *needs* to be said.'

'Good. We all want that.'

Camilla made an effort. She was gathering her strength for some purpose.

'When Adeline was eighteen, she tried to cut herself.'

Fairfax kept his voice steady. 'On her arms?'

'No. Here.'

Camilla pointed to her stomach area, on the right-hand side. Her fingers lingered there.

'Why would she do that?'

'I didn't know, not then. Only later, when her condition became obvious.'

'Her condition?'

'It was a shallow cut, marking the territory, a guideline. It scared me. And when she let me into her room a week or so later, well, that was another shock. She had given up completely on cleanliness. Her hair was long, and filthy, like rats' tails all knotted together. Her teeth were brown, and her breath . . . Well, it wasn't pleasant.' Camilla shuddered a little. 'And so many of her possessions were torn apart, or ripped in two: books, clothes, jewellery, broken in pieces. Only the dressing-table mirror was left intact. That one shining window, ever closed to her. And she turned away from the glass and said, "I have no face, no body. No touch. I am drifting away. Almost gone now, almost gone."'

Fairfax sounded unsure. 'I don't understand what you're saying. What was wrong with her?'

Camilla looked away from him, over to the mirror on the wall. Hobbes stood behind it, out of sight.

She was looking at him, knowing he was there.

She spoke plainly, emotion at bay: 'Adeline was suffering from a condition by which the mind believes the body, the flesh, is dead, or dying, and decaying.'

And then she fell silent, as though her explanation was sufficient in itself.

Fairfax smiled. 'I've never – I've never heard of anything like that.'

'No, it's rare. The Delirium of Negation—'

'And you expect me to believe—'

'Yes, I do!'

She turned back to look at Fairfax. Her voice took on a brittle, angry tone. 'I am saying that it's true. And therefore—'

'It is true?'

'I am the only competent witness of these events. No one else. No one!'

Her raised voice echoed slightly in the room.

Fairfax nodded. He shuffled through some papers on the desk, without aim.

Hobbes watched carefully. Maybe it was time to go in.

But Camilla took charge of the story again. 'There was a hidden room in that house, in Bridlemere. I didn't know it at the time, but now I do. The inside of Adeline's head was off limits, sealed up, locked from the inside. No doors. No windows.'

Fairfax said the strangest thing: 'Was there a light? Was there a light in the hidden room?'

Camilla looked at him curiously. 'Yes. Yes, a tiny one, a candle. A lick of flame but enough to see by . . . not, sadly, enough to live by.'

And her face changed then: it softened slightly.

The most important line of the drama had been spoken.

Fairfax had turned the key in the lock.

And Camilla sat upright in her chair. She spoke clearly. 'Rosamund came to visit. She was alone. I don't know what brought it on, this desire, but she wanted to see Adeline. I was surprised. Adeline opened the door for her. Of course, Rosamund was shocked by what she saw. Very much so. She demanded that Adeline be brought back to life.'

'Brought back to life?'

'Rosamund likened Adeline to a corpse, someone wasting away. Closer to death, than life. Oh, she called her many things. And she blamed me entirely for this.'

Fairfax nodded, giving nothing away. 'Carry on. How did you respond?'

'I told her to leave, of course.'

'Did she obey you?'

Camilla nodded. 'She left. And that night I saw blood on Adeline's dress again, at the stomach. Another cut. I couldn't stop her doing it. Deeper this time.'

'What was she trying to do?'

'She told me once that – that this one spot . . .' – again, Camilla touched the area on her midriff – '. . . this was the only part of her body where she could feel anything, any kind of pain or pleasure. That everywhere else was dead, or dying or – or rotting away . . . Oh, God, I don't know how to say it . . .'

'You're doing well.'

'But that tiny part of her stomach, it had to be torn at, probed, sliced open to make her believe that she still had blood within her, or warmth, the force of life.'

Camilla stopped. She gulped for air. Her face looked ghastly, stark white and drawn at the eyes. She was taking on Adeline's symptoms as she spoke of them.

'I feared for her life, I really did, that she would one day run out of all hope, and take drastic action. I had to stop her doing such a thing. I truly believed that was my only goal, the reason I'd been put on this earth.'

'To protect her?'

'Yes. Absolutely. To look after Adeline.'

'What was the outcome of all this?'

'There was one final time, when the whole family gathered together. And that's when it happened.'

She paused. The silence stretched out.

'Camilla? Do you want to stop?'

A shake of the head. Once more, she looked over to the mirror. And she said, 'He might as well come in now. This should be heard clearly.'

Hobbes took his cue. He walked through into the interview room, and he stood near Latimer, close to the wall, not saying anything.

Camilla began, 'It was 1954, a day in October. I remember it all so vividly, I think I always will. It was the final night of the latest run of *The Moon Awakes*. It hadn't gone well, and Mary Estelle's young replacement had received rather bad notices. But, as always, Leonard liked the family to be together on such occasions. He returned home late from the theatre, and was rather boisterous. He'd been to a party. We were all waiting up for him, myself, Rosamund, Nicholas and Mary Estelle. We'd all been drinking as well.'

Fairfax asked, 'Was Adeline present?'

'Not initially. But I went upstairs to visit her, to see if I could persuade her to join the party. Adeline was standing in the dark, by her bedroom window. The curtains were open. I joined her there, and we both looked down at the lawn, and the flowerbeds and the elm tree, the garden shed. Mummy liked to keep the rear portion of the garden wild, in contrast to the neatness of the beds, and the lawn. And I saw something weird. I looked down and I saw . . . I saw . . .'

Her voice trailed off, and her eyes took on a strange look, the kind that a ghostly vision might bring to a non-believer.

It was quiet in the room. Camilla gave a shiver – it passed through her whole body.

Fairfax whispered, 'What was it? What did you see?'

Her eyes were still unfocused as she answered, 'It was a woman. A woman, standing on the lawn, looking up at the window.'

Hobbes remembered his own experience in the garden, after he'd been affected by the fungi, the spores in the air: the woman he'd seen at the upstairs window. So that was Adeline's bedroom! He took a step forward and uttered his first words since he'd come back into the room: 'Who was it?'

Camilla glanced at him, and then away. And she answered clearly: 'It was Adeline.'

Now she smiled, or tried to: a grim line to the mouth. 'Yes, I'd been drinking, I know that. I admit that. Far too much. We all had. But I know what I saw.'

'But Adeline was standing next to you?'

'Yes, and I turned to her. She was staring out, her eyes unfixed.

I asked her if she'd seen the woman in the garden, and she shook her head. "No," she said, "we're alone here." And when I looked back the garden was empty. I had imagined it, in my drunken state. And, in fact, I did feel faint at that point. I had to hold on to Adeline's arm for support. She turned to me and looked deep into my eyes. Oh, I saw everything I needed to see in that look, all things, all things beautiful and all things deadly and cold. We embraced gently. And she said to me in a lovely, close-up faraway voice, "Don't worry, Camilla, it will all be over soon, all of our troubles." '

Camilla broke away from the spell of memory. 'I'm sorry. I get carried away, when I think of these things.'

Hobbes was close to the table now. He said, 'I believe we're almost finished?'

Camilla nodded. 'I went back downstairs to my family, and I joined in with the laughter, and the joking as I could. There was an odd atmosphere in the room, as though another person was present, in some terrible spirit. I can't explain it. And then Adeline made her entrance.'

'That must have been quite a scene?'

'Oh, it was. She had put on her favourite blue and yellow dress. She looked like Anna Kreeley herself, walking down the stairs and entering the living room. Around her neck she wore a yellow scarf, and on her feet a pair of sky-blue shoes. The perfect combination.'

'How did people react?'

'Not well. At first glance, she looked quite magnificent, but then she came up close, and you could see the terrible affliction, on her face, in her expression, her eyes. The way she held herself. She was dreadfully thin, her cheeks sunken, and her skin had taken on a deathly pallor, grey and drained, marked with tiny wrinkles. But she was only eighteen years old. Eighteen! How could it be? Oh, poor Adeline. That poor girl! Death had taken a premature hold of her, even as she lived and breathed. The dress hung off her like a shroud.'

'How did the family take this?'

'Rosamund had seen her before, remember, if only for a minute. But Nicholas hadn't been home for a while now. And he was . . . well, he was shocked. I had written to him once or twice, telling him about her condition, at length and in great detail, and the trouble she was having. But he'd never replied. Now he was just staring at her, as though he were ashamed of her, or fearful in her company.'

'Fearful?'

Camilla didn't flinch from the truth. 'She looked monstrous.' And then she added: 'To me, she was the sweetest, most beautiful girl in the world, but from the outside, looking in, seeing her through everyone else's eyes . . .' The thought trailed off. 'And so the party began.' Another pause. And then, quietly: 'Within an hour she was dead.'

Camilla's eyes turned to Hobbes. She stared at him, without speaking.

The tape could be heard, turning on its twin spindles.

And then: 'There was a terrible argument. I could not understand what possible right Nicholas and Rosamund had in terms of Adeline's life, or how it was theirs to control, but both of them suddenly took on their parental roles, and started to shout at me, at Leonard and Mary Estelle, at everyone, really, but Adeline. Sweet Adeline . . .'

'What happened? Camilla?'

'She screamed at us to stop! To be quiet! She was crying. Crying. I couldn't bear it, to see her so.'

Camilla was crying herself now, her tears flowing freely.

'Adeline . . . my sister . . . my young *sister* . . . she had a pair of scissors in her hands. They were from my sewing box, my dressmaking shears. She had brought them with her. And I knew what she was planning – I saw it in her eyes, the set of her lips, her expression . . .'

'You'd seen such things before, in her?'

She nodded. 'Oh, yes, many times by now. The hatred of life itself, at the core. But never like this. Never so . . .' She cleared her eyes by blinking. 'You have to understand, this was the first time she had ever confronted her parents, for what they had done, for how she was brought into this world. And once she'd started, there was no stopping her. None! Oh, God!'

Camilla's face and body had taken on the memory of that night, fully. Her brows were furrowed, and the creases ran down into her eyes and her cheeks. Her mouth was a cruel memory of a mouth. Her hands might never have loved or caressed, the fingers were bent so horribly around the invisible handles of the scissors. And she made a sudden stabbing movement, her hand moving at speed across the table. A great wordless shriek escaped from her lips.

Fairfax jerked back in his chair.

Latimer stepped forward. And then stopped, her body frozen.

Hobbes stayed where he was, unmoving.

Camilla was holding herself steady, poised at the moment of pain.

'Adeline went for Rosamund first. The blades almost got her, but Rosamund had fallen backwards in her shock, and crashed against a table's edge. And then Nicholas was yelling at Adeline to stop. Just yelling! It was a terrible noise. It made me close my eyes.' She drew a painful breath. 'I'm not sure – I'm not sure how it all happened. But . . .'

Here she stopped, and looked at the three officers in turn.

'No. I can't remember.'

'You can.' Hobbes didn't raise his voice, didn't insist: he stated the case, as it was, as it needed to be. 'Camilla, you *can* remember.'

She nodded desperately.

'Yes. Yes, when I looked again – I see it now, clearly, from across the room. Adeline had dropped the scissors . . . no . . . not dropped them, but Nicholas had taken them from her. I can see them . . . silver, gleaming . . . the blades, so red . . . dripping . . .'

Hobbes kept his attention on her. 'You mean she had used them on someone?'

Camilla grimaced. 'Herself. She had stabbed herself. Here . . . the place . . .' Her fingers were tracing along her stomach. 'That one sacred place, where the blood still flowed in her, where she still breathed, and thought of herself as being alive and present. Everything else was rotten, all other parts of her, decayed, or decaying, or dead.' Camilla took another breath. 'And then Nicholas stepped forward. Close to her. I thought he was embracing her. But no . . . no. He was . . . he was . . .'

Her eyes told the truth. First her eyes, then her lips.

'He stabbed her. Again. Again. And again.'

Camilla's voice quietened. She could hardly gather a single breath.

'And again . . .' Hushed now. 'He was completing the action Adeline had started. Until she slumped to the floor and lay there, trembling a little . . . and then falling still at last.'

There wasn't a sound in the room.

Hobbes was going to speak, but then he watched in utter fascination as Camilla slowly undid her body from the knot it had contracted into during this long telling. Her shoulders relaxed, the non-existent pair of scissors fell from her empty hands, her arms stretched out and her fingers uncurled. Her head came up and the creases left her neck and brow. Her eyes opened wide. Her lips parted.

'I have told everything,' she said. 'There is no more.'

'You could have gone to the police,' Latimer said.

Camilla's answer was spoken plainly, without a shred of doubt: 'Our family looks after itself. We are self-contained, and self-motivated, our own judge and jury.'

'And what? You found Nicholas innocent?'

Her reply was simple. 'Adeline was at peace. We believed, all of us, that she wanted this to happen. Nothing else mattered.'

Hobbes nodded. He waited for a moment to let Camilla settle. Then he said, 'And each year after that you met up as a family to perform the ritual, with the dress, the tear in the cloth, the spilling of the blood?'

'That's right. Each year, on the same night. Leonard wrote us a script, with the parts we had to play, and the lines to say. You might find it in his papers, somewhere in the house, if he kept it. On the first anniversary we buried the dress in the cellar, her scarf and shoes. And we placed mementoes alongside her, trinkets for the journey, the things we each owned that Adeline liked to play with as a child. I gave her my grandmother's brooch, with its missing ruby. Each object meant something different to each of us. And we buried the dress and said our prayers. It was a proper burial, to replace the one we could not give her, for obvious reasons.'

'The body was elsewhere, hidden away?'

'It was.'

'And the next year?'

'The same ceremony, but a little less grand, less ritualistic, and each year after that, as they went by, with less weeping, more quickly spoken, with fewer mourners, as first Nicholas and then Rosamund made their excuses, and then it was just myself,

Leonard and Mary Estelle. We kept up the tradition for as long as we could, until I left Bridlemere at last, and Mother was put away in the home. And then it was Leonard alone, each year performing his little theatre play, just for himself and for the spirit of the dead girl.'

'What about Nicholas? Did you or Rosamund murder him, for his part in Adeline's death?'

'No. I've told you, we bore him no ill.'

'Death at the hands of a stranger? You're still insisting on that?'

'It seems most likely.'

'And the body of Adeline? Can you tell us where it is, Camilla?'

'I can. I will show you.'

Hobbes studied her. He saw in her eyes the pain of those long-off days; and he saw in her face the scourge of guilt; and he heard from her mouth a whispered prayer for the dead, or the lines from a play, which amounted to the same thing.

Here we lay to rest the body of Adeline Graves.

Our beloved sister, our child . . .

And she spoke on further, and quieter still, the words belonging to herself alone.

The Gathering

It was getting dark. Time had passed in ways they could not comprehend. Dusk. Cold air. A cloudy sky, the moon hidden. The two officers stood close together on the steps that led to the car park, Hobbes staring ahead in silence. A police car exited through the gate, its engine making a rough coughing sound as it drove away.

Latimer waited until she'd smoked her cigarette right down before she spoke. 'Hell of a story.'

'Yes.'

'You believe her?'

'I'm not sure. Some of it.'

'We'll know tomorrow.'

'Perhaps. I hope so.'

Now she turned to look at him. 'You really think it'll be an empty grave?'

'Or another bloody dress.'

'Christ. I hadn't thought of that.' She blinked through the smoke. 'There is one thing, though.'

'I hope it's good.'

'Not really. Just the thought that blaming Nicholas is the easy way out. The dead man.'

'That crossed my mind. I wonder if Rosamund would confirm this story, if we could persuade her to talk.'

Latimer considered the possibilities. 'Maybe. Unless they have a story already written out, a script they all agreed to follow – like one of their father's plays.'

Hobbes nodded. 'I wouldn't put it past them.'

'And we have only Camilla's word for the whole thing. Any member of that family might have lent a hand in ending the girl's life. It feels like they're all capable of it.'

Hobbes thought about this. 'Well, it makes sense, in a way. I got the impression from our brief chats with Nicholas that he felt guilty. And he did give us permission to dig up the cellar.'

'You think he wanted to confess?'

'Maybe. And the opening of the cellar floor . . .'

'An old wound exposed.'

'With people like him – nervous types – it's always one wound at a time, never the full story all at once.'

'The same with Rosamund, I guess. With the scissors to her stomach.'

'The whole family knew what had happened with Adeline. And they were all plagued by it, in their own way.'

'The poor kid.'

'You're right there.' Hobbes shrugged. 'You heading home?'

'I'll take Tommy out for a drink, maybe.'

'Yes.'

'He did all right, I thought. Bloody good, actually.'

'Sure.'

Latimer hesitated. 'It'll be great, having him back.'

Hobbes stayed silent. There was too much on his mind, too many loose ends still, not least the Nicholas Graves case. But he knew the death of Adeline tied it all together.

'I've arranged for the team to start at nine tomorrow. On the dot. Is that good?'

He nodded.

DC Fairfax came out of the building. He was walking with two other officers, both of them laughing at one of his jokes. Latimer took charge of him, offering a smile. They all walked away. Hobbes was alone. He stayed where he was for a moment, until the cold got too much, then went back inside and took the lift up to the bullpen. His desk was littered with papers. Tomorrow, after the search, he'd make a start on—

'Sir. I'm glad I've caught you.' It was PC Barlow. 'I thought you might have left by now.'

'No, lad, still here.'

'I have that report for you.'

'Report?'

'About the plant, the fungus, I mean.'

'Oh, right.' Hobbes had forgotten about it. He took a cardboard folder from the constable and looked inside at the few sheets of paper it contained.

'It's fascinating, sir, actually.'

'Is it?'

'I've found out that fungi aren't plants.'

'That a fact?'

'They don't use photosynthesis. That's the transformation of light—'

'I know what it is.'

Barlow nodded, taking it in his stride. 'Anyway, this particular specimen is new to urban areas. Usually, it's found in the countryside. It's a saprophyte.'

'Elucidate, would you? I've had a hell of a day.'

'I will, sir. It's a species that takes its energy from decomposing organic matter, plant or, as in this particular case, flesh.'

'It feeds off it?'

'It does. Off decaying flesh.'

Hobbes skimmed through the report, noting the use of fancy

words and Latin phrases. Then he asked, 'What's this bit? "Use as a drug."'

Barlow was enthusiastic. 'It's a psychoactive. People have started to use it, just this last year or so, mainly because it's still legal. It's very powerful, but it's not been classified, not yet. It gives the user very specific visions. On the street, it's known as musk.'

Barlow went on his way. Hobbes sat down and tried to write down his thoughts on the Camilla Greene interview, but soon got lost in the words. The page was a blur. His hands shook. A sudden pain had started in his head, and he felt tired beyond measure. He stood up and collected his things. He bought a Mars Bar from the machine in the corridor, and went out to his car. The sugar helped. And the city, of course, as he drove along; this beloved place, the streets, the people making their own way home. Some, a few, were criminals, but most were good people, law-abiding citizens, just going about their business.

It was half past seven by the time he got home. His journey to Margate and Jack Collingworth seemed like a distant memory. Yet the flickers of imagery from *The Spell Makers* remained strong, and became mixed with Camilla's testimony in his mind: brother and sister. Somewhere between the two stories, where they mingled, the truth existed. But Hobbes doubted he would ever find it, not completely, not in all its details.

Still, tomorrow might bring forth miracles.

He turned on the television, just to be with other people, to hear voices other than his own. And he sat down to read Barlow's report. The word *necrophage* stood out: an organism that specifically lived off decaying flesh, that put down roots, sprouted fruiting bodies and sent out spores. And it kept the flesh in a kind of stasis for as long as it could, as it fed off it.

Jesus. They should make a horror film . . .

Under 'Use as a drug', Barlow had written about the addict's intense need to locate any object seen in a hallucination. 'At the height of this desire, users will buy, borrow or steal the object in question.' It sounded crazy. And yet . . . Hobbes turned to view the wall, where a dress hung on a wire hanger, a blue dress with yellow flowers. He had taken it from Bridlemere last night, a souvenir. He remembered the urge to do so. The memory shamed him, the way he'd acted, caressing his face with the fabric. Christ almighty! But now, at least, maybe he had a reason for that, in the effect of the musk on his brain. It felt good to blame an outside source.

He looked down at the coffee-table, at the photograph his son had left in the album, in replacement for the wedding photo, remembering Martin's late-night visit, and his urgent demand to be given the old wristwatch. The wedding photo, the watch . . .

Hobbes returned to Barlow's report. He found the section that detailed symptoms of overuse, or physical changes the drug brought to the body.

. . . highly addictive . . . linked to verbal outbursts, or problems with anger . . . vomiting . . . patches of skin may be tinged with a blue or mauve colouring . . . evidence of contact . . .

The inspector stopped reading as the pieces clicked into place.

Fifteen minutes later he was driving along Upper Richmond Road, heading east. He couldn't remember getting to the car, or setting off, only the action of moving by instinct. One task in mind. The streets were fairly quiet, each lamp a passing blur, the night shops a blaze of colour. Heart pounding, and his hands trembling on the wheel, sticky with sweat. He slowed down and tried to concentrate, leaning forward in the seat, eyes fixed on the road ahead, each junction, each traffic light. Martin's face . . .

Martin's face, that look of need . . .

The wristwatch, the fingertips, the gloves, hiding his shame . . .

Hobbes blinked in the glare of approaching headlights. He was on Peckham Road, heading for the high street, before he relaxed again and felt his hands unclench. He turned on to Cavalier Road and brought the car to a stop outside the squat. Cromwell House. He could hear music from within the archway of the building. People were moving around in the central forecourt.

It was a quarter past nine.

Hobbes got out of the car. He didn't let fear take hold: he was probably beyond such feelings. Instead he marched straight into the place and continued to walk until he met the first group, two boys and a girl. They looked at him with surprise in their eyes.

'I'm looking for Martin Hobbes.'

Not one of them replied. They kept on staring at him. He moved on and approached a couple of girls on their own. They were standing near a brazier, warming their hands at the flames. He repeated his question.

'Who wants to know?'

'Never mind that. Where is he? His flat number?'

The girl who had spoken just smiled at him. Her friend started to laugh. He could see their hands in the flickering light, each finger and thumb stained dark at the tip. The sign. He turned to look elsewhere, and saw a group of young men coming forward, three of them. They wore their best threatening faces, two of them unconvincingly, the other finding it easy. Hobbes concentrated on that guy to begin with. 'I'm a police officer. I'm here for one reason only: to find my son, Martin.'

'Hobbes?'

'That's right. I don't care—'

Pig.

It was more a hiss than a word, but Hobbes ignored the insult. He turned his attention to the weakest-looking of the trio, a boy more than a man. A runaway from a different, more comfortable world.

'I don't give a fuck what you're doing here. I just need to find my son. That's it!'

The lad wavered slightly. The leader of the trio stepped nearer, but Hobbes held him back with a look and a raised hand. His face was set in a fierce mask.

'Kid, if you don't tell me what I need to know, then God help me . . .'

The boy turned and ran. The two remaining just stared at Hobbes, one laughing, the other grinning.

'There's nothing for you here, old man.'

Hobbes moved on. He felt the eyes of the residents on him, and their hatred, and he felt their fear as well, in little pockets here and there, and he felt something else, a tribal nature, a bond between them, whether strong or weak, white or black, male, female, kids out of school, or hardliners in their twenties. An entire world, self-contained, solid in the middle, one-voiced, one-bodied, but brittle at the edges. He had to find a weakness, a way in.

The flames flickered in the brazier, and smoke drifted across the scene.

Music pounded from a nearby flat. He felt engulfed by it, as the volume increased. He didn't feel in any physical danger, not yet anyway, but he was the outsider, completely so, alone against the crowd. And the darkness of the stairwell entrances might hold all kinds of threats. He walked past wire-covered windows, one doorway after another, wondering if he should start knocking on them at random, hoping for answers, or whether he should take one of the stairways up to the first floor, then the second, searching, searching as he may.

Over here!

It was a whisper from the dark near by, a girl calling to him.

He stepped closer to the stairwell and entered the shadows.

She waited for him, her face slowly appearing.

It was the young woman he'd talked to last week, outside the building. What was her name?

'It's me,' she said. 'Do you remember?' Her voice was low, conspiratorial.

'It's – it's Esme, isn't it?'

She nodded. 'Quickly, follow me.'

And he did so.

They ascended a staircase to the first walkway. Many of the flats had boarded-up windows and doors. But the ones taken over were bright and noisy. At the end of the corridor Esme ducked through a doorway into a flat. Hobbes followed her inside, into the darkness, total, and the silence, total. He breathed easily, not daring to move.

'Where are you?'

She was still whispering: 'Just follow me.'

Through an inner doorway. Another room filled with rubbish and broken furniture. No one had lived here for a long time. Stale air, freezing cold. And then another door, another room, where a third door had been crudely cut into one of the walls, making an entranceway to the next flat along. Ragged, exposed brickwork. They were now safely enclosed in warmth and peace, a living area. People were glimpsed through side doors, music still playing, but softer now, and the lights muted, dark red or blue. Faces of young people, their eyes either wide open at the sight of him, such an old person in their midst, or glazed and lost to another world, or closed entirely, cutting out reality. And they moved on. He heard voices, snatches of conversation, saw a man dancing alone in a single room, the walls and floor stripped bare, no furniture, no fittings, only the young man, his naked chest glistening with sweat. And they moved on further, through one door after another, until they came out on to a walkway, and

then another set of stairs. Upwards. Another door. A room lit
with fairy lights, luminous stars painted on the walls and ceiling. Hobbes didn't know where he was. The building was a
labyrinth. Until at last Esme led the way into another space, a
grotto, a sweet-smelling glade lit with purple lamps, lined with
books, and the walls decorated with artworks, amateur paintings and drawings.

'This is where I live,' Esme said. 'Do you like it?' She had a
proud look on her face.

It was a clean room, a delightful habitat. Incense burning.

'Yes,' he said. 'It's a nice room.'

He felt that his speech was slowing. His body was heavy. His
eyes wandered here and there, slightly out of focus. He watched
through a haze as Esme bent down to a tea chest that served as a
table. She opened a wooden box and took something out. He saw
it in her hand, shining in the glow of an Anglepoise lamp. It was
a key.

'Where are we going?' he asked. 'I need to find my son.' He felt
that he'd only just remembered the reason for his visit.

'Sssh. I'm taking you there. Only a little while now.'

And they set off once more, leaving the room by a different
doorway, taking another set of steps, downward this time, until
they reached yet another walkway. Below he could see the central
courtyard with its groups of people, and the flames of the brazier,
and he saw it all through a dirt-covered, rainbow-flecked lens.
Yellow dots of light drifted through the air, inches from his face.
And on they went, the older man following the girl, until she
slipped into another flat, and took a flight of steps that seemed to
be set in the floor of the living room itself. He couldn't make
head or tail of it – where on earth was this place? Which rules of
geometry did it follow? He called her name: 'Esme?' But she
made no answer, only walked on, along a dark corridor now. He

was scared suddenly, not knowing the way ahead, or whether he would ever get out of here, this night or any night, intact or otherwise, mindful or mad. And they walked on until the corridor ended at a sealed door. The dark was lit by a number of glowing yellow dots. They looked like fireflies. He could feel them on his face and hands, and he brushed at them.

Esme stopped, and held aloft the key. 'This might shock you, Mr Hobbes, or scare you even. But I believe it has gone too far, and we are being harmed by it, and I want you to do something about it. Will you help me?'

'I'll try. But I don't know—'

She shushed him once more. 'I'm taking you to see Fabian.'

'Fabian?'

He had heard the name before somewhere. His mind could not fix on the details.

Esme explained: 'Fabian used to be the leader of our clan, and the boyfriend of Nadia. She's the woman in the photograph, standing next to your son.'

'Is Martin here? You said you'd take me to him.'

Esme ignored his plea. Her face took on a cruel aspect. 'Nadia is horrible to us. She sets rules for everyone, and many people here are willing to be told what to do. It saves them from life. But I didn't come here to be told what to do.'

'No, I see that. You wanted to escape?'

'Yes, yes! To escape. Not to swap one set of rules for another, even stricter.'

'I understand.'

Esme nodded. But she was hesitant now, and her will was faltering. 'Fabian died,' she said. 'An overdose. And then Nadia took over.'

'When did this happen?'

'A year ago. And ever since . . .'

And Hobbes saw now that Esme was fearful, dreading what might lie ahead.

He said gently, 'Don't worry. Is Martin close by?'

'I think so, yes.'

'Take me to him, that's all I ask. And, in return, I'll help you all I can.'

She looked into his eyes, he into hers, in the shadowed light of the corridor their eyes shining, white, blue, black. Esme blinked. Was she weeping? He whispered to her, a wordless sound. She nodded and took a deep breath. The key turned in the lock and the door opened. Esme went through first, Hobbes following. But she stopped at the inner threshold and urged him on with a small gesture, and he did so, walking forward.

He saw the light first.

The soft blue light and the yellow sparkles that floated within it.

The whole room was suffused with it.

Hobbes felt dizzy. He was standing in a large room that stretched away, supported by pillars and beams: the cellar of the building, inside the foundations. He walked on.

The blue light came from no obvious source, no lamps or bulbs.

Objects were floating in mid-air, just before him. He couldn't understand it.

His eyes ached, and closed.

There was a singular tone in his head. It wasn't unpleasant, a gentle hum.

He opened his eyes again and tried to be sure of where he was. The objects danced and fluttered, each one tied to a cotton thread or a piece of string, hanging down from the beams above. There were hundreds of them, more even. Too many to count.

He walked among them.

He saw bus tickets, toy cars, a football programme, balloons, photographs, pages torn from books, newspaper clippings, a single shoe, a dead sparrow, an unsigned cheque, more than a dozen vinyl records, items of jewellery – rings, necklaces, bracelets; he saw birthday cards; dice, chessmen, shards of mirrored glass, toffee wrappers, pieces of bone, a teacup, a pair of spectacles, medicine bottles, beads, buttons, baubles, in fact every kind of household or personal item that could be strung from a thread or wire. The floor all around held certain larger items – a radio set, a guitar, a jacket, and so on. Hobbes stepped carefully through the maze, his body setting the nearest items swinging back and forth. It was an art exhibition of a kind, he saw that now, curated by the inhabitants of Cromwell House: a show of treasures, borrowed, stolen or given freely.

There were other people in the room, at the far end, and a second door was visible in the gloom, another way into the exhibition hall. This one was open.

Hobbes approached the other visitors. They were of differing ages and races, and some looked to be from the outside.

No one spoke. There wasn't a sound to be heard. No music played.

It was eerie. Hobbes didn't know what to do. He turned and saw that Esme was still with him. She whispered in a breathy voice, 'We have to bring things here, in homage to Fabian. He demands it of us.'

Hobbes pointed to the side of his brow. 'You mean in here, a voice telling you?'

She nodded. 'It starts off quietly, asking for one thing only, then grows louder, the more we visit. Until Fabian is shouting in our heads. And then the gathering takes place, more and more. I have stolen things.' Her eyes showed her shame. '*Stolen*. I would never have done so before coming here.'

'No, I can see that.'

And he did, remembering again the strange urge that had

caused him to steal the dress from Adeline's bedroom at the Graves family home. The need to *possess* it.

'Where is Martin?'

'He'll be with Fabian. I know he likes to visit at this hour of night.'

'Show me.'

And they moved on, deeper into the tangle of objects. The blue light shimmered and more of the yellow dots floated by. Hobbes recognized them as the spores of the fungus. He covered his mouth but knew that was of little use: there were too many of them – the room was filled with their light. There was a strange otherworldly scent, nasty and rotten and ugly at its core, deep down; and overlying this – hiding it almost – a sweeter aroma, flowery, cloying, off-putting. Hobbes felt like he might retch, but fought against it, and the moment passed. And then, moving forward a few more steps, he saw an object he recognized, dangling on a string: a photograph taken at his own wedding, himself and Glenda, his bride of a few minutes only, standing together proudly, happily, their faces beaming with joy. And next to it, only a few feet away, swaying on its own piece of string, was his old wristwatch, with its silver case and blue face – a treasured object given to Hobbes by his father.

Martin had taken both objects, and placed them here in the cellar of the building.

And then he saw his son, standing with another person, a woman. Other people milled around this central space. Martin had not yet seen his father – his attention was elsewhere. Hobbes came up behind him. He wanted to speak, to call out, but was unable to move his lips properly. His limbs felt even heavier than before. The spores were most concentrated here, glowing with their own light. They made their way inside Hobbes's body, into his bloodstream, casting their spell. He was locked in someone else's dream. The objects danced and swayed around him, made of paper, metal, plastic, wood, bone, glass, all materials. The soft humming sound filled his head.

Hobbes reached out with his hand. It took all his effort to do so. And then he ceased even that movement, for he had seen the body that lay on the low table before him. It was a man, or the shape of a man. But the corpse was covered with a shifting pattern of colour. The horribly sweet scent rose from the mass of rotten flesh, or whatever it was. Hobbes couldn't work it out, not at first. And then he took a step forward. He needed to be close to his son: that was all that mattered.

Martin had bent down at the low table, and was offering something to the body that lay there. Hobbes could see it more clearly now: the torso and limbs were modelled from a plant-like substance or, rather, a fungal substance. The musk had taken over the corpse completely, and the flesh was covered with it, head to foot. Even the face was moulded from the fibrous material. The features might almost be made out.

This was Fabian.

When had he died? Esme had said about a year ago. And yet the process of decay was still active. The musk had taken over the body, every last inch of it, every particle changed in some way, transforming it into a new and strangely beautiful object. Yes, beautiful! There was no other word for it. Here was the true night flesh. The flesh of the body becomes the soil that the fungus grows within, and the spores rise in flight, like insects, glow-flies, like the sparks of the soul cast free . . .

Hobbes touched the surface of the man's body, not the flesh, but the substance the flesh had turned into. His fingers sank into the material, and he felt the fibres close around his fingers, holding them, trying to take them over, drawing them deeper inside. It was sickening. Quickly, he pulled his hand loose, and a cloud of spores rose to meet him. He breathed them in – he had no choice.

Now the woman standing next to Martin turned and looked at Hobbes. He recognized her as the woman in the photograph: Nadia. Her hair was a massed tangle of knotted strands, unwashed for many weeks so that a natural process had taken over. Her face was pitted at the cheeks, with the grey pallor of a long-term smoker. She smiled at the detective and nodded, yet her face gave nothing away. She seemed to be less affected by the spores, and the atmosphere of the cellar, as though she had grown used to it over time. But he saw now that her eyes were intense, staring, fixed on one spot: somewhere inside Hobbes's skull. Unnerved, he moved back a little. His feet almost slipped from under him as he turned, and his mind reeled with a sudden wash of colour and form. Esme grabbed his arm and pulled him away. He lurched forward clumsily, banging into another devotee in his haste. Martin was suddenly close by, his eyes glazed, his mouth twisted into a grim line. And then the young man broke free of his spell, at least for a moment, and his face showed only fear, and anger, as he looked at his father.

Martin . . .

Hobbes could hardly hear his own voice, as he spoke.

Martin, come on. Son, let's get out of here . . .

He reached out, and felt Martin's hand in his, gently closing. He saw the dark-blue colour at the fingertips, the mark of the drug, as their fingers wove together. And Hobbes felt hope. They could walk out of here, father and son. It would be easy . . .

Nadia slapped at Martin's face.

Hobbes heard the sound as a distant report, but the pain was close-up, visceral, shared equally between them.

Nadia loomed close. Her face was speckled with tiny blue patches, where her body had been further affected by the spores of musk. She was speaking, her words a guttural rush of syllables. Her hands raised like claws.

No cops, no pigs, nothing normal, nothing dull or boring, no laws beyond the House and all who live here, as one, working, breathing, loving, dancing, dying!

Her voice wavered, the meaning slurred.

From the roots. As one, as one, alive in death!

She stood her ground, the others with her now, residents and visitors alike, and more of them coming in by both doorways.

Hobbes drew Martin to him. He looked around desperately, hoping to see Esme, his one friend in here, but saw dark shapes only, phantoms in the room. The spores took flight, affecting his sight, his hearing, his sense of taste. They seemed to be closing in, sticking to his flesh, his tongue, his eyelids. He tried to brush them off, in vain.

His vision was blurred.

His breathing slowed. His heart was pounding.

The humming noise filled his head, louder than ever.

He felt unsteady in his feet.

Martin's hand in his, still there, still tight. Hold on!

One more step . . . falling . . . falling . . . one more . . . falling . . .

And then he saw her. Detective Hobbes saw the woman in the blue dress, the blue dress with the yellow flowers, the ghost herself, Adeline, Miss Graves, Miss Adeline Graves of Bridlemere. And she showed him the wound in her side, proud in her movement, displaying the torn cloth, and the flesh itself, opened up to let the blood flow from the wound.

The Blackbird

He made it as far as Camberwell, then pulled over to the side of
the road. His vision was still affected, and it wasn't safe to drive.
He rested for a moment without saying anything, his son beside
him in the passenger seat, also silent. Martin's hands lay twitch-
ing on his lap, and his head was bowed, his eyes closed. By the
dashboard clock it was half past ten. There was a pub close by, its
windows ablaze, music and laughter heard from within as a cus-
tomer opened the door. But Hobbes couldn't face that: too many
people, too much noise. He looked across the street and saw the
lighted window of a café among a row of darkened shops. The
place looked empty, or nearly so. Much better. He had to stir
Martin from sleep, to make him get out of the car and walk
across the road. The café was brightly lit, overly so, and Hobbes's
eyes ached. He could hear the electric buzz of a fluorescent tube
above, like noise touching his skin. They sat at a table and Hobbes
ordered for both of them, coffee for himself and a mixed grill for
the lad. Now his son was eating voraciously. Maybe he'd been
starved in that place, living off air and hope, and shared moments
in the cold rooms.

'Is that good?'

No reply, but let that be. It was enough to have him back in
the world.

Hobbes lit a cigarette and ordered a second coffee. He looked round. There was an old guy at a corner table, and a young couple waiting for their food, with a middle-aged women serving, and a cook heard as a voice from a back room. The smell of fat and the sizzle of bacon as it hit the pan.

Martin finished his meal. There was a moment of awkwardness.

'Why did you come, Dad? I told you not to.'

'Because . . .' It was all Hobbes could manage.

'That's it, that's your answer? Because?'

'Is there any other reason?'

No, none at all. Every further word seemed impossible to say out loud, or even to think about, in case this feeling was broken between them.

And so the silence returned.

Hobbes saw a telephone near the counter, stood up and made a quick call. He came back. His son was looking at him.

'You've called the police?'

'Not yet.'

'Not yet?'

'Tomorrow I'll do it.'

'They'll raid the place.'

'Martin, there's a dead body in the basement. What should I do? Ignore it?'

His son looked out of the window. A few weak patters of rain driven across the glass. The wall clock ticked on. Hobbes felt cold, shivery. He closed his eyes and saw again the vision of Adeline Graves in her youthful vigour, still dancing.

'I don't feel that good, Dad.'

Hobbes examined his son's face. It was clean, still pure, unlined, no traces of infection. And then he looked down at the lad's hands, with their patches of blue. He looked in turn at his own fingers.

Martin laughed a little. It was good to hear. 'You'll have a way to go yet, before it shows.'

'Never again, right?'

'I'm not sure—'

'No, but I am. You see? Do you see? I *am* sure.' His eyes matched his voice, and his hands the same, all clenched tight, firm. 'I won't let anything bad happen to you.'

'I think I'm going to be sick.'

'OK, come on, then.'

He led his son to the gents and waited outside the single cubicle as the lad threw up. The sound of the process echoed in the tiled room. Hobbes read a few lines of graffiti. He felt bilious himself, but knew he had to stay strong until his lad was safe.

'How's it going in there?'

Martin emerged grey-faced, his lips pale, bloodless.

'How's that? Better?'

There was no answer, not until he'd washed his face at the basin. And then he looked at his father and said, 'I need to steal things, take things, the things I've seen tonight, and other nights. I need them to be mine. It won't go away, Dad, it just won't go away. I can't help it, I just need to do it.' His eyes were dark, tightly focused as he spoke.

There was little hope of escape, not yet, but his father took hold of him, and hugged him lightly. Nothing was said between them. Only the touch.

They made their way back to the table. The old man had left, and the young couple were tucking into their meals. The waitress smoked a cigarette. A radio on the counter was playing a song. Hobbes knew it well, a number one earlier in the year, 'Green Door' by Shakin' Stevens: a tinny rattle through the radio's speaker, a distant recall of summer.

'Another drink? Tea? Orange juice?'

A nod, noncommittal. Hobbes ordered him tea, and a chocolate wafer biscuit.

'I didn't know where to go, when I left home.'

Hobbes let him speak.

'And then I ran into a friend and they told me about the squat, about Oliver's . . . That's what we called the house. I was welcomed there. Nadia helped me, a few of the others. It felt safe. I was safe there.' His lips trembled, and his eyes darted this way and that. 'But it all changed when . . . when . . .'

'When you saw the body?'

Martin nodded.

'Listen to me, son. This is very important. Did you see him die?'

A look of fear in response.

'Were you there when he died? How long ago was it? Do you know how he died? Was it an overdose? If so, what kind of drug? Martin! Answer me!'

'No! No, I didn't see. They took me down there to the cellar, Nadia and her friends. They introduced me to Fabian. His body. They called him the dreamer, the sleeping god, the man of flowers, the fisher king, the giver of gifts, the taker, the creator, the lord of the house, Lord Cromwell, the wounded prince, the eternal one, death in life, *death* in—'

He had risen from the table in his anguish as the words tumbled forth, the many names. The two other diners and the waitress were all looking over.

'Martin!' Hobbes grabbed the lad's wrist, hard. And he held on tight.

'Let me go! You can't keep me here, you can't!'

And for a moment, for one long moment, they were pulling apart, separating. But then he felt Martin's body relax, the tension falling away as he looked through the café's window at a car pulling up to the kerb. His mother got out. Hobbes was relieved to see her. Glenda came into the light of the café. She stood at the door looking at her son, and at her husband. She came forward, her expression still unsure. And then she put on her best face, and took hold of Martin, embracing him. Immediately, he sat back down in his seat. Glenda squeezed in next to Hobbes.

'I don't care what you've done, or where you've been.'

That was it. That was all she said.

It was enough.

Glenda smiled, and called to the waitress.

As they waited for her order to arrive, Hobbes told a story. His voice was unsteady, still finding itself. But the words came to him: 'Son, did I ever tell you how we met, your mother and I?'

'Yeah, of course. You met in a picture house.'

'But do you know what kind of picture house it was, and what kind of movies they were showing?'

'Henry! I don't think the lad needs to know this.'

Hobbes laughed gently. 'Oh, I think he does.'

The late-night café was called the Blackbird. Anyone passing along the road at that moment, on that night, might have glanced through the window and seen the three people sitting at the table, chatting to each other. They might have seen them as a family, might have imagined they were close, and loving to each other. They might have imagined them to be happy.

In Blue and Yellow

He got there earlier than expected, considering how little sleep he'd had, bedding down on the settee at Glenda's house, and the state of his head during the night, the visions, the strangeness of his dreams. He'd taken too much stimulus in too short a time. He was fighting it still as he stood in the room on the top floor of Bridlemere, looking around at the peeling wallpaper and the bare floorboards. This was the room with the wardrobe of dresses, where they had found the dress pinned to the floor, after the funeral of Leonard Graves. Hobbes let a picture form in his mind of Nicholas Graves pushing the drawing pins through the cloth into the floorboards. He was attempting to atone for Adeline's death, even after all these years had passed, a need brought on, no doubt, by the suicide of his father. The torn-up letters found in the wastepaper bin at Nicholas's bedsit seemed to confirm this: one last attempt to talk to his daughter, across the years, through the barrier between life and death. Conversations with a ghost.

The only decoration in the room was a playbill fixed to the chimney breast. It depicted Mary Estelle Graves dressed as Anna Kreeley in *The Moon Awakes*. The famous attire, the same pose Hobbes had seen in so many other images around the house. But this playbill was signed by the actress, and dated.

19 October 1954.

He should have read this earlier, on a previous tour of the house, and maybe the story would have come to light. Leonard Graves had killed himself on the same day of the year. And on the anniversary of that day, from 1954 onwards, a torn and bloodied dress had been laid out in a different room of the house. Twenty-seven dresses all told, made by Camilla on her sewing-machine, then hand-stitched where necessary. He could see her clearly, a young woman hard at work to make this symbolic funeral gown for her dead niece, Adeline. Such abstract belief, and all to perpetuate the memory of a girl born in sin, the ultimate sin to which a family could fall prey. A poor, damaged child, hidden for so many years, slowly going mad in her own solitude. He felt like weeping at the pity of it.

He unhooked the playbill from the wall.

For a second he was confused.

There was a hole, a tiny hole, less than half an inch in diameter. Made by a drill bit, from the look of it. Adeline's bedroom was next door: could this be a spy hole, looking into her room? But no: when he put his eye to the aperture, he saw only darkness. It looked through into the hollow of the chimney, nothing more. Another detail in the case, as yet unexplained.

Latimer and Fairfax were waiting for him in the corridor, with the work team standing close by. It was five past nine on 29 October 1981. He gave the order and the men moved into the room. Almost immediately he heard a sledgehammer smashing into the wall, and his ears rang with the noise of it, yet the sound was dulled inside his head, as though his skull was lined with cotton wool or, worse, with the spores of the musk.

'Meg, I'll be downstairs.'

'Sure. I'll let you know if we find anything.'

'Oh, she's there. I know it now.'

'I hope so.'

Camilla Greene was waiting on the second floor, a female police officer alongside. She looked calm, self-contained. He could imagine she felt better for having confessed, or at least that the long-secret story was coming to an end at last. The burden of the years, lifting.

But he didn't want to speak with her, or even be near her.

He moved into another bedroom and looked down at the back garden.

A fleeting image of a young woman moved on the muddy grass.

He didn't bother closing his eyes, or rubbing them. Nothing would make the vision disappear, not until the drug had passed through his body completely. Only then would he be free, at least from the hallucination. But the memory would never leave him, he knew that, both of events here at Bridlemere and of what he had experienced at the Cromwell House squat last night.

Martin came to mind. He hoped and prayed the kid was all right, that he'd get over it. And that Glenda wasn't too harsh on him.

When I was young myself, I never knew such . . .

These thoughts were broken by a noise from upstairs, someone calling. And the sound of the tools quietened. Soon it would be time.

And now, when he looked again at the back garden, it was empty.

He climbed the stairs back to the top floor. DC Fairfax had stepped out of the room. He was standing alone near the open doorway, looking agitated.

'Meg made me leave. Said I was getting in the way.'

Indeed, the detective sergeant's voice was heard from within. She'd taken charge.

Hobbes entered the room.

'What do we have?' he asked.

Latimer wiped dust from her cheeks. 'The fireplace was bricked up. You see here, a different colour of stone from the surrounding wall and much newer.'

'And then plastered over?'

'That's right. And wallpapered. The whole room was redecorated at that time.'

Hobbes moved close to the fireplace. He knelt down.

Partway hidden amid the rubble and the brick dust and the scattered shreds of wallpaper was a large shape, bent over and squeezed into place. It was wrapped in canvas and tied around with string, lots of it. The cloth and string were still fairly intact, but had worn away and even disintegrated in places. There wasn't much to see, as yet.

'OK, let's get it out of there.'

There was a small forensics team waiting downstairs, but he needed to get the body free first. If it was a body. He didn't know which would be worse . . .

This time Hobbes waited in the corner of the room with Latimer. Fairfax was standing by the door. Two men worked on the task, one knocking out any further bricks that needed to be removed, the other slowly pulling the object loose. Suddenly it seemed to slide forward of its own will, slipping free of the chimney. Another cloud of dust rose. Latimer started to cough.

Hobbes stepped forward. 'Thank you, gentlemen.' The two workers left the room.

The shape was wrapped in what looked like tent material, perhaps a ground sheet. It would have offered some protection over the decades. Hobbes bent down, but Latimer said, 'Don't open it, Guv. Let's get Scene of Crime in here.'

He nodded reluctantly.

And so it began: a snip at a piece of string here and there, only enough to allow access. A pulling apart of several layers of canvas, until a larger opening had been made. Fragments of a finer cloth lay on the floorboards, having escaped the makeshift shroud. Hobbes picked one up. It was delicate, fragile, the threads loose, almost decayed. But he saw a hint of blue, and an edge of yellow. Which would make this dress number twenty-eight. Yes, they were close now. The forensics officers kept at their work. It took longer than anticipated – it always did. But Hobbes stayed where he was. He never closed his eyes; he fought back hunger.

'Come on, come on.'

His words had little effect. The officers worked on at the same pace. And then at last something was drawn free from the package. Hobbes smiled – he couldn't help it.

It was a pair of scissors, old, discoloured along the blades.

A weapon.

One of the officers exclaimed. He called for silence.

Hobbes held his breath.

A second object had been exposed, within the layers of canvas.

A human skull. Some areas of brown wrinkled skin still clung to the bone, mummified from being in the wall cavity for so long.

Hobbes turned to Latimer, then to Fairfax. 'Well, then. Here we are.'

Latimer nodded. 'Adeline Graves.'

The three detectives started to chat about the case, but were soon disturbed by a noise from downstairs.

'Who the hell's that?' Hobbes said. 'Keep them away!'

It was too late. Rosamund Graves was already on the landing, her son David close behind. She looked distraught, and she screamed when she saw the body lying on the floor, still in its wrappings.

'My baby! Oh, my poor baby! My baby!'

A female police constable was holding her back, or trying to. Rosamund struggled and almost pulled free. Her voice rose to a howl, calling for her long-lost child, her daughter.

Other Pathways

That night Detective Inspector Hobbes sat alone in his living room. The television was on, but he hadn't heard a word that was being said, not for a while now. The pictures moved on the screen in a blur of black-and-white: a movie of some kind, he'd forgotten the title. A hardback novel lay open on the arm of his chair; he had managed only a paragraph before his mind wandered off. A half-eaten sandwich on a plate. He'd already thrown up twice, clearing his system. Or trying to.

Every contact leaves a trace.

It always came back to that, to Dr Edmond Locard's Principle of Exchange. What was left at the scene of the crime, and what was taken away. But not in terms of physical items, no: he wasn't thinking of dust and fingerprints and shreds of skin, but of the pain left behind, and the love taken. Christ, the way life goes, the way it is.

Every single contact leaves a trace of the person involved.

The people involved.

That family. He'd seen some messed-up individuals in his time, but never so many, so tightly bound together in a shared darkness. Sharing the darkness between them, gleefully at times, then reluctantly, but always coming back to the family's own moral code, passed down from one generation to the next.

It made him think of David Kepple, and their conversation in the art gallery. Even he, the grandchild, still shared that interest: his precious paintings of decomposition. How they tied in with Adeline's view of herself as a living corpse. And what was it he'd said? Yes, something about narrative. How narratives could no longer be trusted,

There is no single truth, only a mist of possibilities.

Something like that.

And then: beware of false endings.

Hobbes made a noise. A sigh, a groan. He broke away from his mood a little. He turned to look at the blue and yellow dress he'd stolen from Bridlemere. He'd taken it down from the wall and now it lay draped over the back of a chair. He'd followed this object for a week and a half, hoping to find the person who had once worn it, or at least its original version. Hopefully, an examination of Adeline's remains would bring an end to the story, especially if they could find dental records. Despite Kepple's insistence, there might yet be certainty in the world.

Still, the doubts remained. In the well-remembered words of Jack Collingworth: *Always doubt, keep asking questions, even when all seems done.* That had been one of his initial lessons, back when he'd first taken on Hobbes as an acolyte. And only yesterday he'd still been giving out advice: 'Sometimes all it takes is brushing away a single layer of dust.' All good stuff, if you knew how to apply it.

Hobbes studied once more the two items he'd brought with him from Bridlemere. One was the framed playbill that had adorned the chimney breast where Adeline Graves had been buried.

Why the chimney breast? It didn't seem right. Why not bury the body in the garden, or under the shed? Or, better yet, take it far afield, out to Epping Forest?

But the house was important. Perhaps they wanted to keep the girl's spirit there.

The other item was a copy of the burial ritual he'd found in the pile of manuscripts in Leonard's old room, on the second floor of the house. Rosamund Kepple had been right: her father had kept the script, six copies in fact. It was only four pages long, and Hobbes had already read through it once that night. Here were the words to be spoken aloud by each member of the family, whenever the annual ritual of the dress took place. There were lines for Mary Estelle, for Nicholas, for Rosamund and Camilla, for Leonard himself. He recognized the words that Camilla had muttered, at the end of her interview: *Here we lay to rest the body of Adeline Graves.*

Our beloved sister, our child.

'My only purpose is to look after Adeline, to protect her.' Those had been Camilla's words, at the interview, or something close to that, that sentiment. So when Adeline dies, where does all that passion, that purpose, go? Into the ritual, the memory. It was a kind of collective madness. But grief makes people do strange things, and how different was it, really, when compared to other rituals around the world, in different cultures and different times? Societies, no matter how big or small, always had to account for and honour the dead, whether as ghosts, souls in heaven, or acts of remembrance.

On page three, Mary Estelle took charge of the soul's passage through the underworld: *May she travel safely, with these gifts to aid her journey . . .*

And the medal, the coin, the brooch, the cigarette card and the lipstick were all mentioned, each relative casting their own spell over the chosen object: magical charms.

Hobbes skimmed the pages a few more times, seeking clarity. Then he picked up the playbill for *The Moon Awakes*. Was it significant? Why this particular bill, on that wall, the only decoration in the room? Why was Adeline associated so much with the play's leading role, Anna Kreeley? He read again the message that Mary Estelle had written on the photograph: *With all my love.* No recipient mentioned. And then the actress's signature, and then the date – the date of Adeline's death.

There was a slight tear in one corner of the playbill, and something was visible beneath the tear. It was only a tiny speck of colour. Hobbes turned the frame over and removed the back. There was another image inside, hidden behind the first, this one also a playbill, and also celebrating *The Moon Awakes*. But immediately he could see that this was a different version of the play, from a different year. It was unsigned. And there was something wrong with Mary Estelle's face. No, not wrong exactly but . . .

And he remembered one more thing, a line that DC Fairfax had spoken, that evening in Richmond Park, when he'd turned up drunk at the scene of the crime. Hobbes had asked him how he'd got past the officer on duty, and Fairfax had answered in a slur, 'There's more than one way through the woods.'

And there was. Hobbes was sure of it.

PART FOUR
THREE DAYS LATER

A House of Twigs

It didn't take him long to find the street and the house number. He parked on the opposite side and waited for a few minutes. Hobbes was nervous, and he wasn't sure why, exactly. There was so much at stake, and here he was, following a hunch. Nothing more. And that was how he chose to view it, as something tentative, fragile.

In fact, he very nearly turned away. He almost started the car and set off again, back to Richmond, and his little flat. It was five o'clock on a Sunday afternoon. Grey skies, low and threatening. Really, this could wait until the morning, but the day had dragged out, and he felt at a loss. And still frustrated, as they waited for the autopsy results. He needed proof! Proof of identity. Only then would he lay this case to rest. And so, instead of taking it easy and putting his feet up, he was following a lead, one that probably went nowhere. He could just imagine Meg Latimer having a right old laugh at his expense.

The house was one of many in a terraced street, two up, two down. Grimy brickwork, windows in need of a clean. But not too shabby.

Hackney Wick. The far reaches of the East End.

He stepped out of the car and walked across the street. He could hear the bell chiming from the hallway inside and soon enough the front door opened. A woman was standing there, looking at him expectantly. She spoke in a soft manner, but with a tinge of working-class Cockney.

'Yes, can I help?'

'I hope so. My name is Hobbes. Inspector Hobbes. I'm a police officer.'

'Oh, yes.'

'I'm looking for Mrs Watts.'

'I suppose that's me.' She smiled.

'Jean Watts?'

'What's this about?' She was suddenly apprehensive. 'Oh, this isn't about Dotty, is it?'

'That would be your . . . daughter?'

'Yes. But Dorothy lives in New Zealand now. She married a young man out there, oh, nearly ten years ago. She's not in any trouble?'

Hobbes reassured her: 'No, no. Nothing like that.'

'Thank God.'

'I'm here to talk about . . .' But then he paused. He didn't know what to say, not really. 'We're making enquiries about a crime. You might have read about it in the papers. The Nicholas Graves case?'

'Oh. I know a little bit about it, yes. The body in Richmond Park. But why . . . ?'

'Look, can I come in? Would you mind?'

'Now you've got me worried.'

This time he didn't respond. He stood there, waiting, keeping his face expressionless. And the woman looked back at him. A moment passed. She gave in with a sigh and opened the door wide. He followed her into the hall and then along, into a living room.

'Would you like a cup of tea?'

'No, that's fine, Mrs Watts. Thank you.'

'People call me Jeannie.'

'Actually, I will.'

'What – call me Jeannie?'

'No, I mean have a cup of tea.'

'Lovely. I'll just be a tick. Make yourself at home.'

She disappeared through the doorway. It gave him a few min-utes to look around the room. It was neat, tidy, a select display of ornaments, a row of five photographs on the mantelpiece, all depicting a young girl, presumably the aforementioned Dotty. He judged Jeannie Watts to be in her mid-forties, so her daughter might be in her twenties now, but there were no pictures of a grown woman, or of a husband. Only the child. There was an upright piano in one corner of the room, old-looking, a little bashed around the edges. It reminded Hobbes of a time when many houses had pianos: he recalled the 'jolly sing-alongs', when he went round to a friend's house for tea. On top of the piano there was a metronome and a small plaster bust of Beethoven. A sheet of music was slotted into the holder: 'Roses of Picardy'. God, that was going back a fair bit.

'Oh, I was just playing that, when you knocked.'

Mrs Watts came into the room, carrying a tea tray.

Hobbes helped her with it. 'It's an old tune,' he said. 'My mum and dad used to dance around the living room to that one.'

'My foster mother used to play it. It always reminds me of her.'

'You were fostered?'

'My parents died when I was very young, in the Blitz.'

'I'm sorry.'

'Oh, hush now. I had a wonderful childhood, despite it all. Now . . .'

She offered Hobbes a seat at a table, and sat there herself. She poured out the tea and put in his milk and sugar, as he wanted. She took a sip of hers.

'Now, what can I tell you?'

'I mentioned the death of Nicholas Graves. Didn't you know him? At least, you met him when you were young?'

'Did I? I'm not sure.' She looked puzzled.

'He was the son of Leonard Graves. The playwright?'

Now her eyes lit up with the memory. 'Oh dear, I haven't thought about Mr Graves in such a long time now. Lenny Graves!'

'You worked with him, I believe. On a play?'

'That's right. But I can't imagine he's still alive?'

'He died recently, actually. About a week before his son.'

'Oh, my. I'm really not keeping up with things.'

'That's OK.'

They drank their tea. Hobbes took a moment to study the woman. Jeannie Watts must have been striking in her youth, and he could see why Leonard Graves might have taken an interest in her. But time had played a strange trick, making her not exactly prematurely old, but twisting her face a little, as though she'd been in an accident at some point. The right side of her face sagged, and the right eye dipped at the corner. Her hair was dark, abundant, with little evidence as yet of grey. There was a slight downward tilt to her mouth, an effort involved whenever she made a smile.

Hobbes was aware, suddenly, that Jeannie was staring back at him.

And her hands came up to her face, to shield it.

He was embarrassed.

'Are you looking at me, Inspector?'

'Sorry. Yes.'

'Inspecting me for flaws, perhaps?' It was said light-heartedly. 'The way men do.'

'Of course not. Force of habit, that's all.'

'Part of the job?'

He nodded.

'Do they give you training in such things, in studying people? I've always wondered, watching *Columbo* on the tele.'

'It's not really like that.'

'No? I'm disappointed.'

'With me, it's just a personal trait. I can't help it.'

'How interesting.'

To get back on track, he said, 'I'd like to know more about your youth, and how you met Mr Graves.'

'Do you think this will be helpful?'

'It might. Nicholas Graves died because of events that happened long ago, we know that now, and I think you were there at the time or, at least, were acquainted with the family.'

'I was. But only for a brief while.'

'Still. It might be useful.'

She nodded, and smiled at him with her usual effort. Carefully, she placed her teacup in the saucer, in a way designed to make as little noise as possible.

'As I said, I was brought up by foster parents, the Mortons, here in Hackney. I haven't moved very far in life, I'm afraid. I was nine years old when the war ended. I used to love hanging around the stage door of the Hackney Empire, and I got to know the doorman there – his name was Albert. Albert Harris. A sweet old man. He'd seen everyone in his time, passing through the doors. Fairbanks, Burton . . .'

'Mrs Watts.'

'Yes, yes. I'm getting to it. But, you see, Albert used to let me in for free. So that's how I fell in love with the theatre. I had a poor education, and the Mortons had only a little money to spend on me. But the Empire was a paradise: the lights, the music, the *thespians*. That was a new word I learned. I would stand right at the back of the auditorium, near the exit, and watch as the play unfolded. Better still, I used to adore going backstage, watching the props being carried on and off, everyone milling around. That room full of costumes! It was thrilling! And for those few hours, I was free. Free of my memories, of Mummy and Daddy. Of the noise of the bombs falling, and the explosions.'

The middle-aged woman's eyes sparkled with the dreams of youth as she spoke.

'So you decided to pursue a stage career yourself?'

'Yes, yes. As I could. The good Lord blessed me with a modicum of looks, and I believe I had a fair enough talent. I put in many hours at the theatre, helping out, learning what I could.'

'You never went to drama school?'

'Good heavens, no! It all comes from a purely natural place.'

Hobbes finished his tea, and refused another cup. 'Did you see Mary Estelle Graves on the stage?'

'I did. Once only. She played Lady Macbeth, in . . . 1947. But she was getting on a bit by then. It wasn't a very good performance, according to the critics. The kinder ones called it her "swansong". The crueller ones . . . Well, she retired from the stage soon after.'

'And yourself? What did you think?'

'Oh, I loved her. She was everything I wanted to be. The very *essence* of glamour.'

'Did you get to talk to her?'

'Not right then, no. My first proper role was young Flora in an adaptation of *The Turn of the Screw*. And then, as I got a little older, a lady's maid in a thriller called *Don't Answer the Door*. It closed after a week. So I wasn't expecting much, but then I managed to read for the part of Imogen in *Cymbeline*. Do you know that play?'

Hobbes shook his head. 'Not in any detail.'

'I was lucky enough to be accepted for the role. My first big break. Here, let me see if I can . . . This is Imogen asking her servant to kill her.' Jeannie's voice took on a different hue, lightening, growing younger, yet touched with despair: ' "Against self-slaughter there is a prohibition so divine, that cravens my weak hand. Come, here's my heart!" ' She held both hands close to her chest as she said this. And then they opened slowly, and moved apart to reveal the target area.

She smiled. 'Have I embarrassed you?'

'No. Not at all.'

'I'm amazed I can still remember the lines! Well, some of them anyway. I was barely eighteen years old, can you imagine? And I received some very good notices. I thought the whole world lay before me.'

'So that would be, what? Nineteen . . . ?'

'1953. Late in the year.'

'I see. And that was when you met Mr Graves?'

'It was during the run of *Cymbeline*, actually. I was living on my own at that time, in a lodging house for young ladies on Wick Lane. I had a job in a corner shop, which supported me as I learned my craft, and auditioned for parts. But I was quite alone, and quite poor. I had few close friends in those days. Such things never came easily to me.'

'Have you always been a loner?'

'If that's the word you want to use, then, yes, I suppose so.'

'But you've been married?'

A shake of her head. Regret in her eyes.

Hobbes couldn't help looking to the mantelpiece, with its row of photographs. And she saw him doing this. Perhaps a certain look was on his face.

'Shall I ask you to leave?'

'Mrs . . . sorry, *Miss* Watts, I'm only concerned about the Graves family, and anything you can tell me about them. That's all.'

'Only, I don't like being treated with disrespect.' That smile came back, her mouth working hard against its defect.

'Of course. I never meant to—'

'If we understand each other?'

He nodded. 'Will you tell me about Leonard Graves, and how he found you?'

With some relief, she answered his question. 'One of his representatives was in the audience one night, and a few days later I was called into his office.' She thought for a moment. 'A couple of rooms on Berwick Street, upstairs, above a Greek restaurant. I didn't have a clue what I was stepping into.'

'And?'

'Oh, I could hardly speak! He, and his casting director, wanted me to read for Anna Kreeley.'

'The main character from *The Moon Awakes*?'

She nodded. 'It was incredible. Such a wonderful chance.'

'Did you know the play?'

'I'd never seen it performed, but I'd read reviews in old copies of the *Stage*, and the playscript a few times.'

'It was Mary Estelle Graves's first big role?'

'It was. It made her a star. And I felt I was stepping into her shoes. Not that I could ever . . . well, I mean . . . the very thought!'

'Jeannie, can I speak freely with you?'

A little fret of worry played around her eyes. 'Of course.'

'Why do you think Leonard offered you the part?'

'Why? I don't know what you mean. Because of my acting talent, of course.'

'For no other reason?'

'What other reason could there be?'

'Your looks.'

She stared at him. Her expression had changed, the polite exterior wavering a little. 'I hope you're not implying . . .'

'I'm saying that when you were young you did bear a resemblance to Mary Estelle when she herself was young.'

The staring match continued. And then she breathed a little easier. 'One or two people had commented as such, yes. But I could never see it myself. Even when . . .'

'Yes?'

'Nothing. It doesn't matter. Look, what is this about? Is all this really necessary?'

'It is. I'm just trying to—'

She stood up. 'I must get things ready. I must get on!'

Now he spoke calmly, with a certain coldness: 'I need to know what happened on that night, the final night of *The Moon Awakes*. That's all.'

'Why?' There was a tremor to her voice.

Hobbes turned in his chair to look at her. He paused to bring his thoughts together, before asking the question plainly: 'Jeannie, did something happen on that night? Something you don't like to talk about? Or even think about too much?'

It took her a while, a long while.

'Yes.'

He could barely hear her. But it was enough.

'Please. Sit down. Let's go through this.'

He waited. Jeannie Watts looked doubtful. She nibbled at her lips, and her hands didn't know what to do with themselves. She picked up a lace antimacassar from the back of an armchair, then put it down again, scrunched up.

Then she wiped at her face and came back to the table.

He opened his bag and removed a sheet of paper. He said, 'I found this recently.'

'Is it a playbill?' She took it from his hands and studied it intently. 'I haven't seen one of these in years.'

'That must have been a very exciting time for you.'

'Oh, it was!' She read out a line of text from it: ' "The glittering debut of a major talent. Miss Jeannie Watts stars in a new production of *The Moon Awakes*, written and directed by Leonard Graves." '

Hobbes watched her carefully. The words emboldened her, and her face relaxed a little. He saw a glimpse of her youth.

'How wonderful it sounds! And rather sad, don't you think?'

'In what way?' he asked.

'The *glittering* debut led to very little else. I performed in a few more plays, and then gave up. I left the theatre, and started a new career, working in retail, clothing stores, fashion houses. These days I work for a mail-order catalogue. I'm a section manager . . .' Her voice trailed off.

'Miss Watts?'

'Yes?'

'Have you ever played a character called Adeline?'

Hobbes was testing her, to see what reaction the question might bring. And it had a profound effect on her. Jeannie Watts looked surprised to begin with, and then a little fearful.

'No . . . no, I don't think so . . .'

'You can't recall?'

'Is this another script by Leonard Graves?'

'Yes, it might be.'

'Let me see . . .' She counted off her roles on her fingers. 'I've played a lady's maid, and poor haunted Flora. I was Imogen, and Anna Kreeley, and . . .'

She stopped speaking. Hobbes could see the puzzlement in her eyes, as his question continued to trouble her. But instead of pursuing it, he drew her attention back to the playbill. 'When I first saw this, I assumed it was Mary Estelle Graves in the photo. But then I looked more closely.'

'It's so irritating to be compared in this way! I am my own

woman. I have lived my life according to certain moral tenets. I will *not* be devalued!'

'I'm not saying that—'

'I think you are. I think you dislike me.'

'Miss Watts. I don't even know you—'

'No. And you never will.'

Hobbes leaned back in his chair. He wasn't yet sure where this was going, but he knew by now one thing: Jeannie Watts knew something of that night when Adeline Graves had met her end.

He concentrated his mind, and asked, 'How did the play go? Was it a success?'

A slight shake of her head. 'No. Regretfully. In Leonard's defence, I think it was the wrong time for a revival. *The Moon Awakes* was a period piece by then, and the public's taste had moved on.'

'But it lasted the whole run?'

'Oh, yes, ticket sales were fair to middling. We muddled along. Old troupers, and all that.'

'Good, good. And then, on the last night of the season, you were invited to a party, I believe, at Bridlemere?'

'Bridlemere? I don't—'

'The name of the Graves family home. On Palliser Road, in Richmond.'

'Oh, right. I didn't know it was called that. I can't remember everything.'

'Of course not.'

Miss Watts had gained a little composure. Hobbes needed all the details he could gather on this case, and he hoped he could tempt them out of her. He asked directly, 'What happened on that night?'

She took a breath to steady herself. 'After the performance we all went for a drink in a pub near the theatre, the whole cast and crew. But there was a sadness to the revelry. And people slipped away one by one, until only the faithful remained. Leonard and the leading man – I can't recall his name, I'm afraid.'

'That's OK.'

'And Betty was there. She was the costume designer. A few others. I was probably a bit squiffy by then. I wasn't used to alcohol. Leonard asked me if I'd like to come back to his house, to meet the family.'

'He mentioned Mary Estelle, I presume?'

'She was the trump card, the reason I agreed. But it wasn't anything like how I expected when we got there.'

'What were you expecting?'

'Something rather grand, and enticing. Carefree. Frivolous, even. It was something I used to dream about, incessantly, when I was a teenager. Being surrounded by creative people all the time, sharing ideas with them. But it was just a family home. A large house, and darkly lit, with lots of corridors. It struck me as being more like the houses I used to read about in Gothic romance novels.'

'And you met the family?'

'I did.'

'Can you remember them all?'

'No, not really. Not clearly. There was a brother and sister . . . I suppose that would be Nicholas and . . .'

'Rosamund.'

'Right. Her name has vanished. And then Mary Estelle, of course. As radiant as ever, if a little frayed here and there. A beautiful specimen.'

'Of what?'

'I'm sorry?'

'A specimen of what?'

'Of . . . Oh, let's call her an ageing queen bee, shall we? Still trying her best to run the hive, and failing a little more each day. She reminded me of some of the older *grandes dames* of the theatre, and the roles they specialized in: cantankerous matriarchs, rigid in their beliefs, grimly hanging on to the past. A little mad. Or quite a lot mad, depending on their mood.'

Hobbes said, 'You're making me think of Norma Desmond in *Sunset Boulevard*.'

'Yes, exactly! That's very astute.'

'How did the family strike you?'

'They were fractious, always on the edge of argument. But I think they made an effort because I was there.'

'And Mary Estelle . . . how did she treat you?'

'I think . . .'

'Yes?'

'I think she was jealous.'

'Of you and her husband?'

'I suppose so, but . . .'

Hobbes glanced again at the photographs of the child, and asked, 'Was there anything going on between you and Leonard?'

Miss Watts shook her head. 'Oh, God, no. Nothing at all. He was a gentleman of the old school. But Mary Estelle had her suspicions, and that was that. She made reference to the newspaper reviews of my performance. Always with a laugh in her voice, but still . . .'

Hobbes thought for a moment. He knew he was coming to the most important part of Jeannie Watts's story. 'Tell me what happened then,' he said.

'Let me think. We all had a drink, and Leonard took me on a tour of the house.'

'All the floors?'

'No, I don't think so. He took me into this one room. It was a kind of study, but with very little furniture in it. And he showed me a series of paintings on the wall, his "greatest treasure", he called it.'

'What was the subject matter?'

Now she looked at Hobbes, and he saw in her eyes an intense look, almost fearful. And she continued, 'It was a series of paintings all showing a human body, a woman's body, slowly decaying, yes, that was it. A dead woman's body decomposing, from solid flesh . . . down to the bare bones, the skull, and all the stages in between. I thought it was horrible, just a really *horrible* thing to paint, and I couldn't understand why anyone would want to depict such a thing, or why Mr Graves would want to collect it and put it on display. And yet, at the same time . . .'

'It fascinated you?'

'It did. It did. Very much so. I couldn't draw myself away.'

And then her gaze came back to the present day, and she blinked a couple of times. It was very quiet now, in this neat and tidy room in Hackney Wick. The only sound was the patter of rain against the windowpane, the droplets casting shadows through the lace curtains.

Hobbes spoke calmly. 'Tell me about the rest of the evening, Jeannie, if you can.'

She stared at him. Her face seemed a little more twisted, that glimpse of her youthful self now long gone.

'I'm still puzzled,' she said. 'Why are you so interested in all this?'

'It's quite simple. I've heard an account of the night from a family member, and for some reason they left you out of the picture. Completely. And I would like to know why that was, and what you saw that led to this denial of your presence.'

A faint smile in response. 'I was a ghost at the feast. If feast it was.'

He could see her excitement at this prospect, of Hobbes investigating a mystery from her life. And now she carried on freely.

'Leonard took me back downstairs. I don't think the sister, Rosamund . . . She wasn't there. But she appeared later on. And we drank some more. I imagine we were all tipsy by then. Oh, yes, at one point I walked out into the back garden. I had gone into the kitchen on my own, to get a glass of water. The back door was open, so I stepped outside. Gardens have always held a magical power for me. I remember now, walking down to the wild area, near the rear wall, and looking back at the house. There was . . .'

Hobbes leaned forward. 'Yes?'

'There was someone at the top window. No . . . two people. Two women, I think. What a strange thing to remember.'

'Not at all. Little details often come back to us, far more than the larger events.'

And he remembered Camilla's story of standing next to Adeline, in her bedroom, and the ghostly figure they had seen in the garden below. How very *alike* Adeline Graves and Jeannie Watts must have looked, in such circumstances, moonlit, on an October evening: one young woman a bearer of her grandmother's great beauty, and the other chosen purely for her resemblance to Mary Estelle Graves. It was uncanny.

An idea formed in Hobbes's mind. It was so strange a thing, he could hardly pursue it, for fear it might break apart.

Jeannie Watts was still talking: 'I went back inside, back to the party. I must have spent some time chatting with Mary Estelle, or trying to, asking for her advice on my career. That's the kind of thing I would have done, given my purpose back then. I was very keen on getting on in life, escaping my loneliness.'

Hobbes knew he was approaching the key moments. 'Jeannie, tell me if you can. Was there anybody else at the party, someone you haven't mentioned yet?'

She took a breath. 'There was, yes. I was coming to that.'

'Who was it?'

'It was a young woman. She came into the room much later on, when we were all quite drunk. I can remember her now, standing at the doorway, looking at us all in turn.'

Hobbes held his breath, as he waited for the story to unfold.

'I didn't know who she was, this new arrival, not to begin with. But I picked up that she was Mary Estelle's third daughter.'

'Can you remember her name?'

'I'm not sure . . .'

'You have to! You have to remember!'

She was shocked by Hobbes's sudden vehemence. 'Please, you're making me . . . Oh, of course, I remember! Yes, *Adeline*, that was it.' And her hands fluttered in front of her. 'So that's why you asked if I'd ever played a role with that name.'

He dismissed the remark. 'Tell me about her, about Adeline.'

'Well, she was an odd girl, I must say, around my age at the time, eighteen or so. But she looked older somehow. Almost . . . What is the word? I don't know . . .'

'She looked ill – is that what you mean?'

'Yes, I think she was. She certainly looked weak, as though she hadn't been eating properly for a while. But it was more than that. Shall I say . . . that life had been *eating* at her? Would that make sense to you?'

'I think so,' Hobbes replied. 'Adeline was suffering from an affliction, a delusion, one that made her believe she was dying, or decaying, or that areas of her flesh were already dead. It was all in her mind, but the thoughts had taken her over so much that her body was following suit.'

'Oh, that's – that's just *horrible* to think about.'

'Yes, it is. But it may be that she was making herself physically ill on purpose to bring her mental state alive in some way in the flesh. There are a number of ways of looking at it.'

Jeannie Watts was lost in the memory, her eyes seeking out some faraway place. 'I can see her plainly, as I think back.' Her voice was soft in the telling. 'So much of that evening is coming to me now.'

'What was Adeline wearing?'

'Oh, I don't know. A dress of some kind, I imagine.'

'Was this the dress?'

Hobbes's hands opened. He had brought the dress from his own rooms with him, and now he unfolded it in front of her.

She stared at it with fevered eyes. 'Yes, it might be. Where did you get that?'

But Hobbes diverted her: 'What was the effect of Adeline's sudden appearance?'

'I don't know what you mean.' She spoke without purpose: her gaze had not yet given up on the dress.

'Nothing unusual happened?'

'Like what?'

Hobbes felt a sudden frustration. He drew back a little. 'You said before that the family was arguing.'

'Did I?'

'You know you did.'

'I can't recall. Not precisely. It's so many years ago!'

'It was 1954, we discussed that.'

'I never said *arguing*. I said fractious, that they were almost arguing, but –'

'Miss Watts—'

'– but they held themselves back, because I was there. That's what I said.'

'I know that. But—'

'And I left soon after Adeline . . . soon after she appeared. The atmosphere had soured.'

Hobbes placed the dress on the table in front of her. He asked, 'And what about the scissors?'

'I don't understand what you mean! Why would you mention—'

'The dressmaking scissors. Adeline was holding them when she came into the room. Don't you remember?'

'Yes, but—'

'And she threatened someone with them. She threatened Rosamund.'

'Rosamund?'

'You saw it all. You were there—'

'No! I left the room, I got my coat from the hallstand, and I went outside. Nobody noticed me leaving, nobody cared. They were all tied up in their own hatred.'

Hobbes started to speak, but decided against it. The room was darkening around them. He stood up, and made to click on the light. But Jeannie Watts worried herself over this.

'No, please don't do that. It's too early.'

Hobbes turned on the light anyway, and saw her flinch in its glow. He returned to his seat at the table. Their faces were only inches apart. Spitting distance. In fact, he could see flecks of saliva on her lips. He could see every line around her eyes, every mark, the places where the effort was strong, and where it was weak. One of her cheeks was trembling. Her hands were balled into fists on the tabletop. Her whole body seemed paused to collapse, especially when Hobbes spoke again.

'Tell me about the child in the photographs. Dotty in New Zealand.'

'What about her?'

'Who is the father?'

'Why does that matter to you?'

'Is there really a child?'

She could not look at him now.

The suspicion grew in Hobbes's mind, a new and quite shocking way of seeing the events in the Adeline Graves case. But he still wasn't sure.

'Miss Watts? It's best to tell the truth. A murder has been committed.'

Her fingernails tapped at the tabletop repeatedly. It took a moment, and then the relief played freely across her face as she admitted at last: 'No. No child. No Dorothy. Only some photographs I found in a wastepaper bin at work. I thought she looked rather beautiful, and I couldn't understand why anyone would want to throw them away. If I admitted that I was incapable of bearing children, would that explain my actions to you?"

'I would think that you're lying.'

She was genuinely surprised by this. Her face gave everything away, and she stuttered, 'How – how dare you? Dorothy is—'

'Your name isn't Jeannie Watts.'

'What?' The word came out in a gasp.

'What is your real name?'

'My name?'

'Your real name? The name your parents gave you?'

'Oh, I see what you mean. It was Nell. Yes. Now I see why you're confused, Inspector. I was born Eleanor Smith. But everyone called me Nell. My mum, my dad. God bless them in heaven. And my foster parents . . . one family, and then another. They all called me the same thing. Nell! Nell Smith! I changed it when I started on my career. I needed a new name for the theatre, a stage name, something that would stand out.'

'I don't believe you.'

'But you must! You have to believe me! Nell Smith at first, then

Jeannie Watts ever after. This is the truth. There is no other truth!'

Hobbes made to protest, but she cut him off. Her fist banged down on the table, and she started to cry out: 'I am Jeannie Watts, I am forty-five years old. I live at twenty-nine Monastery Road, Hackney, London, postcode E9 5SZ. Jeannie Watts! I was born some few streets from here, on White Post Lane, near the train line. As a child, I heard the trains from my bedroom, coming and going in the night. I could smell the steam in the air.'

It was an enchantment against pain, a consolidation of a learned identity.

'My parents were killed in 1942. They didn't like the idea of me being evacuated, of being separated from me. We used to hide in the cellar of the local pub, the Star and Garter, whenever the sirens went off. It was so exciting! But then one night the all-clear was sounded, and we went up again, on to the streets. There was a bomb in the rubble of a house, and it . . . it . . .'

'The bomb exploded?'

'Yes. That's right. And I lost everyone!'

Hobbes's face was brutal in its look. 'I don't care about your past. Only about what happened that night, at Bridlemere. I think you stayed in the living room. You saw the arguments flare, and the shouting begin. I think you—'

'Please—'

'No, listen to me! Jeannie, don't turn away. You were there, you saw everything. You did meet Adeline Graves. You talked to her. You said something to her, something that upset her. Is that right? And you saw her approaching with the scissors in her hands. You saw the look on her face. What was it? Sheer hatred? Or something more? Something . . . hopeful?'

He paused. He was exhausted. His muscles had tightened into knots.

The rain was pelting down now, loud against the window like shots of lead.

Jeannie Watts was shaking terribly.

Her mouth cracked open.

Her eyes, unblinking.

Hobbes told the story of that night, as he saw it, speaking coldly now.

'Adeline drew close and she attacked you. Did you place your hands over the wound in your side, just here, in the midriff?'

He showed her the place on his own body.

And she copied his movement on hers.

'How did it feel, can you remember? Can you remember that moment, Jeannie, as the blood left you, as it drained away? What was it like, when the darkness closed in?'

Her face was frozen. All traces of emotion gone.

She might have been a statue at that point, or a broken machine.

Only the quiver of her lips gave evidence of life.

Hobbes asked again, fiercely now: 'How did it feel, when Adeline attacked you, when she killed you?'

The whole conversation rested on this one statement.

He waited, hardly breathing.

Everything he'd suspected, or dared to suspect, was now coming true.

Jeannie Watts frowned.

The drama was coming to its final act. One of her hands came up to her face, to rub at her cheeks, her brow, the area around her mouth. To all intents and purposes, she was removing traces of stage paint from her skin.

And she spoke. Her voice was quiet. 'I would not die, not as quickly as they hoped. The blood flowed too slowly from my wound. I watched as Nicholas bent down beside me and placed a cushion over my face. I could not breathe. It was painful. At first. And then . . . and then . . . blissful.'

Hobbes didn't dare to reply.

'I lay there unmoving, with barely a heartbeat, and I saw in the shadows of myself that Adeline was waiting for me. She was gentle at first, and then a little more forceful, as she stole my spirit from me. As she took from me the last thing I had left, my soul. And then . . .'

She took one great breath, to force out these last few words.

'And then the darkness was complete. And the silence.'

She paused. Another breath. Softer than before.

'The stillness . . .'

Her eyes closed. And remained so.

Hobbes watched her.

She was murmuring to herself.

He couldn't hear the words.

A change was taking place, inside her head, in her mind.

God knew what she was thinking.

And then her eyes opened again, wide this time.

She was staring ahead, not at Hobbes, not even at the wallpaper, but at another person close by, invisible as yet, but also sitting at this table.

A third person.

Hobbes could only imagine that Adeline Graves was there as well, conjured into being by Jeannie Watts's powerful imagination. The two women were perfect reflections of each other.

And Hobbes leaned back, leaving them facing each other.

He observed the change in the face before him: the tilt of her head, the sagging flesh on her cheek, the curl of her mouth, the look in her eyes, they all righted themselves, a former appearance restored as the mask was dropped.

And the two women became one again.

Hobbes said, 'Tell me your name.'

'Adeline.'

'Adeline Graves?'

She nodded. But that wasn't enough.

'Say it!'

'Adeline. Adeline Graves. What have you done?'

Her voice, too, had taken on a new colour, more refined, more like Rosamund's tone, or Mary Estelle's upper-class accent. Her face, her accent, her life: all had been constructed around her true self.

'I will disappear.'

Hobbes held her stare. He could see the pain in her eyes. 'No, I don't believe you will.' He said, 'You've played your part wonderfully, for so many years. Isn't that true? But now, now it's time to give it up, to step down . . .'

Adeline was trembling. 'To step down from the stage?' She laughed at this. Her voice took on a strange lilt, the kind an actress might use to convey a certain mood. 'I assure you, the stage is my world. I am the parts I have played, nothing more.'

'The one part, yes. The one role. You've rehearsed your lines well, I see that. I admire you for it. The time and the effort you've put in, Adeline, the facts you've learned, and memorized, about poor Jeannie's life, the life you stole! But it's more than that, isn't it? You actually *became* Jeannie Watts. You became that person when the real Jeannie was murdered on that night in 1954. Only by doing this could you battle the rot that devoured you, that plagued your mind, and then your body. And only by taking on this other woman's life could you, finally, have a life of your own.'

Adeline laughed at this explanation, a soundless laugh.

She was picking at the skin of her palm with the fingers of her other hand, peeling the skin away. It seemed to come easily.

Hobbes looked on, horrified. 'Adeline . . .'

Her nails dug in. She was hurting herself, drawing blood.

But her face showed no pain, only the silent fixed laugh, a cruel grimace.

She spread a little of the blood on to the dress, where it lay on the table.

'Whose idea was it? Tell me the truth! Who thought of this? Was it Leonard, or your mother, Rosamund?'

The fingernails stopped at their progress. She stared at him then, the look in her eyes abstracted and distant. 'It was Camilla.'

'Camilla?'

'My sister Camilla . . .'

'You mean your aunt?'

'Camilla went to see the play and she saw what Leonard had done, how he'd chosen a young version of his wife for the part of Anna Kreeley. And she learned of the actress's life, her loneliness, how Leonard had found her, a pitiful girl, an orphan, without friends or relatives. She was perfect in every way for Camilla's purpose.'

'Which was?'

'To give me life.'

'So, in your room that night, when you and Camilla looked down into the garden, and you saw Jeannie Watts, is that what you talked about, killing this woman, this guest in your house?'

'Yes. Exactly.'

'Who else knew about it?'

'Nobody, not to begin with, but Camilla drew them in, one by one at the party. Only Nicholas was doubtful.'

'Mary Estelle and Rosamund, they were both complicit? And Leonard as well?'

A nod.

'And Camilla's been looking after you ever since. Using the family money.'

'She's very sweet to me, very kind.'

'Has she been staying here with you, these last days, since Leonard died?'

'We have our games, sister and sister.'

'Where is she now? Is Camilla still here?'

'No, gone now. Back home.'

Adeline's voice was weakening, her lines broken into fragments. Her body continued to sway back and forth. 'I am not myself.'

'Adeline—'

'I am *not* myself. I need . . . I need to be myself again. I need to be Jeannie again. I need to live again!'

She was crying out. The chair creaked as she rocked on it. Her hands held on to the edge of the table.

'I should have gone round to see him, to see Leonard.'

'This time?'

'We should have performed the ceremony.'

'Why didn't you?'

'I was sick, sick of it all. And I wanted to be free. But now . . . now I know, I've made a mistake.'

Her voice took on a chant-like quality. 'We need to bury the dress again. Over and over again. I need somebody to read the script for me, to say a prayer for the dead, that I might rise.'

Hobbes tried to hold her, but she was too strong, driven by her desperate needs, her mind cast into darkness.

'I need to live!'

She grabbed the dress, stood up and moved to the nearest doorway. Hobbes went with her into a kitchen at the rear of the house. The lights were off but Hobbes could hear her in the dark, moving about, opening a drawer. His hand searched for a light switch, without luck. The rain dribbled down the window-pane, casting strange patterns on the walls, and on the grey-lit face of Adeline Graves. She pulled the wig from her head, revealing her auburn-coloured hair, or what remained of it, for it was ragged and short, badly cut, dirty and greasy. It stuck up in little tufts.

Hobbes watched her, fascinated.

She was caught in a great struggle to survive, one expression mixed with another, both vying for dominance.

Jeannie Watts, Adeline Graves. She was an actress caught exactly between two states, two roles.

Hobbes asked her a question, hoping to keep Adeline in view. He said, 'What about Nicholas? Did you kill him as well?'

'He had to die! He wanted to tell everything. He wanted to show the world what I was, what I'd become. He mentioned you, Inspector. Inspector Hobbes. He wanted to confess, and tell all.'

'You couldn't let that happen, could you?'

Her head shook from side to side. The rain painted her face with ever-changing shapes. She looked to be dissolving.

'I shut him up. I closed his mouth. My father's bloody mouth.'

'In the park?'

She nodded eagerly, proud of her achievements. 'I'd brought one of the dresses with me, just to make him remember everything that he'd done.'

'There was no one else involved?'

'Alone, all alone, little Jeannie Watts, all alone.'

There was one more thing he needed to know. 'What about Camilla? She came to us, and confessed. You didn't punish her.'

'It wasn't a confession. It was an act, a script we made together, that the family made together. For our protection.'

'I think she went too far, revealing the body in the wall.'

'Poor woman, she thought she could end the story, once and for all.'

Hobbes forced himself to stand tall, to speak with conviction. 'I'm going to call my colleagues. They will need to question you further. Will you come with me?'

'I'm sorry. That's simply not possible.'

Her voice wavered, from one accent to another.

And then she shifted slightly, and her right hand came up, to reveal a pair of scissors in her grasp. Kitchen scissors: she must have grabbed them from the drawer as she came into the room.

'I'm not leaving without you,' Hobbes said. 'So how do we play this out?'

'To the end. The closing line.' And she smiled at the idea.

Hobbes felt both compassion, and rage. The emotions troubled at each other, without hope of either winning out.

He had a sudden vision of his own child, of Martin.

And he said with passion, 'You killed a poor young woman, in cold blood.'

'I brought her to life. I gave her a child, Dorothy, and lovers, one, two, three. I gave her a job, and a house, a roof and walls to shelter within. What else could I do?'

And Hobbes knew there were no options left. Only to make an arrest.

He stepped forward.

Adeline cringed. The skin was flaking on her face, her flesh soft and ready for decay to take over. The spell was weakening. Hobbes saw in her eyes the depths of despair, and her madness. It was driven deep, with no other outlet but self-harm, to let the night flesh fall away until only the bones were left, to crumble into dust.

She turned the blades of the scissors towards her own stomach area, just to the side. She was still holding the dress in the other hand.

'I watched you from the shadows.'

Her voice had taken on its former tone, and Adeline's looks settled on her face, at least for the moment.

'No one can see me, not when I wish it. I have no form in the world, only what I have stolen, and the mask I wear. And so I move in silence, unseen, when I desire to. And I did so, I desired to watch you, Detective, after Nicholas had told of your interest in my case. I waited in the niches and alcoves of Bridlemere, all those places where Camilla and I used to play our games of Hide and Seek.'

'You visited your family home?'

The woman's face shifted, and the patterns of rain trembled down her. Her teeth were visible as she smiled in delight. Her mouth broadened further, into a snarl.

'You were standing only a few feet from me, and I saw you shiver, as though a ghost had visited you.'

'I don't believe in ghosts.'

'I watched you a second time, when you took the dress in your hands, and rubbed it against your face. I saw your look of pleasure. How wonderful. And yet how ashamed you must feel! How alone!'

'You were there? You followed me?'

'I saw you at the funeral of my grandfather, when you chased that silly little girl with her pretend dress. What a fool you made of yourself that day.'

'What else have you seen?'

'I looked at you from my little house of twigs.'

'I don't understand.'

'You leaned over and looked into my room of branches, and my carpet of dried leaves, my walls of glass. Don't you remember? When David introduced me?'

'Of course. He called you Nell.'

'Like I said, my first name. Nell Smith.'

'So David Kepple's involved?'

'In his ignorance, yes. Ignorant of all things, only that I exist, and must be loved. And fed. And praised. And prayed for. And kept warm. The family deemed it so!'

That one phrase contained the whole meaning of this case.

The family deemed it so.

Hobbes felt sick.

Adeline's hands trembled on the scissors. He really thought she was going to damage herself now, but before he could move to stop her, Adeline had twisted away, or slithered away, or floated away, for her body had taken on a liquid quality – *she was hardly there at all*. And she made for the kitchen door, her feet soundless on the stone floor. Before Hobbes could even turn, she had wrenched open the door and run outside.

He stepped out. The rain hit him immediately, drenching his hair and face. The sky was low and the darkest grey, almost black. He could see only a few feet ahead. His shoes sank into the muddy soil as he moved forward, calling her name.

'Adeline. Adeline!'

His voice was lost in the murky air, in the slanting lines of rain.

And then he saw a movement, a blurred shape emerging from the darkness, and he ran towards her as best he could, almost slipping.

'Adeline! Wait. Don't—'

But now she had vanished once more. She cried out in alarm. And so he stood where he was, then took a few tentative steps towards the sound. He found her lying on the ground, near a patch of lawn, tripped by a large branch lying next to her feet. Her face was pelted by the rain, wet and glistening, and her short hair was matted close to her skull. But her face was the worst to look at, for the skin was pitted, and some of it had come away in shreds of flesh. She was sobbing. Drops of rain ran into her mouth. Her features slipped from one expression to another. One mask, another mask. One woman, another woman. Hobbes could hardly make it out. Was it an effect of the rain, the mud and the dim light? Or something real, something drawn from her mind, and manifested on the body? There was no way of knowing, not clearly.

The dress was still clutched in her hands.

She clung to it dearly, the only thing she had left.

Spells Against Darkness

From statements made by Adeline Graves during her interrogation, from the words of her grandmother, Mary Estelle, in her moments of clarity, from the confessions of Camilla and Rosamund, now they knew it was all over, from testimonies given by all parties at the murder trial, and from journals found in Adeline's home in Hackney Wick, from all these sources, and from his own thoughts on the matter, Hobbes put together a version of the twenty-eight rituals, as undertaken over the years. Above all, he needed to know the story, or at least a variant of it, to picture the events in his own mind, this shared obsession of a family – and an idea, a spell, that drew people like a pull of nature, bringing with it both death, and life.

It goes like this:

Year zero. 1954. The corpse of Jeannie Watts is wrapped in Adeline's favourite dress. She's interred in the chimney breast. A prayer is said, improvised by Camilla. A prayer for her niece's continued life.

1955. For the first six months, all is well. But the spell lasts for only so long. Adeline struggles to accept this new identity. She is wasting away, as her condition reasserts itself. Negation. The family prepare a special ceremony, to take place on the first anniversary of the death. Jeannie Watts will die again, in a symbolic manner, and her 'body' will be reburied in the cellar, dressed in blue and yellow, accompanied by five magic charms. A pigeon, found dead in the attic, is added to the pile of grave goods. A set of wings for the journey. Prayers are chanted. Leonard writes a script for this act of magic, and Adeline takes a full measure of life from it. The family see how she is now, how *alive* she appears, how vibrant. Decay is kept at bay. And they promise always to come back to this moment – to meet on this day, to perform the same ritual every year. And so Adeline will live on, in this new guise.

1956. All the family are present as the third dress is torn and bloodied. It is hung on the wall of Adeline's bedroom, a constant reminder of the spell that renews her. She is now calling herself Jeannie, and asks that her relatives do the same. They are happy to go along with this.

1957. Mary Estelle Graves begins her novel, *A Spell of Darkness*. She uses her own family as a template, and Bridlemere as a model for the novel's Gothic mansion. The story of Nicholas and Rosamund's encounter is coded in the pages, as is the death of Jeannie Watts, and the ceremony of rebirth that follows it. And another dress is torn, and daubed this time with red paint. It is laid out on the floor of the attic.

1958. *A Spell of Darkness* is published. The critics take it to be a work of fiction. Camilla makes another dress at her sewing-machine, following the usual pattern, using the same cloth as before. It is torn, painted, prayed over, folded neatly and placed in a drawer in the master bedroom of the house. There it rests.

1959. Another dress is made, and torn. This time Nicholas makes a cut in his arm, and his own blood is used as the magical element.

1960. This year Nicholas stays away. He no longer thinks of himself as part of the family, and all that it stands for. The ceremony goes ahead without him.

1961. Nicholas starts to think about making a film of his life, his family, and the terrible events they go through. Another dress is buried, this time in the back garden. Later that year, Camilla digs it up and displays it in her room, dirt, insects and all.

1962. Nicholas directs and shoots his low-budget experimental film, *The Spell Makers*. He uses amateur actors, including, in a bit part, a young man called George Collingworth. The film is never truly finished. Again, Nicholas stays away from the annual ceremony. The family continue, as always. Another dress is prepared, another symbolic death undertaken.

1963. This year Rosamund stays away. Adeline frets over this, worried that not enough people are present: the ritual's power will be weakened. She especially regrets the absence of her mother and father. But another dress is torn and prepared, this time with Mary Estelle's blood as a sacrament. The matriarch's energy will surely reinforce the spell. Surely.

1964. The tenth anniversary. Leonard and Mary Estelle exert all their influence to draw the family together. Nicholas and Rosamund return to the fold. The ceremony takes on an extra significance. Leonard rewrites the script, adding more lines, more images of extreme poetic symbolism. The dress is torn, bloodied, and hidden under a bed.

1965. Nicholas and Rosamund stay away. Adeline is distraught, but she takes her usual strength from the ritual death. The day after the ceremony, Camilla announces that she's leaving home. Adeline retreats to her room, and cries in her solitude. Her 'sister' will no longer be there to protect her, to look after her.

1966. Camilla returns for the special day. She brings with her a supply of dresses, all handmade, and she promises to keep the house supplied, no matter how long it takes. Adeline smiles. And Jeannie Watts dies again, for the thirteenth time.

1967. Camilla returns, but only for an hour or so. Long enough for the ceremony to take place. There is no sign of Nicholas or Rosamund. It seems the family has lost them for ever. Adeline weakens. She stares into the mirror, and fears that the rot might return to her body, that she might begin again to die, to fade away into dust. Leonard writes a will, leaving all his goods to Camilla. He expects her to look after Adeline, whatever the future might hold. This will is never made official.

1968. Leonard exerts his authority, wishing that all attend the ceremony this year, all his children. Rosamund relents, but Nicholas stays away.

1969. For the first time Camilla stays away. The dress is torn and bloodied, this time with tomato ketchup only. Leonard, Mary Estelle and their granddaughter Adeline are the only members of the congregation. There seems little use for the magical script, and so the ritual takes place in silence.

1970. Silence. Cloth, blood. Three people. The dress hung in the garden shed.

1971. Mary Estelle is too ill, too listless to attend. She stays in bed, asleep, as Leonard performs the ritual for Adeline's benefit, quoting only his own lines. His granddaughter is grateful, and she promises always to love him.

1972. The day arrives, and passes, and no ritual takes place. *Surely now we have done enough! We have brought her fully back to life!* But Adeline suffers, and cries out in the night, so the dress is torn and bloodied, a day late. Leonard resolves never to ignore the spell, not until his dying day.

1973. Mary Estelle, Leonard and their granddaughter gather in the cellar. A neighbour's cat is caught, and killed. And drained of a little blood. Nobody speaks. The dress is laid out on the floor, on the same spot where the second dress is buried. Adeline goes up to the room where the real Jeannie Watts lies at rest, hidden behind the chimney breast. She asks a favour of her grandfather, that he drill a small hole in the wall. This he does, to please her. By this method, 'Jeannie' can now speak to her former self, to 'Adeline', the conversations always taking place at night. They talk in whispers.

1974. Two decades have passed. And for the first time in years, all members of the Graves family make an effort. Leonard, Mary Estelle, Rosamund, Nicholas, Camilla, Adeline. The thirty-year-old David Kepple attends. He is drawn into the family's secret. All are present; all the lines of the script are intoned, as written and directed by Leonard. Adeline takes great power from this, and is rejuvenated. Everyone is happy. They drink freely and play parlour games late into the night. This is the last time they will all be together, in this manner. A week later, Adeline surprises them all by announcing her leave-taking from Bridlemere. A small terrace house is bought for her in Hackney.

1975. Adeline returns for the day. Her grandparents are shocked by her appearance, for she has taken on Jeannie Watts's identity fully, calling herself by this new name, in a new voice, and making no reference at all to Adeline. Even her face looks different. The spell has a power beyond anything the family may have envisaged. Another dress is prepared. It is folded and laid out on the floor of a cupboard, one in which Adeline used to hide when she was a little girl.

1976. Adeline returns. As do Camilla and David. Mary Estelle acts strangely at the ceremony, saying her lines out of turn, or forgetting them completely, instead making bizarre noises. She is losing her memory, and asks her husband why he is tearing a perfectly good dress like that, and why he is wiping his own blood on the cloth. A month later the family decide to send Mary Estelle to a nursing home.

1977. Leonard, Adeline, Camilla. They do not speak to each other. The dress is hardly touched: the tear is feeble, the blood a few spatters of paint. It will have to do. That week, Leonard moves into a downstairs room. He tidies away all the dresses still on view, placing them in drawers, in cupboards, in the attic. He can't bear to witness them. He has never lived on his own before, and sometimes he imagines that Adeline is in the house with him, hiding from him, like she used to do as a child. And sometimes she is a child again, and he can hear her laughter down a corridor, or around the next corner.

1978. Leonard and Adeline. Half-forgotten lines, wrong cues. All the magic of the years has been reduced to a pitiful act.

1979. Twenty-five years. A quarter-century has passed. Despite this, the family stays away. Only Adeline turns up. She can see that her grandfather is struggling. He can't remember where he placed the key for the cellar door, so Adeline breaks the lock for him, using a kitchen skewer, and they conduct the ceremony down there, in the cold. Leonard insists on presiding over the ritual, as usual, his voice feeble but resolute on every word. He is determined to protect his granddaughter, above all else. He will never stop, never . . .

1980. Adeline enters the house. She finds her grandfather asleep in his armchair in the living room. She rouses him, with some difficulty, and together they perform the ritual, as it used to be performed, each taking the lines of the missing family members. Briefly, the passion of the early years is brought to life. And the dress is torn, bloodied, arranged with its attendant scarf and shoes, and laid out on the floor of Leonard's bedroom.

1981. One person alone. He gets up late that day, weary in his bones, and he struggles to clean the lower rooms of the house, ready for Adeline's visit. He has prepared a few of the older dresses for her, in their favoured locations. He really is looking forward to seeing her. Every so often, he stops to catch his breath. The appointed hour comes, but his granddaughter has not yet arrived.

Can she have forgotten? No matter, he must continue: the spirit must be roused. He lays out a new dress on the floor of the living room, in front of the fireplace. He has already torn it at the midriff, the spot he knows so well, the site of the first ever wound. But something takes him over: perhaps a feeling of loneliness, or a sense of futility. He takes a razor blade to his arm, and allows the droplets of blood to fall on the blue cloth and the yellow flowers. This will be Leonard's last ritual. The years weigh heavy. A sticking plaster stops the flow of blood; he would hate his best white shirt to be ruined. His blazer fits as it did ten years ago. Yes, something to be proud of. He has kept himself trim. And then he sits at the kitchen table, drinking vodka and swallowing sleeping pills: one, two, three, and then a handful. The note to Adeline is safe in his pocket. *I'm so sorry. For everything.* In other words, for allowing all this to happen. The curse of the family.

I have tried my best to serve you, but can do no more.

Leonard sprays his wife's favourite perfume on to one of her handkerchiefs, and revels in the scent. He remembers so well when they first met, in the foyer of the Palace Theatre. April 1917. They were married within a month! He smiles at this. But now the darkness is taking hold. Perhaps he recites Prospero's lines of farewell from *The Tempest*, speaking them quietly: *These our actors, as I foretold you, were all spirits, and are melted into air, into thin air.* How gentle it all seems. These moments. Her name. Yes, he would like her name to be the final word spoken. *Adeline.*

And then silence.

SLOW MOTION GHOSTS

Jeff Noon

A vicious murder.
A curious clue left on the body.
The soundtrack to the murder still playing . . .

It is 1981 and DI Henry Hobbes is still reeling in the aftermath of the fire and fury of the Brixton riots. The battle lines of society – and the police force – are being redrawn on a daily basis.

With the certainties of his life already sorely tested, a brutal murder will shake his beliefs to their very core once more. The staged circumstances of the victim pose many questions to which there are no obvious answers.

To track the murderer, Hobbes must cross boundaries into a subculture hidden beneath the everyday world he thought he knew. His investigation takes him into a twisted reality, which is both seductive and devastating, and asks him the one question he has been dreading: how far will he go in pursuit of the truth?

'An utterly brilliant crime fiction debut'
WILLIAM SHAW

'Assured and compelling . . . it's a belter'
GUARDIAN